a Love Letter to Whiskey

5TH
ANNIVERSARY
EDITION

a Love Letter to Whiskey

5TH
ANNIVERSARY
EDITION

KANDI STEINER

Dedication

To Sasha Whittington, my very best friend
and the only girl who loves the burn of whiskey
just as much as I do. This one's for you.

One day, whether you
are 14, 28 or 65,

you will stumble upon
someone who will start
a fire in you that cannot die.

However, the saddest,
most awful truth you will
ever come to find—

is they are not always
with whom we spend our lives.

— Beau Taplin

FORWARD
from the Author

ON OCTOBER 13TH OF 2016, I published my seventh book.

Although I had gone through the writing, editing, and publishing process six times before, I just knew in my gut that something was different about this one. It felt closer to home.

It was real, raw, emotional, and absolutely excruciating to write.

I think that's when you know you've created something magical – when the pain outweighs the pleasure.

A Love Letter to Whiskey was born during a tumultuous time in my life. I was in the middle of an ugly and heartbreaking divorce, while also on the cusp of discovering a part of me that had been dying to break free. The same way Jamie and B struggled against their warring emotions, I did the same with my own.

I'll never forget the day this book was published, how I cried tears of joy and celebrated both *my* birthday and the birthday of a book I knew would hold a special space in my heart forever.

But the way you, the readers, received this book?

I never saw that coming.

And it absolutely blew me away.

Since its publication in 2016, *A Love Letter to Whiskey* has been made an Amazon Top 10 Bestseller in the United States, an international bestseller in Italy, Israel, Canada,

Australia, and the United Kingdom, an audiobook that brought me to tears the first time I listened to it, a limited-edition cover for the Hello, Lovely Box, and perhaps more than anything – *the* book everyone thinks of when they hear my name.

To say it has been an honor is the biggest understatement of all time.

When I attend book conventions, this book is *hands down* the one most frequently brought up by readers meeting me for the first time. I have held you as we sobbed together over how close to home some of these painful moments hit, and your stories have stayed with me long after our interactions. The countless social media messages, emails, and handwritten letters could wallpaper an entire room, and still, I can't find the right words to thank you for sharing those confessions with me.

Through all this, however, there has been *one* rather big complaint over the years...

The ending.

How could I do that, leave you with just six little words to wrap up eleven years of torture?

In my heart, that was the right ending. And from the emotion it evoked in many of you, I think you agree – even if you also want to strangle me, which is completely fair.

Still, I wanted to do something special to celebrate the fifth anniversary of this precious book baby coming to life.

And so, it is with deep pleasure that I present to you *Love, Whiskey* at the end of this special five-year anniversary edition.

Love, Whiskey is Jamie's side of the story, as well as an extended epilogue to show you more of what happened *after* that torturous end.

You'll also find bonus content with letters I've written over the years, a few behind-the-scenes fun facts, and a letter from Lauren Sweet, the narrator of the audiobook, as she shares how this story has stayed with *her* through the years, too.

This edition is for you, my lovely readers. Thank you for screaming your love for this book at the top of your lungs, and for showing me more joy and gratitude than I ever imagined possible. I am humbled by your passion and truly honored to share a connection with you through the written word.

Here's to another shot…

Because let's be honest – the addiction never dies.

All my love,
Kandi Steiner

PROLOGUE

Relapse

IT'S CRAZY HOW FAST the buzz comes back after you've been sober for so long.

I opened my door and felt tipsy just at the sight of him, eyes blurring and legs shaking. It used to take me at least a shot to get to this point, but my tolerance level had been weakened by distance and time, and just seeing him warmed my blood. I gripped the knob tighter, as if that'd help, but it was like trying to chug water after passing the point of no return.

Whiskey stood there, on my doorstep, just like he had one year before. Except this time, there was no rain, no anger, no wedding invitation — it was just us.

It was just him — the old friend, the easy smile, the twisted solace wrapped in a glittering bottle.

It was just me — the alcoholic, pretending like I didn't want to taste him, realizing too quickly that months of being clean didn't make me crave him any less.

1

But we can't start here.
No, to tell this story right, we need to go back.
Back to the beginning.
Back to the very first drop.

ONE

First Taste

THE FIRST TIME I tasted Whiskey, I fell flat on my face.

Literally.

I was drunk from the very first sip, and I guess that should have been my sign to stay away.

Jenna and I were running the trail around the lake near her house, sweat dripping into our eyes from the intense South Florida heat. It was early September, but in South Florida, it might as well have been July. There was no "boots and scarves" season, unless you counted the approximately six weeks in January and February where the temperature dropped below eighty degrees.

As it was, we were battling ninety-plus degrees, me trying to be a show off and prove I could keep up with Jenna's cheerleading training program. She had finally made the varsity squad, and with that privilege came ridiculous standards she had to uphold. I hated running — absolutely *loathed* it. I would much rather have been on my surfboard that day. But fortunately for Jenna, she had a competitive best friend who never turned down a challenge. So when she asked me to train with her, I'd agreed eagerly, even knowing I'd have screaming ribs and calves by the end of the day.

I saw him first.

I was just a few steps ahead of Jenna, and I'd been staring down at my hot pink sneakers as they hit the concrete. When I looked up, he was about fifty feet away, and even from that distance I could tell I was in trouble. He seemed sort of average at first — brown hair, lean build, soaked white running shirt — but the closer he got, the more I realized just how edible he was. I noticed the shift in the muscles of his legs as he ran, the way his hair bounced slightly, how he pressed his lips together in concentration as he neared us.

I looked over my shoulder, attempting to waggle my eyebrows at Jenna and give her the secret best friend code for "hot guy up ahead," but she had stopped to tie her shoes. And when I turned back around, it was too late.

I smacked into him — hard — and fell to the pavement, rolling a bit to soften the fall. He cursed and I groaned, more from embarrassment than pain. I wish I could say I gracefully picked myself up, smiled radiantly, and asked him for his number, but the truth is I lost the ability to do anything the minute I looked up at him.

It was an unfamiliar, warm ache that spread through my chest as I used my hand to shield the sun streaming in behind his silhouette, just how you'd expect the first sip of whiskey to feel. He was bent over, hand outstretched, saying something that wasn't registering because I had somehow managed to slip my hand into his and just that one touch had set my skin on fire.

Handsome wasn't the right word to describe him, but it was all I kept thinking as I traced his features. His hair was a sort of mocha color, damp at the roots, falling onto his forehead just slightly. His eyes were wide — almost too round — and a mixture of gold, green, and the deepest brown. I didn't coin the nickname Whiskey until much later, but it was that moment that I saw it for the first time — those were whiskey eyes. The kind of eyes you get lost in. The kind that drink you in. He had the longest lashes and a firm, square jaw. It was so hard, the edges so clean that I would have sworn he was angry with me if it weren't for the smile on his face. He was still talking as my eyes fell over his broad chest before snapping back up to his sideways grin.

"Oh my God, are you fucking blind?!" Jenna's voice snapped me from my haze as she shoved Whiskey out of the way and latched onto my hand, ripping me back to standing position. I'd barely caught my balance before she whipped around to continue her scolding. "How about you brush that long ass hair out of your eyes and watch where you're going, huh champ?"

Oh no.

I didn't even have time to call dibs, I couldn't even *think* the word, let alone say it, before it was too late. I watched it, in slow motion, as Whiskey fell for my best friend before I even had the chance to say a single word to him.

Jenna was standing tall, arms crossed, one hip popped in her usual fashion as she waited for him to defend himself. This was her standard operating procedure — it was one of the reasons we got along. We were both what you'd call "spitfires", but Jenna had the distinct advantage of being cripplingly gorgeous on top of having an attitude. She flipped her long, wavy blonde ponytail behind her and cocked a brow.

And then he did, too.

His smile grew wider as he met her eyes, and it was the same look I'd watched fall over guy after countless guy. Jenna was a unicorn, and men were enamored by her. As they should have been — she had platinum blonde hair, crystal blue eyes, legs for days, and a personality to boot. Now, before you go thinking that I was the insecure best friend — I had it going on, too. I worked hard, I was talented — just not at the things traditional high school boys valued.

But we'll get to that.

"Hi," Whiskey finally said, extending his hand to Jenna this time. His eyes were warm, smile inviting — if I had to pick the right word for him, just one, I'd say charming. He just oozed charm. "I'm Jamie."

"Well, *Jamie*, maybe you should make an appointment with the eye doctor before you run over another innocent jogger. And you owe Brecks an apology." She nodded to me then and I cringed at my name, wondering why she felt the need to spill it at all. She always called me B — everyone did — so why did she choose the moment I was face to face with the first boy to ever make my heart accelerate to use my full name?

Jamie was still grinning, eying Jenna, trying to figure her out, but he turned to me after a moment with that same crooked smile. "I'm sorry, I should have been watching where I was going." He said the words with conviction, but lifted his brows on that last line because he and I both knew who wasn't paying attention to the trail, and he wasn't the guilty party.

"It's fine," I murmured, because for some reason I was still having a difficult time finding my voice. Jamie tilted his head just a fraction, his eyes hard on me this time, and I felt naked beneath his gaze. I'd never had anyone look at me that way — completely zeroed in. It was unnerving and exhilarating, too.

But before I could latch onto the feeling, he turned back to Jenna, their eyes meeting as slow smiles spread on both of their faces. I'd seen it a million times, but this was the first time I felt sick watching it happen.

I saw him first, but it didn't matter.

Because he saw her.

• • •

It was just over a week later that Jenna and Jamie put a title on the flirting relationship they'd been having for a solid eight days. That's how it was when we were in high school — there were no games, no "let's just hook up and see where this goes." You were either with someone or you weren't, and they were very together.

I had the privilege of watching them make out between classes, and as much as I wanted to hate them together, I

7

just didn't. In fact, I'd pretty much forgotten that I'd seen Jamie first because they were disgustingly cute together. Jenna was taller than me, but she was just short enough to fit perfectly under Jamie's arm. She was a cheerleader, he was a basketball player — different seasons, but popular and respected nonetheless. His dark features complimented her light ones, and they had a similar sense of humor. They even *sounded* good together — Jenna and Jamie. I mean honestly, how could I be mad at that?

So I dropped it, dropped the idea of him, moved easily into the third wheel position I was used to with Jenna and her long list of boyfriends. Jamie was the first of them who seemed to enjoy me there. He was always talking to me, making jokes, bridging the gap between awkward and easy friendship. It was nice, and I was sincerely happy for them.

Still, I had opted out of tricycling that particular afternoon after school. Instead, I swung my Jansport onto my bed and immediately started ruffling through the clothes in my top drawer for my bathing suit, desperate to get some time on the water before the sun set. Daylight Savings hadn't set in yet, but the days were slowly getting shorter, reminding me that summer was far away.

"Hey sweetie," my mom said, knuckles rapping softly on the panel of my door frame. "You hungry? I was thinking we could go out for dinner tonight, maybe to that sushi bar you love so much?"

"I'm not really hungry yet. Going to go check out the surf," I replied, my smile tight. I didn't even look up from my drawer, just pulled out my favorite white, strappy top

8

and avoided her eyes. It wasn't that I was a dramatic teen who hated her mom, I wasn't — I loved her, but things were different between us than they had been just two short years before.

Okay, this is the part where I warn you — I had daddy issues. I guess in a way, mommy issues, too.

But let me explain.

Everything in my life was perfect, at least in my eyes, until the summer before my sophomore year of high school. That was the summer I opened my pretty gray eyes and looked around at my life, realizing it wasn't at all what it seemed.

I thought I had it all. My parents weren't married or even together, but then again they never had been. I was used to that. It was our normal. Mom never dated anyone, Dad dated but never remarried, and somehow we still always ended up together — just the three of us — every Christmas. I'd always lived in my mom's house, but I'd spent equal time at my dad's. My parents never fought, but they never really laughed, either. I assumed they made it work for me, and I was thankful for that.

We were unconventional, me bouncing between houses and them tolerating each other for my sake, but we worked. Dad's skin was white, pale as they come, freckled and tinged pink while Mom's was the smoothest, most delicate shade of black. Ebony and ivory, with me the perfectly imperfect mixture of the two.

They may not have made enough at their respective jobs to shower me with birthday gifts or buy me a shiny new car on my sixteenth birthday, but they worked hard, they paid the bills, and they instilled that mindset in me, too. The Kennedy's may not have been rich in dollars, but we were rich in character.

Still, not everything is as it seems.

I never understood that saying — not really — not until that summer before tenth grade when everything I thought I knew about my life got erased in a violent come-to-Jesus talk. My mom had drank too much one night, as she often did, and I'd humored her by holding her hair back as she told me how proud she was of me between emptying her stomach into our off-white toilet.

"You are so much more than I ever could have wished for," she kept repeating, over and over. But then the literal vomit turned to word vomit, and she revealed a truth I wasn't prepared for.

You see, the story I'd been told my entire life was that mom and dad were best friends growing up. They were inseparable, and after years of everyone around them making jokes about them dating, they finally conceded, and it turned out they were perfect together. They had a happy relationship for several years, a bouncing baby girl who they both loved very much, but it just didn't work out, so they went back to being friends. The end. Sounds sweet, right?

Except it was a lie.

The truth was much uglier, as it so often is, and so they hid it from me. But mom was tequila drunk that night and apparently had forgotten why she cared so much about lying to me. So, she spilled the truth.

They had been best friends, that much was true, but they had never dated. Instead, my dad had turned jealous, chasing every guy who dared to talk to my mom out of her life. But he didn't stop there. One night, when she was crying over the most recent guy who'd dumped her, my dad had come on to her. And he didn't take no for an answer.

Not the first time she said it.

Not the eleventh.

She counted, by the way.

Mom was seventeen at the time, and I was the product of that night — a baby not meant to be born from a horror not meant to be lived.

I guess this is the part where I tell you I immediately hated my dad, and in a way I did, but in another way I still loved him. He was still my dad, the guy who'd called me *baby girl* and fixed me root beer floats when I'd had a bad day. I wondered how the soft-spoken, caring man I'd grown up around could have committed such an act.

For a while, I lived in a broken sort of limbo between those two feelings — love and hate — but when I finally had the nerve to ask him about it, to tell him that I knew what happened, he had nothing to say. He didn't apologize, he didn't try to defend himself, and he didn't seem to hold any emotion other than anger that my mother had told me at all. After that, I slipped farther toward hate, and I stopped talking to him a short five months after the night my mom told me the truth.

And though I shouldn't have resented my mom for not telling me sooner, I did. She didn't deserve me to blame

11

her for letting me think my father was a good person, but I did. And so, my life was never the same.

Like I said, it wasn't that I hated my mom, because I didn't. But there was a raw wedge between us after that night, an unmovable force, and I felt the jagged splinters of it scrape my chest every time I looked at her.

So, more often than not, I chose not to.

"Okay," she replied, defeated. "Well, I hope you have fun." I was still rummaging, searching for my bottoms, and she turned to leave but paused long enough to call back over her shoulder. "I love you."

I froze, closed my eyes, and let out one long breath. "I love you too, Mom."

I would never not say those words. I loved her fiercely, even if our relationship had changed.

By the time I found my suit, dressed, strapped my board to the top of my beat-up SUV and made it to the beach, the weight of the day was threatening to suffocate me. But as soon as I set my board in the water and slid on, my arms finding their rhythm in the familiar burn that came with paddling out, I began to breathe easier.

The surf in South Florida was far from glorious, but it worked for my purposes. It was one of my favorite ways to waste a day, connected with the water, with myself. It was my alone time, time to think, time to process. I used surfing like most people used fitness or food — to cope, to heal, to work through my issues or ignore them, depending on my mood. It was my solace.

Which is why I nearly fell off my board when Jamie paddled out beside me.

"Fancy meeting you here," he mused, voice low and throaty. He chuckled at my lost balance and I narrowed my eyes, but smiled nonetheless. Everything I thought I knew about his body was erased in that moment and I swallowed, following the cut lines along his arms that led me straight to his abdomen. There was a scar there, just above his right hip, and I stared at it just a second too long before clearing my throat and turning back toward the water.

"Thought you had plans with Jenna."

He shrugged. "I did. But there was a cheerleading crisis, apparently."

We met eyes then, both stifling laughs before letting them tumble out.

"I'll never understand organized sports," I said, shaking my head.

Jamie squinted against the sun as we rode over a small wave, our legs dangling on either side of our boards. "What? You'll never understand having a team who works toward the same goal?"

I scoffed. "Don't be annoying. You know what I meant."

"Oh, so you hate fun?"

"No, but I hate *organized* fun." I glanced sideways at him then, offering a small smirk, and I grinned a little wider when the right side of his mouth quirked up in return. "I didn't know you surfed."

"Yeah," he answered easily. "Believe it or not, us organized-fun people enjoy solo sports, too."

"You're really not going to let this go, are you?"

13

He laughed, and I relaxed a bit. So what Jamie was impossibly gorgeous and had the abs of the young Brad Pitt? I could do this, be friends, ignore the little zing in my stomach when he smiled at me. It was nice to have a friend other than Jenna. Where she made friends easily, I tended to push people away — whether by choice or accident. Maybe the Jamie-B-Jenna tricycle wouldn't be so bad, after all.

But when I truly thought about that possibility, of having a guy as a friend, my stomach dropped for a completely different reason. A flash of Mom bent over our toilet hit me quickly, her eyes blood-shot and her truthful words like ice picks in my throat. I swallowed, closing my eyes just a moment before checking the waterproof watch on my wrist.

"We should try to catch this next wave."

I didn't wait for him to answer before I paddled out.

We surfed what we could, but the waves were sad that day, barely offering enough to push our boards back to shore. So eventually, we ended up right back where we started, legs swinging in the salt water beneath us as we stared out at the water. The sun was slowly sinking behind us, setting on the West coast and casting the beach in a hazy yellow glow.

"Where do you go when you do that?"

"Do what?" I asked.

"You have this look, this faraway stare sometimes. It's like you're here, but not really."

He was watching me then, the same way he had the first day we met. I smoothed my thumb over one of the black designs on my board and shrugged.

"Just thinking, I guess."

"Sounds dangerous."

He grinned, and I felt my cheeks heat, though no one would know but me. My skin didn't reveal a blush the way Jenna's did. "Probably is. You should steer clear."

Jamie chewed the inside of his lip, still staring at me, and opened his mouth to say something else, but didn't. He turned, staring in the same direction as me for a few moments before speaking again.

"So what are you thinking right now?"

I let out a long, slow breath. "Thinking I can't wait to get out of here, move to California, and finally surf a real wave."

"You're moving?"

"Not yet. But hopefully for college."

"Ah," he mused. "I take it you have no interest in going to Palm South University, then?"

I shook my head. "Nah, too much drama. I want a laid-back west coast school. Somewhere with waves that don't suck."

Jamie dipped his hand into the water and lifted it again, letting the water drip from his fingertips to the hot skin on his shoulders. "Me too, Brecks. Me too."

I cringed at the use of my name. "It's just B."

"Just B, huh?"

I nodded. "You want to go to school in California, too?"

"That's the plan. I have an uncle out there who has some connections at a few schools. You have a specific one in mind yet?"

"Not yet. Just somewhere far from here."

He nodded once, thankfully not pushing me to expand on that little dramatic statement. We sat in silence a while longer before paddling back in and hiking our boards up under our arms as we made the trek back to the cars. The sand was a bit course under our feet, but I loved the way it felt. I loved everything about the beach, especially surfing, and I glanced over at Jamie, more thankful than I thought I would have been running into him.

He helped me load up after we rinsed off, strapping my old lime green board to the top of Old Not-So Faithful. And just like the reliable Betty that she was, the 1998 Kia Sportage failed to turn over when I tried to start her up.

"Great," I murmured, my head hitting the top of the steering wheel. Jamie had just finished loading his own board a few cars away, and he made his way back over.

"Not starting?"

"Seems to be my lucky day."

He smiled, tugging the handle on my door to pull it open. "Come on, I'll drive you home."

I didn't know it then, but that one small gesture, those six small words, they would be what changed everything between me and Jamie Shaw.

TWO

AS MUCH AS I loved the beach, I hated what it did to my hair.

I was a product of my parents, taking equal features from each. I had my father's eyes, my mother's hair, a smooth mixture of their skin tones. With my dad being white and my mom being black, I fell right in-between them with a creamy mocha latte. I was short like my mom and stubborn like my dad, and somehow I inherited the fiercest combination of their work ethic. My mom was petite, with virtually no curves to speak of and I mirrored her in that respect. I loved my athletic build, even if it didn't grab the attention of boys the way Jenna's hips did.

All that being said, salt water mixed with my hair about as well as water mixed with oil. I tried my best to tame it in the small visor mirror in the passenger seat of Jamie's Jeep, using my fingers to try to breathe life back into the tight spiral curls. I wiped my fingers across my cheeks next, rubbing the leftover salt away. My gray-blue eyes looked tired that day, and I let them flick to the freckles on the apples of my cheeks for just the shortest second before flipping the visor back up and settling back in the leather seat.

I'd never seen a Jeep that nice, let alone ridden in one. It was brand new, cherry red, with black leather seats and a tricked-out dashboard. It seemed a little much to me, especially for a highschooler. Did a seventeen-year-old really need such an expensive car?

The answer was absolutely not.

But I'd learned a lot about Jamie in those eight days since we'd first met, thanks to a little social media stalking. Our school was ginormous, there were more than six-hundred kids in mine and Jenna's grade alone. But, I wasn't too proud to surf the Web to find out more about my best friend's new guy, and I learned a good amount. Enough to know that his father owned one of the top privately-owned accounting firms in Fort Lauderdale and Jamie would want for nothing the rest of his life. I *hoped* to go to college in California, but there was no doubt in my mind he would get there if that's what he decided he wanted.

I half-wondered what that would be like, growing up knowing finances would never keep you from anything, but mostly I didn't care. I was brought up with the mindset that you work hard for what you want in life, and that's what I intended to do. I was already well on my way, focusing on my grades and getting involved in what school activities I could stomach to build my resume for college applications.

I also discovered that he had a dog named Brutus and two sisters, both younger, both just as gorgeous as him.

That was as far as I let my stalking go before I could no longer claim it wasn't creepy.

"So just take this all the way to Scenic Drive?" Jamie asked, turning onto Cherry Street.

"Yep. Take a left on Scenic and I'm the fourth house on the right. It's bright yellow, can't miss it."

A soft silence fell over us and I ran my hands over my hair again, smoothing it down, wondering if Jamie even cared what it looked like at all.

"This is a really nice car," I said stupidly, breaking the silence. Jamie's eyes lit up a bit and he shifted, switching hands on the steering wheel.

"Thanks. I had to work my ass off for three summers to earn it, so I appreciate it."

I cocked a brow. "You paid for this yourself?"

"Well, kind of. I worked for my dad at his firm for three summers without being paid. I just told my dad I wanted a Jeep, a nice one, one that I could use to tote my board around but also be comfortable in for a long road trip." He turned to me then. "He finally bought if for me after this past summer."

"Nice. And why exactly does your car have to be road trip proof?"

Jamie noticed me crossing my arms, goosebumps breaking on my skin from the salt water drying. He leaned forward to adjust the air. "I don't know, just in case, I guess. I love to drive. Helps clear my head."

I nodded. "Yeah, I get that."

"It's also about the only time I get to listen to the music I actually want to listen to. You know, when no one else is in the car to say anything about it."

"Okay, now I'm curious," I said, uncrossing my arms and tucking my legs beneath me. "What exactly do you listen to?"

Jamie pressed his lips together in a tight line. "Promise not to laugh?"

"No."

He chuckled. "Then I can't show you."

"Fine, fine. I won't laugh." He eyed me, debating whether to trust me or not. "At least, not loud enough for you to hear."

"Fair enough." He smiled, but it dropped quickly as he plugged his phone into the auxiliary cord and thumbed through his music. Each time he flicked his thumb up, scrolling through the playlists, a long indented line would break on his forearm where the muscles worked. I let my eyes stay there, watching that muscle, until the first note played as we pulled up to a stop light.

It was soft, soothing, familiar. *Really* familiar. When it sank in what song it was, I couldn't hold back my reaction.

"No fucking way."

"Yeah, I know, it's nerdy." Jamie reached for the volume knob but I smacked his hand away.

"No, no it's amazing. I just, I can't believe *you* listen to classical music. This is Brian Crain, right?"

It was his turn to blanch. "Yes."

"I love him," I said excitedly, sitting up straighter. I might have even bounced a little. "He's incredible. *Please* tell me you listen to The Piano Guys, too."

His mouth fell open. "I fucking *love* The Piano Guys."

We both laughed, our eyes bright, searching each other as if the other didn't truly exist. "This is crazy! I've never met anyone else who loved this kind of music. Like... ever."

"That makes two of us," he said as the light turned green. He didn't go right away, just kept his eyes on mine, staring at me that way he did that made me wonder what he was thinking. It was as if I were a painting and he a curator. I felt him debating, circling, wondering if he should collect me or pass me by.

I prayed for the first option, even though I knew I shouldn't.

The Mazda behind us honked and Jamie blinked, the spell broken. For the rest of the ride home, we didn't say another word, just enjoyed his playlist and the wind in our hair. It was strangely comfortable sitting in silence with Jamie, as if we didn't need words, especially with a piano version of "Bring Him Home" from *Les Misérables* serenading us as he drove.

When he pulled up to my house, I smiled, my head still laid back against the headrest as I turned to face him. "I can play this one."

"Play it?"

I nodded. "Mm-hmm, on violin."

"You play the violin?"

"No."

He opened his mouth, shut it again, and then laughed. "Okay, color me confused."

My smile grew. "I don't play violin. But, one day I was sitting next to this kid in band at lunch and he heard me

21

listening to this. He plucked my earbuds out and thought he was so cute, talking in my ear about how he could play this song on violin. He thought his game was smooth." I shrugged. "But I wasn't impressed, told him anyone could learn to play it. He gave up on flirting then and started taking offense, told me there was no way I could learn to do it, so we made a bet. And five weeks later, I strode up to the same table where he sat, pulled out his violin that was propped up next to him, and played it."

"No you didn't."

I pulled my lips between my teeth in a smile. "I did. I'm a very competitive person, Jamie Shaw. And I never turn down a challenge."

His eyes were a sort of golden green in what light was left from the day, dusk settling in around us, and his skin crinkled at the edges as he let his head fall back to mirror mine. "I'll keep that in mind, Br—" He paused. "B."

For just a second, I let myself stare at him, then I unclicked my seatbelt and grabbed my beach bag, pulling the strap up over my shoulder. "Thanks for the ride home." I sighed, shaking my head. "Jenna is going to kill me when she finds out I can't go to the game tomorrow."

"What do you mean?"

"Well, I'm going to call my dad to see if he can go get my car and get it into his friend's shop, but there's no way it'll be fixed by tomorrow night. Jenna is cheering in our first home game. I promised her I'd go, but unless my mom gets off work early, I don't see that happening."

"I'll take you," Jamie offered quickly.

"No, no, it's okay. You don't have to—"

"I want to. Seriously. I'm going anyway, and it'd be nice to have someone to sit with." He smiled, that lazy, crooked smile that made my legs tingle.

"Okay."

He grinned wider. "Okay."

Mom was already in her room by the time I'd hung my board in the garage, so I made myself a grilled cheese and ate alone in my bedroom. I didn't turn on my TV or look through the notifications on my phone. I just ate it slowly, one bite at a time, staring at my closet door and replaying every moment of the evening. Then, after taking as much time as I reasonably could to eat, I called my dad. He must have known when he answered that I needed something — it was the only time I called anymore — and I cut straight to the chase. He told me he'd take care of it, because that's the kind of guy he was.

But he was also the kind of guy who could rape my mother, and sometimes I had to force myself to remember that. Especially on nights when he called me "baby girl" and my heart surged with the love I'd always had for him.

My vision was blurry, likely from the salt water, so I ran myself a bath as soon as I ended our call. I'd always loved baths, only taking a shower when I was in a rush to be somewhere. It was nice to soak in the hot water, to take time to think. If I only had those thirty minutes to myself a day, it was enough.

But that night, as I wiggled my toes beneath the faucet, the water slowly filling in around me, I felt different. The heat was a little hotter, the lights a little brighter, and my vision still wouldn't quite clear. I thought a little too hard about the one person I knew I shouldn't, and a new buzz

23

I'd yet to experience rushed over me as I let him sink into my system.

I should have cleared my mind. I should have called Jamie and told him not to pick me up for the game. I should have pulled up a picture of him and Jenna to remind myself where I sat on this tricycle.

But I didn't do any of those things.

And I only wished I felt guilty about it.

• • •

As much as I detested school spirit, there was something to say for the energy of a home high school football game in South Florida. Students were painted brightly in our teal and white colors, cheering loudly and blaring fog horns. The band played upbeat music that was hard not to dance to and everyone high-fived each other when our team did something right, bringing a camaraderie to the stands that I wasn't expecting.

South Springs High School hadn't won a single game the season before, but we had a halfway decent team this year, which was great for me since I'd likely be at every game watching Jenna cheer.

Jenna Kamp was the kind of friend you latched onto and never let go of. She was fiercely loyal, hilarious, and driven — which was exactly the kind of person I wanted to surround myself with. She never slept on her dreams and never let me sleep on mine. All that aside, she was the only person in my life who took me for who I was — exactly who I was — and loved me completely. She knew about my parents, about my name, about my less-than-stellar car. She didn't care that my mom smoked cigarettes in the house and so my clothes smelled like smoke or that I didn't learn how to do anything with my hair until we were eighth graders. She loved me through the awkward stages and I knew she'd love me through much worse. She was my forever friend.

Which is why I felt supremely shitty that I was focusing on the place where my knee touched her boyfriend's as we watched her cheer from the stands.

The bleachers were packed, so Jamie and I had wiggled our way into a small open space on the third row up. It was either touch the random freshman on the other side of me or touch Jamie, and I opted for Jamie.

Out of pure familiarity, of course.

"You surviving over there?" he asked, sipping on the red slushy he'd purchased at half-time. "I know all this organized fun can be torturous."

"You're totally judging me for my lack of school spirit, aren't you?"

"Only a little bit."

I sighed. "And all this after I promised not to judge you for your musical taste. You don't play fair, Jamie Shaw."

He moved his straw around, a smirk crawling up on his lips. "You have no idea."

I narrowed my eyes, ready to ask what the hell that meant when the cheerleading squad started up a new cheer. Jamie's eyes found Jenna's and he zeroed in on her, sexy smile in place, their eyes staying connected the entire time as she moved. I watched her too, mesmerized by her flawlessness. Seriously, I'd yet to meet another person more beautiful than her — including Jamie. She just dazzled.

When the cheer ended, Jenna blew Jamie a kiss and he grinned as she turned back toward the field, her short skirt twirling with her.

And then, he turned back to me.

"So are you involved in any clubs or anything?"

My cheeks heated. "Okay, seriously, don't laugh, because what I'm interested in and what Jenna is interested in are completely different."

"I'm not comparing you."

I chewed my cheek at that, noting the sincerity in his eyes. "I'm in Debate Club. And Interact."

He barked out one, loud laugh. "Of *course* you're in Debate Club."

"What's that supposed to mean?!"

Jamie laughed harder, his hand coming down on my knee as he doubled over. I tried not to feel the burn through my jeans. "Nothing, it just makes sense. You and that mouth of yours." He removed his hand, but now his eyes were on my mouth he'd just mentioned, and I could barely breathe.

He sniffed, looking back out at the field. "What is Interact?"

"Basically a community service club. I want to beef up the resume before senior year, you know?"

Our team scored and everyone jumped up, cheering loudly, Jamie and I a little delayed. We shared high-fives with a few people around us and watched Jenna perform a toe touch jump before settling back in on the bleachers.

"Yeah, you told me how you want to go to school in California, but what exactly do you want to go to school for?"

I stole his slushy then, pointing the straw at him before taking a sip. "You'll have to get in line to get the answer to that question, right behind my mom."

Jamie snatched the slushy back and immediately took a pull, which made me realize we'd shared a straw. I couldn't figure out why that made my stomach flip. "Can you share a little insight with the back of the line, at least?"

"I just don't know yet. I'll probably go in undecided, take my general education requirements and figure it out from there. I love to write, but I also enjoy the objectivity of solving a math problem. I get amped up over public speaking but I also take solace in the quiet hours spent on a solo project." I sighed. "I just think it's stupid to narrow down my options. Is it so bad to be passionate about more than one thing?"

He tilted his head. "Not at all. I think that makes you rare."

"Great. Rare. Like a steak. Sounds like when my mom used to tell me I was 'special.'"

Jamie laughed. "You are. You're unique, B. I like that about you."

My breath got stuck somewhere beneath my chest bone and I inhaled deeply, tucking my hands under my thighs and pulling my knee from where it touched his. It was suddenly too much, and I focused instead on where the cool metal of the bleachers touched my skin.

"What about you? You have it all planned out, don't you?"

"Kind of. I mean, for me, it's always been sort of easy. I want what my dad has, you know?" His eyes were bright, animated. "I'm not sure if I told you or not, but he's an accountant, owns his own firm in Fort Lauderdale."

"You don't say?" I acted surprised.

Jamie sat a little straighter, talking with his hands. "He started that firm when he was twenty-six, B. Twenty-six. Can you imagine?" He shook his head. "It almost went under twice, but he fought for it, and now he's one of the best firms in town. I want to continue that, work for him until he hands it over to me, work even harder once it's mine to keep the reputation he worked so hard to build. I want to meet the love of my life, marry her, fill our house with kids and do what I need to do to give them everything they need."

"You want those things? Or does he want them for you?" The other team scored a touchdown and the crowd around us booed, halting the conversation for a moment. When the noise died down, Jamie continued.

"*I* want them," he said with absolution. "I love what my dad has built with my mom, what they've both done for me and my two sisters — Sylvia and Santana." He shrugged, and I watched a single strand of his hair fall out of place and onto his forehead. "I've worked at the firm for three summers now and I love it. I'm good at it. I don't know, it just makes sense for me, I guess."

"It must be so comforting, to know what you want the way you do."

He swallowed, his eyes focusing on the game and not on me anymore. "Sometimes it's harder than you think. There's always this fear that even though I may know

28

what I want, I may never actually make it a reality." Jamie glanced at me then. "Sometimes it's more complicated than just wanting something and making it happen."

I nodded, at least I think I did. He was looking at me in that way he did, and when that happened, I couldn't be sure I was actually moving the way I told my body to.

"I think you'll find a way."

He smiled, an easy smile, one that erased the tension of that moment. "Thanks, B. I think you will, too."

We ended up winning the game, twenty-four to fourteen, and Jenna sprinted off the field and into Jamie's arms at the sound of the final whistle. He picked her up easily, swinging her around before kissing her to a collective "aww" from those in the stands who witnessed the movie-like moment. It was that kiss that stunned me back to reality, the reality where Jamie was my best friend's boyfriend. Jenna turned to me next and I slapped on a smile as quick as I could before she wrapped her arms around me.

"I'm so glad you came! I know this isn't exactly your scene."

I shrugged. "It wasn't all that bad." My eyes flitted to Jamie's and he smirked, but I looked away quickly, back to Jenna, my best friend, who I loved, who trusted me. "Still want to stay the night tonight?"

"Duh! We need a bestie night. *Please* tell me you have gummy bears and Mountain Dew ready for consumption."

I scoffed. "Come on now, is that even a question?"

She smiled radiantly, her blue eyes shining under the stadium lights. "I just have to finish up here and I'll be over. See you in an hour or so?"

"Perfect."

She leaned up on her toes to kiss Jamie once more before trotting off, and Jamie took longer than necessary before turning back to me. Our eyes met, saying more than words could, and I turned before he did, making my way to the parking lot with him not far behind.

• • •

It was silent in Jamie's Jeep on the way to my house — completely silent — both of us caught up in our own thoughts. That was, until my phone rang.

"Hey Dad."

"Hey, baby girl. How was the game?"

"Fine," I clipped. To say that my relationship with my dad was strained after Mom's confession would be an understatement. I probably drove him insane with my whiplash, because one moment I would forget for a while, let everything be how it used to be, and other times it was all I could do to talk to him without vomiting. I didn't know how to just snap my fingers and suddenly hate my dad, though I tried more often than not to do so. I guess there was no "right way" to handle it, at least not that I'd found.

"That's good, I'm glad you got out of the house." His tone had changed, probably because he'd picked up on mine. He knew what kind of day it was for me. "Listen, I have some news on your car."

"And?"

"And... we can't figure out what's wrong. Not yet, anyway. We checked the battery, the alternator, the timing belt — Nick thinks it might be something electrical."

30

I sighed, pulling my legs up into Jamie's passenger side seat and setting my chin on my knees. "So what does this mean?"

"It means we'll need more time with it to figure out what's going on. Nick is about to leave town for a couple of weeks but when he gets back, he's going to make it his number-one priority."

"Two weeks?!" I yelled a little louder than I intended and Jamie's brows furrowed, asking if I was okay. I just shook my head. "Well this sucks."

"I know. But in the meantime, you and I can start saving."

I swallowed. "How much do you think it's going to cost?"

Dad was quiet for a long moment, and I pictured him running a hand over his red beard. He always did when he had bad news. "I can't be sure, but I'd bet on at least a grand."

"Fuck my life."

"Language, Brecks."

My cheeks heated with anger. "Don't call me Brecks."

He sighed. "It's your name, baby girl."

"No. My name is B. And you know that by now, so stop acting like you don't."

"I'm just trying to help here."

He sounded defeated and I gritted my teeth, clenching my fist around the phone before letting out a long exhale. "I know, Dad. I have to go, but thank you. I'll call you tomorrow."

"Okay. I love you."

I paused. "You too."

The silence was too much when that phone call ended and Jamie seemed to pick up on it, because he hooked up his phone and started playing The Piano Guys without saying a single word. I was thankful as their version of "With or Without You" slowly faded in over the speakers, but didn't say so. Instead, I racked my brain for ways to come up with the money I'd need to get my car fixed. I'd worked at a grocery store chain over the summer, but was hoping to take the school year off to focus on school work and maybe having a little fun.

So much for that.

I shot out a text to my old manager and she responded back almost immediately, telling me I could come back on Monday after school.

Jamie pulled into my driveway this time, turning his Jeep completely off and staring at me until I conceded and returned his gaze.

"Why do you hate your name, B?"

A heavy weight dropped in my throat and I shifted, debating on what to tell him. Did I tell him the truth? Did I tell him it was none of his business?

I was too exhausted to lie, so I inhaled a shaky breath and let my head fall back against the head rest like I had the evening before. "My dad forced himself on my mom the night she became pregnant with me."

"Jesus," Jamie whispered under his breath, but I kept going.

"I only found out about it a little over a year ago. Up until that point, I loved my name. It was short, cute, fun.

32

But one night, my mom got sloshed and decided to tell me that everything I thought I knew about my life was a lie." I laughed, a manic sort of laugh. I had no idea why I was spilling this to Jamie, but for the first time since the night my mom had told me, I was starting to feel something. It started as a pressure in my chest, but with every word I spoke it bloomed, filling the space meant for air with an uncomfortable sting, instead. "You know he wasn't there when she had me? No one was. Not my grandma, not any of my mom's friends — it was just her and me. The nurse placed me in her arms and Mom said she cried."

Jamie didn't say anything, just reached his hand out to rest it on my thigh.

"My dad is Irish, and he has all these freckles all over his face. So when Mom saw the freckles on my cheeks, she thought about him, about that night, about the freckles she counted to get her through the eight minutes of him violating her." My eyes flooded with tears and I batted at them hastily. I couldn't believe I was crying, that I was finally *feeling* something after I'd been almost numb to it for so long. "She named me Brecks because it's Irish for 'freckled.'"

He squeezed my leg tighter and I fought the urge to grab his hand with my own.

"Once I found out, I couldn't stand my name anymore. I hated it. I hated the meaning of it. I hated what my father did to my mom and I hated what she did to me by naming me after something so monstrous." I laughed again, shaking my head and swiping at the tears that wouldn't stop. Jamie Shaw had spotted a wound not even I knew I had, and it was like telling him about it gave me permission to bleed. "God, I'm sorry. I don't know why I'm telling you this."

"Because I asked."

I sniffed, eying him then. "Doesn't mean I had to answer."

Jamie lifted his hand from my thigh, his thumb wiping away a tear I'd missed as it ran along my jawline. I leaned into his touch, closed my eyes, and let out a shaky breath.

"I'm glad you did."

I chewed my bottom lip, his hand still on my face, and I tried not to feel guilty.

But this time, I did.

"Thanks for the ride, Jamie," I said quietly, breaking our contact and pulling on the door handle.

"Hey," he stopped me as I stepped out. I shut the door but leaned in through the window, waiting. "My passenger seat is yours until your car gets fixed. If you want it."

He was watching me closely — too closely — and I let my eyes fall. "I think we both know that's a bad idea."

Jamie started to speak, but it was too soft for me to hear and he trailed off, not finishing his thought. I used my wrist to wipe at my nose and offered him a weak smile.

"See you at school."

Jenna showed up thirty minutes later, which was just enough time for me to wash my face and change into an oversized t-shirt and spandex shorts. We ate gummy bears and watched MTV while she gushed about how incredible Jamie was. I nodded along, smiling and commenting where appropriate, knowing all too well what she meant.

She'd just fallen asleep when my phone pinged with a text from him.

— **I meant what I said earlier. Let me drive you until your car is fixed. We can be friends, B.** —

I didn't answer, but took my phone with me into the kitchen to pour a glass of water. I chugged the entire thing and then my phone screen lit up again.

— **Please. Let me be your friend.** —

I knew it was a bad idea. There wasn't just a red flag, there was a warning bell and alarms and whistles and neon lights with DON'T DO IT in all capital letters. But sometimes, even when we know something is bad for us, we do it anyway. Maybe for the thrill, maybe to cure our curiosity, or maybe just to lie to ourselves a little longer.

I'd like to tell you I told him no, that I deleted his number and turned off my phone and crawled into bed with my best friend who was dating him. But instead, I curled up on our old couch, laid there alone for what felt like hours, and finally responded with just one word.

— **Okay.** —

THREE

Just One Shot

FALL FADED SLOWLY INTO winter, the weather not really changing much in the process, blurring the seasons together in my mind. Jamie drove me to and from school every day, even when basketball practices picked up, and he never complained when I shared yet another unfavorable update on the status of my car.

It worked out, actually, because he stayed for practice while I volunteered with Interact or stayed after to help the Debate Club. We would meet in the parking lot, him dripping in sweat that somehow made him more attractive rather than less and I dripping in sarcastic remarks geared toward the drama on his team.

Sometimes, when he could, he would drive me to work or pick me up after a late shift at the grocery store. He would drive me to the football games, too, and we'd sit side-by-side, drinking slushies and watching Jenna cheer. We talked more and stared at each other less, which made my conscience feel better. When we both had time, he would even drive us out to the beach to catch the surf, both of our boards fitting easily on top of his Jeep.

So as the seasons changed, we fell into a routine. And he and Jenna fell in love.

I had an up close and personal seat to watch it happen, and I was genuinely happy for them. Jamie was hands down the best guy I knew and Jenna was my best friend. I couldn't have picked a better match.

At least, that's what I told myself.

My car was finally fixed on December fourth, a whopping three months after my dad had taken it into the shop. When I'd told Jamie, he seemed happy — not necessarily relieved, but happy — and that upset me. There was a part of me that hoped he might be disappointed, that he might miss our drives spent talking and listening to music, too.

And when I realized that was how I felt, I was even more upset. Because I didn't have the right to wish those things any more than he had the right to feel them.

When fall semester ended, Jenna left town for her family's annual ski trip in Colorado. I didn't expect to hear from Jamie over break, since Jenna was out of town, and I didn't — until Christmas Eve.

It was after midnight, but I was wide awake, my stomach in knots knowing my father would be sitting at our kitchen table the next day. Our family was always together on Christmas — no matter what — and while it used to be a tradition I loved, it was one I dreaded now. They used to do it to put on a show for me, to make me feel like our family was somewhat still a unit, but now that I knew everything? I just wondered what the point of it was. I didn't want to play the game, anymore. So I was tossing and turning, not really even trying to sleep when my phone pinged with a text from Jamie.

— **Are you awake?** —

I squinted through the darkness at the screen, debating whether to answer or not. There was a strange twist in my stomach urging me not to, but another, more powerful part of me somehow knowing he needed to talk to someone that night. In the end, I gave in to curiosity.

— **Indeed I am.** —

— **Take a drive with me?** —

There was that little twist again. The warning bells.

— **Sure.** —

Less than fifteen minutes later, I was buckled into Jamie's passenger seat as he cruised the ghosted streets on my side of town. Everyone was asleep, waiting on the big man in the red suit to sneak in through the doggy doors since no one had chimneys in South Florida. We had the town to ourselves, and Jamie took his time, driving slow, no destination in mind. His music was louder that night, William Joseph's "Standing the Storm" spilling from the speakers as he shifted his grip on the steering wheel over and over. His usual carefree expression had been replaced by a more pensive one, his brows pinched together and his eyes hard on the road in front of us. Every now and then he would sigh, but he still didn't say a single word. I let him drive in our comfortable silence for almost an hour before I reached forward to lower the volume.

"Did I ever tell you about why I hate cats?"

My words seemed to snap Jamie out of his haze, his head jetting back as a grin split his face. "Oh this ought to be good."

"See, I had a cat once," I said, sitting up straighter and tucking my feet under my thighs. I'd already kicked my shoes off, finding my comfortable position in my seat next to Jamie. It felt almost like home after that semester. "Her name was Aurora, like the princess, but we called her Rory. Only she wasn't a princess. Like, at all. She was actually the devil."

A loud laugh boomed out of Jamie's throat and I smiled inside, knowing my story was working — at least at the moment.

"She refused to shit in her litter box. I'm serious — *refused.* She would shit right outside of it instead. And because I'd begged my mom for the damn cat, guess who got stuck picking up after her?" I poked both of my thumbs hard into my chest. "This girl. But that wasn't the worst of it."

"Should I pull over for this?" Jamie teased.

"This is serious, Jamie Shaw!" I smacked his bicep and he chuckled, holding the steering wheel with his thumbs but lifting the rest of his fingers as if to say "my bad."

"*Anyway,*" I continued. "So, Rory would always find small ways to torture me. Like she would eat her string toys and then throw up on my favorite clothes. Or wait until I was in the deepest part of sleep and jump onto my bed, meowing like an alleycat right up in my ear."

"I think I like this Rory."

I narrowed my eyes, but Jamie just grinned. "You think you're hilarious, don't you? Do you just sit around and laugh at your own jokes? Do you write them down and re-read them at night?"

Jamie laughed, the corners of his eyes crinkling.

"As I was saying," I voiced louder. "She was a little brat. But for some weird reason, she always loved to be in the bathroom with me when I took my baths."

"You take baths?"

"You're seriously missing the point of this story!"

"There's a point to this story?"

I huffed, but couldn't fight the smile on my face. "Yes! The point is, I thought that was our bonding time. Rory would weave around my legs while I undressed and she'd hang out on the side of the tub the entire time I was in the bath, meowing occasionally, pawing at the water. It was kind of cute."

"So you bridged your relationship with your cat during bath time?"

"Ah, well see, one would think that. But, one night, that little demon hopped onto the counter and just stared at me. I couldn't figure out why, but she just wouldn't stop *staring*. She kept inching her paw up, setting it back down, inching it up, setting it down. And finally I realized what she was going to do — and she knew I did — because as soon as realization dawned, Rory smiled at me — swear to God — and flipped the light off in the bathroom."

Jamie doubled over that time, and I spoke even louder over his laughter.

"I'm terrified of the dark, Jamie! It was awful! And so I jumped up, scrambling to find a towel so I could turn the

40

light back on. But because I'm a genius, I yanked on the shower curtain to help me stand up, but that only took it down and me along with it. I fell straight to the floor, but I broke my fall with my hands instead of my face."

"Luckily."

"Oh," I chided. "Yeah. *So* lucky. Except guess where Rory's litter box was?"

Jamie's eyes widened and he tore his eyes from the road to meet mine. "No!"

"Ohhh yeah. My left hand landed right smack in the middle of a steaming pile of poo. And Rory laughed inside that little manic head of hers as she watched the whole show."

"This seriously has to be made up," Jamie wheezed as we pulled up to a stoplight, his free hand gripping his stomach.

"I only wish I was that creative."

We both laughed together, the silence in the car finally warmed over. When the light turned green, Jamie eased on the gas, but didn't reach for the volume to crank the music again.

"So. Baths, huh?"

I nodded, untucking my legs and resting my bare feet on his dash. "Yep. I do my best thinking submerged in a tub of hot water. Bubbles are an added bonus." I winked.

"Baths are to you as driving is to me."

"Mm-hmm," I agreed. "Which brings us to the purple elephant in the car." I leaned my head back, eying Jamie as the smile slipped from his face. "Care to tell me the reason we're driving around this dead ass town in the middle of the night?"

It was the small movements that always gave Jamie away. He never really exaggerated anything — but there were subtle shifts that always tipped me off to when something was on his mind. His thumb would slowly slide along the steering wheel, or his left brow would dip just marginally before evening out again, and sometimes he would crack his neck — quickly and quietly. That night, I'd seen all three, and he knew to not even try to tell me there was nothing wrong. I knew better.

"I don't know, B. I just… ever since school let out, I can't stop thinking about how fast everything is changing. I mean, it's Christmas, my last Christmas home with my family. In six months, I'll no longer be in high school. In eight, I'll no longer be in Florida. It feels like my entire life I've been aching to grow up and move on and now that it's all here, I'm dreading it. It's too soon. I'm not ready." He swallowed, taking a left turn and steering us toward the beach. "I'm scared."

"It's okay to be scared," I whispered.

"Is it?" he challenged, parking the Jeep in a free spot in front of a beach bar. He rolled down his window to check the parking meter, but I guessed it was probably free parking at this time of night. He didn't make a move for cash, but left the window down, his elbow resting on the edge. "I've always been so sure of everything. Confident. And here I am at one of the most exciting times of my life and I feel like hiding."

I rolled my window down too, and Jamie took it as a cue to cut the engine. The distant sound of the waves behind the bar replaced the cool hum of the engine and we both relaxed into the comfort it brought.

"I think it's normal, to feel both excited and terrified of the future. And I'd be willing to bet every senior goes through what you are right now. You're excited to get out of high school, but also sad, because as much as it's sucked, it's been fun, too. I mean look at you — you're this big basketball star and you're playing your last season, your hot little girlfriend is a junior, so you know she's not coming with you, and you're going from a familiar city and state to one you've only visited before now."

He shifted when I mentioned Jenna, but I tried to move on quickly.

"What I'm saying is it's okay to feel what you're feeling. I'd be more concerned if you weren't scared."

For a minute we were silent, and Jamie ran both hands back through his long hair. I wondered if he'd cut it when we graduated. I hoped he wouldn't.

"What if I fail? What if I hate college and all the pressure and I just crack?"

"You won't."

"But what if I do?"

"You *won't*, Jamie," I said again, leaning over the consul. I waited until he looked at me to continue. "Over the past few months, I've learned a lot about you. I know that when you want something — truly want it — there's no chance in hell you'll ever give up on it. Like when you wanted me to go watch one of your stupid basketball games even though you knew how much I hated it and you found new ways to pester me every day until I finally gave in." I chuckled, but he remained stoic, so I cleared my throat and leaned in a little closer.

43

"I know how much your family means to you, how much the firm means to you, and since you never play fair," I teased, "you don't have to worry about not succeeding." The corner of his mouth lifted, but fell too quickly. I reached out then, just barely placing my hand over his. "In all seriousness, you're not going to fail. Because that's not who you are. And I think once your feet hit California, you're going to buzz to life with the energy there and use that to drive you forward. And you're going to drink too much and stay up too late but you're also going to study hard and work harder and one day you'll be back here, running the firm, with the wife and kids you've always wanted." My throat felt thick at the mention of him building a family. "And I'm going to be sitting right here saying, 'I told you so.'"

Jamie turned to me then, and I realized how close we were. Too close. I felt his breath on my lips, but my eyes never left his. He smelled like fall — not like pumpkin and freshly fallen leaves, but like fall in Florida — salty like the beach air, earthy like the palm trees, with a sweet spiciness that reminded me of the honey whiskey my dad always drank after Thanksgiving dinner.

"I hope you're right," he finally said, voice just above a whisper.

My heart was racing, my hand still touching his, and he moved his fingers beneath mine as if he were about to grab me in return. But I took my chance to put distance between us, sitting back in my seat with a grin and a wink. "Always am."

Jamie turned on a new playlist after a while and we sat together, letting our minds race as we watched the waves gently roll in. It was too dark to really see them, but we could hear them, smell them, feel them. It was almost dawn by the time Jamie turned the Jeep back on to drive me home, and my eyelids were heavy when he pulled into the driveway.

"Can I ask you something?" Jamie asked as my hand found the door handle. I nodded. "What happened to Rory?"

I smiled, feeling the sleepiness tighten my skin. "My grandma came and stayed with us not too long after the bathroom incident and she and Rory fell in love. I suggested she take her, and I'd barely gotten the sentence out before Grandma was loading her up in the car."

Jamie looked tired, too — his honey eyes rimmed with red. But he was smiling at me so genuinely, watching me so closely — like he always did.

"Can I ask you something now?" I whispered.

"You can always ask me anything."

I hated the way those words both stung and exhilarated me, like a stiff shot of liquor.

"If Jenna wasn't out of town, would you have texted her tonight instead?"

Jamie's brows bent, and I hated the way my breath shallowed as I waited for him to speak. But when he finally did, I wished I'd never asked at all.

"Don't make me answer that."

His eyes were focused on mine, looking for my reaction, and I did my best not to have one. Nodding, my lips spread into a quick smile, but it slipped just as quickly as it'd appeared. "Goodnight, Jamie."

With that, I opened the door and closed it as quietly as I could behind me before sneaking back into my room. The sun was already starting to rise and I knew I didn't have much time to sleep, yet still, I couldn't even shut my eyes. I just stared at my wall, knees tucked up and covers wrapped around me tightly.

Of course he would have called her if she were here. Jenna was his girlfriend, and I was just his friend. Which was fine, I reminded myself. It was more than fine. It was the way things were meant to be. Jenna and Jamie just made sense, and I was happy to be a part of the tricycle.

Everything was *fine*.

My eyes were fluttery, exhaustion seeping in, but just before I could doze off, my phone pinged from my bedside table. I tilted it up, my heart stopping at the text on the screen.

— **Thanks for tonight... You're my best friend, B.** —

I stared at those last two words before my name, reading them together and then dissecting them until they blurred and I dropped my phone back to the nightstand, finally surrendering to sleep.

• • •

It was less than a month before the end of the school year when Jenna told me she was breaking up with Jamie.

"What?!" I exclaimed, a little too loudly, my burrito half-falling out of my mouth. I scrambled for my napkin, wiping at my mouth with wide eyes still locked in on Jenna's unfazed face. "What are you talking about? Why? What happened?"

"Isn't it obvious?" Jenna asked, diving into the guacamole with one of her chips before popping it into her mouth. We were in the middle of the food court at the mall, hundreds of people around us shopping away, not knowing my best friend was dropping astronomical news on me mid-Mexican Fiesta. "He's leaving, B. Jamie is about to graduate and move to California. It's been fun, but it's over. I mean, I knew this was coming. He was a great boyfriend, but it is what it is."

She said it so nonchalantly, dressing up another chip while I gripped my foil-wrapped burrito so hard the fillings oozed out onto my hands. I dropped it to my plate, grabbing more napkins, mouth still open wide. "Jenna, you can't break up with Jamie. You guys are perfect together."

Jenna scrunched her nose. "I mean, we're cute together, yes, but he's going to college, dude. He's going to want some sorority girl or something. And I'm going to be a senior. The last thing I want is a long-distance relationship."

"But this is *Jamie*!" I argued. "We're talking about hilarious, down-to-earth, smart and driven Jamie. The guy who brought us chick flicks, french fries, and chocolate when it was period week. The guy who went to every single football game to watch you cheer. The guy who wore a freaking hot pink tie to match your prom dress." I was waving my arms around like a mad woman, but Jenna didn't bat an eye.

"Like I said, he was a great boyfriend. Amazing, even. But we both knew it wasn't going to last. And it's totally okay."

"No it's not!" I couldn't figure out why I was so horrified by her news, but I just couldn't let it go. "He listens to classical music, Jenna. Like come on, what other guy do you know who listens to classical music?"

"Um, no one?"

"Exactly!" I said, exasperated. "And he has goals. He wants a family. He has the best sense of humor but he can also be serious when he needs to be. He's like the pegasus to your unicorn."

"Okay…"

"And he's a good friend. Like, the best kind. He treats his mom like a queen and that says something about a man. And he drives a bright cherry red Jeep, Jenna! He surfs!"

"Oh my God, I get it!" she finally huffed, tossing her hands up before crossing them over her chest. She rolled her eyes. "Jeeze, maybe you should date him."

I had nothing in my mouth to choke on, but I choked anyway. "What? No, no way. He's, no Jamie is *your* boyfriend. You guys are perfect together. Jamie and I? No. We couldn't, we'd never. No way." I was stumbling over my words, slurping my drink too hard in-between sentences. I was officially the furthest thing from cool about the whole situation.

And Jenna noticed.

She narrowed her eyes. "I was joking, spazz. What is up with you? Why does this bother you so much?"

Jenna was scrutinizing me, waiting for a confession of some kind. I stared back at her for a minute, frozen, and then finally forced a long, deep breath before covering my face with my hands. "Ugh, I don't know. I'm sorry. I just really thought you guys were good together." I sighed, scrubbing my hands down my face and letting them slap into my lap. "I just want you to be happy. But clearly you're fine with this and it's what you want, so of course I support you. It's just my job as your best friend to question big decisions like this and make you think about them."

She was still watching me, eyes wary, but she smiled. "I love you, B. Even if you are thirty-five shades of weird."

"Love you too, bestie."

I forced a smile and changed the subject, all the while replaying our conversation in my head and wondering how Jamie would take the news.

I must have texted Jenna a million times that night asking if she'd done it yet, but she hadn't. She waited four days to break up with him, and once she told me it was done, I waited again — for him to text, for him to show up at my house, to want to take a drive. But he didn't. He didn't say a word to me. Not the night it happened, or the night after, or the week after. Jamie completely ignored me and Jenna both until the night he graduated.

And that was when I met the other side of Jamie Shaw.

• • •

It had been more than three months since I'd had a Friday night off.

Since I needed every single Friday off in the fall semester for the games, I had to make up for it once football season was over by picking up the Friday slack at the grocery store. But now, school was out, the seniors were currently walking across the stage at our high school gym, and I was less than an hour away from stepping into the role they just left vacant.

Senior.

It felt strange, calling myself a senior, like when you say a word too many times out loud and it stops making sense. The plan for that night had been to crash the grad parties, say goodbye to our senior friends and toast our new reign. But Brad Newman's parents had surprised him with a trip to the Bahamas, flying out immediately after graduation, and so the biggest grad party of the night had, in turn, been cancelled.

Jenna made a joke earlier that week when we found out, saying that we should throw a party at my house. I don't think she expected me to say, "Let's do it!" Hell, *I* didn't expect me to say it. But I was high that week, feeling the rush from the transition, and my mom was going to be out of town. Why not throw a party?

So instead of getting ready to go out, Jenna and I were setting up my house, lining the counters with booze most of the seniors had worked together to get for the occasion and cranking the music on my mom's old five-CD changer stereo. We were both dancing as we mixed punches with too much alcohol, broke out my mom's favorite shot glasses, and put on lipstick that smeared too easily on the rims of our red plastic cups.

"To us," Jenna said, her cup tapping mine. "The new seniors."

"*Seniors*, Jenna!" I squealed, sipping my drink quickly before wrapping her in a crushing hug. "Can you believe we've made it? From pigtails and sandboxes to high school seniors."

"I know, it's crazy to think about," Jenna agreed, her eyes glossy as she shook her head. We were standing in my small kitchen, her leaned back against the counter while I straightened everything for the fifteenth time. "I couldn't have gotten through all these years without you."

I paused, smiling at my best friend. "Me either." Lifting my drink to my lips again, I kept my eyes on the counter when I asked, "Do you think Jamie will show?"

It seemed I was more affected by that possibility than Jenna was, because she simply shrugged, shaking her blonde hair over her shoulder and adjusting the spaghetti straps of her thin tank top. "I doubt it. He went ghost on us after I broke up with him. I imagine he'll probably end up at a different party, if he even goes out at all." She frowned. "I think I broke his heart, B."

I took another, longer drink, letting the fruity sting of the alcohol sink in. "I should turn the air down. It's probably going to get pretty hot in here."

I couldn't have known how right I'd be about that.

The party kicked into gear slowly, a few people trickling in around nine followed by a few more and it continued like that until my house was completely packed. The music was too loud, thumping through every room as tables were cleared of picture frames and knick knacks and replaced instead with drinking games of various types. With how often the front door opened to let new people in and the back door opened to let people out to smoke and drink in the back yard, it became a pointless task to try to keep it cool. South Florida was hot in June, plain and simple, and I gave up trying to fight that.

Still, if I wasn't able to control the temperature inside, I needed to find another way to stay cool. The alcohol was cold, but still sent a heat wave through me with each new sip. I was in the middle of a flip cup game with Jenna and a slew of people I didn't know very well when I gave up and decided to go for the next option — taking clothes off.

I had a thin tank top on underneath my shirt, so the strip show would be PG-13, at best. I pulled the loose v-neck over my head, vision temporarily blocked by the lavender fabric before I dropped it to the floor with a smile, those in close proximity cheering over the music at my little stunt. I felt instantly cooler for all of three seconds before my eyes landed on the newest arrivals at the party and my smile slipped, along with the cup in my hand, its contents crashing to the table.

Jamie looked different. I knew it had only been a few weeks since we'd hung out, I knew he was the same age, but there was something different about him. It was the way he carried himself, the cocky half-smile he was flashing me as he high-fived a few of the guys in my living room, the challenge in his eyes before he tore them away from me and turned to a tiny brunette on Jenna's cheerleading squad, instead. I don't know how long I stood there staring at him with my mouth open, but clearly it was long enough for Jenna to notice, because she followed my eyes and gasped.

"Holy shit, he showed."

I swallowed, finally ripping my eyes away and stacking cups for a new game. "Mm-hmm."

"He looks hot."

"Everyone does, it's a hundred degrees in here."

Jenna smirked, nudging my elbow before letting her eyes find Jamie again. "Man, maybe I should have waited until after graduation to break things off. Would be nice to have one more night with him…"

"I'm going to go figure out what to do with my hair," I said quickly, giving up on setting up a new game and ducking through the crowd to my room. There were several signs on the door with warnings of those who dared to enter, clearly marking it as a NO PARTY ZONE, which I was even more grateful for when I slipped inside and felt the only air-conditioned relief in the house. I sighed, back against my door, and took a few much-needed breaths through my nose before opening my eyes again.

I fanned my neck, crossing to my small vanity mirror and taking a pulse check of my appearance. My makeup was somehow holding up, eyes dark and dramatic like Jenna had shown me how to do, but my hair was frizzy and unruly, so I twisted it into a tight bun on top of my head and secured it with a few bobby pins before reapplying lipstick. The deep, dark red almost made my freckles pop more under my gray eyes, but I embraced them.

Turning in the mirror, I eyed the wet spots on my tank top, debating changing, but knowing that would earn me a few raised eyebrows from my classmates. I'd just called attention to what I was wearing and it would be weird to walk out in something new now.

Once I had regained my composure, I slipped back out to the stifling heat of the party and made my way to the kitchen, a new idea for cooling myself sparking to life. Frozen margaritas. That's what this party needed. But first,

I had to get to my mom's blender, which was conveniently placed on the very top shelf of our top right cabinet.

I opened the cabinet wide and eyed the edge of the blender peeking out over the shelf, hands on my hips, debating options. I'd just braced my hands on the counter and was about to lift myself up when strong hands found my waist.

"Here," he said, voice low and husky. "Let me help."

His hands gripped tighter and he lifted me, my knees finding the counter as I tried to find my breath and a little balance. For a second I just stayed there, staring at the blender within reach now, but not being able to focus on anything other than where his hot skin touched mine. My tank top had risen, his grip on the slick skin of my hips. I forced a breath, grabbed the blender, and made to turn but was stopped by him once more.

He had stepped closer to the counter and every inch of my body brushed his as he lowered me down. First just my hips in his hands, but then my ass rubbed against the front of him, causing him to groan into my neck as my toes finally found solid ground. I turned, his hands still on me, my breath still caught in my throat as I lifted my eyes to his.

"Hi, Jamie."

He smirked down at me, his eyes too heated, too low. "Hi."

I cleared my throat as a sign for him to drop his hands from where they seared themselves to my skin, but he didn't catch the cue. Or he didn't care. So I slipped out of his grasp and plugged the blender in, reaching into the freezer for ice and searching mom's cabinets for margarita mix. I found some, blessedly, and snatched what was left of a Jose Cuervo bottle on my way back to the blender.

Jamie stood next to it, casually leaned up against the counter, arms crossed. His hair was longer than I remembered, curling at his ears and laying in a perfect wave across his forehead. He hadn't changed out of his graduation clothes, but he'd loosened the tie around his neck and unbuttoned the top button of his shirt, rolling the sleeves up to cuff just below his elbows. It was clean, crisp, and white, calling attention to the tan he'd clearly been working on since I'd last seen him. I wondered if he had been surfing, work keeping me from doing the same.

"You're wearing makeup," he said as I sidled up beside him, dumping ice cubes into the blender and covering them in tequila.

"And you're wearing dress shoes."

He looked down, chuckling, before lifting his hazy eyes back to mine. "We should dance."

"Wh—"

I didn't have the chance to ask my question because Jamie grabbed my wrist and twirled me before pulling me flush against him, attempting some sort of drunken version of a waltz in my tiny kitchen as high schoolers weaved in and out around us, oblivious to the way he was making my heart race. I giggled, breaking free after another spin and finding my place back at the blender, topping off the tequila with margarita mix and snapping the lid in place.

"You're drunk, Jamie Shaw."

"And are you, B Kennedy?"

I clicked the blend option and spoke over the noise of ice breaking. "I'm getting there." I eyed him, my head tilted to the side as I tried unsuccessfully to figure out what had changed. Jamie seemed more dangerous that night. He stood too close, watched me for too long. It was unnerving, but in an oddly pleasing way. "What have you been drinking, anyway?"

"Whiskey," he answered easily, and a short laugh escaped my lips.

"Of course. I should have guessed."

"What's that supposed to mean?"

I shrugged, using a spoon to break up a large ice chunk before replacing the top on the blender and turning it on again. "Just makes sense. You're practically whiskey on legs, anyway. The color of your hair, your eyes, the way you smell — it's like your spirit drink."

"I remind you of whiskey?"

"In every sense of the word," I murmured, maybe too low for him to hear. I thought of how his skin burned mine when he touched me, how just being in his vicinity made my limbs tingle.

I realized then that it was harder pretending like he didn't affect me when he was no longer tied to my best friend.

"We should do a shot." Jamie pushed off the counter and grabbed the only bottle of Jack Daniel's, filling two of my mom's shot glasses to the rim before turning back to me. He slid the one branded with the downtown casino's logo into my hand and lifted the other.

"I'm making a tequila drink," I pointed out. "Mixing will probably screw me in the long run."

"Nah, you'll be fine."

"I don't know, Jamie…"

"Oh come on," he challenged, taking a small step toward me. It was tiny, barely even an inch, but suddenly I felt the heat from him surrounding me and I picked at my tank top with my free hand, desperate for a breeze. "Don't you want a little whiskey on your lips?"

My eyes shot to his, because I knew as well as he did that there was more than one question beneath the one he'd voiced out loud. He cocked a brow, waiting, and though I should have pushed him back, made space, poured up a margarita and walked away from him, I lifted my glass to his instead.

"To bad decisions."

His grin widened, his eyes never leaving me as I tilted my head back, letting the amber liquid coat my throat. Jamie took his slower than I did, inhaling through his teeth as the burn settled in.

And just like that, I'd taken my first shot. I didn't tell Jamie it was my first one, I didn't think I needed to. I wanted to hate it, to detest it, to grimace and wipe my mouth with the back of my hand and reach for a chaser. But we set the glasses back on the counter slowly, our fingers brushing, and Jamie's eyes were on my lips where leftover whiskey remained. My tongue traced the liquid, and he inhaled stiffly, eyes snapping up to mine.

Cat, meet mouse.

• • •

My mom was going to murder me.

Nearly everyone was gone now, the time on my phone reading 3:47AM. Everyone except for Jenna, who was passed out in my bed, Ali, a basketball player in my grade, who was curled around the same toilet Mom had been hugging the night she told me about Dad, and Jamie, who had stayed to help me clean what little we could once the last of the party had cleared out.

The carpets were ruined, that much I could tell for sure. I could probably salvage the cabinets and tables with a good scrub down and I'd need to search every corner for trash. Sticky cups had been gathered and thrown away, but shot glasses still littered the kitchen and various spots in the living room. It reeked of alcohol, a smell I wasn't exactly sure how to get rid of at the time, and I was supposed to work in seven hours.

"I have to call out," I finally said, blowing out a breath as I surveyed our surroundings.

Jamie looked around, too, running a hand through his long hair. "When does your mom get home?"

"Late tomorrow night." I checked my phone again. "Or should I say, late tonight."

"You've got time. It's not too bad." I leveled my eyes and he bit back a smile. "Okay, so the carpet is shot, but everything else is fixable."

"My TV remote is missing."

"Replaceable."

"There's a mustache made out of spitting tobacco on my face in one of the only family pictures we have."

Jamie tucked his hands into the pockets of his dress pants. "Yeah, you're kind of screwed."

"I told you what would happen if I mixed alcohol," I teased, trying to find humor in the situation while I still could.

Jamie crossed the living room to where I was standing, his eyes bloodshot but still beautiful. "Let's get out of here for a while."

"Are you crazy? I need to clean. I need to…" I waved my hands around. "Do something. About all of this."

"You've already admitted that you're screwed, B. What you *can* do is only going to take you a few hours, so why not send out tonight with a bang?"

I chewed my lip, knowing he was right and hating it all the same. "What do you have in mind?"

• • •

Jamie thumbed through his phone as we settled in on a blanket in the sand, feet facing the waves, the beach still dark. He landed on Chad Lawson's *The Piano* album, adjusting the volume before setting his phone down between us and reaching into the brown paper bag on his lap. He handed me one burrito before retrieving his and setting the brown bag aside, using his shoes to weigh it down against the wind.

I couldn't believe he'd convinced the cab driver to take us through the only 24-hour breakfast drive-thru in town, but I was happy he had been smart enough to realize neither of us was in shape to drive. He cracked the seal on a Vitamin Water and took a long pull before passing it to me.

"Think this will save us from a hangover?" I asked, taking a sip before passing the bottle back to him. He replaced the lid and we both went to work unwrapping the tin foil around our breakfast burritos — mine bacon, his sausage.

"I think it's one of my more brilliant ideas. What cures a hangover better than greasy eggs, Vitamin Water, and the beach?"

"So modest," I chided, taking my first bite. The sarcasm died on my lips after that. "Homahgawd." I groaned, taking another bite as Jamie watched me, chuckling.

"You're welcome."

I grinned through a full mouth, but didn't say anything else. For a while, we just listened to the smooth melodies flowing from Jamie's phone as we ate and shared that one drink between us. Dawn was on the horizon, the beach glowing first in a cool pool of blue before taking on a soft purple hue. I was still in the thin tank top I'd stripped down to at the party and I shivered a bit against the cool breeze rolling in off the waves.

"Here," Jamie said, unbuttoning his shirt the rest of the way down. He yanked his tie off before shaking one arm out and then the other. I tried to argue with him, at least I thought I did, but my voice must have been just as stuck in my throat as my eyes were on his chest. His bare, beautiful chest. He draped his shirt over my shoulders, the fabric still warm from him, dripping in his scent, and I sighed with the comfort it brought.

"Thank you." I peeled at the foil covering my burrito, eyes on the water. "So, you excited to get out of here? Ready to cause trouble at UC San Diego?"

He smirked, but offered a single shrug. "Yes and no. Remember our talk over Christmas break?"

I nodded.

"I'm still feeling a bit of all that. Don't get me wrong, I'm excited for this next chapter and all that, but it's still a little scary."

"It'd be weird if you weren't scared," I reminded him, and he gave me a small smile. I could tell he didn't want to talk about the future anymore, and in a way I didn't blame him. Up until that point in our lives, high school had been our biggest and best experience. It was hard to imagine a future where the things that mattered to us then would only be a distant memory.

When we finished our burritos, we both leaned back on our palms, watching as the sun began its slow ascent. There was always so much hype around sunsets on the west coast of Florida, but I found even more beauty in the sunrises on our coast. There was something about being so close to the ocean at the dawn of a new day, filled with new possibilities.

"You've been avoiding me," I said after a while, keeping my eyes on the horizon just past my toes.

"Not just you."

"I know," I clarified. "I just thought maybe you'd call me. Or want to go for a drive. Or..." I didn't know what else to say, so I let my sentence fade on the breeze.

"I wanted to," Jamie said, adjusting the weight on the heels of his hands. "I don't know. Jenna hit me at a time that was already so hard for me, you know?" A line formed between his brows. "My parents were high school sweethearts."

61

The weight of that statement hit me hard in the chest. What he meant to say was that he wanted what his parents had, and he thought Jenna was the key to that. I suddenly realized her breaking up with him was the best thing that could have happened to me. Even then, when I was still in denial about my addiction, the thought of him marrying my best friend nearly caused me to gasp out loud.

"It's okay that Jenna wasn't the one."

"I know," he said quickly. "I think I always knew. She was fun, we clicked, had some great times together. But there was something missing." He turned to me then, eyes boring into the side of my face because I refused to meet that stare.

"You'll find someone," I said softly, eyes still on the waves. They were bathed in a pinkish-orange glow as the sun struggled to wake up our part of the world.

"Well," he said loudly, sitting up straighter. "I don't like leaving my life to chance. So, I have a proposition." I met his eyes then, and they were playful — mischievous. "If you're game, that is."

"Why do I feel like I should run right now?"

Jamie laughed, and it was the first time I'd seen his real smile break through that night — teeth bright, skin wrinkled at the corners of his eyes. "I say we make a pact."

"A pact?"

He nodded. "If neither of us are married by the time we're thirty, we marry each other."

"Oh my God," I scoffed, leaning up to mirror his new posture. "That is so stupid, Jamie. It's also the plot line for every cheesy Rom Com ever."

He shrugged, wiping the sand from his hands and gazing back out at the water. "Sounds like someone is scared."

"I'm not *scared*. It's dumb."

"Mm-hmm."

"I'm going to be married by thirty, Jamie. And you're *definitely* going to be locked down by then."

"So then you have nothing to worry about." He challenged me for the second time that night, eyes sparking to life as they met mine. He extended his hand. "If we're not married in twelve years, you become Mrs. Shaw."

I swallowed hard at his words. *Mrs Shaw.* "That's not fair. You turn thirty before me."

Jamie shrugged again. "My pact, my terms. Do we have a deal?" He thrust his hand out farther, and I stared at it, brows bent as I chewed my cheek. Finally, I rolled my eyes and gripped his hand with my own, shaking it three times. "Fine. But this is dumb, and pointless."

Jamie just grinned.

"You're so weird," I said, getting in the last word on my feelings about the stupid pact.

"Yeah, but you love me anyway." He winked, stealing the Vitamin Water from the space between us and draining the last of it before leaning back on his hands again.

I didn't think too long about the fact that he'd said I loved him, or the possibility that he might be right. I didn't think about the pact or what would happen in twelve years, because Jamie was leaving, and I was staying.

Mom grounded me for the first month of that summer and I had to pay to replace the carpets, but I didn't even care. It was worth it to have that first shot of Whiskey, to eat breakfast burritos on the beach and make stupid promises we wouldn't keep.

That was supposed to be the last night I saw Jamie Shaw.

I let him go, just like I was supposed to, and I did my best to never think about him again. Not that summer when I saw him around town, not that fall when he left for California and I stayed behind, not even when I applied to Alder University knowing it was in the same city as the University of California San Diego. I avoided looking at his social media, too. Eventually, as senior year kicked into gear and my focus became my *own* graduation, I really did start to let him go.

But as fate would have it, that wasn't my last night with Jamie Shaw.

Not even close.

FOUR

Barrel Aged

THE THING ABOUT WHISKEY is that the longer it sits in the barrel, the more it changes — and it never stops. Whiskey aged for two years is different from whiskey aged for ten, and no matter what year you decide to throw the towel in and pour up a glass, you can't go wrong. Whiskey at a ripe age, young and full of character, is buzz-worthy. But whiskey aged, even just a little bit? Pure bliss.

And don't let the fact that some of the alcohol evaporates over time fool you, because when you taste that aged whiskey, it'll burn just as deliciously as it did when it was young.

I was strolling the rows of tables lining the student union walkway at Alder University in San Diego, taking fliers from a few of them, passing by others, when the barrel cracked open.

"Hi!" the blonde seated behind the Campus Housing table said excitedly. "Are you picking up your housing information?"

I did my best impression of Ryan Atwood from *The OC*, channeling the lip tuck and eyebrow raise of indifference. I *was* in California, after all. "Indeed I am."

"Great!" she answered too quickly, clapping her hands together. "Last name?"

"Kennedy."

She went to work searching through the various envelopes lined up on her table and I bounced on my heels, enjoying the warmth of the sun mixed with the cool breeze. It was the last week of August, a normally hellish time in South Florida, but the weather was still mild in San Diego. Sun bright, a few white clouds floating by, breeze rolling in off the coast. It couldn't be more than eighty degrees and I smiled at the feel of the light air, the humidity so much less stifling than that of Florida. I was officially in my new home for the next four years, and I knew immediately that I'd made the right choice choosing Alder.

Alder University was a small, private campus, but a prestigious one. Tucked between the heart of San Diego and Imperial Beach and stocked with a plethora of options for undecided undergrads, it was the perfect college for me. I smiled again, hiking the same Jansport I'd used all through high school up higher on my back just as the perky blonde snapped her fingers.

"Ah! Found it!" She plucked the folder out, checking its contents before looking back up to me. "Brecks, right?"

My smile immediately fell with her question, along with my mood. I somehow forced a tight smile, but before I could even nod, another voice boomed my answer from behind me.

"It's B," he said. His voice was smooth, oak infused and deeper than I remembered. I turned, words stuck in my throat, eyes wide as I drank him in. Every single inch of him, from his worn sneakers and basketball shorts to the soaked Alder t-shirt he wore, sticking to the defined ridges of his abdomen. My eyes trailed up over the faint stubble on his neck and jaw before they found honey whiskey pools. He slid up beside me then, crooked smile in place as he held my stare. "Just B."

Time stopped in that moment, and I couldn't keep my eyes from tracing his features — his new, shorter hair, his biceps that had filled out considerably since the last time I'd seen them propping him up on the beach in Florida, the few inches he'd grown. His aura was different, cockier, more sure. I wish I could tell you I'd been smoother than the first time I'd met him on that running trail, but the truth was I couldn't have been more obvious in my eye-assault, and he noticed, because when my eyes found his face again, he just cocked one brow and widened his grin.

"You cut your hair," I finally breathed, my body rejoining the world in a whoosh. It was like all the sounds of students and the birds in the California trees found me all at once, attacking my senses along with the brightness of the sun through my cheap sunglasses.

Jamie chuckled, lifting his hand to just barely touch my face. "And you got a nose ring."

I smiled, still staring at him, still not listening to the blonde behind the table who was trying to give me important information about my new dorm room. Luckily, Jamie was listening, and he reached over to take the envelope and keys from her. He winked, at her, not at me, and that's when I finally looked at her again.

"Good to see you, Jamie. How have you been?" she asked, too eagerly, and I eyed her up and down slowly. Big blonde hair, 80's-style curls, with bright blue eyes and skin tan enough to make me think it might be fake. She wasn't as pretty as Jenna, but she had similar features, which made me turn to Jamie to study his reaction with her.

"Oh you know, same old same. I think I got this," he said, holding up the envelope in his hands. "Take care, Melanie."

Melanie all but swooned as we walked away from the table, and I fought hard not to roll my eyes. "I take it you two know each other?" I asked, nodding back to where she was still staring at him.

He shrugged. "You could say that."

And the urge won over.

I let my eyes roll, and Jamie laughed, hard and solid, the sound booming. Then, he stopped, eyed me, and opened his arms wide. "Come here."

"Ew," I said quickly, shaking my head and walking forward. "You're sweatier than two rats fucking in a gym sock."

"Oh come on," he teased from behind me. "It's just a little perspiration." And then, I was off my feet and in the air, back pressed against the damp fabric covering his chest as he spun me around. I squealed, laughing and flailing until he put me down.

"Why *are* you so sweaty? And why are you here?"

"I just finished playing basketball out at the courts. And I go to school here. Which, I guess that makes two of us now," he added, holding up the envelope from Campus Housing. I snatched it from his grip and flipped through the contents, holding out my hand for him to drop my keys into as my mind raced.

"I didn't know you went here."

"Sure," he said. "It's okay that you're stalking me, B. Maybe I kind of like it."

"You wish," I replied, nose still in the papers. "Seriously though, you were supposed to be at UC. What happened?" My fingers filtered through the folder as I waited for him to respond. There was information about my Resident Assistant and various activities planned for the semester as well as safety protocols. I was one of the few freshmen lucky enough to land a dorm room where I had my own room, but shared a kitchen and bathroom space with three other girls. I'd met one of them at orientation earlier that summer, but the others I'd only looked up on social media, so I was anxious to meet them.

"Remember my uncle I told you about? The one who had connections at a university in California?" I nodded, and he grinned, opening his arms to gesture to the campus around us. "You're looking at the same university my dad and uncle graduated from, both with their degrees in Accounting. At first, my application was waitlisted, but my uncle knows a few of the guys on the Admissions Board, and he worked some magic."

"And now here you are," I said, peeking up at him.

His grin widened. "Here I am."

I shook my head, dropping my eyes to the housing packet again while my stomach did backflips. Jamie Shaw went to the same college as me. I didn't know whether to feel lucky or cursed, and the ache in my chest wasn't helping me decide. I'd avoided him since that night on the beach, letting him go, letting the *idea* of him go. He was Jenna's, and then he was gone — end of story.

Except now, it wasn't.

"So, you made it to California after all."

I looked up then, catching Jamie's amused eyes with my own. "I guess I did."

Though so much had changed about Jamie, one thing that hadn't was the way he stared at me — that expectant way, like he knew something I'd yet to figure out. I shifted under his gaze, suddenly hot, and was just about to ask how he liked it at Alder when I was picked up from behind for the second time.

Mid-air, I knew exactly who it was who had me pressed against them as they spun me around, and it almost killed me that for the past ten minutes since I'd run into Jamie, I hadn't thought about that person once.

Because you see, I didn't expect to see Jamie at Alder, but I *was* expecting to run into someone that day.

My boyfriend.

"Oh my God, I almost forgot how beautiful you are," Ethan said when he dropped me back to the ground. He immediately dipped me back, pressing his lips hard to mine as a blush crept up on my cheeks. He stood me back up, hands framing my face, before Jamie cleared his throat.

Ethan perked up at that, tucking me into his side and smiling wide at Jamie. "And I see you met my roommate!"

I blanched at that, my eyes wide while Jamie's were shielded beneath bent brows.

"Jamie is your roommate?" I squeaked.

"Yeah," he answered, pointing his finger between the two of us. "Y'all know each other?"

Jamie's eyes hadn't left mine, but they'd changed, grown cooler in tone somehow. "We went to high school together," he clipped.

I swallowed, studying Jamie's face, wondering why he suddenly looked ready to kill something. "Yeah. He dated my best friend back in the day."

"Huh!" Ethan mused, grin still in place. "What a small world!"

Jamie's nose flared, his eyes bouncing between Ethan and me before they stuck hard on where our hands had laced together. "I was just heading back to the dorm to shower. I'll see you later, Ethan."

"Later, bro."

Jamie glanced at me one last time before jogging off, leaving me stunned to silence beside his roommate.

My boyfriend.

Jesus.

"Let's get you moved in, babe," he said, kissing my hair as he steered us away from the union.

I had driven a tiny U-Haul truck here, convincing my mom that I wanted to do the trip by myself. It took almost a week with how often I stopped, but it was a nice road trip to do alone. It gave me time to think about the next chapter in my life, and I was excited to start writing it.

I pointed the U-Haul out to Ethan when we reached the parking lot near my dorms. He got to work, talking to me the entire time about everything he couldn't wait to show me as I tried to stay focused and present. The truth was, I could only think about one thing. One person. The boy I wasn't supposed to ever see again.

I would never admit it, but even then, I was already itching for another taste.

• • •

Jamie did a pretty good job of ignoring me after that.

I'd see him around campus sometimes, usually with his arm around a curvy blonde, which I'd learned quickly was his "type." But whenever we'd find ourselves in the same place, whether it be his and Ethan's dorm or a neutral space on campus, he somehow found an excuse to leave as soon as I showed up. We'd spent a total of maybe three minutes together since that first day on campus, and I was convinced he hated me.

But I didn't know why.

The most obvious answer would be that he didn't like that I was dating his roommate. But again, I found myself asking *why?* He'd dated my best friend in high school and I'd been nothing but supportive. Did he not like Ethan? Was he upset that I was a link to his past life in Florida, suddenly showing up to cramp his style? Was he upset I didn't tell him before I got here? We hadn't talked since that last day on the beach after his graduation, and I'd just met Ethan over the summer. I didn't know Jamie even went to Alder, let alone that he was Ethan's roommate, and it wasn't even like Ethan had much time to tell him, seeing as how he was in Florida for the summer while Jamie had stayed at Alder.

I worried myself sick with questions for a few days after our first encounter before worry turned to anger. This was Jamie, the boy I used to ride around town with, the boy who called me his best friend. And suddenly he was the world's biggest prick. He'd gone from smiling and joking with me on that first day to avoiding me completely, save for the glares he would occasionally throw my direction on his way out when I'd be hanging out in his and Ethan's dorm room. It was maddening.

Whatever. He wanted to ignore me? Fine. I would ignore him right back.

I was studying for my first sociology test about a month after school started when Jenna called. I smiled at the screen on my phone, flopping back on my bed to take a break and talk to my best friend who was an entire country away.

"I miss you!" she squealed as soon as the line connected.

"I miss you, too! How's New York?"

She huffed. "The city is amazing, the school work sucks, and the weather I haven't decided on yet. How about you? How are classes? How's Ethan?"

"Classes aren't bad, and Ethan is amazing. He's been really busy with Student Government, but I see him almost every night and he's been showing me a lot of the campus."

"You guys boning a lot?"

"Oh my God, Jenna." I rolled over, fingers tracing the lines of my pale-yellow comforter. My dorm room was small, but it had a door that separated me from my roommates, which was all I really needed in life. I had minimal decorations, my laptop the only thing that sat on my desk other than a photo of Jenna and me, and I had two motivational posters on the wall. The biggest embellishments were my throw pillows, yellow and white, and my lime green surfboard that leaned against the inside of my closet, begging to be used.

"What? You lost your v-card this summer, B. I'm finally allowed to ask you about your sex life and I'm taking every opportunity to do so."

I rolled my eyes. "We're boning a consistent amount, doctor, and I'm taking my birth control. Can we move on to something else now?"

Jenna laughed. "Fine. If you were wondering about me, I haven't hooked up with anyone yet, but I have my eyes on a few prospects."

"Thanks for the update, scout."

"So what else is new?"

Jenna was attending New York University, on the literal opposite side of the country from me, and the more we talked about professors and campus dining, the more I missed her. It was the first time we'd been apart since we were toddlers, and I was still having a hard time building a friendship with my roommates. I had three of them, one a volleyball player here on scholarship from Virginia, one an animal-rights' activist from northern California, and the other a soft-spoken Christian from Kansas. None of us had found much common ground to walk on yet, but I was trying to be hopeful.

"When can I come visit you? I miss the beach already," Jenna said with a longing sigh.

"My twin bed is yours to cuddle in anytime you want it."

"I'm serious, I'm going to just pop up on your doorstep one day."

I smiled. "And it'd be the best day ever."

After our phone call, I shot off an email to Mom with details on how classes were going. Our schedules hardly ever lined up enough for phone calls, but we had been emailing pretty steadily. Interestingly enough, our relationship had grown stronger during my last year of high school. Part of that might have been me disconnecting my father from my life completely while the other part was likely from me finally forgiving her for my name. I wasn't ready to embrace it again just yet, but after many late-night talks, I understood her motives. My mom had been a young, scared teenager when I was placed in her arms. And though I was born out of a tragedy, she found beauty in me, and she'd given up so much for me to chase my dreams.

I earned a few scholarships that helped get me to California, but I had still fallen short of what I needed. That was, until I found out Mom had been saving for my college fund religiously since I was born. Dad didn't have anything to offer me, other than a pat on the back at graduation, and I hadn't spoken to him since.

It hurt letting go of my dad, because for so long I'd lived in that space in-between, where I wasn't sure how to feel about him or what he did to my mom. But even in that space, we'd grown apart, and I didn't want the good memories I had with my dad to be replaced by awkward, tension-filled ones. So, I decided after graduation to just let him go. He'd only called once since then and I ignored it. Maybe we could reconnect later, but right now, I was content focusing on me for a while.

I'd just picked up my flashcards again when my bedroom door swung open.

"Ethan's here," Marie said without looking up from her phone. She was the animal-rights' activist and the one I thought I'd get along with the easiest. I mean, I was getting a minor in Women's Studies, embracing my feminist side, and she was trying to save kittens. We were a match made in heaven, right? Except she hadn't said more than thirteen words to me. Including the two she'd just used to introduce my boyfriend.

"Hey, beautiful," he crooned as he let himself into my room, closing the door behind him.

I smiled as he leaned down to kiss me, running my hands up his arms to hook around his neck. Ethan was strong, built, not much taller than me but so solid. His skin was the same as my mom's, dark and smooth, and he had full lips that I loved to kiss. He also had what I liked to call a "News Anchor Smile", blinding white, almost too wide and genuine for comfort.

We met the summer after I graduated high school when he was in Florida for an internship, after he spent a night at a Palm South University party sweeping me off my feet with cheesy pick up lines and random fruit facts. I shit you not, the man wooed me with mango and nectarine trivia. He kind of tasted like nectarines, actually — a tangy sort of sweetness.

"Please tell me you're almost done studying," he sang into my neck, still holding me close.

"I'm almost done studying."

"Yes!" he celebrated, pulling back to face me but keeping his arms around my waist. "We're going to a beach house party tonight."

"We are, are we?"

He nodded. "We are. It's casual, there's a pool and stuff, so just dress in a bathing suit and cover-up or whatever. I can pick you up and we can ride together."

I chewed my lip. "I don't know, Ethan. I may be almost done studying, but I still have that paper to write before Monday."

"And? Come on, it's Thursday, and I happen to know you don't have classes on Friday, and you don't work this weekend," he pointed out. I couldn't argue that. I'd picked up a job at the coffee house and bookstore on campus, but I'd requested the weekend off to write my paper and get in some last minute studying. "So take tonight to have fun with your sexy, eager-to-party boyfriend and then you can work the rest of the weekend and I won't bother you. Promise."

He puckered out his lower lip and batted his eyelashes over dark midnight eyes. I just laughed.

"Fine."

"I win!"

I swatted at his arm but he caught my hand, placing a kiss on the back of it. Ethan was always sweet that way. He touched me gently, whispered sweet nothings into my ear, always called me names like "beautiful" and "gorgeous."

"What time should I be ready?"

"Let's say around six. Jamie will be there, too, so you'll have both of us. And this is the perfect chance for you to get to know more people."

I swallowed, my pulse racing at the mention of Jamie. *You'll have both of us.* Now that was a fantasy I could get behind.

"Sounds good."

He smiled, pecking me once more before letting me loose. "See you tonight."

Ethan let himself out and I plopped down at my desk, staring at my flashcards for fifteen seconds before giving up and packing them away. I grabbed the key to unlock my bike, the only transportation I'd brought to California after my car pooped out senior year, and made my way to the bike racks. I had about four hours before Ethan would be back to pick me up, and I had some shopping to do. The only bathing suit I brought was my old black top and two mismatching bottoms from high school, and neither would do for the party.

It might have been the wrong person to be thinking about in that moment, but I couldn't stop obsessing over how Jamie had been ignoring me. If he was going to keep with that plan, I was going to do everything I had in my power to make it damn hard to follow through with.

• • •

I was ready early, which was surprising for me, and I tried chalking it up to eagerness to see Ethan and not nervousness to see Jamie. The truth was probably somewhere in-between. I pushed all thoughts to the back of my mind as I checked my outfit in the one mirror in our dorm. It was a shared mirror, laid out in front of two sinks between our two showers and it cut off at my knees, but it was enough.

I'd spent fifty hard-earned dollars on the coral top I was sporting, but it was worth it. I didn't even know they made bathing suits with underwire, but my barely B-cups were pushed up to the heavens, making them look fuller than I'd ever seen before, and the bright orangish pink was blazing against my mocha skin. It tied around my neck and clasped in the back, and I'd paired it with simple black bottoms that tied at each hip.

Makeup was still sort of a challenge to me, since Jenna helped me more times than not in high school, but I'd played up my gray eyes with a smoky eye and nude lip gloss. My hair was natural, spiral curls jetting off in different directions but framing my face in a tame enough way. I took one last look and slid into my gold sandals just as Ethan knocked on the front door.

Marie let him in before I could slip on my black, mesh lace cover-up and he stalled, his eyes trailing. "Damn."

I laughed, because I had no idea how to react to the way he was staring at me. I reached for my coverup resting half in the sink, half out and pulled it over my head, but his hands were on my hips, stopping it from falling the rest of the way down.

"Maybe we should skip the party," he murmured.

I lightly shoved him toward the door and he dropped his hands, my coverup hitting my thighs. "Nuh-uh. I'm giving up a full night of studying, mister. You're taking me out."

Ethan looked pretty enticing himself, dressed in patriotic board shorts that just hit his knees and a plain white t-shirt. He kissed my nose before grabbing my hand and leading me through the door and out to his car.

The drive was quiet, the wind whipping around us in his convertible Mustang. He said it was a gift from his father for high school graduation, and that was all I needed to know to guess what kind of upbringing he had. Still, we hadn't really talked much about where we'd come from. For the both of us, it was more about where we were going. He asked me a lot about my major, which I still hadn't decided on, and he loved to tell me his plans to make a difference in our country. He was going into politics. He knew that with *certainty*. I was a little jealous of that.

What I loved most about Ethan was how much he believed in me, even when I didn't believe in myself. He challenged me to ask myself what I wanted out of my life, and no one had really made me think about it before I met him. He didn't just see the girl in his car tonight, he saw the woman she would become in ten years. I was a vision to him, and he was a comfort to me.

We pulled up to a large, rustic gate less than half an hour later and Ethan entered the code before driving us up a long driveway shielded by trees on either side. When the mansion it lead to came into view, my jaw dropped.

I'd been to beach houses before in Florida, but nothing compared in size to this one. It was two stories, at least a football field in width, off-white with deep-red paneling. Ethan parked his car and held the door open for me while I continued to stare.

"Come on, time to show you off." He grinned, offering me his arm, and I hooked mine through it to let him walk me inside.

I expected marble floors and high chandeliers, I expected fancy artwork on the walls and vases more expensive than my tuition on every table, and I found all of that. But what I also found that I was not expecting was a full-blown house party. The music blaring from the DJ set up in the far corner of the massive living room was deafening, lights streaming from his table across the crowd of students. It looked like a club in the space that had been cleared out in front of his table and the rest of the house was packed with different groups of people talking, playing drinking games, or doing drugs.

"Wow," I breathed.

Ethan ran a hand over his barely-there buzz cut as he followed my eyes. "Yeah, I guess I forgot to mention it gets kind of crazy out here." He looked back to me, at my stunned expression I'm sure, and grabbed both of my hands. "Are you okay? We can ditch. It's fine, really."

"No!" I said too quickly, but we both just smiled. "I'm excited to be here. It looks... fun." It was hard to hear my own voice over the music, so I leaned in a little closer to Ethan. He kissed me, short and sweet, and then we joined those in the kitchen filling up red plastic cups.

It really was something attending that first party. Sure, I'd snuck into a few Palm South University parties over the summer, but this? This was on a whole other level. This wasn't some frat party, though it had many of the same elements. No, this was an *elite* college party. I was fascinated, but I'd be lying if I said I didn't feel a little out of place.

I did a lot of looking around for the first hour, hanging onto Ethan's arm as he walked around to different groups. Everyone knew Ethan, mostly because of his position on Student Government, and it was magical watching him talk to so many diverse groups of people. He just clicked with everyone.

I joined him for a few dances in the middle of the makeshift dance floor before the music and the heat inside got to be a little too much. It wasn't that I wasn't enjoying myself, because I was, but I just needed air — a little silence — a little calmness.

"I'm going to step outside for a sec," I screamed over the music into Ethan's ear. He nodded and I kissed him on the cheek before pushing my way through the crowd. I passed a coffee table lined with four lines of coke and tried not to stare as four eager girls made them disappear to a roar of applause around them.

This was *definitely* not a PSU party.

As soon as I shut the sliding glass door behind me, it was like shutting off the entire world. Silence. Beautiful silence.

I actually sighed, taking one deep inhale of the salty air before turning to find one of the most beautiful pools I'd ever seen. It was just below the balcony where I stood and was set in gray rock, with a swim up bar to the left side. There was a waterfall just above the bar, and a mini bridge that connected the two sides of the pool. To the right, it had the illusion of completely dropping off into the ocean that lay spread out below it. The moon was bright that night, and it lit up the ocean in a straight line that continued through the top of the pool to the exact spot where I stood.

It was odd. Everyone was dressed for a pool party, but not a single soul was actually in the pool.

"Pretty amazing, isn't it?"

I probably should have jumped at his voice, but I think my body already knew he was there. It was buzzing, just slightly, like when in the presence of a ghost.

Jamie leaned over the railing to the right of the sliding glass door I'd just exited, his back to me as he lifted his beer bottle to his lips. I slid up beside him, resting my elbows on the lip of the rail to mirror his and breathing in a deep inhale. The air was so fresh in California, so light. It was warm and salty just like Florida, but it didn't have the same weight.

"It is," I finally answered, turning to face him. I always loved that, the first sight of him, the first hit. It was a little jarring, like a slight burn, but the aftertaste was smooth, welcoming, like an old friend calling me home. "So you're acknowledging my existence now?"

He tipped the bottle again with a shrug, but his eyes hadn't left the ocean yet.

"Stop being a brat, Jamie Shaw," I said, sipping on my own drink. He smirked then, I saw it out of the corner of my eye.

"I can't believe you just called me a brat."

"I can't believe you're acting like one."

"How so?" he asked, finally facing me. He was on the defensive, but the line between his brows vanished once he really looked at me. I fought the urge to shield myself as his eyes trailed a fire down to my chest. I knew the top had paid off because he swallowed, eyes heated, and I suddenly wondered why I'd wanted that attention. I had a boyfriend, and yet this was it — this was the exact reason why I'd shelled out fifty bucks for a bathing suit top. For the look Jamie was giving me now, for the rush I felt along with it.

"By ignoring me for the past month," I whispered, my voice failing me in my time of need, but it was enough to snap his attention back up to my face.

He scoffed. "I haven't been ignoring you. I've been busy. And I figured you probably were, too." He didn't finish that sentence, but I knew what he wanted to say was that I was probably busy *with Ethan*. He took a long swig from his bottle before bracing his elbows on the railing again. "How are you liking San Diego?"

I hated this conversation. It sounded forced, like two strangers instead of two people who used to share the deepest secrets. "It's fine. I haven't really seen much," I replied flatly, one hand on the rail and the other on my hip as I remained facing him.

"Ethan's not showing you around?" I didn't miss the slightly mocking tone when he spoke Ethan's name.

"He is," I clarified. "He's been taking me to a lot of places on campus. He's been telling me a lot about the traditions on campus and giving me some ideas of organizations to join. I got a job at the coffee shop, too, which is great since he has the Student Government meetings there."

Jamie's profile was so strong against the moonlight, his jaw defined by the shadows that fell beneath it. "Sounds like you're well on your way to becoming the senator's wife."

"Hardly," I choked out on a laugh, and that finally made him look at me again. "I'm nineteen, Jamie."

"And?" he answered quickly. "Ethan is already building that life. He's working on the ultimate plan — right positions in SGA, right classes, right internships with notable politicians…" he paused. "Right girlfriend."

I glanced through the sliding glass doors where Ethan stood in a group, laughing, telling a story that had everyone around him enthralled. Was that true? I knew he was into politics, knew that was where his future existed, but was he really planning it all out already? Was I part of that plan?

"So he's serious about his future. Nothing wrong with that."

He laughed. "How much do you really know about him?"

This time it was me on the defensive, and I crossed my arms beneath the coral top biting into my skin. It drew Jamie's eyes down again, just for a second, but I smiled at the victory. "I know enough. And I like him, so drop it."

When Jamie's eyes met mine again, they were different. They reminded me of the night after he graduated, the hint of mischief, the glint of challenge. "What are you drinking?"

I opened my mouth to reply, but it stayed open, and I fought the smile threatening to break through. When I pressed my lips together to bite it back, Jamie grinned.

"B," he said, and I felt the moment he stepped into my space, that familiar burn washing over me before the haze set in. "What are you drinking?"

I let out a long exhale. "Whiskey."

A wide smile split his face just as the sliding glass door slid open, mixing our silent oasis with the chaos inside. Someone yelled something — what, I couldn't be sure — and then bodies were splashing into the pool. It seemed it finally was an actual pool party, and just in time to save me from letting myself brush past the tipsy threshold with Whiskey.

"Let me show you around San Diego."

Jamie was still standing close enough that I felt his breath on my lips with the words.

"I have to study."

He laughed, but moved just a millimeter closer. The heat multiplied. "It doesn't have to be tomorrow. Just let me take you out, show you your new home city. I bet you haven't even surfed yet, and that's just a crime."

He was right, I hadn't taken my board out yet, and I was itching to. My grip tightened on the rail, keeping me in place. I wanted to pull away, I wanted to lean in closer. I had no fucking idea what I wanted.

Finally, I found my voice long enough to answer. "Okay."

"B!" My name found us from across the pool and Jamie and I both snapped our necks in unison to find the source. Ethan waved from where he'd slid up on a bar stool in the pool, calling me over. I nodded, smiling, and turned back to Jamie.

"I guess I'll see you around."

Jamie's eyes were still hard on Ethan, but he finally ripped them away to look down at me once more. "Yes, you will." He watched me for a minute, and I couldn't shake the way his eyes had changed. They were a darker, deeper brown, shaded with bad intentions. "Remember how you used to say I don't play fair?"

I cocked a brow. "Yeah…"

His eyes smoldered as he stepped away from me, and I felt the loss of energy instantly. He wet his lips, and my eyes followed the sweep of his tongue.

"Just wanted to make sure you didn't forget."

With that, he gripped the Alder t-shirt he was wearing by the back collar and stripped it over his head, letting it fall beside his feet. My breath caught at the sight of his abs on full display, their definition stronger than the last time I'd seen them. I noted the scar just above his hip, the one I wanted so desperately to trace with my fingers, and I found his eyes again just in time for him to wink. Then, he climbed onto the railing and jumped into the pool to the sound of a roaring crowd.

You know those gut feelings you get that warn you of impending doom? I had swarms of them that night as we danced around each other at the party, never getting close enough to talk again, yet never getting completely out of the other's sight. I stayed close to Ethan and Jamie kept his distance, but whenever our eyes met across the crowd, my stomach twisted in warning.

I should have listened, but if you haven't learned by now, caution signs didn't work when it came to Jamie.

F!VE

Stained

EVEN THOUGH I KNEW eventually I would cave, I did resist the first few times Jamie asked me to hang out after that night. The first time, not even a full week later, I said I was studying. The time after that, I was with Ethan. And, the third time, I claimed period cramps. I thought for sure he'd let it go after that last excuse . But the thing about whiskey is that it's a stubborn drink that refuses to be ignored. It doesn't just sit on a shelf in a pretty bottle and wait patiently. No, it clamors for attention, and that was just shitty news for thirsty fools like me.

It was only ten in the morning and yet I'd already worked a full six-hour shift at the coffee shop. Opening sucked, especially since the biggest rush of the day came between six and nine. Thankful as I was for the job, I missed sleeping in something fierce.

I was yawning, ready for a Friday spent curled up in my tiny twin bed when I rounded the corner to my dorm and saw Jamie leaned up against the same cherry red Jeep he'd driven in high school. He wasn't even in a parking spot, just pulled up against the curb closest to the entrance of the community where my dorm was housed.

He didn't see me at first, and I took those few stolen moments to shamelessly check him out. He was still just as lean and tall as he was in high school, but his arms had filled out since then. In fact, it seemed all of him had filled out — even his neck, which was a strange thing to notice about a person, but I did. He was in a weird state of being between the high schooler I'd left on the beach over a year ago and the man I wasn't sure I'd have the privilege of knowing five years from now.

When he noticed me approaching, Jamie stood straighter, a shit-eating grin in place. "Hey, sleepyhead," he offered as I approached him with another yawn.

"Pretty sure this is illegal," I spoke through it, my voice morphed, pointing to his Jeep in a sweeping motion.

"It's okay. No chance of being caught since we're about to move."

"We?"

He nodded. "We. Hop in."

"Jamie…" I started to argue.

"Nope. No excuses. I've heard enough of those over the past few weeks." He pushed off his Jeep and circled to the other side, opening his passenger door. "Let's go."

"I'm so tired. And I'm not dressed for anything." I motioned to the white jean shorts and pale-green polo I'd worn to work.

"What you're wearing is fine. And we'll get coffee."

He lifted a brow, nodding toward the front seat again. "Come on. In."

I debated arguing again, but at that point I knew it was useless. "Brat," I huffed as I slid inside.

Jamie smirked, but didn't press his luck, simply shutting the door behind me and jogging around to the driver side. I have to admit, it was surreal being back in that seat, in that Jeep. A rush of memories flooded in, of long nights driving around our lazy beach town in South Florida, talking about our fears, our secrets, our dreams.

"She's missed you," he said, watching me as my fingers traced the dash.

"She?"

"ScarJo," he answered, opening his arms wide to gesture to his car.

"Oh my God, you can't be serious. Like Scarlett Johansen?"

"Hey!" Jamie defended. "Don't judge! I was a horny sixteen-year-old when I got her."

"Nerd," I teased, but when I ran my hand over the door panel, I sighed contently and leaned back into the seat, kicking off my sandals and propping my feet on the dash. *Home*. "It does sort of feel like this seat belongs to me."

I glanced over at Jamie and he was watching me in that peculiar way, just the slightest hint of a smile resting on his lips. I wanted to ask him what he was thinking, but before I had the chance, his hand found the gear shift and he threw us into drive.

"Let's go see San Diego."

• • •

For the first hour, Jamie just drove. I don't even think he really had a place in mind. His Jeep slowly cruised the streets of the different areas of San Diego, moving us through Chula Vista into the heart of downtown. We both stared out at the city, pointing here and there, rarely ever saying anything. Claude Debussy mixed with the California wind, which made for the most incredible soundtrack for our drive. It was sunny, but the clouds were puffy white that day and they gave us reprieve from the sun.

For a while, I didn't even think about being tired. San Diego was such an artsy city, and there was something colorful and eye-catching around every corner, it seemed. Still, eventually, the yawns caught up to me again, and Jamie said he knew the perfect place to get coffee.

When we reached the destination he had in mind, my feet hit the floorboard and a laugh ripped from my throat. "You have got to be kidding me."

"Don't you mean, 'You have *cat* to be *kitten* me?'"

"You're not cute, Jamie Shaw," I retorted, shoving my sunglasses on top of my head to get a better look.

The Cat Café.

"Am too. And what? I thought we could honor Rory's memory. Plus, if you fall asleep on our first date, I'll never live that down."

I rolled my eyes as he circled to find parking. "This is not a date."

"It's a boy and a girl out doing fun things together."

92

"As *friends*."

"Or…" Jamie teased, finding a spot. He whipped the Jeep in with a crooked smile on his face.

"I have a boyfriend."

He was unbuckling his seatbelt, but paused a moment, his eyes on where his hand still held the buckle. He sniffed, cracked his neck, and then let it go. "Come on. Let's get you caffeinated."

I let him avoid the statement, mostly because I was dying for coffee. You would think working in a coffee shop would make me not want it as much, but it was quite the opposite, actually. I started every morning with a cup of Joe and I was far from opposed to an afternoon pick-me-up at the moment.

Jamie seemed in his thoughts as we walked the street up to the café, his hands tucked in his pockets and eyes on the cobblestone below our feet, but when we opened the door to the café, he perked up again.

It looked a little strange to me. We sort of walked straight into a decision in the form of two, rather unimpressive hallways. Jamie led me down the one straight ahead where a counter that looked similar to a concession stand at a high school sat. We placed our orders as I took in the paw prints on the wall and the snacks for purchase. In the end, Jamie opted for black coffee while I chose the Americano, and hot drinks in hand, we made our way back to the other hallway. When we emerged into an open room with seating along the walls, I nearly dropped the cup in my hand.

"Holy shit!" I said, louder than I intended, definitely loud enough for the couple sitting at the first table to hear me. "There are actual fucking cats in here!"

Jamie barked out a laugh, pausing at the entrance with me so we could both look around. The inside of the café was quaint, sort of rustic, with wood browns warming the walls and floors of the room. But there were pops of color — a red door near the back, bright orange pillows plopped on the floor here and there, and brightly colored cat havens and toys littered the entire area.

And there were cats *everywhere*.

"When it said Cat Café, I didn't know I was supposed to take it so literally," I mused, eyes still wandering the space as a black and gray striped tabby wove itself between my ankles. She arched her back as she rubbed against my bare leg, then sauntered off, plopping down on one of the empty pillows and looking back at me as if to ask, *"What are you waiting for?"*

"Careful. I think that one is plotting how to get you alone and in a bathtub." Jamie cracked a smile at his own joke and I glared at him before pushing forward to claim one of the last tables available. Some customers were sitting down on the floor with the cats, playing with different toys or posing for pictures, while others sat at small tables like the one Jamie and I had selected.

"How do you even remember that story, anyway?" I asked, sipping my Americano to the symphony of soft mews and human chatter around us.

"How could I not? You fell butt ass naked into a pile of cat shit."

"You're the worst."

Jamie laughed. "Oh come on, you can't hate cats forever." He set his coffee down carefully and picked up a tiny black cat that had wandered over to our table. "Look. This one is so sweet."

He cradled the little guy in one arm like a football, scratching behind his ear before rubbing his belly and repeating the process. And as if Jamie Shaw wasn't already hot, melted sex on a stick, he was holding a little kitten inside a coffee shop with a five o'clock shadow teasing his jaw.

Lord help me.

We drank our coffee slowly, filling each other in on the last year and a half. I loved hearing about Jamie's family and he entertained my stories of Jenna and me during senior year. He was impressed she'd gone off to NYU, and I tried not to feel that familiar pang of jealousy when he asked a dozen questions about her.

It was so comfortable between us, even in the silence, and that's what I loved most about our time together. It never felt forced.

Yet, there were these small, almost microscopic moments of charged energy between us that broke the comfort from time to time. They came when one of us would stare a little too long, or smile just a little too big, or think just a little too hard. They were almost like little shocks to our system to make sure we were paying attention, that we didn't slip too far, and I think it was those moments we craved the most.

When our cups were empty and we'd made the rounds to play with each and every cat in the café, Jamie checked the time on his phone.

"Do you still write?"

I was still kneeling, petting that same tabby that had greeted us at the door, and I peered up at him. "Yes?" I couldn't believe he remembered that. I'd just started writing that year I met Jamie, and since he left, I'd slowly found myself writing more and more. Usually it was just poetry or assignments for school, but I could see myself building a world one day — telling a story that meant something to me. "Why?"

He held out his hand and I let him help me up, brushing the fur off my palms as a grin played on Jamie's lips. "How'd you like to visit the most popular author in the city?"

• • •

It took everything in me, including a hand hard over my mouth, not to laugh.

Jamie's fists were clenched, his face red as he listened to the librarian tell us for the eighth time that there was no way in hell we were going to see the Dr. Seuss collection.

"As I've explained, sir, it isn't open to the public. We offer exhibits during his birthday month of March and sometimes over the summer, but at the moment—"

"This doesn't make any fucking sense!" Jamie's voice had always been smooth, low, but right now it was booming, and while I was close to laughter, the tiny librarian was not. She had wide, owl eyes that, even narrowed at Jamie, took up her entire face. She was also about as tall as I was in fifth grade, but she wasn't backing down. "So you're telling me the collection is still here. It's all *here*. But for some fucking reason it's blocked off and no one can see it?"

"Sir, the collection is very fragile. Only researchers who have obtained permission can gain access to the collection."

"We just want to see it," he pleaded. "We won't touch a thing."

"I'm sorry," she said again. "Now, if you continue to raise your voice, I'll have to ask that you kindly leave. This is a library."

Jamie scoffed, throwing his hands up in surrender. "Exactly! A library! But you won't let us see the fucking books!"

The librarian rolled her eyes with exhaustion just as laughter won me over and I grabbed Jamie's arm. "Come on, it's fine. Let's go."

He pointed a finger at her nose as I yanked him away. "Karma is real, Mrs. Seuss Security. Just remember that."

I laughed even louder then, tugging on him harder to pull him out the front door and back into the walkway of the UC San Diego library — the Geisel Library, to be exact — named after the one and only Theodore Seuss Geisel.

Dr. Seuss.

"As amazing as it would have been to see that collection, it's not worth getting you arrested," I said through my laughter, looking back at him. Jamie was still scowling and I learned quickly that looking back while trying to tug him forward and walk at the same time proved to be too much for my hand-eye coordination. I tripped over my own feet, shooting forward before Jamie's arms were around my waist, catching me, steadying me.

And then, I was facing him. My eyes on my hands that had found his chest. His hands on my hips. I glanced up at him, and immediately wished I hadn't.

"Thanks," I murmured, putting some distance between us. "Can you take a picture of me?" I pulled out my phone and handed it to him before he could answer. Before he could stare any longer. Catching my breath, I put on my best smile and held my arms up high to frame the sign with the library name above me.

"She was a Doc Blocker," Jamie said, and he waited for me to crack up before snapping the picture.

"That's actually kind of clever."

He took a bow, handing my phone back to me, and I felt his calm settle in. Getting him out of that library had been step one, and he seemed to be shaking it off now.

"There's a snake path over here," Jamie said, pointing off to the side of the library. "It winds through some fruit trees. I didn't get a chance to check it out when I came for the campus tour, and since I ended up at Alder, I haven't made it over here. Want to walk for a bit?"

"Sure."

It was a neat place, not just the library but the college campus, too. I loved the idea of an entire library being dedicated to an author. To be able to write stories that inspired the way his did? That moved people? *That* was something special.

"So," Jamie said as we made our way toward the path. I could see the snake head peeking out over the sidewalk ahead of us, different color tiles creating the illusion. "What do you write?"

"It depends. Mostly poems right now, but I think I'd like to write a novel one day. Maybe."

"Possible major?"

I scrunched my nose. "I don't know about all that."

Jamie grinned. "Ah yes, I almost forgot. Ms. Indecisive." I stuck my tongue out and he flicked his sunglasses over his eyes. "Well, do you like to read, too?"

"Of course."

He shrugged, steering us between the first two fruit trees. "Could always go into publishing."

"Yeah?" I brushed my hand against one of the leaves. "I never really thought about that. That could be cool. I love to read, and I think I could be a pretty good salesman."

"Oh yeah," Jamie said, and I nudged him at the joke that rested beneath his comment. "So what do you like to read?"

"I read a lot of things. A lot of genres. Right now I'm really into romance."

"Romance?!" Jamie exclaimed with a laugh. "Oh man. Does Ethan know?"

"I don't know, I'm sure he's seen me with my books a time or two. Why does that matter?"

He shrugged. "I'm just saying, I would want to know if I wasn't pleasing my girl enough and she needed a steamy sex book to get her rocks off."

"Oh my God, Jamie!" I halted our walk then, just as two girls with books pressed to their chest rushed past us. "It's not even like that. At all."

"Sure," he said with an amused smirk. *Bastard.*

"It's not. I read romance because it's fun to fall in love. And with romance books, I get to do it over and over. I get to be different types of lovers, I get to feel the heartbreak of love and the successes. Love is the most powerful and real emotion we feel, and I think it's sort of magical that we can experience some of the greatest loves of all time through books."

"Except they're not real."

I huffed. "You're impossible."

We started walking again and Jamie apologized. "I'm just kidding. I'm sure they're great." He paused, but curiosity got the best of him. "So Ethan is satisfying you between the sheets then, huh?"

"We are not talking about this."

"Oh come on," he pleaded. "I told you all the dirt when I was dating Jenna. You owe me."

That was true. He had told me more than I wanted to know about his and Jenna's... adventures.

"Yeah, that wasn't exactly saint-like, either."

"True," he conceded. "But lines always have been pretty blurry with us, haven't they."

It wasn't a question. It was a statement. And it was the truth.

I sighed. It *was* just Jamie. I mean, this was the guy I'd shared the story about my name with — the most personal story of my life. He'd called me his best friend. And in a way, he'd always kind of felt like mine.

"Fine. But no teasing."

"I swear."

I rolled my eyes, because I definitely didn't believe him, but let out a long breath anyway. "I don't really know what to say."

"Tell me how Ethan is in the sack," Jamie said simply.

I balked at his forwardness, shaking my head.

"I don't know." I was flustered, stalling. "He's fine."

"*Fine?* This is sex we're talking about, B. Not china."

"You said no teasing!"

"I lied."

"Clearly."

"Seriously," he said, pulling us to a stop again. We were right in the center of the snake path, the trees shielding us from the outside world — even if just for a moment. "Come on. Sex isn't a taboo thing. It should be talked about. It's about finding what works for you, what brings you pleasure."

God, just hearing that word roll off his lips sent a rush of heat from my face all the way to my toes.

"He's fine. Good…" I trailed off. "I just, I wish it was more… exciting. He's so sweet, gentle, and that's nice but…" I blushed. This was the most I'd ever talked about sex, including the few times I'd opened up to Jenna, and I didn't want to feel embarrassed, but I did. "There's no real passion. There's no urgency. I'm all for sweet nothings whispered in my ear, but sometimes I just want to be thrown onto the bed, you know? Ravaged. Like he can't fathom the thought of taking his hands off me."

I was babbling, looking around the garden, afraid someone might overhear us. But when I chanced a look at Jamie, everything stopped. The heat of the sun closed in around us and suddenly the symbolism of where we were clicked into place. A snake path, in a garden. I felt like Eve, and here Jamie was — the juicy red apple — taunting me. Daring me.

His eyes were hooded, and I'd never been so fascinated watching someone breathe before, but there was a dip that appeared over and over at the base of his neck as he inhaled. It disappeared when he pushed the next breath out, and I counted that motion nine times before he spoke.

"I get that."

He only said three words, low and breathy, and I knew it was because he didn't trust himself with more than that.

"It's probably too late to go surfing, huh?" I asked, looking at how low the sun was in the sky.

"Today?" He asked, snapping out of our haze. "Yes. But, we could go tomorrow. Get up super early, catch the morning waves. What do you say?"

I didn't even hesitate. "I'm in."

Jamie smiled, that bright, all-teeth smile, and then we walked back to the Jeep in comfortable silence.

He dropped me off at just past five o'clock after I declined his invitation to dinner. I was exhausted, and if we were waking up early in the morning, I wanted to sleep.

Ethan texted me twice — once while I was still in the Jeep with Jamie and once after I was back in my dorm. He wanted to hang out, but I denied him, too. I told him I was tired, which was true, but what I didn't tell him was that I just needed a minute. My day with Jamie didn't change anything I felt for Ethan, but it did remind me of everything I'd always felt for Jamie. All the thoughts I'd let go of on the beach the morning after Jamie's graduation had been rounded up again, and now here they were, prevalent in my mind and waiting for me to address them.

I desperately wished I had a bathtub, because all I wanted to do was run a long, hot bath and soak for hours — in the water and in my thoughts.

I couldn't believe Jamie remembered so much about me. About us. And it somehow brought me more comfort than anything because I remembered, too. It turned out a Whiskey stain was just as permanent as ink, and I wondered if I would ever truly wash myself clean.

Or if I even wanted to.

SIX

"B, WAKE UP."

"Mmmm," I murmured, reaching out to hit snooze on the alarm clock that was saying my name. My hand found a warm, hard body, and I tugged at the t-shirt wrapped around it. "Sleep."

There was a chuckle, and my eyes flitted open, my room still dark save for the night light I had plugged in.

"Come on. We should get going if we want to catch the morning surf."

Jamie.

My hand retracted backward and I threw the covers off, confused.

"How did you get in here?" I grabbed my phone next. 5:35 AM.

"You let me in, goofball. I called you."

"What?" I scrolled through my call log and sure enough, his name was there, not even five minutes earlier. "I'm so confused."

Jamie sat on the edge of my bed and I suddenly wished I had the comforter still. I was dressed in nothing but boy shorts and a crop t-shirt. "You let me in. Then you grabbed my hand and pulled me back here before crawling back into bed."

"Oh my God." My hand found my forehead with a smack and Jamie chuckled again. I loved that sound. The throatiness of it.

"Relax. You're just tired. We can do this another time, if you want to rest."

"No," I said quickly, scooting past him. I grabbed my bathing suit from the top drawer of my dresser, not even bothering to hide my ass in the tiny shorts I was wearing since apparently I'd already paraded it around that morning. "Give me a sec to change."

"You don't have to, we can—"

"I want to. I've been here almost two months now and still haven't surfed. And that's one of the biggest reasons I wanted to come to California, anyway."

Jamie nodded, standing from his perch on the bed and grabbing my surfboard from where it leaned against my closet. "Alright, then. Go get dressed. I'm parked in the G Lot."

He tugged my board up between his arm and ribs and I held the door for him to exit before excusing myself into the bathroom I shared with Marie.

Plopping down on the toilet, I forced three, long breaths. I was excited to go surfing, but being woken up by Jamie in such close proximity and me in so little clothing had my blood pumping. I decided not to think too much on it, changing quickly and brushing my teeth before jogging out the door to Jamie's Jeep. It was a sight I missed, both of our boards attached to the top of it, and Jamie waiting inside, window down, smile on his face as the sky just barely broke with the first light-blue hues of daylight.

Today would be a good day.

"What's that?" Jamie asked, eying my old simple bathing suit I was wearing under my t-shirt and shorts.

"My swim suit?"

He chuckled. "You're going to freeze. Do you have a wetsuit?" I shook my head and he kicked the Jeep into drive. "Alright then, that will be our first stop."

The conversation on the way to the beach was easy, mostly Jamie telling me about his favorite surfing spots he'd found since he'd been there. He was taking me to Windansea, which was insane in itself considering how many times I'd heard about it from watching pro surfing on TV. It wasn't that I was obsessed with watching surf, because surfing was always more of a personal release for me, but I did catch it from time to time. And Windansea was often mentioned as home turf for big-time surfers.

My phone pinged with a text from Ethan just as we arrived at the beach, my brand new wetsuit folded across my lap and waiting for me to slip into it. Jamie hopped out of the Jeep quickly to get to work on taking our boards down while I stared, wondering what to say back.

— **Hey, just tried to surprise you with breakfast in bed. Where are you?** —

I thumbed out a response, but debated the last part. Deciding against adding *who* I was with, I stuck to just answering his question.

— Decided to finally check out the surf. Call you when I'm back on campus? —

— Sounds like a plan. I wanna take my girl to dinner. —

I smiled.

— I'd like that. —

— Then it's a date. Have fun out there! —

I tucked my phone into the pocket on my beach bag and sighed, feeling a strange pang of guilt twist in my stomach. I wasn't doing anything wrong by surfing with Jamie, so then why did I feel inclined to keep his name out of my answer to Ethan?

"Ready?" Jamie popped up beside me, opening the passenger side door wide as I hopped out. And that's when it hit me.

I was about to surf the waves in California.

My smile felt too big for my face as I picked up my board from where it leaned against Jamie's Jeep. "Let's do this."

We made our way down to the beach, which was mostly rock and looked nearly vacant as the sun rose behind us. There were a few surfers already out in the water, but it was nowhere near as crowded as the beaches back home would have been. Then again, it was October, and we were early. I imagined it'd fill up soon enough.

Jamie and I wasted no time, dropping our bags near a small surf shack and pulling on our wetsuits. It felt weird to me at first, but the minute my toes touched the icy water, I was instantly thankful for the coverage. I hissed, stepping back at first, and Jamie laughed.

"Told you you'd freeze."

Thankfully, the sun was already starting to warm the air around us, and the cold water wasn't enough to keep me from one of my dreams — surfing in California.

The minute I laid my board down and climbed on, strap around my ankle and arms on each side ready to paddle, I instantly felt at home.

"God, I've missed this," I whispered.

"Me too," Jamie answered, but he wasn't on his board yet. He was staring at me, instead. I sat up, straddling my board, and smiled back at him. His hair had grown out a bit since I'd arrived on campus, and in that moment — in the water, climbing onto his board — he felt like my Jamie.

I learned a lot about myself that day. Like that no matter how big my mouth was, it was tougher surfing in California than I thought. Not that I couldn't do it, because I did, but paddling out wasn't as easy as it was in Florida, and the waves were bigger here, which meant adjusting my knowledge on when to catch them and how to ride. I got the hang of it soon enough, and Jamie and I caught wave after wave all morning and well into the early afternoon.

Still, we had to take a lot of breaks. My stamina was sad compared to what it had been in the Florida surf. But Jamie had packed us a lunch, so we spent a lot of time on the beach, laughing and soaking up the sun — which I was the most grateful for. I hadn't expected the water to be as cold as it was, and that combined with the intensity of the surf was exhausting in the best way.

We slowed down after lunch, taking our time, sitting side by side on our boards and talking between catching waves. When the sun was high in the sky and the waves more crowded, I knew we needed to head back to campus so I could get ready for my date with Ethan. I didn't want to leave the waves, but then again I knew they'd be here, and I hoped Jamie would want to bring me out again soon.

"Next time, we should check out the Imperial Beach Pier. It's a little more crowded, but fun. We can grab lunch after, too. Lots of great fish joints."

"I'd love that," I answered honestly before sighing. "I don't want to leave, but we should head back."

"Aw, you tired? California waves too much for you?"

I rolled my eyes. "I have a date with Ethan tonight," I said, turning to Jamie then. I don't know why I expected some sort of reaction from him, because I found nothing.

"Oh. Okay. Well let's catch one last wave then." He smiled, falling forward on his board before paddling out.

And that was it.

It felt a little surreal as we made the hike back up the boardwalk to where we'd parked. I had finally surfed in California, and the day had rushed by so quickly I almost forgot to take it in. So, after we loaded up the boards and Jamie tossed on a t-shirt, I walked back over to the top of the boardwalk and gazed out over the waves, watching the surfers ride them in.

I was shivering still, even with my wetsuit abandoned in the Jeep and a light sweater thrown over my bathing suit. My curls were big and frizzy from the salt water as they blew in the sea breeze around me, blocking my vision from time to time and reminding me of home.

I felt Jamie slide up beside me and we both rested our elbows on the rail, eyes on the water.

"I can't believe we're in California."

Jamie smiled. "Together."

I squinted against the sun as I turned toward him, my sunglasses still in the car. "Thank you for today, Jamie. Yesterday, too."

"We're just getting started," he answered, and I felt those words in my core. *We're just getting started.*

We stood there a moment, both of us silent, and then he leaned against the railing with an easy smile again.

"By the way, I have to ask. How come you left the push up bra at home? I was kind of looking forward to seeing you try to surf in it."

I nudged him, eyes narrowed. "It was a pool party, okay? I needed something a little more showy than my surf tops that make me look like a boy." I glanced down at the top I was wearing beneath the mesh sweater, a black and lime green halter that matched my board and made me look as flat as one.

"Oh, so you were putting on a show that night, huh?"

"Well, you see, someone had been ignoring me," I teased back. "So I needed to find a way to get some attention." I scrunched my nose, tongue between my teeth. I loved bantering with Jamie, but hated the way my stomach dropped right along with his smile as a more serious tone set in around us.

There it was — that signature stare from Jamie. The way it combined with the sunlight burned my skin, and suddenly I wasn't shivering anymore.

"You don't look like a boy, for the record," Jamie said, his voice low again.

I laughed, not believing him, but then he stepped closer and his hand weaved into my salty hair. I stopped laughing. I stopped *breathing*.

"And I wasn't ignoring you. I was avoiding you. I was trying to stay away." He swallowed, his eyes holding mine before flicking to my mouth and back as his other hand slid up to mirror the first, framing my face. "I was trying to stop myself from doing this."

He pulled me into him and before I could register it all, his lips were on mine.

And my world tilted, taking me with it.

Jamie had held his breath on that kiss, and for a moment I held mine, too. But when I lifted up on my tip toes, pressing my lips harder against his and fisting my hands in his shirt to pull him even closer, we both exhaled together. Our breaths rushed out around us and Jamie sucked my bottom lip between his teeth, letting it go with a groan as he kissed me again, this time sliding his tongue in to find mine.

I was spinning, tipsy, teetering on the edge of being wasted on Whiskey. I'd dreamed of kissing Jamie so many times, but nothing could compare to how it really felt — his hands on me, so strong, his mouth skilled and passionate. My legs were weak and he felt it, taking the weight of me in his arms, kissing me like he'd waited his entire life to have the chance.

"Fuck," he groaned, pulling back and pressing his forehead against mine. We were both panting, trying to stabilize.

"Jamie, I—"

"Have a boyfriend. I know." He let me go then, pulling back and spinning to face away from me. He ran his hands through his hair roughly and paused, hands still on his head. "Goddamnit. I'm sorry."

My heart fell through the boards where we stood and crashed somewhere on the rocks below us. He was sorry. I'd just had the best kiss of my entire life, and he was *sorry*.

I watched his back, not knowing what his face looked like, not knowing why it wasn't until that exact moment that I realized it was me who should be apologizing.

It was me who had just cheated.

"We should go," I whispered, and I didn't wait for him to respond, just made my way back to his Jeep. I slid inside right away, but Jamie took his time, and when he finally fell into the seat next to mine, he didn't look my way. He started the Jeep silently, pushed it into gear, and then we drove in silence. No music, no words, just wind.

My phone rang, startling us both, and Ethan's name filled the screen when I pulled it from my bag.

"Hey babe," I answered. Jamie fisted the steering wheel tighter.

"Hey, you almost home?"

"On my way now. Listen, I'm really exhausted, could we maybe go to dinner another night?"

I felt Ethan's disappointment through the phone and Jamie looked at me then, brows pinched together.

"I miss you, B. I haven't seen you all week. Can I at least come over? I'll bring a movie and you can fall asleep on my chest, if that's what you want. I don't care what we do. I just want to be with you tonight."

Tears pooled in my eyes and I blinked rapidly, keeping them at bay. Ethan was the best guy I had ever dated, the guy whom I'd trusted enough to give myself to. He'd cherished my virginity, and he continued to practically worship me every day. He was sweet, he was kind, he had a plan. And for some reason he wanted me to be a part of it. He was everything I could have ever hoped for.

I was so, so stupid.

"I miss you, too. Give me an hour and then you can head over."

He sighed, and I could see his smile as if I was there with him. "Can't wait. See you soon."

I ended the call just as Jamie pulled onto campus. Jamie parked in G Lot again and when I went to reach for my handle, he locked all the doors.

"I'm sorry, B."

He said the words again, and they burned even more the second time I swallowed them.

"Ethan is a great guy and he cares about you, and I know you care about him, too. And what I did today was selfish. It was foolish. I'm not sorry I kissed you," he clarified, and my eyes found his then. "But I'm sorry I did it when you weren't mine to kiss."

I chewed my lip, fighting back the emotions I was feeling. "I'm sorry, too. I think maybe this was a bad idea."

"No," Jamie argued, shaking his head as he turned to face me completely. "Listen, I promise, I won't pull that shit again. But please, don't push me away. We can still be friends, B. I don't want to lose you." I had a flashback to the night he texted me after our first football game together, the night we went to watch Jenna but watched each other, instead. "Please, let me be your friend."

Could we be friends? Could we hang out together like we did in high school now that we had kissed, now that we had crossed that faint line that had always been drawn between us? I wasn't sure, though the bigger part of me thought I probably didn't want to know the answer.

Still, I nodded. The thought of losing him crushed me, too.

"Okay."

Jamie breathed a sigh of relief, but I sat up straighter.

"But we can't…. I can't…" I gestured behind me, back to the beach, back to the kiss.

"I know."

I nodded again, feeling solid in our understanding. "Help me with my board?"

An hour later, I was freshly showered, lying in my twin bed with my head on Ethan's chest as we watched a horror film. He held me close, his fingers lightly tracing the hem of my sleep shorts for the first thirty minutes of the movie, and I didn't tell him about the kiss. I should have, but I didn't want to hurt him, and at the time, I was still lying to myself, repeating the words Jamie had said in the car. *We could be friends.*

Before long, Ethan was hovering over me, kissing me softly as he moved between my legs. He promised me the world between kisses and I drank him in eagerly, desperate to believe him, to want what I knew I should.

But the truth was still there, stuffed under my pillow, tucked away in my mind.

I drank Ethan in that night, every last drop, but when we finished and I rolled to one side, him pulling my back against his chest, I traced my mouth with shaky fingers.

It was the aftertaste of Whiskey I still felt on my lips.

S E V E N
Water of Life

IT TURNED OUT MY fear of not being able to be normal around Jamie was unfounded, or so it seemed at first.

I avoided Jamie for a few days after the kiss, but when we did eventually hang out again, it was as if it had never happened. Conversation was easy, we saw each other when we could and, even around Ethan, Jamie seemed normal. We went surfing a lot, and since Ethan didn't like to surf or even be at the beach at all, that was usually mine and Jamie's time just the two of us. It was fun — we explored new places, tackled new waves, and Jamie even broke in a new board. I, on the other hand, felt like I could never part from mine.

Jamie was true to his word. He didn't try to kiss me again. In fact, he'd pulled back completely. It felt like I was more inclined to be the one caught staring or standing too close. Jamie, on the other hand, would keep his distance. He kept conversation at safe levels and every touch between us was nothing but friendly.

As if to prove he was serious, Jamie even dated — well, I say *dated* lightly. He never put a title on his escapades with the parade of blondes he had coming in and out of his and Ethan's apartment, but I received the message loud and clear. I think, looking back, he thought it would solidify his promise he'd made to just be my friend. And it did. But, it also made me question why he'd ever kissed me at all. I looked nothing like those girls. They were all light skinned, curvy, blonde. Clearly it had been a mistake for him, which is why he had apologized so quickly.

It was just a kiss, a harmless mistake.

We were fine as friends.

It was easy, being with him — just like it always had been. And so, almost exactly like we had in high school, Jamie and I fell into an easy routine. Surfing, exploring new places in San Diego, studying — we even flew home for holiday break together. I was the most thankful for that, especially after my mom and I spent our first Christmas alone together. Even after I found out about what my dad did, we'd still all been together at Christmas. But this time I'd told him not to come, and even though I was solid in that decision, it still killed me. Jamie picked me up that night and we drove around our old hometown, just like we had that Christmas Eve his senior year.

We really had fallen into a friendship, or at least, we'd convinced ourselves we had.

But see, what you likely already know about liquor that I had yet to realize at that time in my life is this: each type of alcohol affects you in a different way.

Jamie was whiskey, that much I was sure of. I couldn't deny the way he burned, the way his taste lingered. Still, no one warned me that once a whiskey girl, *always* a whiskey girl. But I was figuring it out.

Ethan was like rum. He was sweet and fun, like a fruity cocktail on the beach. He said all the right things, took me to the right places, gave me the right gifts on holidays we celebrated together. For all intents and purposes, he was a perfectly fine libation.

But I didn't get drunk off rum the same way I did off Whiskey.

One particularly late night in February, Ethan showed up unannounced at my dorm. Marie and I had actually formed a friendship by that point, and we were making spiked apple ciders in the kitchen when he knocked.

I opened the door, a little buzzed, and smiled wide when I saw him standing there.

"Hi, baby!" I threw my arms around his neck and giggled, but he just barely hugged me in return. When I pulled back, there was a thin line forming between his brows and his eyes wouldn't fully meet mine.

"Can you take a walk with me?"

"Right now?" I asked, turning back to Marie in the kitchen. She was stirring her cider with a cinnamon stick and singing Katy Perry. "Why don't you come inside? I'll make you a drink."

"B," he said, and the way my nickname left his lips sent a shiver up my spine. I crossed my arms, trying to find warmth in the oversized sweater I was wearing. "Please. I just… I need to talk to you."

I stared up at his frown, missing the smile that usually held its place. "Okay. Let me put on my boots."

Marie just grabbed my cider, now holding one in each hand, and raised both eyebrows at me as she passed into her room. I laughed, tugging on my boots quickly and meeting Ethan outside. My stomach was in knots as we started walking, the campus dark save for the streetlights and dorm windows. When Ethan reached for my hand and gripped it tightly in his, I breathed easier, but only marginally.

"I need to ask you something, and I need you to be one-hundred percent honest with me."

I squeezed his hand in return, trying to swallow down the thick ball of cotton stuck in my throat. It was cold, especially for San Diego. I learned that, just like Florida, Southern California earned about a month and a half of moderately low temperatures. At the present moment, it was just over fifty degrees, but it wasn't just the cool night air giving me a chill.

"You and Jamie spend a lot of time together. And I get it, I understand that you guys were close in high school. I get it that you both like to surf, and I don't want you to stop hanging out with him or anything. But..." Ethan stopped, pulling us over to a bench and sitting down first. I stayed standing, and Ethan continued to look anywhere but at me. "B, I can't compete with Jamie." His eyes finally found mine, and what I saw behind them nearly broke me. "I just can't. So if I'm not enough for you, just tell me now."

"Ethan," I sat then, both of my hands reaching out for his. He held them tight, his teeth hard on his bottom lip as he stared at where our fingers met. "You are more than enough for me. Hell, *I'm* the lucky one trying to figure out

118

what the hell it is you see in me." I laughed and Ethan forced a smile, but it fell quickly. "I'm serious. Ethan, Jamie and I, we're just friends."

He nodded, sniffing, and I watched the cloud of air escape his lips with his next question. "Promise?"

A knife twisted in my heart, and I fought against it to smile. "I promise. You have absolutely nothing to worry about."

Ethan traced the skin of my palm with his thumb before pulling me closer. He wrapped his arms around me, resting his chin on my head as he exhaled slowly. "Can you... I know you guys have a lot in common. But, I need you to just put me first a little more, okay? I need to feel more important than him. I know it sounds juvenile and needy but I don't care. I can't keep comparing myself to him in my head. I just want to look at you and see more in your eyes than I see when you look at him."

I physically cringed then, shaking my head against his chest and tangling my hands in the pocket of his hoodie. "God, Ethan, I'm so sorry."

"It's okay, you're not doing anything wrong." He pulled back then, his dark eyes finding mine. It was complete silence around us, a late Tuesday night on campus, a cold night that called for snuggling on couches, not on benches. "I just need a little reassurance sometimes. I—" he paused, as if he caught himself about to say something he'd regret. "You just mean a lot to me, okay? And I want to know if you feel the same."

I smiled, framing his face with my hands and pulling his lips to mine. "I do."

It occurred to me then that it didn't matter that Jamie and I had made a promise to stay friends or that we'd kept it, not if our friendship was still strong enough to make my boyfriend feel like our relationship wasn't.

When Ethan pulled me against his chest again, his fingers lazily running through my hair, I stared across campus toward the apartment where I knew Jamie was lying in bed. I didn't know if he was alone. I didn't know what he was thinking. I didn't know if he was waxing his board or breathing seductive words against the neck of a girl he'd just met. I had no idea if he still thought about our kiss or if he'd hate the new lines I was about to draw in our friendship.

All I knew was that I couldn't enjoy the spicy sweetness of rum if I was drinking it while still staring at a neat glass of Whiskey.

And so, I did what I needed to do.

I poured that last glass down the drain, twisted the cap on the bottle, and put it back on the shelf, locking the doors to the liquor cabinet up tight.

When I peeked back up at Ethan, he moved my hair aside before kissing me, soft and sweet, like coconut and strawberry. He was my Miami Vice, and he had my full attention.

For now.

• • •

Jamie didn't really seem to notice me pulling away — at least, not at first. We just hung out a lot less and my texts were few and far between. But it worked out because I was busy with Ethan, and Jamie was busy with his flavors of the week.

What I started to discover as I spent more time with Ethan was that he really *was* serious about his political life plan. He was in full-on campaign mode, running for SGA Vice President since he was about to go into his junior year. And even though most of our newfound time together was spent designing and printing posters, running over speeches, and building a website complete with a booming social media campaign, I was enjoying it. I even helped run a few of his pizza stops on campus. He would hand out free pizza to hungry college students passing us between classes and I would talk to them about their vote, promising he was the best candidate and knowing in my heart it was true.

That's what I loved most about Ethan — he was solid in his decisions. He had already made so many changes on campus in the year he'd been a class senator, and I knew if he did get the vice presidency, he would bring even more to the table. The girl he was running under as the presidential candidate was amazing, too. Her name was Shayla Hart and together they were the first black president and vice president nominee team. I wanted this win for them, and I could feel it — our campus did, too.

I was handing out the last of our HART I HAMILTON stickers on a Thursday afternoon when I got a text from Jamie that made my stomach drop.

— Where are you? I'm coming to pick you up. —

It was the first time since I'd pulled back that he didn't ask me to hang out — he told me. And I knew before

my fingers even moved over the keys on my phone that
something was wrong.

— I'm with Ethan doing campaign stuff. Rain check?
—

I shook my head, shoving my phone in my back pocket
and slapping on my smile to hand out more stickers. The
last one left my fingers just as my phone buzzed again. I
tried to ignore it, asking Ethan if there was anything else
he needed me to do, but he was deep in discussion with
Amelia and simply kissed my forehead, saying I'd worked
hard enough for the day and I should go home and get
some rest. We were going to a bonfire that weekend, and I
was definitely looking forward to a long night of sleep to
recover from the campaign craziness.

Giving in, I grabbed my backpack from behind our
booth and started the trek across campus to my dorm. I
made it all of ten steps before my phone practically burned
a hole in my pocket.

— Aren't you almost done for the day? I can wait.
Just take a drive with me. —

I thumbed out three different responses — all of them
excuses, none of them strong enough to send — before I
tucked my phone away again without responding at all.
Maybe I could just ignore him. Maybe if I didn't answer,
he'd just let it go and find someone else to ride around
with.

Even as I thought the words, I didn't believe them.

I dropped my bag on my bed as soon as I got home
and stripped my clothes off, aching for a shower. It was
late February and I'd been told we were almost out of the

122

"cold season", but after standing outside in the mid-fifties with a pretty stiff windchill, I was ready for a hot shower.

I took my time, letting the water rush over my skin while trying not to think of how much I'd rather be soaking in a bath. When I made my way back to my room, towel wrapped around my body and my hair still tied in a shower wrap, my phone buzzed from inside my bag.

I had six missed calls, all from Jamie, and one lone text that changed my plans for the evening.

— I need you, B. Please. —

My gut wrenched so violently I bent at the waist, bracing myself with my hand before taking a seat on my bed, not really caring that my damp towel was surely leaving a mark.

I told myself not to respond, fake that I fell asleep, but I knew Jamie, and he'd never say he needed me when he truly didn't. Something was wrong, and it was that feeling alone that let me not even think twice before sending a text back.

— See you in twenty. Lot G. —

• • •

Did you know whiskey in Gaelic means *Water of Life*?

I didn't learn that little fact until later in life, but I remember thinking how magical whiskey must have been the first time those monks tasted it that they coined it with that terminology. It must have been life-altering. It must have made them pause, gasp, and declare that they could no longer live without it. After all, we can't live without water, right?

I wish I would have known that before that night. Before I dressed in simple sweat pants and an oversized sweater, foregoing makeup and sneaking across campus to where I knew Jamie would be waiting. If I would have known, if someone had warned me, I might have been able to save myself from the precise moment my true addiction started.

Maybe.

I watched my breath in little puffs of white as I made my way toward Lot G. The lot was full, yet still I spotted Jamie immediately. He was leaned up against his Jeep, hood up and hands stuffed in the pocket of his navy blue Alder hoodie. He had gray sweat pants on, too, and I couldn't deny the surge of comfort I felt when I saw him.

He waited until I'd nearly reached him to lift his head, and the pain behind his eyes made me stop in place. Something was wrong, *really* wrong. I opened my mouth to say the first word, but was at a loss, so I closed it again. I stood there, waiting for his cue.

Jamie's brows bent together as his eyes scanned me slowly. Then, he pushed off his Jeep in one swift move and his arms were around me. He dropped his head to mine, grip crushing, like he was gripping onto me as his last lifeline. My arms snaked around him hesitantly and I squeezed him in return, letting him feel that I was here. Jamie held me like that for what felt like hours. He didn't speak, didn't cry, just kept readjusting his grip around me, pulling me as close as he possibly could. I breathed in the scent of his cologne against his chest, smelling fall in Florida with a spicy mix of cedar.

"Jamie," I breathed after a while, trying to pull back.

He sighed, the force of his breath moving my hair around it. "Not yet, okay?"

I nodded, face still against his chest, and he quickly pressed a kiss to my forehead before letting me go and motioning to the Jeep. He climbed in first, but my skin was burning from where his lips had touched it. My fingers rubbed the spot as I circled the Jeep before sliding into the passenger seat and buckling my seatbelt.

Jamie turned on his playlist and shot the volume up to seventeen before even putting us in drive. Andre Gagnon started off the soundtrack for the night, *Like the First Day* serving as a beautiful backdrop to a not-so-beautiful feeling building in my stomach.

It was different being in Jamie's Jeep without the top down. All the windows were up and the heat was on low, making the music sound even louder than usual. But there were some things that never changed, like the way Jamie's thumb just barely slid up and down the steering wheel, giving him away. Or how he cracked his neck quickly and quietly, just like he had in high school.

At first I sat rigid, waiting for Jamie to tell me what had happened, but after twenty minutes had passed without a word, I knew he needed time. So, I kicked off my boots and propped my sock-covered feet up on his dash. Jamie didn't smile or turn down the music to talk, but he let out a long, slow exhale, and I knew in that moment that just me being beside him was setting him at ease.

That knowledge made my chest tingle.

It wouldn't be much longer until the weather would even out again. Southern California was mild practically

year-round, but I actually kind of enjoyed the cold front
we were having. It was nice to cozy up, even if just for a
few weeks.

We drove in that same pleasant silence we always
found when we were together, enjoying his playlist and
avoiding real life for a while. After an hour, I thought
about reaching for the volume knob, but I didn't have a
cat joke this time. I didn't have the right words to tackle
what Jamie had on his mind. This time, I'd have to wait
for him, and I was okay with waiting all night if he needed
me to. I guess I should have been thinking about Ethan,
wondering if he would find out, if he would be mad —
and in a way I did worry about those things. But it wasn't
enough to keep me from Jamie when I knew he needed
me.

Two hours passed faster than I thought they could. It
was easy with great music and new sights. Jamie didn't
seem to have any destination in mind as he cruised the
streets of San Diego. We drove slowly through Mission
Valley and Pacific Beach before winding up through
Bird Rock toward La Jolla. Eventually we both rolled our
windows down, me hanging my hand out the window
and surfing the air waves as the heat still blasted high
enough to keep me from freezing.

I was in a daze, lulled by the music and the steady
hum of the engine when I realized we were slowing down.
Jamie pulled into a parking space on the side of a street
and I could smell the salt of the ocean. He didn't speak,
just cut the engine before hopping out and grabbing a
large bag from the back. I rolled out after him, following
his steps without a word.

He wound us through a few small houses and a grove before walking onto a secluded little beach. It couldn't have been more than two-hundred feet in length, half that in width between the grove and the water. There were a few lights on in the houses off in the distance, but nothing on the beach itself. It was just us, the sand, the water, and the moon.

Jamie dropped the bag he had in the sand and pulled out a thick woven blanket, spreading it out on the beach. He sat down without hesitating and looked up at me, pulling a second blanket out and patting the spot next to him. I tugged my boots off again, falling down next to him, and he covered us both with the spare blanket. It had to be in the low fifties now, maybe high forties, but with the layers of clothes we were wearing and the blankets, it wasn't so bad.

I leaned back on my palms, watching as the gentle waves rolled in and waiting for Jamie to speak. He seemed to be waiting for something, too — a sign, maybe — but eventually, he sighed, long and slow, and broke the silence.

"What would you do if everything you had planned for your future went up in flames and there was nothing you could do about it?"

I shifted on my hands, uneasy at the loaded question. "Find a new future, I suppose."

"What if there wasn't one?"

Leaning up, I hugged my thighs to my chest and leaned my cheek on my knees. "What's going on, Jamie?"

He swallowed, the motion visible in the shadow the moon was casting off his jaw. I couldn't shake how tired his eyes looked, how sad, how defeated. Jamie was sitting there, right beside me, yet he seemed so far away.

"Things have been hard, you know? I mean, we're in college, but we're not too dumb to see how the economy is suffering right now. But I never thought it would directly affect me. I think we're at that age where we just feel invincible, like nothing can touch us, but it can." He shook his head, picking at the strings on the edge of our blanket. "My dad's firm is going under. It's going fast. And I'm here, in California, in fucking *college*, powerless to do anything to save it and yet depending on it all the same."

My hand moved of its own accord, reaching out for his. He turned his palm up to meet me and the moment my hand slid into his, he gripped it tight, just like he'd held me in the parking lot. Jamie held onto everything fiercely and unapologetically that night.

"How bad is it?"

"Bad," he croaked. His hand squeezed and I moved closer, leaning my head on his shoulder.

"But is there a chance it'll be okay?"

He shrugged. "I guess there's always a chance."

"So focus on that," I said, my eyes on the waves as I breathed in his scent. "Jamie, your father built that firm. It's been a part of him since he was twenty-six years old. He's put blood, sweat, and tears into it. Do you think a little recession is going to kill his dream? His baby?" I didn't wait for him to answer. "No way. Because the Shaw's are fighters. When you see something you want — truly want — you go after it. All of you. And your dad is going to find a way to keep the firm alive. There is no other option for him."

"It's not that simple," Jamie argued, free hand still picking at the blanket. "There's less of a need for high-end accountants when businesses are tanking. The few clients they have left are seeking out cheaper options, if not battling their own demise."

"Okay, but this recession isn't going to last forever. If your dad can just hold on—"

"And what if he doesn't, B?" Jamie turned to me then, frustration in his voice. "What then?"

"Then he starts over, *Jamie*." I sat up straighter, facing him, too. "And so do you. And you figure it out. Because that's what life's about. It's about paddling out and fighting the waves until you find the perfect one to ride home on."

"I don't know if I could start over," he said dejectedly. The brokenness in his voice was enough to make me move until I was positioned right in front of him, forcing him to look at me. I was so used to seeing Jamie carefree, surfing or driving his Jeep or charming the panties off of every blonde on campus. It was rare to catch him in a moment like this, and I wanted to bring the real Jamie back to the surface.

"Don't you remember what I told you Christmas Eve when we were in high school?" The line between his brows eased at that, and he nodded. "I meant it then, I mean it even more now. You're only a sophomore in college and already you've done two internships and started preparing for your Certified Public Accountant examination, which you don't even need to *think* about until grad school. You're acing your classes and building a network by attending all those fancy events downtown.

You're *doing* it, Jamie. You're making your own dreams come true, just like your dad did. This recession will pass, and you'll come out on top no matter what because that's just who you are."

He was nodding along with me, bottom lip sucked tight between his teeth and eyes on where my hands had wrapped around his. "You're right. I can do this."

"You can," I said, squeezing his hands.

He looked at me then and his nose flared. "I'm not going to lie and say that I'm not scared, but I believe you when you say I can do it. I believe you when you say it will be okay."

"Good. Because I'm right, like, ninety-seven percent of the time."

He cracked the smallest smile at my lame attempt at a joke. *There he is,* I thought. *There's my Jamie.*

"I think I'm going to go home this summer, try to help my dad turn it around."

"You should. It'd be a great experience for you and I know your dad would love having you around."

"Would you come with me?"

His question knocked the breath from my chest, as if I'd forgotten I was alone on a dark beach with him until that exact moment. I pulled my hands from his and tucked them in my lap. "I don't know what my plans are for the summer yet. But you'll be fine without me."

"You've been pulling back lately," Jamie whispered. I shook my head, not ready to have this conversation. "You have. Don't lie to me."

"I never could."

"So then tell me what's going on."

I sighed, debating how likely it would be that Jamie would let me change the subject, but I knew Jamie well enough to know he wouldn't let this go. A part of me was ready to talk about it, though — to tell him why I'd been staying away. Maybe if I got it all out in the open, he would respect my decision. Maybe he'd understand.

"Ethan feels threatened by you, I think." Jamie's eyes widened at that and I shook my head. "That's the wrong word. He just... I don't know. He feels like he has to compete with you. And I hate that I made him feel that way. I just need to focus on my relationship with him and I can't do that if he sees me spending all my time with another man."

"But we're us," Jamie argued. "It's always been us."

"Has it?" I argued, peeking up at him through my lashes. "Seems to me like it's always been us and other people." I cringed a little as the words left my mouth, but I didn't take them back.

The greenish-gold of Jamie's eyes was glowing fiercely in the bright light from the moon, but they shifted in that moment. I watched in what felt like slow motion as the vulnerability that existed in them just moments before was replaced by an insatiable hunger.

"It's just us right now," he said, voice low.

"Jamie..."

"You said you could never lie to me."

The air around us was tightening, catching fire. "I couldn't."

"So then tell me, B," he urged, reaching out for my hands that were tucked in my lap. He grabbed me by the wrists and pulled me closer. "Is it Ethan scared of you being alone with me, or is it you who's afraid?"

My breaths were hollow, especially when his jaw ticked beneath the skin as he waited for my answer.

"Both."

He licked his lips. "Why?"

Each breath I sucked in through my nose burned, like it was poisonous, like the next breath might be my last. "Because I don't trust myself when I'm with you."

Jamie squeezed his eyes tight and blew out a hard breath through his nose, his right hand dropping mine and running up my arm before sliding to my neck. When his eyes shot open again, they were dangerous, thirsty, ravenous. He leaned in closer and I pulled away, farther and farther until I was leaning back and he was on his knees in front of me.

"Would you be mad if I kissed you right now?"

"Yes," I lied, proving my previous statement wrong. I wanted him to kiss me — *God*, I wanted him to kiss me. It was all I could do to pull back from the way he pushed himself into my space. But a normal girl with a boyfriend would have been mad. That's why he asked me. And that's why I lied. I tried to hold onto the last thread of morality I had, but he snapped it in half with his next sentence.

"Then I hope you'll forgive me later."

Jamie closed the distance between us and I opened my mouth to stop him, but he was already there, catching my words with the sweep of his tongue against mine. I gasped into his kiss, pushing up onto my knees to meet him and he groaned at the sound, his hands sliding under my sweater to grip my waist.

He didn't ask if it was okay to keep kissing me. He didn't need to. I was tugging at his hoodie, wanting him closer, wanting more of his tongue, his touch, his scent. He broke our kiss long enough to trail his teeth down my neck, sliding his hands up my waist until his thumbs brushed the lace of my bra.

My heart was a snare drum, pounding erratically against the confines of my rib cage. Jamie traced his fingers along the lacy edge before he gripped me again, this time spinning me to face the ocean. I lost my balance, falling back against him, and his mouth found the base of my neck once more. He bit the tender flesh before sucking it between his teeth and I moaned, letting my head drop back.

"Is this the passion you've been missing? The urgency?" he asked, his lips on the skin beneath my ear. Chills broke on my skin and he sucked my earlobe into his mouth as his thumbs hooked under my bra. He didn't take it off, just pushed it up enough to expose my breasts, and his large hands palmed each one easily. He rolled my nipples with a pinch and I arched my back into him, feeling his hard on pressed against my ass as he inhaled a stiff breath. His hands were cold. His kisses were hot. "Because I can't fathom taking my hands off you right now."

I bit my bottom lip, dragging my teeth across it slowly as Jamie's words ripped me at the seams. I was completely open, completely exposed, raw and uninhibited with the power from his hands surging through my core. My first taste of Whiskey had been nothing. My first shot? Child's play. I'd been holding back, delicately balancing on the line, afraid of drinking too much — but this was it. I knew it. I felt every inch of the fall from tipsy to drunk. I was completely wasted, and all I wanted was to feel this way forever.

Jamie dropped his hold on my breasts and snaked one hand into my hair, tugging it back until his mouth could catch mine. I moaned louder and his other hand slipped slowly down, catching on the skin of my stomach before finding the hem of my boy shorts that were peeking out above my sweat pants. His fingers dipped beneath the fabric as he ran a line from hip to hip and I bucked against the touch, his hand fisting in my hair, holding my head back, leaving me completely at the mercy of his touch.

I was writhing, waiting, my hands on his thighs as I braced myself for his touch. He dipped his hand under deeper, then withdrew it, running it back up my ribs to palm my breast again. I groaned, impatient, and grabbed his hand with my own before forcing it down again. He smirked against my mouth, tugging my bottom lip between his teeth and letting it go with a pop as I moved us beneath my boy shorts. The moment his fingers slid between my thighs, we both moaned.

"Oh fuck," Jamie breathed, kissing me as I pulled my hand back to brace myself again. He slid his fingers down my slit and one finger entered me slowly. I gripped his thighs hard, my nails digging into the fabric of his sweat pants. He worked slowly, his one finger moving deeper and deeper each time until he thrust another inside and I broke our kiss, crying out loud at the sensation.

"Shhh," he ordered, hand dropping its hold on my hair to cover my mouth. I bit down on his fingers, sliding my hand between his thighs behind me to grip him through his sweats. Jamie groaned, thrusting into my touch as his head fell back, and then, all at once, his hands were gone.

My body convulsed at the loss of him, but when I turned on my knees, his shirt was already over his head and I followed suit, stripping my clothes off as he did the same. His eyes never left mine, gaze only broken by curtains of clothes flying between us. When he dropped his boxer briefs, my mouth hung open at the sight of him and I swallowed. He was staring at me, too, chest heaving, and then our eyes met and we crashed together again.

My hands weaved into his hair and I pulled him down on top of me. He moved easily between my legs, blindly reaching for the top blanket and tugging it up over where our hips met and running the length of his erection along my wet slit. He slowed then, breathing hard between softer, longer kisses.

"We need to slow down," he breathed.

"Like hell we do."

He smirked against my lips, slowing my kisses. "I don't have a..." He pulled back, our chests heaving together as he stared down at me. The moon lit him from behind, his strong jaw pronounced against the dark blue of the sky. "We don't have protection."

My eyes bounced between his. "It's okay," I dug my heels into the hard muscles of his ass, bucking my hips up to meet him again. "I'm on birth control. And I'm clean. Are you?"

"Yes."

He said the word like a curse, squeezing his eyes shut

and letting his forehead drop to mine as I dug my nails into his shoulders.

"Jamie," I breathed, wrapping my hands around his neck and pulling his lips to mine again. "I can forgive you for kissing me, but I can't forgive you if you stop right now."

He groaned, low and throaty before he kissed me back. And then, with the slow steadiness of an expert, Jamie filled me, and we tumbled into hell together.

We both gasped, open mouths against each other, my hands on his neck and his forearms braced on either side of me. He withdrew even slower before pushing in again, this time hitting deeper than before.

"God, B," Jamie hissed. "I've dreamed of what this would feel like, taking you, feeling you wrapped around me. But it doesn't even compare. I can't…" He shook his head, moving just a little faster. I felt each thrust through the movements of his thighs, his back, his shoulders, and I wrapped my legs around him tighter. "I'll never—"

"I know," I stopped him, because I did know.

He would never be the same, and neither would I.

If you asked three different whiskey distilleries what the best kind of whiskey is, you'd find three different answers. Some like their whiskey sweet, infused with honey or fruit and smooth on ice. Some prefer their whiskey bold, with sharp spices and mint. Me? Personally, I preferred whiskey that burned — slowly — in an all-consuming fashion.

And that night, I felt every inch of my body catch fire as I drained the bottle.

Jamie took his time, finding what worked for me and what didn't. He explored my body, tasted my skin, and exposed me to a passion unfounded in my life before that night. I came first, tightening around him and fisting the sand at the edge of the blanket. Jamie followed closely, and I nearly lost myself again at the sound of my name on his lips as he fell apart.

He held me close as we climbed the stairs back to Earth. He was still inside me, and he kissed me softly, his eyes lingering on mine. I think Jamie was drinking me in that night, too. I wondered if I burned. I wondered if he liked it.

So you see, the addiction was born on a chilly February night in the soft sand of a private California beach. In that moment, wrapped in his arms under a woven blanket, I felt euphoric. But as we all learn at a young age, what goes up, must come down.

And oh how we crashed.

EIGHT

FOR THE FIRST THREE minutes of consciousness that next morning, I lived in complete and total bliss.

I lie in bed, stretching my arms high above me and flexing my toes as a sleepy smile moved in on my face. I was deliciously sore, aching both physically and yearningly. I wanted more, I wanted to relive last night, I wanted to stay in that memory forever.

After three minutes, my eyes shot open, and dread rushed in like a hangover.

I sat up straight, clutching my sheets in one hand while the other found my forehead. Gazing around my room, I tried to guess what time it was. Jamie and I had stayed out late — too late — the sun already rising when he dropped me off. We'd both been quiet on the ride home, and even though he held my hand the entire way, I worried what he was thinking. Was he feeling guilty about Ethan? Did he regret making the move? Or was he high off life like I was, even if what we had done was wrong?

I couldn't tell, and since it was daylight when he dropped me off, we didn't risk another kiss or even a hug. He simply squeezed my hand before letting it drop and I snuck back into my dorm.

Reaching for my phone, I groaned at the time — 1:42 PM.

I'd missed my Sociology class and I was about to miss English Comp I if I didn't get my ass across campus in less than twenty minutes.

I jumped up, throwing my hair in a sorry excuse for a bun and rushing to brush my teeth before dressing in the first pair of jeans and long sleeve shirt I found. Even though I was in a hurry, it wasn't enough of a distraction from the thoughts racing through my mind.

Adjusting my book bag on my shoulders, I pulled out my phone again, checking for a text from Jamie that still hadn't come in. The dread I'd been feeling low in my stomach all morning made enough room for doubt and anxiety to slink in with it.

Last night had been amazing, and Jamie had seemed so sincere, but what if it was all an act? What if he planned that — the whole opening up to me thing before making his move?

Even as I thought it, I knew it couldn't be true. But what *could* be was that Jamie felt like last night was a mistake. Or worse, that last night didn't mean anything at all to him — that he wasn't even thinking about me at all. That was probably why he hadn't texted.

Or he could be sleeping still.

But he's likely stripping off Melanie From Orientation's bra.

Maybe he's just in class. Did he have classes on Friday?

Nope. He was definitely putting another notch in his headboard. Right next to the one he carved out for me last night.

I stopped dead in my tracks.

Wait, it's Friday?

I smacked my forehead hard with my hand and dragged it down over my face slowly, biting my forefinger as it ran across my lips.

I don't have classes on Friday.

Grumbling, I turned back toward the dorm but took the path that crossed past the coffee shop. Clearly I needed caffeine. I was losing my damn mind.

My pace slowed a little then, but the thoughts buzzing around in my head like wasps only zoomed faster. How was it that everything had felt so right last night, yet felt so wrong now? How was it that the safety of Jamie's arms was somehow lost after a few hours of sleeping on my own?

I blew out an exaggerated breath, deciding to put myself out of my misery and text him first. But when my fingers hovered over the keys, I realized I had no idea what to even say.

— **Wow. Didn't even get me breakfast the morning after. What a let down.** —

Lame. I deleted it.

— **So... last night was fun.** —

Ugh, too desperate. I shook my head, settling for one word.

— **Hey.** —

My throat tightened as I hit the send button, knowing I couldn't take it back now. Part of me was convinced I was acting crazy and he'd text back in a matter of minutes, but the other, louder part of me said nothing is ever certain when it comes to Jamie Shaw.

I tucked my phone in my back pocket just as I rounded the breezeway that led to the coffee shop, desperate to get some caffeine in my system. But when I spotted Jamie walking out the door, I paused.

It wasn't as cold at that time in the afternoon, and Jamie had already shrugged out of his jacket. It was draped lazily over one arm while his other arm rested easily around the shoulders of one of the girls he'd hooked up with earlier in the semester. I thought her name was Tina, but I couldn't be sure. I didn't care, honestly. All that mattered was that she was laughing, head tilted back as Jamie grinned down at her, his mouth too close to her neck.

I swallowed, trying to shake the icky feeling climbing from the tips of my cold fingers to the warmth of my neck. But when Tina placed her hand gently over Jamie's chest, both of them still laughing, I lost any fight I had left to convince myself whatever I was seeing was innocent.

I was going to be sick.

Ducking inside the doors of the breezeway bookstore before he could see me, I sprinted to the first trashcan in sight and heaved, my stomach too empty already to cooperate. A few girls scurried away from me as one of the cashiers rushed over to see if I was okay, but I brushed him off, bracing both hands on the trashcan for a moment to steady myself before racing out the door again.

Each step vibrated from the sole of my foot up between my aching thighs, still sore from him, and I dug my thumbs into the loops of my backpack straps, pulling them tighter and tighter as I walked. I'd never experienced anxiety like that — the crippling kind, the kind that makes every rational thought literally impossible to grasp.

Jamie never did text me back, not in the time I walked back to the dorm or later that night when I stayed wrapped in my comforter, staring at the phone, hoping for something — anything — to prove my gut instinct wrong.

Reassurance never came, no one to break up the party dread, anxiety, and doubt were throwing in my stomach now. Guilt moved in next, and there was only room for one more. I curled in on myself, squeezing my eyes shut and rocking gently, holding out for hope. Finally, at just past midnight, I gave up on waiting. With a shaky sigh, regret slipped in, stealing the last spot.

I didn't sleep that night.

• • •

I peeled myself out of bed early the next day, showering off the sand and smell of Jamie I'd let myself sleep in all night. The day before, I had practically been a spazz, but a new calmness had settled in, and my stomach had evened out. I was almost sluggish, my body reluctant to wake to the harsh reality of it all.

It was a mistake.

It was a stupid, heat-of-the-moment lack of judgment.

And that was fine.

142

It was clear Jamie wasn't bothered by what had happened, so why should I be? Maybe I was young, naive, making it into a bigger deal than it needed to be. So what, we'd hooked up? It happened all the time.

I repeated those words, over and over, washing them into my skin as I scrubbed Jamie off. And as each layer of him swirled with the water into the drain at my feet, I discovered the other layers that rested beneath — the guilt, the shame, the fear, the hurt.

By the time I'd dressed and finished my hair, my biggest concern had drifted to Ethan. He'd asked me to come over to their place for some last minute campaign preparations before the fire pit party that night and I was terrified of seeing him. I'd been set on telling him the truth about Jamie and me, but that was when I thought there *was* a Jamie and me. Now that there wasn't, that I realized the mistake I'd made, I felt sick at the thought of losing Ethan, too.

I knew it made me a shitty person, I *knew* he deserved the truth and I deserved whatever resulted from that, but it didn't make me feel any better about the idea of it. Still, I had made enough mistakes in the last day and a half, and after a night of agonizing, restless "sleep", all I wanted was to do something right.

I had to tell him, and I had to be okay with whatever happened after I did.

I picked up lunch from the favorite taco place on campus and made my way to Ethan's, planting the seed and watering it with every step I took.

It was just a mistake. It's fine. Shit happens. Don't make a big deal out of it.

I wasn't sure if I truly believed it or if I was just slowly putting up a wall, brick by brick, hoping it was strong enough to keep me from my true feelings. But I kept repeating those words, those sentiments, laying the bricks and topping it all off with barbed wire.

I was *fine*.

By the time I used my spare key and pushed through the door of their apartment, I almost believed that.

"I brought tacos!" I announced, kicking the door closed behind me and holding up the two bags. I felt him in the room as soon as I entered, but I didn't dare chance a look in his direction. I found Ethan instead, and my heart warmed at the sight of his smile.

"You didn't."

I nodded, setting everything in my arms down on the counter and waving hello to Shayla who was sitting crosslegged on the floor next to a stack of posters. "I did."

He was there, in the corner, right next to where Shayla was tapping on her laptop as she sorted through materials, but I still didn't look at him.

Ethan picked himself up from the floor and rushed over, wrapping me in his arms and greeting me with a long, slow, heated kiss. "Marry me," he murmured against my lips and I giggled, guilt surging as he kissed lips that were still swollen from Whiskey. I pushed him back playfully before digging through the bags.

"I'll get this all set up. Whatcha working on?"

"Just going through inventory, figuring out next week's plan so we can have some fun and *not* think about this election tonight at the party."

"Amen!" Shayla yelled and I chuckled.

I smiled, but it was weak, my stomach like a hive of bees as I stepped in closer to Ethan. "Do you have a second to talk? I... I need to tell you something."

His brows turned in, hands finding my arms in a comforting embrace. "Is everything okay, babe?"

"Yeah, I'm fine," I said with a swallow. "I just, there's just something we need to talk about."

"Okay," he said, eyes flickering between mine before he turned to glance over his shoulder at Shayla. "Would it be okay if we talked later tonight? We're really trying to get all this done before the party. I mean, that is if you're sure you're okay and it can wait?"

He was still staring at me from the corner of the room. I felt his eyes burning craters into my skin as Ethan waited for my response.

"Yeah, sure. Yeah it can wait." I forced another smile. "Go get back to it. I'll make everyone a plate and then come help."

"Thank you," he whispered, kissing my cheek once more before jogging back over to take a seat on the floor next to Shayla. They bent their heads together, pointing at something on her screen and talking numbers. It was then that I finally let my eyes drift to Jamie.

His face was stone, eyes intense as they bored into me from beneath his furrowed brows. I let my eyes fall to his mouth, lips set in a firm line, and then I swallowed and turned, reaching into the cabinet for plates.

What, he thought I was going to walk in here devastated? Crying and begging him to tell me why he never texted? Why he never called? He thought he had the upper hand, and maybe he did, but I was determined not to let that show.

It was just a mistake. It's fine. Shit happens. Don't make a big deal out of it.

I repeated the same thoughts, again and again, willing them to be true.

"What are you doing?"

I jumped a little at the boom of his voice, the plates rattling in my hands as I pulled them from the shelf.

"Making tacos. Want some?" I avoided his eyes, setting the plates on the counter before opening each styrofoam takeout box with the ingredients.

"Don't play dumb, you've never been good at it."

"Because you know me so well."

"I do," he said loudly, grabbing my wrist that had just been reaching for the taco shells. We both glanced up at Ethan and Shayla, but it was like we weren't there at all. "I *do* fucking know you," he said again, his voice lower. "What's wrong?"

"Nothing."

"B," he warned, and I tugged my wrist from his grip.

"Nothing. I'm fine."

"You're fine," he deadpanned.

I sighed, piling the first shell with grilled chicken before dropping it to a plate and facing Jamie. I set my face first, hoping like hell he wouldn't see the way he'd hurt me. "Yep. Are you going to help me with these or not? Because otherwise you're kind of in the way right now."

Jamie let out a sharp laugh. "That's fine, I don't mind

146

being in the way. Seems to be my favorite place to be actually."

I narrowed my eyes at his insinuation.

"What's gotten into you? Did I do something?"

"Why would you think that?" I brushed it off, still aiming for calm, unaffected.

He scoffed, crossing his arms before stepping closer. "Oh, I don't know, less than thirty hours ago you were forcing my hand between your thighs and now you won't even look at me? Yeah, maybe that."

"Shhh!" I scolded, my eyes flicking to Ethan, who was oblivious, before snapping back to Jamie. He was standing so close, his words like flames that licked at my stomach. "Stop. It was a mistake."

His head snapped back like my words had struck him. "A mistake."

"We were both vulnerable, it was a heavy moment. Shit happens."

"Shit hap—" he didn't even finish the sentence, just threw his hands up, raking them through his light brown strands before clasping them to rest on his head. He let them fall again, hands hitting his thighs. "What are you even saying right now? Do you hear yourself? Do you *see* yourself? You're shaking, B."

He went to reach for me and I backed away, my lower back hitting the counter. "I see just fine, thank you. Well enough to see that whatever happened the other night clearly didn't stop you from shacking up with Tina yesterday." I met his eyes then and watched the argument drain from them.

"What? *Tina?*"

"It's fine, Jamie. I saw you two together, but it's okay. What happened with us... it didn't mean anything to me either," I lied. "So we're cool. Like I said, shit happens." I kept plating the tacos, done with the conversation, done with him.

"Wow." Jamie shook his head before sliding closer, invading my space. "I don't know what you think you *saw*, but if this is really how you feel, I'm glad your twisted little mind made this shit up to make you feel better about it."

With that, he pushed off the counter and walked away. I watched every move, every flex of every muscle in his back until he disappeared inside his room, slamming the door behind him.

"Jesus, what's wrong with him?" Shayla asked.

Ethan looked at me, brows bent, asking me the same question. I just shrugged.

"Guess he doesn't like tacos."

Shayla laughed and Ethan offered her a forced smile, but his eyes found mine again and I felt the accusation in that gaze. I ignored it, finishing their tacos and hand delivering them along with two bottles of water. Then, I made my own plate, sat down next to them, and talked campaign plans.

It was almost five when I made my way back to my own dorm, mind heavy with Jamie's words as I walked. I'd been so set on seeming indifferent to what had happened between us, but now I wasn't sure that what I'd seen had really been what I thought. But if it wasn't, then why didn't he ever text me back? Why didn't he call? Why didn't he do *something*, anything to reassure me that what happened between us had been real?

I'd never been so fucked up mentally in my life. Nothing made sense, and for reasons I couldn't explain, the first person I wanted to talk to about it was my dad. I wanted a man's opinion. But as I pulled out my phone and brought up his contact, I paused, heart breaking as I realized he wasn't a man — not a real one. A real man wouldn't do what he'd done to my mother. A real man would have owned up to his mistakes, would have asked for forgiveness, would have given the explanation he owed to his daughter.

I felt sick again as I tapped out of my dad's contact, pulling up Ethan's, instead. My fingers were typing out the text message excuse about how I didn't feel well enough to go to the fire pit party when a familiar voice squealed my name. I glanced up, and then I almost dropped my phone. There were two large suitcases propped up next to my dorm room door and a long pair of tan legs I'd know anywhere stood right beside them.

"Surprise, bitch!"

Jenna.

NINE

Jack Daniel's

I'D NEVER SIPPED WHISKEY from a flask so angrily.

Jenna was filling up her cup from the keg, going on about one of her professors whom she swore was hell bent on failing her, and I was trying to get my shit together. My best friend had flown across the country to surprise me and my brain decided to fill itself with Jamie, instead. It was annoying. I didn't want to think about him, and every time I tried not to, it became more and more impossible to accomplish.

He'd yet to show to the party, and I had a feeling it was because he knew I was here. I'd had no choice but to come, especially after Jenna showed up, but I was still uneasy from what had happened earlier.

I didn't know what possibility bothered me more — that he would go out somewhere else tonight or stay inside because of me, or that he would show up and I'd have to be around him and Jenna and Ethan all at once.

I took another shot.

"So yeah, I'm pretty sure he wants to bang, but he's *pissed* that he wants to bang me so he's making my life a living hell," she finished, sucking the froth from her new beer.

"So basically you're going to have sex with your teacher."

She shrugged, steering us toward one of the fire pits. "Probably."

We both laughed, and I tried for the fiftieth time to relax and have fun. Jenna was blown away by the fact that Alder was a wet campus and we could just have a kegger out by the fire pits on the edge of campus. We still had to register it as an event, and there were limitations, but it was pretty awesome. Still, I wasn't in the mood for beer that night. I needed something stronger.

Hence, the flask.

I tipped it to my lips once more and sucked a breath through my teeth as the whiskey burned its way down. I hadn't even sprung for a nice bottle, just opted for good ol' Jack Daniel's. One day I swore I'd have an entire cabinet dedicated to high-end whiskey, just so I'd always have some ready for an occasion such as this.

"You've been quiet," Jenna observed. "Everything okay?"

I forced a smile. "Of course. My best friend is here!"

"But?"

Dropping the act, I dropped onto one of the benches by the far fire pit and Jenna took the seat next to me. It was one of the last chilly nights we'd have in San Diego and the fire was a welcome warmth. "I'm so sorry, Jenna. I really am excited you're here. I'm just…" I debated telling her, spilling everything right then and there. The truth is I *wanted* to tell someone, but it wasn't the right time. "Tired. I've been helping Ethan with all this campaign stuff and it's just kind of exhausting."

"Ah," Jenna mused, her eyes scanning the gathering crowd until she spotted Ethan. He and Shayla were now camped out at the keg we'd just been at, filling cups and handing them out, clearly not taking the night off like they'd said they would. "Pretty impressive that he's running for Vice President. He seems like a good guy."

"He is," I agreed, my voice like sandpaper rubbing together. Ethan was an incredible guy, and when he found out what I'd done, I'd lose him. My stomach rolled, and I clutched the flask tighter.

"Are you happy?" Jenna asked casually, tossing her long blonde hair over her shoulder as she sipped from her beer. The sun was just setting, the sky fading into a deep navy blue behind the fire. Her question should have been easy to answer, but I made a strange noise before smiling and shrugging. She cocked a brow. "What the hell does that mean?"

"I'm happy," I said quickly. "I am. Like I said, he's amazing."

"You are the worst liar."

I laughed. "I think it's just the campaign stuff. I'll be happy when it's over."

Jenna narrowed her eyes, but let me drop it. "Okay, fair enough. So," she said with a pop, sitting up straighter. "I'm here for a week. What are we doing first?"

I perked up at that, excited for a week with her and plenty of distractions. "Well, we obviously have to hit the beach so you can see what the west coast has to offer. There are a few fun clubs downtown we can get into, and I have at least four places you have to eat at before you can leave the city — starting with The Taco Stand in La Jolla."

Jenna squealed excitedly. "Can we go dancing somewhere?!"

"Duh!"

We laughed, and as the noise faded, I took in the moment to truly appreciate the fact that she was there. "I'm so glad you came, Jenna. Your timing actually couldn't have been better."

She nudged me. "Must be that best friend ESP stuff hard at work."

"Must be." I unscrewed the metal cap off my flask and tapped her red plastic cup with it. "Cheers, bitch."

"Cheers."

We tilted our drinks back, and Jenna opened her mouth to say something but was cut off.

"Well I'll be damned."

Jenna turned and I closed my eyes, pushing an exhale out through my nose as my stomach somersaulted.

"*Jamie?!*" She jumped up, throwing her arms around his neck as I held tight to my flask and lifted it to my mouth again. "What the hell? What are you *doing* here?"

He laughed, and I finally chanced a look at him. He had on the same hoodie from two nights ago and memories hit me like flashes of lightning, quick and beautiful, one right after another. His hair was disheveled, his eyes low, lazy smile in place. One glance, that's all I needed for two things to sink in — one, he was drunk, and two, I was in trouble.

"What do you mean? I go to school here."

Jenna's mouth gaped open and she turned to me, brows pinched together in confusion. "What? Oh my God, B, how did you never tell me Jamie went to the same school as you?"

Jamie turned to me then, an easy, cocky smile playing at his lips. "She never told you, huh?"

My fingers nervously played with my curls and I shrugged, smile tight. "I figured you saw on social media or something."

"Yeah right," she giggled the words. "This asshole deleted me after he broke my heart."

Oh God, she was flirting.

Jamie lifted one eyebrow, his smile growing as his eyes swept Jenna's body. "I seem to remember being on the other side of that heartbreak."

Now I was having a different kind of flashback, to that first day on the trail, the way they were looking at each other, studying each other, wondering where the other had been hiding. I tried to swallow, but came up empty. Shooting to my feet, I forced a smile and looped my arm through Jenna's. "We should make the rounds, I want to introduce you to everyone."

She was still looking up at Jamie, but she spoke to me. "Yeah, in a minute. I think Jamie needs a drink."

I knew by the glazed look in his eyes that he had already had plenty, but his hands *were* currently empty. Our eyes connected, just for a second, and the anger I'd seen earlier had completely vanished. I tried to ask him something in that short moment I had his eyes on mine, but I wasn't sure what. He dropped his gaze back to Jenna too quickly for me to figure it out.

"That I do. Escort me?" he asked, holding out his arm. Jenna dropped mine like a hot rock and took his offer.

"Of course." They started walking, and Jenna turned over her shoulder to mouth *oh my God* to me before waggling her eyebrows and smiling back up at Jamie. I just watched them leave, flopping down on the bench with a sigh.

Fuck.

I realized quickly what kind of night it would be, so I drained three long shots from my flask and gritted against the sting. I needed an escape, I needed a break from my thoughts.

I needed to get drunk.

For the first half hour after that, I watched them together, sipping from my flask every other minute. I watched as they filled their cups, as they talked and laughed, as Jenna took every chance she could to reach out and touch him. When they made their way over to a bench at the fire pit opposite me, I stood abruptly, pausing a moment as the whiskey hit me all at once. Shaking it off, I scanned the fires until I found Ethan, weaving my way through the crowd toward him.

I was not going to torture myself. Jamie was my friend, Jenna was my best friend. They'd been together once before, so what if they rekindled that flame for the next week that she was here? It would be just like high school.

Except back then, I hadn't slept with Jamie. I hadn't felt him burn himself into my skin, brand me, *ruin* me.

I huffed, shaking my head. It was one night, and it wasn't a big deal. It clearly didn't matter to Jamie and it shouldn't matter to me. I had Ethan, and Jamie had every other blonde bunny on campus. Things were back to normal.

I repeated that as I drained the last of my flask.

"Hey, there you are," Ethan said with a smile as I wrapped my arm around his shoulders and slid into his lap.

"Here I am." I kissed him hard, fists gripping his shirt to pull him closer. I needed him, I needed to fill myself with his scent and erase Jamie's.

"Whoa," he said against my lips, but I just pressed my lips into him harder. "Hey, you okay?" He'd pulled back, scanning me, judging my intoxication level, no doubt.

"Peachy. Just kissing my boyfriend." I smiled and he returned it, but hesitantly. "What are you guys talking about?"

Shayla had turned away at some point, probably feeling a little awkward at my public display of affection, but she lit up then. "Oh! We were just talking about switching things up at our tents next week, really ramping up before the election, you know?" I nodded, reaching for my flask before realizing it was empty. "What do you think of *ice cream* instead of pizza?"

She was smiling so big, her and Ethan both waiting for my answer. I sucked my lips between my teeth before letting them go and clapping my hands on my thighs. "I think that sounds amazing! I need a drink. Be right back."

I hopped up before either of them could say anything else and made a beeline for the keg. It wasn't whiskey, but it'd do.

After I filled my drink, I wandered around for a while, deciding not to worry about Jenna. She was a big girl, and clearly she knew what she wanted to do tonight. Thinking about it just made me sick so I avoided it, prancing from group to group before finally making my way back over to Ethan.

Except Jamie and Jenna were at the same fire pit now. *Perfect.*

I took my place in Ethan's lap again and his hand found my hip, pulling me closer. "Hey," he whispered.

"Hey."

"I'm sorry about earlier. I don't want you to think I didn't enjoy that kiss, because I definitely did," he said, pressing his lips to my shoulder. "It's just that Shayla was in the middle of that whole campaign conversation and I was worried she'd feel weird."

"It's fine, I probably should have taken a breath before mauling your face."

He smiled, teeth bright even in the low light from the fire. "I kind of like when you maul my face." He leaned in then, taking my chin between his thumb and knuckles and kissing me sweetly. My eyes flitted to where Jamie sat on the bench catty-corner to us, but his were on Jenna — focused, like he always was.

Ethan still held my chin as he pulled back, eyes searching mine. "Did you want to talk now?"

"What?" I asked, returning his gaze but still somehow acutely aware of Jamie's movements.

"You wanted to talk earlier. Everything okay?"

Shit. Suddenly, the idea of telling Ethan terrified me — especially after the amount of Jack Daniel's I'd consumed. Seeing his gentle face in the light of the fire twisted the knot in my chest. He deserved to know, and I still planned on telling him.

But not tonight.

"You know, it's nothing really. Let's just enjoy ourselves tonight."

Ethan's eyebrows pinched together. "You sure?"

Nodding, I leaned in for another kiss, silencing his worry with my lips. "I'm sure."

Even with my heart breaking over what I was keeping from Ethan, I still wondered if Jamie was watching us kiss, and I almost couldn't hide my disappointment when I pulled back from Ethan's lips and discovered that he wasn't.

I might as well have been dead to him.

Maybe I was.

"We should play a game," I announced to the group, sipping from my cup.

Jenna clapped her hands together. "Oh! Yes! How about Never Have I Ever?"

"Classic choice, bestie," I air-cheers-ed her and she winked, lifting her cup, too.

"We're a little old for games, don't you think?" Jamie's voice boomed. He was finally looking at me for the first time since he and Jenna had walked away, but I shrugged, keeping my eyes on the fire.

"You don't have to play. Tina just showed up, why don't you go get her a drink and leave us kids alone?"

I said it with a smile, but my condescending tone was evident.

Jenna eyed me before turning her gaze to Jamie. "Girlfriend?"

Jamie was frowning, but I kept smiling sweetly. "No. B has some weird obsession with my Economics project partner and can't let it go."

I rolled my eyes. "Whatever. Stay or go, I don't care. Ethan, you go first."

Ethan looked uncomfortable, his eyes wary as he glanced around the fire, but he conceded. "Okay. Never have I ever had a one-night stand."

Jamie and Jenna drank, smiling at each other over the rims of their cups. Jamie's eyes fell on me next, and I saw the challenge in them before he even spoke. "Not drinking, B?"

"Nope." The word popped off my lips. "Your turn."

"You've *never* had a one-night stand?" he questioned, leaning his elbows on his knees. One eyebrow lifted as he waited for the response stuck in my throat.

"I was her first," Ethan said confidently, pulling me in close and kissing my neck. "Her only."

Guilt rolled through my stomach like a rock slide and I hastily kissed him back, keeping my eyes off Jamie's.

"How sweet," Jenna cooed.

"Yeah. *So* sweet," Jamie agreed. "So, my turn, huh? Hmmm... Never have I ever had a threesome."

Jenna and I smiled across the fire at each other, thinking about the promise we'd made to each other years ago that if we ever had a threesome, it had to involve the other. But the smile slid from my face when Ethan took a drink.

"Wait, seriously?"

Ethan cringed, like a dog with his tail between his legs. "I was a freshman, I thought it was cool at the time. It didn't mean anything."

"Oh," I replied softly, wondering why he'd never mentioned it before.

"Are you mad?"

It clicked then why Jamie had asked that question and I glared at him over the flames. He just smirked.

"Of course not," I assured Ethan. "It was before me. No big deal." I smiled to seal that lie and he pulled me in closer, kissing my neck as I took a drink and nodded to Jenna. "Your turn."

"Oh! Never have I ever gotten a tattoo," she said excitedly, scanning the fire. When none of us drank, she pouted. "Damn, we need a little excitement in our lives."

I laughed, but then snapped my fingers together. "You know what? We should get tats before you leave."

"Seriously?" she squeaked.

"Hell yeah! Why not? We'll go tomorrow."

"Oh my God! I'm in!" Jenna bounced as Shayla slid into the open spot next to Ethan, handing him a new beer and taking a drink of her own.

"What's up?"

"We're playing Never Have I Ever. Wanna play?" I asked.

"Sure!"

I waved my hand, tilting my cup to my lips. "Floor's all yours."

"Hmm.... Never have I ever had sex on the beach."

KANDI STEINER

I choked, beer filling my nose as Ethan rubbed my back. "You alright?"

Nodding, I stood quickly, keeping my eyes off Jamie. I didn't need to see his cocky smile to know it was sitting on his perfect face. "Fine. I'm going to get a refill."

Ethan tried to tighten his grip on me but I slunk away from him, storming toward the keg. Jenna followed.

"Hey, are you okay?"

"I'm fine!" I yelled. Jenna's brows shot up and I huffed. "Sorry. Everyone's been asking me that tonight and I'm just annoyed."

She laughed. "Okay, note to self — you're fine. Come on, let's get drinks."

Jenna led the way to the keg and filled up first, taking her first drink and looking back toward the fire pit as I filled mine.

"So, Jamie."

"What about him?" I tried for indifferent. I wasn't sure if I landed there.

"I just… I forgot how *hot* he was. He's gotten even better with age. Like fine wine."

Or whiskey.

"Yeah. He's a stud," I said flatly.

"I think he might be up for a little *blast from the past* action tonight. Would you be mad? If I maybe left with him?"

I dropped the nozzle on the keg, an ache burning my chest at the thought. Chugging half of what I poured, I started filling again, but didn't look at her. "Of course not. Have fun."

"Are you sure?"

161

I didn't get to answer because Jamie had shown up, holding his hand out for the nozzle as I finished filling my cup. I thrust it into his hands.

"You girls up for a swim?" he asked, nodding toward the pool not even a hundred feet from the pits.

"It's freezing," I deadpanned.

He just shrugged. "So? Live a little."

"Because that always works out so well," I murmured, lifting my cup to my lips.

Jenna narrowed her eyes. "Why are you being weird tonight?"

"I'm not being weird," I gritted through my teeth, my head swimming from the alcohol. I realized the longer I stood that I'd successfully fulfilled my plan to get drunk.

"I don't know," Jamie offered, standing up straight with his beer now full. "You are kind of being weird."

I glared up at him then and he just smirked, taking a sip. I opened my mouth to pop off some sort of smart remark, but decided better, shaking my head instead. "I'm going to find Ethan. You two have fun catching hypothermia."

Jenna called out to me but I ignored her, deciding at that moment that what Jamie and Jenna did that night didn't matter.

But no matter how much I repeated that to myself as I finished beer after beer and the night turned to early morning, I couldn't stop watching them. They were like a car wreck or a drunk guy preaching on the sidewalk. No matter how I tried, I couldn't tear my eyes away for more than thirty seconds, and the more the night went on, the more they touched, the more they laughed, the more I wanted to vomit.

Even worse, Jamie's eyes never found mine again. Not when I danced with Ethan, grinding my ass into his groin, or when I straddled him on the bench, kissing him with fervor. He didn't glance over when I laughed loud or glare when Ethan's lips found my neck and collarbone. It was like I didn't exist, and the more I drank, the more that bothered me.

Everyone has that one night they can trace back to in their mind, that first night they drank too much and made a complete ass of themselves. Well, this was that night for me, and I was about to find out the hard way that, contrary to popular belief, "liquor before beer" did not always mean "in the clear" — especially when it all started with Jack Daniel's.

"I want to go swimming," I sang into Ethan's lips as we kissed, the party in high gear around us. Jamie wanted to go in the pool, and I wanted Jamie's attention. Science.

Ethan laughed. "A little too cold for that, babe. Maybe in a week or two."

"No, I want to go now," I argued, pouting.

A freshman sprinted past us, ripping his clothes off and flinging them behind him, screaming something about skinny dipping. I perked up, eyes on him as everyone laughed around us and I turned back to Ethan.

"Come on! Let's go!" I jumped up, tugging my boots off and following after the naked freshman. Ethan hooked his arm around my elbow.

"B, no, you're not going skinny dipping."

I didn't know why, but his demand didn't sit right with me, and I scowled. "I can do whatever the hell I want."

Ethan's eyes were hard, unbudging. "I'm serious. There's too many people here, and it's a campus party. There's campus police like two streets away and you're already drinking underage. Don't be stupid."

I ripped my arm away from his and saw Jamie and Jenna both stand in my periphery. "What, afraid I'll damage your perfect reputation before election?" I was sneering, and I knew I was being ugly, but I couldn't stop it. I was out of control. "It was embarrassing to kiss me earlier, guess it'd *really* be embarrassing if I took my clothes off." I didn't know why I wanted to push his buttons, but I stripped my sweater off to prove the point, leaving me in just the tank top I was wearing underneath. A few guys whistled and I tossed a wink in their direction.

"Okay, come on. We're leaving." He went to grab my arm again but I dodged it.

"You can go if you want. I'm not ready to leave."

"That wasn't a request."

"And mine wasn't a suggestion."

"Damnit, Brecks!" He screamed my name like a curse word. It might as well have been. "You're not getting in that pool. End of story."

He was talking to me like a child, scolding me by using my full name. I glared at him, mouth open, wondering how he could do that. He didn't know about my parents, but I'd told him my real name in confidence, telling him there was a very real reason why I never went by it.

And he'd betrayed that trust.

164

"B…" Jamie flanked me, holding his hands out like I was dangerous. "Come on. I'll walk you back to your dorm."

"I can walk myself," I spat at all of them, snatching my sweater and boots off the ground. Then, I turned on my heels and tore through the crowd that had been staring at us, pushing down the emotions building inside of me and focusing on not stumbling as I pulled my boots back on.

I didn't even make it through the parking lot before I heard his steps behind me.

"Go away, Jamie," I threw behind me, still stalking toward the path that led back to my dorm. The university was set up in a circular fashion, with different sidewalk circles connecting the inner and outer parts of campus. We were on the outside, and so was my dorm, just a short ten-minute walk away, and I found solace in that as I brushed past the cars parked in Lot A.

"What? Nothing to say now?"

"I said go away."

"Oh come on," he chided, his long legs letting him catch up to me easily. "You've been doing your damnedest to get my attention all night. Well, you've got it."

I scoffed. "Contrary to your belief that the world revolves around you, Jamie, you were the last thing on my mind tonight."

"Bullshit."

I spun then, stopping us mid-stride, practically seething. "Just leave me alone! Go back to Jenna and give her the *Tour De' Jamie's Bedroom*. I've heard it's *quite* the tourist spot on campus."

Jamie's lips flattened and he slammed his hand against a random truck. "Damnit, B!" I flinched, waiting for the alarm to sound, but it didn't. "What the hell do you want from me? You give yourself to me after all this time and then treat me like scum the next fucking day, saying it was a mistake and didn't matter to you. But then, you act like a goddamn fool when you see me with your best friend." He stepped into my space and my breath caught in my chest. "You think I slept with Tina? I didn't. She's in my class, nothing more. You think that night didn't matter to me? It did. It's all I've thought about since. You think it doesn't *kill* me to see Ethan's hands on you?" He stepped closer, eyes wild. "It does. It fucking *murders* me. You think what happened between us wasn't real? It was." His chest was heaving as everything faded out around us and his eyes fell to my lips. "And it still is."

He broke the space between us, crushing his mouth on mine. His lips sparked the fire and I sucked in a breath through my nose, head spinning, before my hands found the center of his chest and I shoved him back hard. He hit the truck and threw his hands up, eyes an inferno as we both panted.

I watched him, my conscience telling me to walk away while my body screamed for me to never let go. Nothing made sense. *Everything* made sense. The whiskey clouded my head and I stopped trying to fight the fog, launching myself at him and yanking his sweater until his mouth was on me again. He lifted me, spinning us and pinning me against the truck. His lips traveled down my neck to my collarbone, my chest, the swell of my breast. He sucked the skin hard, trying to brand me, but I wasn't his to mark.

"Stop," I breathed, and he groaned, taking it as a challenge as his hand slipped under my tank top. I moaned, breathing hard into his mouth as he slid his tongue inside mine. I was dizzy. I wanted to give in. I wanted him. *Badly*.

But this was wrong.

"Stop!" I said again, this time pushing him off and dropping my feet back to the ground. "We can't do this."

"Why not?" he panted.

"B?"

Jenna's voice startled us both and I closed my eyes, leaning my head against the truck before turning to face her.

She crossed her arms, eyes bouncing between the two of us. "What the fuck is going on?"

Jamie forced a long exhale through his nose, and I couldn't even look at him again. I didn't want to see the pain, the resignation.

"Come on, Jenna. Let's go." I reached for her hand and she took it, eyes still wild under bent brows as I tugged her away from Jamie. To his credit, he didn't follow this time.

When we were out of ear shot, Jenna pulled her hand free and picked up our pace. "You better have some fucking booze in your dorm room because you've got a *lot* of explaining to do."

I glanced back at Jamie, who hadn't moved. He just stood there watching us leave, and I knew nothing would be the same after I told Jenna. She would make me choose. She would be the voice of reason I was running from.

"All I have is Whiskey," I whispered, tearing my eyes from Jamie to the path we were walking. I meant that sentence in more ways than one, and I knew before telling Jenna anything that I couldn't ever lose him.

But that meant I'd have to lose someone else.

T E N
Hangover

THEY SAY TIMING IS everything, and I was beginning to learn that timing was everything but kind to Jamie and me.

I woke up that next afternoon hungover as hell, but finally feeling relieved from the pressure that had been crushing my chest. The sun was shining hot through my dorm window and I kicked the covers off. Jenna grumbled, rolling away from the light as I stared up at my ceiling, going over my plan for the day.

After talking to Jenna until nearly five in the morning, spilling everything, I felt better. I expected her to judge, or hell — to maybe be mad, seeing as how she had dated Jamie in high school — but she didn't, and she wasn't. She listened to me sob and break down and she held me through all of it, and then she did what I knew she would.

She made me choose.

I thought it would be harder, I thought it would kill me to say out loud who I wanted, but after confessing everything and feeling the whiskey and beer leave my system gradually, it was like walking out of a foggy haze into the purest clarity. I knew what I had to do, and even though I knew it would hurt, I was ready to do it.

Crawling out of bed, I padded to the bathroom and popped two ibuprofen before attempting to wrangle my hair. As I did, I cringed at my reflection. I looked like absolute shit, and I knew I deserved it. Ethan shouldn't have had to put up with my dramatics last night, and he shouldn't have to be lied to, either. I hoped he would understand. I hoped he would forgive me. I hoped he would move on, finding a girl who could treat him better than I did.

More than anything, I hoped he'd be happy.

And then there was Jamie. My stomach lurched at the thought of him. After last night, I didn't know if he would hear me out — if he would give me a chance to explain myself or if he'd give a shit after I did. But I had to try. One thing was certain after talking to Jenna all night — I wanted to be with him — needed it, really. I just hoped I wasn't too late.

I remember the next sixty seconds like a slow motion car wreck.

Me, staring at my reflection in the mirror, planning out all the words I would say. Jenna, sprinting up behind me with my phone in her hand. Her voice, panicked. Her hair, wild. My mom's cries on the other end, loud and jarring, pounding against my head that the ibuprofen had yet to help ease. It happened all at once — all of those things — but I remember them singularly, morphed, almost as if I'd dreamed them.

I had everything planned out — what I would say to Ethan, what I would say to Jamie — but I never got the chance.

In that moment, everything in my life shifted focus. What I thought was important was trivial, what was last on my mind became first.

My dad died on the day I realized I loved Jamie Shaw.

Love pulled my soul one way and grief yanked it another, and so it ripped in two, split into jagged, irreparable halves. One floated high, calling me up with it, while the other sank into a bottomless black hole.

But I was too weak to fly.

The heavier half dragged me with it and I didn't cry, I didn't scream, I didn't fight. I drowned easily, staring at the floating half on the way down, wondering if we'd ever meet again.

• • •

I felt everything alive inside of me slowly slipping away as I stared out at the choppy water. A storm was rolling in, the gray clouds lurking off in the distance as the sun began to fade. It wasn't as cold as the night before, and I stood where the water met the sand, my board under my arm, wetsuit zipped up high to my neck.

It was as if each time the water rose high enough to lick at my toes, it stole a little more of what was left alive inside of me, leaving dead driftwood in its place. My eyes grew hollow, my breaths grew steady, and my heart grew weak.

I could still hear my mother's words, and they still didn't make sense. *A freak accident*, she'd said. It sounded like a horror movie, or a newspaper article about a distant human being whom I didn't know personally. It didn't sound like my life. But it was.

My dad's parents had a house on a lake in Central Florida. We used to drive up on the weekends to ride the wave runners and go swimming. Every memory I had there as a child was filled with joy. Mom said Dad was there for Nana's birthday, swimming just off the dock like we always used to. He was just swimming, just enjoying a weekend at the lake, and then his life ended. Cords plugged into the dock and house boat had slipped into the water, electrifying it, and he'd suffered from electric shock drowning. I didn't even know that was possible, and maybe that's why I couldn't process it.

Maybe it was a combination of everything in that moment — the guilt from what I'd done to Ethan, the ache of what I felt for Jamie, the shock of my father's death. Everything had been thrown into a blender, dial set to shred, and now it was all I could do to stand near the edge of the ocean and not wish to drown in it.

I left Jenna in my room, packing my bags because I couldn't, and caught a cab to the beach to try to feel. I just wanted to feel something — *anything*. I wanted it to sink in. I wanted to cry. I wanted the numbness to go away, but it was only plunging deeper, seeping into the cracks between my joints, settling into its new home.

"You can't go out there."

His voice was steady, low and oaky like always. My lip quivered at the sound of it and I nearly dropped my board. Fastening my grip, I hiked it higher, not turning to see him for fear of a completely different emotion sinking in. "I'll be fine."

"It's about to storm, and it's getting dark," Jamie warned, and I felt his arms hook around my board from the other side. I gripped it tighter at first, but then my shoulders fell and I released my hold, letting Jamie take it away. I instantly felt empty as he set it easily in the sand, and I kept my eyes on the swell to avoid looking at him.

He stood beside me, gazing out at the water with me, and for a moment he let the wind and the waves be the only sound. His hand reached out, just barely, his pinky brushing mine before I slid my palm into his and held on tight.

"Jenna called me. She... she told me what happened." I didn't respond, but my thumb rubbed his.

Thunder rolled low and menacing in the distance, and I felt its cry deep in my stomach.

"Talk to me," he pleaded.

A sickening ache spread through my chest and I fought against the sob. "I don't know what to say."

"Don't worry about it making sense, just talk. Just... get it out."

I nodded, over and over, my lips between my teeth as I held his hand and watched the sun set behind a wall of storm clouds. I didn't know where to start, but as the last sliver of gold fell behind the gray, I took a breath, sharp and unsteady, and then I spoke.

"I'm supposed to hate him," I started, sniffing. "I was named after the freckles on his cheeks, the same ones on

mine, and I'm supposed to hate him. He raped my mom,"
I choked out, and the emotion started to surface, tears
welling and blurring my vision. "And I never knew. I
never knew that the hands that taught me how to ride a
bike were the same ones that held my mom down the night
I was conceived. I never knew the eyes that cried with
tender joy the day I lost my first tooth were the same ones
that watched my mom beg for him to stop hurting her." I
shook my head, and Jamie's hand gripped mine tighter.
"He was always there. He was the one to buy me my first
notebook and pen and tell me to write. He was the one
who took me on a shopping spree the day my childhood
best friend moved away. He was always there," I covered
my mouth with my free hand, squeezing my eyes shut.
"And then he wasn't, because I pushed him away, because
I was supposed to. I haven't talked to him since the day
I graduated high school. I ignored his phone calls. I told
him not to come to Christmas dinner for the first time in
my life." My throat constricted, and I squeezed my eyes
harder, trying to block out the truth. "I didn't talk to him,
Jamie. And now I'll never talk to him again."

The tears built up enough to spill, and I felt them
hot on my cheeks as Jamie pulled me into his chest. My
arms wrapped around his waist, cries staining his t-shirt
as he held me tight. I felt the first drop of rain fall on my
forehead, but I didn't brush it away.

"It's okay to love him," Jamie whispered, and another
deep roll of thunder sounded with his words.

"No it's not," I breathed, lifting my head from his
chest. I met his eyes, their greenish-gold glow bringing me

the strength I needed to say the next words. "Just like it's not okay to love you."

His nose flared, and his hand found my chin, tilting it up before sliding to cradle my neck. "You love me?"

I nodded, biting my lips together as a sob threatened to break through. A new stream of tears slid down the same path as the ones before them and he used his thumb to wipe them away.

"Why is that not okay?"

"Because," I tried, my fingers playing at the hem of his t-shirt, but I didn't have the words to explain. I couldn't use letters and syllables and sentences to string together the thoughts in my head, the feelings in my heart. "I can't be with you right now, Jamie. I'm going home tomorrow for the funeral and I just… I can't promise you anything. I can't…" My words faded off, because speaking them out loud hurt. I couldn't promise Jamie anything because I had nothing left to give, not now that everything had changed.

Not even five hours before, everything important to me was centered around a nineteen-year-old girl's universe. I wanted to declare a major, I wanted to party all week with my best friend, and more than anything, I wanted to set things right with Ethan and Jamie.

But that universe seemed so far away now.

Now, all that mattered was that my father was gone. He was dead. I'd been ignoring him, thinking I had all the time in the world to figure out what role he would play in my life. But I was wrong.

Like I said, my father died on the day I realized I loved Jamie Shaw.

It was as simple and as complicated as that.

Jamie lifted his other hand to mirror the first, framing my face. His eyes bounced between mine, his brows bent together as he studied me, focused like always, trying to break through the wall I was slowly building between us. "Is it okay that I love you back?"

A short cry left my lips but he didn't let me answer before his mouth met mine. He kissed me like he was losing me, like that kiss was his last chance to keep me, and I didn't have the heart to tell him that it wasn't. I broke on that day, on that beach, and though I tried to fight it, the numbness of it all had blanketed me completely.

"Stay with me tonight," he whispered against my lips, pulling me closer, trying to meld our bodies together. I nodded, still crying softly, and he tried with every ounce of power he had to kiss away my tears before they could fall. He kissed me all night long. He kissed me until my lips were chapped and my heart was bruised. He was desperate to leave his mark, and this time I let him.

The next day, I left for the funeral and I never came back.

Jenna flew with me, handling everything I couldn't — the paperwork at school, the questions from my mom, the outfit for the funeral. She held my hand through the service, through the stream of people offering their condolences, and that night when we made it back to Mom's house, I sat down at my computer, and I wrote.

I wrote page after page of absolutely nothing, but everything to me in that moment. Every word made me feel better and worse all at once, and so I chased one feeling and ran from the other, round and round until my fingers ached. I think I needed that first, true heartbreak to feel enough to write the way I did that night. Words don't get written from a heart that's never felt. They come from pain, from love, from unspeakable depths — and they were my only release.

That was also the night I pledged myself dry.

With that last taste of Jamie still fresh on my lips, I shelved him, knowing I'd suck him dry if I didn't let him go. It took writing my feelings for me to be able to name why I'd left Jamie behind. The truth was I believed him when he said he loved me, and I knew he loved me enough to let me bring him down along with me. I could barely get out of bed every day. What kind of person would I be if I let Jamie love me in my condition?

It turned out I was water, he was whiskey, and I couldn't dilute him — not now that I knew he loved me enough to let me. I needed to be stronger, to be ice the next time I melted with him.

I did make one phone call back to campus, to Ethan, telling him over the phone what he deserved to hear in person. Then, I finished school at Palm South University, and always made sure to be out of town for the summers when I thought Jamie could maybe come back.

He called me twice a year, every year — once on my birthday and once on the anniversary of my dad's death. I never answered. And I never called him back. It seemed I was trying to let go of Whiskey and he was trying to hold on to me.

It was just a matter of time before we figured out who would win.

E L E V E N

Sober

EVEN AS FAR AWAY from shore as I was, I could still hear the ring of my cell phone. I could still feel it vibrating like it had that morning, just like it had every year on this day since I'd left California. And just like always, I'd let it vibrate and ring, not silencing it but not answering it either. I'd stared at his name on the screen and thought to myself that I was almost there — I was *almost* to the point where I'd be able to answer. I was closer, but I still wasn't there just yet, and so that phone call sat at the front of my mind while I swung my feet lazily in the water on either side of my board.

There were only two times when I had felt okay over the past three years: when I was writing, and when I was surfing. Each of them provided their own, unique kind of solace.

When I was writing, I was facing my fears — my anxieties, my feelings. I was putting them into words, giving them life, letting them know I recognized they existed. It was therapeutic and even if no one other than my professors had seen anything I'd written, it felt good just to get it out of my system.

Surfing, on the other hand, was the step before writing. It was what I did when I needed to avoid a feeling, or when I needed to allow myself time to think on it before I could point my finger into its chest and call it what it was. Right now, I was taking a pulse check, celebrating how far I'd come while also recognizing I still had a ways to go to be completely whole again.

The swell was smaller than California, but it was enough. As a perfect wave started forming, I bent forward and paddled out quickly, popping up on my board just in time to catch it and ride it back to shore. For the few moments I glided across the top of that wave, the wind in my long, wet hair, I felt free.

Then, I paddled out a bit, sat up, and straddled my board once more, my eyes on the sun that was still struggling to wake up with me.

It'd been exactly three years since my father's death.

How drastically my life had changed since that day.

I still remembered every aching moment that lined the path of healing I'd been walking since then. I remembered the break on that beach with Jamie, the numbness after the funeral, the denial and desperation that followed me around for nearly a year before I finally started accepting and adjusting. Writing and surfing — they were my only release.

At first, I'd driven myself mad searching online for answers about my father's death. I'd researched everything there was to know about electric shock drowning, as if that would help, as if that would bring him back or make it any less difficult to hear those who knew him best say how tragic it was to lose him in a *freak accident*. I hated when they said that. I hated that stupid phrase and the fact that there was no comfort or clarity to be found within it. It was just a callous way to make sense of something that never truly would.

Next, my mother convinced me to try therapy. She'd finally gone, after all those years of shouldering what my father did to her. It seemed like his death had killed her and freed her in equal measure, and her therapist helped her address those feelings. Still, after just two sessions, I knew it wasn't for me. I didn't want to talk.

And so, I wrote.

Eventually, *slowly*, writing started to really help — especially once I declared English: Creative Writing my major at Palm South University. Once writing assignments started to come and I was tasked with reading other works of fiction that made my emotions feel more in reach, everything started clicking together, and I started to feel okay.

Mom helped, too — along with her boyfriend, Wayne. They'd met at the beach one morning when she came to watch me surf, and he'd been nothing but a positive light in both our lives. It was the first time in my entire life that I'd seen my mom in love, and I wondered if it took my father's death for her to be *able* to love at all. Up until that point, I hadn't really thought about the fact that Mom had spent nineteen years of her life in close proximity to a man who had violated her in the most personal way — all for me. She tried to keep us a family unit, to ensure I grew up with both parents in my life. Now, she was finally focusing on herself, and seeing that made me feel like it was okay to focus on myself, too.

I'd dated, just like she had — and by *dated*, I mean I let two different boys take me out to dinner and then take me back to their beds. Neither had filled the gap left by the last man who'd touched me, but they'd been a nice distraction, at least.

Ethan called me sometimes, too. I only answered his call once, the first time he called after I'd explained why I left — after I told him the truth about Jamie and me. He called less than a week later, drunk as a twenty-one year old in Vegas, his words slurring together as he cursed me for breaking his heart. I cried with him, ashamed of what I did to him and still in pain over my father. After that, I stopped answering his calls, too.

Three years.

I still remembered that day, the feel of it, the pain. It was as if I was a ball of yarn, and that was the day I'd become completely unraveled, my string frayed and worn. Over the past three years, I'd slowly pulled myself together, forming the same ball of yarn I'd been before yet one that was wound differently. I was almost okay again.

Almost.

In just two months, I'd be graduating college and heading to Pittsburgh, ready to start the next chapter in my life. I rode in one final wave with that thought reverberating through me. When my feet hit the sand again, my board tucked tight under my arm, I had an overwhelming urge to face one last challenge before graduation.

I dropped my board into the sand next to my beach towel and rifled through my bag, searching out my cell phone. It was hot in my hands, the sun warming it even through the cool February chill. I thumbed through my missed calls log and hovered over his name, finger shaking at the thought of dropping just a centimeter more to dial his number. *Was I really ready to talk to him? What would I say? What could I offer?*

I didn't have the answers to any of those questions, so I sighed, flipping over to my voicemail log instead as I fell back onto my beach towel. I clicked on the message saved from my first birthday after I'd left California, my favorite message from him, and put the phone on speaker as I laid back and gazed up at the pinkish-blue sky.

Hey, B. It's me… Jamie… but I guess you already know that, huh? He sighed, and I'd listened to that call enough to know exactly how long the sigh lasted before he spoke again. *I know you're hurting. I know you're pushing me away because you think you should handle this all on your own. And honestly, I don't know, maybe you're right — maybe I'm not the person who can help you right now.* There was a shuffling noise then, and I had theories about what it was — him running his hand over his face, maybe? Or was it the wind? Was he at the beach where we'd said goodbye? *But I want to be. So please, just… call me back. I miss you.* My chest always ached at that part. *Happy birthday.*

The voicemail ended, and I closed my eyes, letting the sound of Whiskey soak into my skin like sunshine, hoping it would be enough to keep me dry a little while longer.

• • •

"To college," Jenna said, lifting her shot glass filled with chilled Patron high in the air. "May it remember us fondly as it kisses our sweet asses goodbye!"

"Cheers!" I yelled in unison with the table as we all clinked our glasses together before tapping them on the table and throwing them back. I hissed as the tequila stung my nose and throat, quickly reaching for a lime and sucking it dry.

"Shit, that burns," Jenna laughed, her blue eyes watering.

"I hate tequila," I agreed, dropping the dry lime in the bowl and reaching for my beer.

"Same, but it gets the job done," Kristen said. Jenna and I both tilted our beers in a *touché* before taking a sip. Kristen slid off her bar stool and pointed at both of us. "Be right back, I have to pee."

Kristen was my project partner in one of my capstone classes. We'd gotten to know each other a lot over the last few years, especially being that we were two of the maybe five minorities in the English: Creative Writing program. She was from Brazil, and I loved her unique outlook on literature — especially modern American literature. I was going to miss her, but damn was I ready to get away from Palm South University.

I adjusted my graduation cap on my head, still annoyed that Jenna was making me wear it out all night. I always thought it was silly when grads did that, as if they were begging for attention or a pat on the back from every patron in the bars they attended on their graduation day. Still, I was in a good mood — I guess walking across the stage will do that to you. So, I indulged her, wearing my cap with a smile as we celebrated surviving the past four years. At least she'd let me change out of my gown and into a cute pair of jeans.

"So you're booked the rest of the weekend until you leave Sunday night?" Jenna clarified again, her pouty lip protruding.

"Yes ma'am. Mom has a small family party planned tomorrow and then we're driving out to the beach for the night and all of Sunday until I leave."

"Well, I guess I can't be mad at mother/daughter time," Jenna compromised with a sigh. She lifted her beer to her lips but spoke again before taking a drink. "She's going to miss you, you know."

I joined her sigh. "I know." Picking at the label on my beer, I thought about how close Mom and I had become over the last three years since I'd flown home from California. We'd grieved together, healed together, and grown together. I ended up living at home while I finished out my schooling at PSU, and as much as I loved reconnecting with Mom and growing even closer than before, I was ready to take on a new chapter. I was ready for a new city, for new people, for a new chance at finding myself. "She'll be okay, though. She has Wayne."

"Ugh, don't remind me. Lucky bitch."

I laughed and Jenna smirked, clearly not ashamed in the slightest that she had the hots for my mom's boyfriend. They'd been dating for almost a year now, and he was good for her — he was good for both of us. He helped me apply to grad schools out of state when I was terrified to leave, and I was forever thankful for that.

"I'm still mad at you, you know," Jenna added. "Here I am finally coming back home and you're leaving."

"Maybe I'll come back after grad school. Who knows."

Jenna grumbled. "Just save me a spot in your bed, okay? And for the love of God, *don't* become a Steelers' fan."

"That's baseball, right?"

Jenna groaned just as Kristen rejoined us and I laughed, uncrossing my legs just to cross them the other way.

It felt good to laugh, to have fun. It'd taken me so long to get back into a headspace where I *could* laugh. Losing my dad had fucked with my head more than I thought it would, and it was only in the last year that I truly felt myself learning to let him go — to let the guilt go. I loved him, and that was okay. I was angry with him, and that was okay, too. But now, it was time to leave him here in Florida and find out who I was — who I could be — in a new city and state.

"Oh my God," Jenna whispered, dropping her beer to the table and tugging on the belt loop of my jeans. She leaned in close, her eyes somewhere behind me. "Don't look, but Jamie is here."

"*What?!*" I whisper-screamed.

"Who?" Kristen asked simultaneously, cranking her neck in the same direction as Jenna. She told me not to look, but of course I didn't listen — how could I? A ghost had just walked into the bar, and I had to see for myself. As soon as I spotted him, my heart jumped, and the hole I'd felt growing since the last time I'd seen him filled, warming my blood.

It had been three years. Or had it been just yesterday? I wasn't sure. I felt both measurements of time, noting his differences but feeling his familiarity even from across the bar. In Scotland, you can only classify whiskey as Scotch once it's been aged in casks for a minimum of three years. I realized it in that moment that Jamie was a young Scotch now, a blended whiskey promising experience and flavor. My mouth watered and, like a magnet, his eyes found mine just as the door swung closed behind him.

He was with a group of men, all dressed in suits, and one clapped him on the shoulder before nodding to the other end of the bar. He nodded, but didn't follow as they made their way in that direction. Instead, he kept his focus on me, tilted his head as if he wasn't sure I was actually there, and then he took the first step.

I inhaled, holding that breath as Jenna freaked out beside me and Kristen looked between all of us wondering what the hell was going on. I couldn't tear my eyes away from him, and I drank him in like I was privileged to do so as he crossed the room. His tie was loosened around his neck, the sleeves of his light gray dress shirt rolled up to his elbows, but it wasn't what he was wearing that kept my attention. It was his auburn hair, slightly darker than I remembered and styled carefully. His broad shoulders, fuller than the night I cried on them three years before. It was his jaw, still so square and set, now shadowed with just a hint of stubble. And his eyes, a deep amber, shaded with fire and tinged with both pain and curiosity as he stepped into the space right in front of me. He didn't look like my Jamie, and yet I still saw him there, under the surface. I felt him, that vibration from his presence. His scent invaded next, spicier, but with the same notes of honey.

Finally, I let my breath go, slow and steady as it left my lungs.

I'd turned on my bar stool, legs still crossed and hands folded tightly in my lap, and he casually tucked his hands in the pockets of his dress pants as his eyes raked over me.

"You changed your hair," he rasped, his nose flaring as his gaze made the leisurely ascent back to my face. I felt want radiating off him like a heat wave, and my skin slowly defrosted the longer he stood there. My hair was bigger now, longer — flowing down to the middle of my back in the same soft, small spirals I'd always had.

"And you got a tattoo," I mused. I could see the edges of it peeking out from where his sleeve met his forearm, and he glanced down at it with a barely-there smirk before he looked at me again.

For a moment, we just stared, both smiling, both adjusting to the new buzz blending with the all-too-familiar one. Then, Jamie shook his head, and a grin split his face. "You have two seconds to get off that bar stool and into my arms before I drag you off it."

I blushed with a smile that mirrored his, looking down at my heels before easily stepping down and closing the space between us. The moment our bodies met, his arms wrapping around my small frame and mine resting around his neck, we both sighed, and peace settled in just as the rest of the bar came back into focus again.

I suddenly heard the loud rawr of laughter from the group of guys he'd walked in with, and the commotion of glasses and ice behind the bar. I heard Jenna clear her throat behind us and listened as the pop song playing grew louder and louder. Still, Jamie just held me, and I squeezed him back.

"Oh hey Jamie, nice to see you, too," Jenna finally chided. Jamie loosened his grip and I slid out of his arms, reaching for my beer but not taking my seat just yet.

"Hi Jenna," Jamie replied, smiling at her briefly before turning his gaze back to me. "So, celebrating tonight?"

He flicked my grad cap and I groaned, embarrassed. "Yes. I got a piece of paper that says I'm great at pulling all nighters and regurgitating textbook notes."

Jamie chuckled. "Congrats."

"And she got into grad school," Jenna added. "In Pittsburgh."

"*Pittsburgh?*" Jamie repeated, eyebrows shooting up before he tilted his head. "What's my surfer girl going to do in a city like that?"

My cheeks warmed and I picked at the label on my beer again, tilting it to my lips instead of answering.

"And you?" Jenna asked. Kristen was still just staring at us, asking me questions with her eyes that I only answered with a shrug. "What are you doing back in Florida?"

"I'm celebrating, too, actually. Passed my CPA exam and accepted a job offer from my dad."

"Really?" I asked with a wide smile, pride I wasn't sure I was allowed to feel surging through me. "Wow, that's amazing. I'm so happy for you."

"Thanks."

Jamie wouldn't stop staring at me. *God*, how I loved the way he looked at me — focused, and unapologetically so. Jenna went to ask another question but he cut her off.

"Want to get out of here?"

My heart thumped hard against my ribs and I fought back a smile. "You know I hate clichés."

He shrugged. "I also know you'll make an exception for me."

"Oh? Do you now?"

Jamie tucked his hands back in his pockets, his stance confident. "I do."

Chewing my lip, I kept his eyes a moment longer before turning to Jenna. She threw her hands up before grabbing her beer. "Oh for God's sake, go. Go before he gets *me* pregnant with that fucking look of his."

I covered my laugh with my hand, mouthing a *sorry* to Kristen before grabbing my purse off the bar. Her eyes were wide, but she smiled and tipped her beer to Jenna's. "We'll be fine. Go."

And so, I turned back to Whiskey, feeling him close enough to taste after three years of being dry, and I smiled.

"Lead the way."

TWELVE

One Night with Scotch

I LOVED EVERYTHING ABOUT that moment.

I loved the way Jamie's one hand rested easily on the steering wheel while the other held the gear shift. I loved the way the warm breeze whipped in through the windows of his new Jeep. I loved the view of my feet on his dashboard as the same roads we'd driven at seventeen stretched out before us. And most of all, I loved the easy conversation, and the easy silence — because we fit so well into each.

Years had passed, there were still words left unsaid, but all that mattered right then and there was that we were together. I felt it, I knew he did, too. It was a night meant for us, and I had no intentions of wasting it.

Jamie let me choose the playlist as we caught up, him filling me in on his dad's firm surviving the recession while I painted the picture of how I'd ended up an English major. Peter Jennison's *Longing for Home* album played softly in the background of our conversation, and I couldn't help but note the difference in tone from the last time Jamie and I had been in the same place. We were both grown now, both free from what had been wearing on us the last night we'd spent together. It was like the universe shoved us together at exactly the perfect moment, and I was thoroughly enjoying the alignment of the stars.

"I can't believe you traded in ScarJo," I commented, running my hands along the edge of my seat. His new Jeep was literally brand new, decked out even more than his first, and it was dark and edgy. The interior was leather and sleek, the dashboard advanced, and the paint job was matte black. Even his rims were a dark charcoal gray, and I loved the way he looked in the driver seat — relaxed, confident, sexy as hell.

He chuckled, adjusting his grip on the wheel as we took a turn. "Yeah, well ScarJo started getting cranky in her old age. I held onto her until about two months ago before giving in and upgrading."

"Oh, I'm sure it was *so* hard to do," I teased, waving my hand over the dashboard of his new baby.

He sniffed. "Yeah well, there were a lot of memories in that Jeep. I didn't want to let her go, not until I had to."

A heaviness settled in around us at that comment, and I felt it — I knew where the conversation was leading. We were past catching up on family and school and surfing. Jamie was about to ask me the questions I wasn't sure I could answer, and my stomach turned with the thought of trying.

"You never came back," he whispered. I just barely heard him over the music and I lowered the volume,

191

pulling my feet off the dashboard and tucking them under my legs, instead.

"I know."

"And you never answered my calls. You never called me back. You never…" his voice faded and his knuckles whitened around the gear shift.

"I know."

I closed my eyes, resting my head against the leather and inhaling a long breath. He didn't ask me why, he didn't beg for an explanation even though I knew he needed one. We pulled up to a red light and I turned my head to the side, opening my eyes to look up at him.

"Nothing I say is going to make you feel better, Jamie. I have excuses, I have reasons why I pushed you away, but none of them will make up for the fact that it was shitty of me to do. I was young, I was hurting, and I didn't know how to handle my new reality. I ran away from you, from California, because I thought it was the right thing to do. And in a way, I'm glad I did, because I needed to heal. But in a way I hate myself for how I left you."

A muscle popped under his jaw and I tentatively rested my hand on top of his.

"My dad's death changed me, Jamie," I croaked, my voice unsteady. "And what I did to Ethan, it was against every moral code I had and I hated myself for losing control, for loving you when I was supposed to be loving him. It was just…" I closed my eyes again and Jamie turned his hand in mine, squeezing it, asking me to continue. "I was fucked up. And I needed time."

The light turned green and Jamie turned his hand again, shifting the gears while my fingers rested over his.

"And now?" he asked, glancing at me briefly before his eyes found the road again. I thought about his question, wondering what exactly he was asking.

"Now, I'm sitting in your Jeep, and nothing has changed, yet everything has."

He nodded, brows bent together as he digested my words.

"And I'm wondering how much longer you'll fight the urge to kiss me before you finally give in," I breathed, and he snapped his eyes to mine. "Because I leave in less than forty-eight hours, Jamie. And I *need* you to kiss me before I board that plane."

Jamie tore his eyes from mine just in time to take a sharp turn. He cracked his neck, accelerating with a rev of the engine, and I watched as the want that had been hovering above us fell, drenching us completely, neither of us seeking cover.

"I'm taking you to my place. Now," he rasped. It wasn't a question, it wasn't a request, and it wasn't optional. "If you didn't mean even a word of what you just said, you have roughly seven minutes to take it back. After that, you're not allowed to say another word, not even my name, because I'm going to fuck you speechless."

His words unleashed the need and it coursed through me, pooling between my legs as I forced a breath. His jaw was set, and he didn't smile as he turned to face me, waiting. His eyes held the challenge, and he dared me to accept it, to give into him. I think he wanted me to fight him, to argue why it was a bad idea, how our timing still wasn't right and we were only setting ourselves up on a higher shelf to fall and shatter once more. But I didn't care. I would suffer the break if it meant I could feel whole with him for just one night.

And so, I chose my last two words carefully.

"Drive faster."

• • •

As soon as Jamie's front door closed behind us, he had me up against it, his mouth crushed hard on mine as he tossed his keys on the small table next to us. They slid across the wood surface and crashed to the floor but neither of us cared. Jamie lifted me and I hooked my ankles behind his back, my high heels digging into the hard muscles of his ass and pulling him closer.

He groaned, pinning me with his hips as he tore his shirt over his head and let it drop to the floor. His mouth trailed from my lips to my neck and he sucked hard, biting my collarbone before breaking back again long enough to pull sharply on my strapless top until I lifted my arms and let him peel it off. I wasn't wearing a bra, and he hummed with approval as his hands palmed me, thumbs brushing my nipples as I arched into him.

"Jamie," I barely moaned his name before his mouth covered mine.

"Shh," he said, lifting me and carrying us to his kitchen. It was pristine, wood floors and sleek granite counters, and he dropped my feet to the ground in front of the island. "Take these off," he tugged at my jeans and then started working on his dress pants, eyes falling to my heels. "Leave those on."

Scotch was so much stronger than the Whiskey I'd let intoxicate me three years ago. He was more confident, more experienced, and I knew tonight wasn't going to be anything like our first time. Jamie was eager to burn me and I was desperate to let him.

I slipped the top button of my jeans through the slit and unzipped them slowly, tugging them down my hips one side at a time, inch by inch, my eyes on Jamie as he watched me. When I let them fall past my thighs to my ankles, I stepped out of my heels, kicked my jeans off leg by leg, and stepped right back into the six-inch black pumps.

"Good girl," Jamie mused as his eyes trailed up my body. He dropped his boxers to join his pants on the floor and stepped out of them, kicking them away, and then he was in front of me, palming himself as his teeth dug into his bottom lip. I reached for my panties next, but he shook his head. "Leave them. Turn around."

I spun, looking back over my shoulder as my hips met the cool granite. Jamie stepped up behind me, sweeping my hair to the side before kissing my neck as he continued stroking himself. I gasped, and he dropped himself long enough to grab both of my wrists and guide them up to grip the other side of the island. I was bent over, breasts flat against the counter, ass pressed against his hard on. He kissed down my back and bit the flesh just beneath the lace of my thong and I winced, the pain shocking but welcome.

He stood again, trailing his hand over my ass before popping it swiftly. I jumped, but loved the way it stung, and I moaned loudly, my cheek hot against the granite. Jamie gripped the crease of my hip with one hand, hooking one finger from the other under the g-string and tracing it down until he met my opening. He sucked in a breath as he felt how slick I was already, and he pressed two fingers inside me with a roll of his hips behind his hand.

"Fuck," he dragged the word out, withdrawing his fingers before sliding them in again as I gripped the counter tighter. He tapped the insides of my thighs, letting the lace fabric pop against me. "Open."

I did as he said, widening my stance as he tugged my hips back just enough to give him the space he needed. He dropped to his knees, and then the lace was gone again and his tongue swept along my slit and I rolled against him, meeting his mouth with my flex just as it closed around my clit. He sucked, and my thighs shook around him. I felt him smirk, his breath still hot against my center as he repeated the process, licking and sucking and biting me closer to the edge of release.

My teeth dug so deep into my lip I nearly drew blood and I released it mercilessly, crying out and bucking my hips against his mouth. I was close, *so* close, and Jamie knew, because he stood again and I glanced back over my shoulder just as he licked his lips and wiped at his chin with the pad of his thumb.

"Don't move."

He retrieved his pants, pulling a foil packet from his wallet before letting it drop again. I went to push myself up off the counter but his hand found my back and he pressed me back down gently, his cock settling between my cheeks.

I heard the condom wrapper tear open and felt his brief absence before he ran his wrapped member against my opening, teasing me with just the crown. He bent forward, fisting my hair and wrapping it once around his wrist.

"All this fucking hair," he rasped, sucking the lobe of my ear between his teeth. Chills raced from the point of contact to my toes, and he pulled, my head coming up off the counter with the force. I gazed up at the light fixture above us as Jamie filled me from behind, all the way to the hilt. Jamie groaned, dropping his forehead to the back of my neck as he pulled back and flexed into me again. "God, I've been fantasizing about my hands in your hair like this all night. And these fucking heels," he moaned, standing straight and pulling my hair with him so that my back arched. He slammed into me harder and I cried out, already on the brink of coming undone.

He worked with such skilled control that I wondered how busy he'd been the last three years, but I chose to ignore that, focusing instead on the fact that he'd clearly been studying and I was the exam, his chance to prove what he'd learned.

When he dropped his grip on my hair, his hands found my hips and he pulled me onto him with each thrust, pinning me against the counter and driving into me harder each time. My clit rubbed against the smooth surface and I trembled around him as my orgasm built. I chased it, desperate to find it, but Jamie pulled out, leaving me gasping as my eyes flew open.

"Not yet." He spun me around and bent, swooping me up into his arms and carrying me through the back hall. He kissed me the entire way and I hooked my arms around his neck, yanking him closer, panting against his mouth as he kicked us through the last door and dropped me down into the plush comforter.

I landed easily, gazing up at him and backing myself up to the headboard as he dropped down between my legs and followed. My shoulders hit wood and he used his thighs to spread mine before entering me again, his lips finding mine just as he bottomed out. I shook at the intensity, digging my nails into his back as he flexed again.

"Goddamn, B," he growled, his arms shaking as he held himself steady over me. My legs were already useless from the kitchen, but I wrapped them around his waist and dug my heels into his hips. He hissed, biting my neck in return, and that combined with pelvis against my clit was all it took to send me spiraling. Black invaded my vision and I held my breath, catching my climax with his name on my lips.

I dropped my hands from his back and fisted the comforter, twisting it and pulling the corners free as I held on tight, riding out my orgasm. He kept the same pace, the same pressure, until my legs fell lax. Then, he kissed me, long and slow, steadying his pace, letting me parachute down.

He was still working between my legs, and he hooked his forearm under my left knee before guiding my ankle to rest on his shoulder. He kissed my ankle, sucking the soft skin there, and then he picked up his pace, reaching new depths in that position. It took only four pumps for him to find his own release, and one hand tightened around my ankle as the other held him steady over me. He groaned, flexing into me even deeper one last time before letting my leg fall and collapsing down on top of me.

My legs ached, but I wrapped my arms around him, fingers softly brushing the ridges of his shoulders. He trembled under the touch and kissed my neck. Jamie was panting, his breath hot against my skin, and I struggled to find balance in my own breathing. He propped himself up on his elbows and kissed my lips, shaking his head. "Well damn."

I giggled, and he kissed my nose. "My thoughts exactly."

"You have to be mine after that," he breathed. He was still inside me and the intensity was too much to think, but I forced my way through the haze.

"I can't."

"Fuck that," he argued. "You can. You are."

"I'm leaving Sunday night, Jamie," I said seriously, breaking our kiss so that he'd look at me.

He exhaled, furrowing his brows. "So be mine for the weekend."

I hated the way he looked at me, even more knowing I couldn't give him that, either. "I can't. I have plans with my family. This is it… this is all I have."

"Why can't we be long distance?"

I laughed, wrapping my left hand around my right wrist behind his neck. "Because that's a guaranteed way to get our hearts broken." I saw the disappointment in his eyes and quickly followed that statement. "But I'm not running from you anymore, Jamie."

"Does that mean you'll answer my calls?"

I smiled softly and nodded. "Just... let's not try to put a name on this. On us."

That seemed to ease him a little, and he blew out a long breath through his nose, eyes bouncing between mine. "Alright, then. I need you to give me two things." I waited, and his tongue rolled over his lips before he spoke again. "Tonight, and one day."

"Tonight," I repeated, breathily. "And one day."

He nodded. "I have to have both."

I considered him, thought too hard about what he was asking before deciding I didn't need to dwell on it right now. I answered with one nod before pulling him down until his mouth met mine again. He kissed me with intent, and I felt him harden where he still rested inside me. My body achingly stirred back to life, and I knew I was in for a sore weekend after that.

So that's what I allowed myself — one night with Scotch. He made the most of it, not letting me sleep until the sun was already peeking through the dark curtains in his bedroom. I tried not to hold onto his words with too much hope, because the fact was that I was leaving for Pittsburgh, and he was staying here. It was just like that night on the beach five years before, except this time the roles were reversed, and I knew he wouldn't follow me to Pennsylvania the way I followed him to Alder.

I kept that in mind as we made love that night, over and over, yet still it was impossible not to hold onto him too tightly. I'd let him go three years before and I was terrified to do it again, even though I knew I had to. Looking back, that was the night my hate for timing truly manifested. That was the night I realized that no matter how easy it seemed to be to form a long-standing relationship with Whiskey, the truth was that it wasn't simple at all, not even a little bit.

He asked me for two things: tonight, and one day.

But one day never came.

THIRTEEN

The E in Whiskey

"WELCOME TO RYE PUBLISHING," Mona said quickly, ushering us off the elevator as she adjusted the tight, dark bun on her head. "This is going to go quickly because I have shit to do, okay? So pay attention."

I nodded feverishly, popping the end of my pen on the notepad hooked in my arm just in case I needed to write anything down. It was my first time in the office, my first day of my internship, and regardless of Mona's bored eyes and bubblegum popping, I was excited to be here. Hell, I was *honored* to be here.

Rye Publishing was very well known and sought after. It was hard to land an internship role and even more impossible to get hired on full-time. Though they were stacked with clients, the payroll list was small, exclusive, and top-notch. I wanted a spot so badly I could taste it like the iron from blood on my tongue. I was going to make a name for myself at Rye Publishing if it was the last thing I did.

"This is my desk, reception. I handle all the clients and guests who come through as well as administrative tasks. Clearly, I love my job," she said with a roll of her eyes. "Our office is a big square, cubes all in the middle and offices on the outside with the exception of two meeting areas. This is one of them," she gestured to a conference room with a long, rectangular table and dozens of leather chairs on either side. One giant screen sat on the far wall and a whiteboard wall with writing scribbled all along it took up the back space not occupied by a window. "It's almost always booked, so don't plan on using it unless you're invited. But the one on the opposite end of this hall is a more relaxed meeting space with hammocks and such, you can almost always get in there."

Mona was clicking down the hall in front of me, her years of perfecting striding in heels leaving me looking even less coordinated than usual. I scurried to keep up with her as my eyes took in the offices we passed. There were books *everywhere* — shelves of them, frames holding manuscripts, classic covers blown up to poster-size. Every window had a different, beautiful view of downtown Pittsburgh and the entire office had a modern, sleek feel to it. There were chalkboards and whiteboard walls here and there, and Mona walked me past the "break room" that looked more like a rustic bar than anything else.

She showed me where each department housed themselves within the office, from the agents to the media team, and then she pointed to a tiny half-desk in the corner of the central cube area. It had a computer and an empty pencil holder along with an all-black filing cabinet that matched the black leather chair.

"This is you," she said, glancing down at her nails as she used her other hand to wave at the desk. "Don't get too comfortable. I'm sure I don't have to tell you that the likelihood of you getting hired is slim to not happening."

I swallowed, but felt that resolve sink in deeper. She said I couldn't do something and my mind immediately went to all the ways I'd prove her wrong.

"To be honest, I have no idea who is supposed to tell you what you're doing but I imagine they'll be by eventually. Bathrooms are that way," she added, pointing back toward the elevator. "If you need me, I'll be at the front." She gave me a pointed look then, arching one of her dark, perfectly manicured eyebrows. "But do your best *not* to need me. Kay?"

I fought back a smile, nodding once in answer. "Thanks for the tour, Mona."

She waved me off, clicking away with a slight sway in her pencil skirt. She was beautiful, exotic, and I suddenly felt a little under dressed in my dress slacks and flowy top.

I dropped my purse onto the desk and looked around. It was early, I was one of the few people in the office, and those who *were* there weren't paying attention to me — not yet, at least. I made a promise to myself then that by the time my internship ended in August, they'd know my name. They'd know exactly who I was.

My phone pinged and Jamie's name lit up the screen, making me smile. I slid the bar on the screen and his message filled it.

— Sign any NYT bestsellers yet? —

No matter how often or little he texted me since our night together back home last weekend, it always warmed

204

the skin of my cheeks to see words from his fingers. It was even better when he called me, which had been nearly every night since I'd flown out to Pittsburgh.

— **Working on it. Pondering if I should aim for top agent or CEO. Have to align the strategy accordingly, you know?** —

— **Go get 'em, tiger. Call me tonight.** —

My heart flipped at his request and I bit my lip, staring at the message. I loved our late night phone calls. I was learning more and more about him, just when I thought I knew all I needed to. It wasn't that I changed my mind about the long distance thing, but where was the harm in talking and texting? In seeing each other when it made sense? I wasn't expecting any more of Jamie and he wasn't asking any more of me, which was exactly what I needed at that point in my life.

"I see you've just been blown away by the welcome committee," someone said behind me. I jumped, tucking my phone back in my purse and whipping around. It was a boy, or should I say a man — he couldn't have been much more than two or three years older than me. His dark blonde hair was parted at the side and flowing in a swoop like he worked all morning to get it that way. His eyes were bright blue, kind and inviting, and he had a wide grin that reminded me a little of Ethan's. "Hi."

"Hi," I said, reaching out my hand and returning his smile.

He took it, giving it a light but firm shake before eying the few people at their cubes over my shoulder. "Sorry about them. It's busy for us lately, and I guess that gives them all an excuse to forget their manners." His eyes found mine again and he dropped my hand, resting his elbow on the wall of my cube. "I'm sure after a riveting tour with Mona, they feel like a field of puppies."

I laughed at that, but I was nervous. "Oh no, she was great. I really love the hammock room." I cringed. *I really love the hammock room?* Cool, B.

He cocked a brow. "She was great?" He shook his head. "Anyone ever tell you it's terrible to lie to your boss on the first day?"

My stomach rolled and I blanched, stammering. "Oh, I mean, it really wasn't that bad. I think she's just busy. It's actually—"

"Relax," he said with a chuckle, pushing off his casual stance on the wall of my cube. "Coffee?"

"Please," I breathed.

He led the way, introducing me to a few of the associates he'd been referring to as we passed them. When we made it back to the chic break room, he popped a new cup into the Keurig and leaned against the counter to face me, folding his arms. "So, Brecks Kennedy, you ready for your first day?"

My name didn't sting as much as it had when I was younger, but it still unnerved me, and I brushed a long chunk of hair over my shoulder before correcting him. "It's just B, actually. I don't really go by my full name. But yes, very honored to be here..." My voice faded when I realized I didn't know his name. Mona had been the one to handle my hiring paperwork over email, and I had no idea who I was reporting to.

"River," he said, pulling the fresh cup of coffee from the coffee machine and handing it to me before starting another for himself. "River Godsby."

"*Godsby?*" The Chairman and CEO of Rye Publishing was Randall Godsby, and my wheels started turning before River could even respond. Not just about the fact that they were surely related, but the fact that his parents had named him *River*. His name sounded as expensive as the Zegna suit he was wearing.

He nodded, a smile playing at his lips as he turned to face me again. "Indeed. Randy is my father."

"Oh." That's all I said. I wasn't really sure how to respond to that.

River chuckled. "Yeah, I guess it's kind of a family business. I've been in the literary world since I was in the womb, practically." He smiled that wide, genuine smile again and I relaxed a bit.

"That's neat, actually. Are you… what's your position here, if you don't mind me asking."

He smiled. "Not at all. I'm an agent right now, but on my way to vice president if I have anything to do with it."

"Impressive," I said, taking the first sip of my coffee. I wasn't sure where any of the creamer or anything else was and it was scalding hot, so I flinched, but tried to hide it.

River laughed, grabbing his own coffee and guiding me to a cabinet that held what I was looking for. "Here," he said, handing me a few creamers and packets of sugar. "Fix your coffee up and take a few minutes to get settled at your desk. Your login info should be on a sticky note on the keyboard and you can change your password then.

Get your email set up and I'll be over to touch base in fifteen or so, okay?"

"Sounds great."

He turned, but paused. "And B?"

"Yeah?" I asked, mid-tear on the first sugar packet.

River eyed me curiously, in a way that reminded me way too much of the first time Jamie had looked at me. "Welcome to Rye Publishing."

• • •

I moaned out loud as I slipped off my first high heel and let it fall to the floor just inside my apartment. Stretching my toes, I pulled the bobby pins holding my hair up before tugging the other heel off and letting myself fully sigh with relief.

It had been a long, hard first day — but an amazing one, too. I smiled as I picked up my shoes and padded into my bedroom, tossing them to the bottom of my closet before turning and heading straight for my freshly stocked fridge. There was a cold slice of pizza and chilled beer in there with my name on it.

My head was still spinning with all the information I'd had shoved at me that day as I took the first bite and popped my beer open. I looked out the large window on the far side of my small studio apartment, loving the floor-to-ceiling view of Market Square. It was the main reason I decided to live here, even though it was more expensive than every other place I looked at. It was worth it to me, to spend a little more but get a view like that. Plus, it had a bathtub, and that was a *necessity*.

I think there are some times in life, seemingly insignificant snapshots of time, where a sizable shift takes place. Standing barefoot in my kitchen overlooking downtown Pittsburgh while I ate cold pizza and chased it with cheap beer was one of those times for me. This was it — I was on my own, for the first time in my life, and I was doing it. No mom, no roommate, no boyfriend — just me — and I was going to show the publishing world who I was in that summer I had their attention if it was the last thing I did.

When I finished my pizza, I texted my mom quickly before calling Jamie. My fingers still shook slightly when I called him, or in the few seconds it took me to answer his call, instead. After three years of ignoring him, I was finally at the point where I felt like we could be good for each other — even if just in the friendly way. I'd missed him, missed our conversations, and if I got to have his hands on me occasionally, too? It was an all-around win.

"I just rode the best wave," he answered, breath heavy in the receiver. "You should have been here. For South Florida, it was like surfing gold."

"Rub it in," I teased.

"Okay. Did I mention I'm not wearing a shirt?"

I chuckled, tapping the speakerphone button before dropping my phone to the bed so I could undress. "You never did play fair, Jamie Shaw."

"So you've told me." I swear, I could feel his grin through the phone. "How was the first day?"

"Long, but amazing. My boss is young and really cool. He seems eager to have me start on projects, which eases my initial worry of being a paper-pusher all summer."

"Yeah right. Like they'd stuff you behind some desk. You'll probably be opening another office in NYC by next week."

I smiled, both at the image he'd painted and the faith he always had in me. "How was your day?"

"Meh," he answered as a soft dinging noise rang out behind him. I heard the Jeep door close and the ringing stopped as he thrummed the engine to life. "Work was work, but I got out of the office early enough to get in some surf time. So life is great."

"I miss the beach already," I said with a sigh, pulling my loose silky blouse over my head.

"It misses you, too. Not as much as me, though."

My cheeks heated and I unzipped my pants, wiggling them off my hips before letting them fall and kicking them near my clothes hamper.

"Are you getting undressed?" Jamie husked.

"Maybe."

He groaned. "That's just cruel."

"Relax. I'm just taking a bath."

"Of course you managed to find a place with a bathtub."

"You know I wouldn't live without one again. The seven months at Alder were torture enough for life."

Jamie was quiet then, and I wondered if hearing me speak so casually about that time in our lives stung. I felt it a little, like an electric shock when you touch a freshly-laundered pair of jeans.

"I want to see your new place," he finally said.

"So get your ass up here."

Jamie laughed. "Oh sure, I'll be on the next flight. Who needs a job, right?"

"Exactly."

I peeled off my panties and unhooked my bra, and then an idea sparked to life. I bit my lip, wondering if it was stupid, but grabbing my phone and clicking on the video chat option before I could talk myself out of it.

"Turn on your video and I'll give you the virtual tour."

"Hang on, I'm just pulling into my house. Give me a few minutes."

I set up the camera on my end, making sure it was facing away from me as I walked naked back to the kitchen to open a new beer. When Jamie's video clicked in, I saw his face, and he saw my view of Market Square.

"Damn," he said, dragging the word out as he slung his own keys down on the same table he'd missed the night he'd taken me home. "Look at you, big city girl."

"Pretty, right?" The sun was hanging low over the high buildings, casting shadows between the streams of golden rays of light. It seemed the entire city bled black and gold always.

I walked him through my tiny space as he kicked back on his bed, excited that he loved my first apartment as much as I did. Even though it was only about the size of my dorm room at Alder, it had hardwood floors and modern appliances. I'd decorated it simply in the week that I'd been there, but it was just enough for me. My bed had the same view through the large window and the more the sun set, the more rustic my place felt.

"Alright, I know you're dying to show me the bathtub."

"Of course. Had to save the best for last." I still had the camera angled away from me and I walked him into

211

the bathroom head on, giving him only the view of the toilet at first, then turning left and revealing my beautiful, freestanding claw bathtub. "Ta-da!"

Jamie exaggerated a long gasp followed by an "*oh*" and "*ah.*"

"Isn't it *gorgeous*?" I scanned the tub from faucet to back like it was a tropical scenery. Leaning forward a bit, I turned the water on and adjusted it to the hottest setting before standing again. "Totally worth the extra five-hundred bucks a month."

He chuckled. "You're right. I'd pay at least a thousand."

"Glad we're on the same page."

I chewed my lip for a moment, second-guessing my next move. Hesitantly, I pulled my long hair forward over my breasts and turned the phone slowly until we were both facing the mirror. Jamie's eyes widened as they scanned me — makeup still in place from work, hair kinked from the bun I'd had it in all day, the mirror cutting off right at the bottom of my belly button and my hair staying in place over my modest cleavage. .

"Jesus," he breathed. "You really did save the best for last."

I watched as he swallowed, the movement highlighted by the way the shadows of his bedroom framed his jaw and throat. The fingers of my free hand played at the ends of my hair and I kept my eyes on the phone screen. I'd made the first move, and now I was waiting. I needed him to take control, and he must have sensed it.

"Pull your hair back."

The mirror was starting to steam lightly, and I let the heat soak into my skin as I used one hand to gather my hair and pull it back, letting it fall to rest against my lower shoulders. The ends of it hit the middle of my back and chills followed as Jamie groaned.

"Now I *really* wish I was there."

For a moment he just scanned me, slowly, as if he didn't get a good enough look the weekend before. Then he scrubbed a hand hard down his face before it disappeared out of camera view and he moved a bit. It only took a second for me to realize he was taking off his swim trunks.

"What are you doing?" I asked, my voice low.

"I'm going to make you feel good," he answered confidently. "Get in the tub."

I couldn't take my eyes off him, but I did as he said, switching the view on the camera to be on my face as I slowly sank into the half-full tub. The water filled the space around my body all the way up to the top of my chest and I used my toes to shut the water off as I heard Jamie fling his shorts to the side.

"Do you want to see what you do to me?"

It felt so dirty, answering his question with his face locked on mine. I nodded, and Jamie dragged his teeth along his bottom lip with force before flipping his camera. The screen filled with a close up of his abs that led down to his hard shaft, the scar on his hip that I loved so much serving almost as an arrow pointing my attention where Jamie wanted it. He ran his hand across the ridges of his abdomen and down the deep V of muscles that led to his hips before wrapping it around himself. Just seeing him hard and ready, gripped in his large hand and throbbing for a release was enough to make me moan.

"Fuck, Jamie," I whispered, sinking farther into the water. I angled the phone to hold a better view while my free hand found my breast. I massaged it, rubbing my thumb over the nipple and arching my back into my own touch as if it was his. He stroked himself and I gasped at how big he was, how much he wanted me.

"Pretend that hand is mine," he said, low and smooth. "Touch yourself the way I would if I were there."

My hand immediately slipped into the water, and I rolled into the touch, mind racing with memories of how Jamie's hands felt. I remembered the roughness of his palms, the confidence in his grip, his unquestionable knowledge of what I wanted. I let the camera follow it down between my legs, not even sure if he could see it clearly through the water as my fingers found my clit and I circled softly. We both moaned together and I knew that whatever he could see was enough.

It was one of the most intimate moments of my life.

I was sweating, working myself under the water while Jamie stroked himself closer to release. He said exactly the right things to turn me on, to work me up, and when the moment was right, he spoke the words that gave me permission to fall apart under water. We were both panting by the end, caught up in each other, in our independence and the lust that always sparked to life between us.

What ifs are cruel motherfuckers.

That night is one I always look back on, wondering if I'd played the next moments differently, if everything would have fallen perfectly into place. I guess we're all guilty of that, of stringing a list of what ifs together, hoping that if we find the right combination it will somehow have the power to actually take us back. But the reality is I can't go back to that night to tell myself not to be stupid, to tell myself how perfect that moment was, to smack myself into some kind of common sense.

"Be with me," Jamie said sweetly as we both crawled between our sheets on opposite sides of the country later that night. My hair was still damp from the bath and I'd have bet money on the fact that his skin still tasted like salt from the ocean.

"I am with you."

"No, I mean really be with me. Be my girlfriend."

My stomach dipped and I tried not to show it, taking my time situating myself under the covers before responding. "Why do we have to put a title on it? Can't we just… I don't know. We're friends, Jamie. Best friends. I love talking to you, I miss you, I like making you feel good." I blushed a little at that last part.

"Exactly, so why does it freak you out so much to be official?"

"It's not that it freaks me out," I argued. "It's just that this is the first time in my life that I've ever been completely on my own, Jamie. I need to just be myself for a while. You know how the last few years have been for me," I added, and Jamie's mouth thinned into a line, probably because he didn't know — not really — and that was because I hadn't let him in. "Let's just exist, and let it go where it will go. No sense in putting pressure on either of us right now."

"Are you hooking up with other guys?"

"What?" I shook my head. "No, of course not. I don't even *know* any other guys out here."

"That's not the point."

"I know, but I'm just saying."

He huffed. "Would you be okay if I hooked up with other girls?"

My stomach dipped again, this time forcing me to sit up with it. I blew out a breath, physically ill at the thought of him with someone else but knowing that if I couldn't be his exclusively, I couldn't ask him to be mine, either. "Yeah. I mean, I guess. I get it. You have needs."

"Again, that's not the point." He ran a hand roughly through his short, neatly styled hair. I missed it long. "I know it sounds stupid, but when I lost you three years ago, I told myself I'd never let that happen again. It's important to me to be with you, B. But I can't be if you don't let me."

I exhaled slowly, softly, thinking back to the first time he'd told me what he wanted in life. I'd always been unsure, up until this point in my life, but he'd always known. He wanted to work at his dad's firm, make partner, take over, and have the same family life that his dad did. He thought he'd marry his high school sweetheart, and here he was a college graduate and single. I knew what he wanted, what he needed in life — but I also knew I couldn't be that for him. Not yet, at least.

"I'm not going anywhere," I assured him, and I sealed that promise with a sincere smile. "But I can't give you my all right now. I'm here to work, to get my graduate degree, and to find the rest of myself that's still floating just out of reach. I want you, I do," I said again. "Just give me some time to figure out my new surroundings, okay?"

Jamie still looked disappointed, but he nodded. "Whatever you need, I'll give it to you."

I believed him when he said that, but sometimes we say things we don't mean. We may mean them in the moment the words leave our lips, but as time goes on, good intentions get rubbed raw by failed expectations. Those on the promising end forget why they promised at all, hearts jaded — for good reason.

The Scottish are the only ones who can technically spell whiskey as "whisky." They claim more vowels wastes good drinking time, and I wish I could have realized that then, because that's exactly what I was doing — wasting time. Letting days and weeks and months of incredible, soul-shattering love pass me by because I thought I knew the right way to spell out the path of my life.

Turned out I was wrong.

Turned out I had a rare, deliciously aged bottle of whiskey in my grip, but I let it slip through my slick fingers and crash to the floor.

And I wasn't the one allowed to pick up the pieces.

F O U R T E E N

On the Rocks

JAMIE PULLED AWAY AFTER that.

Not all at once, but slowly and surely.

Sometimes he seemed normal, sometimes we'd talk for hours and fall into that same easy friendship that'd always existed between us. He never did make it out to see me in Pittsburgh, but I did fly home one weekend, and we spent the entire time tangled in his sheets, save for the one lunch with Mom and Wayne and the dinner with Jenna. And when I got back home, we made tentative plans for him to come see me next, when things slowed down at work. One night, we sat up a movie on each of our screens and hit play at the same time, being as together as we could be through video chat while it played.

And those were the good times.

But mostly, Jamie was absent — thinking to himself even if he was on the phone with me. I knew it was killing him to not have me the way he wanted. It felt like rejection to him, I can see that clearly now, but I was selfish back then and I didn't see a damn thing — maybe I didn't *want* to see it.

Eventually, the calls and texts became fewer and fewer, and I guess I kind of knew that would happen. It was my fault, really — I was the one who asked for the distance, the one who kept it in place, and even though I missed him the more he pulled away, I filled the space he left with more work instead of working to keep him as the occupant.

The summer flew by in a heated streak, blinding me like the lights from a camera flash. Between the internship and my online courses for my grad degree, free time was practically nonexistent. Before I knew it, it was August, and I was in the last two weeks of my internship with a huge open agent event to host before I rounded out my time with Rye Publishing.

I was right in the middle of a particularly stressful Thursday afternoon when Jamie texted me that he needed to talk. I was already busy, stretched thin and on the verge of proving that I could be a permanent employee at Rye, and the last thing I needed was the stomach somersault that came with that text from him. The attention I'd garnered as an intern was unprecedented, and I could feel success nipping at the tips of my fingers, waiting for me to latch on. Still, that could all be gone if I let my emotions get the best of me.

I debated type-screaming at Jamie, telling him I didn't have time for his shit, but the truth was I was scared of what he had to say. In a way, I knew what was coming, at least I could guess — and I guess that's why I wanted to be angry. Being mad would be easier than being breakable.

In the end, I just responded with an "okay" and a promise to call him as soon as I got home that evening. I had just thrown my phone on my desk screen-side down with a long sigh when River propped his forearm on my cube.

"You need a break."

"No," I corrected him as I logged back into my computer. "I need more hours in the day, actually."

He chuckled. "Come on. Food. Now."

"I'm fine."

"Did you forget who your boss is?" I finally looked up at him and he cocked one beautiful blonde eyebrow with a stupid smirk on his face.

"Way to pull the *I pay you* card."

"Well, I'll *pay* for your lunch. How's that?" He snagged my umbrella from where I'd propped it at the corner of my desk and handed it to me. "You've been here for over two months and you still haven't eaten a Primanti Brothers' sandwich. We're fixing that today."

I let myself smile, realizing at the mention of food just how hungry I actually was. Maybe I did need a break, even if it was only for an hour. I took the umbrella from his hand and grabbed my purse off the cube hook. "Well how can I say no to sandwiches piled high with french fries and coleslaw?"

"You can't. Another trump card."

He smiled, motioning with his hand for me to take the lead. I looked back at my phone on the desk but decided to leave it behind. If I was taking a break, I was taking it from everything — and *everyone*.

The walk through Market Square to Primati Brothers was wet, and surprisingly chilly for the time of year. I was used to sweltering Augusts, but it was in the sixties and drizzling all day that day. River and I walked side by side with our umbrellas popped open, talking about the event coming up and other small conversation bits. I loved walking through downtown. In fact, I loved everything about Pittsburgh. I was surprised by how much it had evolved to feel like home.

"Okay, now once you walk through this door, you're on a break. I'm serious. No work talk," River said when we reached the entrance. He held his hand on the door until I agreed, and then he opened it and the smell of heaven invaded.

It was a small place, limited seating mostly at the bar that surrounded where all the cooking was happening. River and I slid up onto two barstools at the far end and a smiling waiter dropped off our menus before turning back to the flat-top to flip an egg.

"What are you guys having to drink?" he yelled over his shoulder. He had long, dark hair, pulled back into a low bun and tattoos lining his arms. The entire crew behind the bar was shouting orders to each other and cracking jokes in-between. I already felt at ease.

I opened my mouth to reply, ready to ask for a water, when River answered for us, ordering two local beers.

"I know I'm at the end of my internship, but don't tell my boss I'm drinking on the job, okay?" I teased.

"Something tells me he won't mind. So, what are you going to order?"

I looked over the menu, scanning the options. "The Pitts-burger. Number two bestseller." My eyes read over the other options, and I frowned when I couldn't find any other menu items with callouts like that. "What's the number one bestseller?"

River and the waiter exchanged grins as our beers were placed in front of us, the froth spilling over the side a bit. "You're looking at it, sweetheart."

I was confused, but when River's eyes crinkled at the edges and fell to the beer I'd just wrapped a hand around, it clicked into place. "Ohhh," I mused, holding mine up. "Beer. Number one bestseller. I get it."

"Faster than most, actually," the waiter agreed. "So, what will it be?"

I ordered the Pitts-burger and River opted for the Cajun Chicken and Cheese, and then we relaxed, drinking our beers and talking about everything *but* work. I hadn't really stopped to make friends in Pittsburgh, throwing all of my energy into work, but I had taken all the time that I could to get to know Pittsburgh more. I loved the fanfare, the local eats, the hidden gems. It was such a fascinating city, and knocking another place off my bucket list with River seemed like the perfect way to spend my lunch break.

"So, I couldn't help but notice you left your right hand behind," River said as he drank the last of his first beer. He waved his hand at our waiter for another while he waited for my response.

"Right hand?"

"Your phone."

222

"Oh." I ran the pad of my finger over the sweating glass of my beer and shrugged. "Yeah, just needed a break."

"Boyfriend?"

I laughed, cocking a brow at my boss. "No, but slick way of asking if I had one."

I wasn't blind to River's attraction for me. I didn't ever see him acting on it, but he would flirt from time to time, or let his eyes wander over me a little longer than they should. Still, he took me seriously as a professional, and that's what mattered most to me.

"Wow, I didn't think you could impress me more."

"It impresses you that I'm single?"

He chuckled, thanking the waiter for his new beer before turning to me again. "No, it impresses me that you're out here on your own. I've never had an intern with as much tenacity as you, and to find out you haven't been living with a roommate or going out every night or spending your weekends with a boyfriend to keep yourself sane has me wondering how you do it."

I smiled at his compliment, but lifted my shoulders again. "I don't know, I'm not completely alone. I talk to my best friend a lot."

"Jamie, right?"

My stomach dropped. "Yes…"

River put his hands up. "Chill, I just see her name on your phone screen a lot in meetings."

"Oh, it's a… I mean Jamie's not a…"

He waited as I stumbled for words, but then recognition set in. "Wait, is Jamie a guy?" He groaned. "Oh no, please don't tell me you have a guy best friend."

"Why?"

River shook his head, eyes on the hand wrapped around his beer. "My mom always told me to never give my heart to a girl with a guy best friend, because her heart isn't really hers to give in return."

He couldn't have known how those words would sit with me. He couldn't have known that they'd snake their way in-between the bones of my ribcage, winding tight, cutting off my ability to breathe with their truth. I swallowed, the familiar burn of Whiskey invading my tastebuds. I chased it down with beer, wondering if River was right, wondering even more if it was okay that he was. Jamie wanted my heart, right? Would it be so bad if it was already his? Did I have a choice in the matter?

"Good thing you're not trying to give your heart to your intern then, huh?" I winked, and River sat back on his bar stool, a small smile playing at his lips as he watched me.

"Yeah. Good thing."

My sandwich was amazing, everything I thought it would be. Piled high with french fries and cole slaw, I was barely able to scarf down half and finish my beer, too. On the way back to the office, I was rubbing my stomach, surprised to find it still flat after that meal.

"So, there's another reason why I wanted to take you to lunch," River said as we rode the elevator back up to the office.

"Besides ruining me for all other sandwiches?"

He grinned. "Yes. Besides that."

Silence fell between us, and I looked over my shoulder as if I'd find the rest of his sentence there. "Okay... so..."

We hit our floor and the doors opened to the office just as applause broke out. I jumped back, but then my hands flew to cover my mouth as I read the banner strung high above Mona's desk.

YOU'RE HIRED.

"What is this?" I whispered, stepping off the elevator as everyone continued cheering. Mr. Randall Godsby made his way through the masses, wide grin that matched River's firmly in place. The agents I'd worked with all summer were there, along with the media team and vice presidents. It wasn't a huge office, but it felt big in that moment — like a family.

"Congratulations, Brecks," Mr. Godsby said as he extended his hand for my own and I fought against the natural urge to cringe at my full name. I took his hand, looking back over my shoulder at River, but he was just smiling as he glanced between his father and me. "River has told me more than once how crucial you've been to the team this summer, but even if he hadn't, I would have noticed for myself — and that's saying something. If you're looking to hole yourself up in Pittsburgh a while longer, we'd like to offer you a full-time job — as an Associate Literary Agent."

I squealed, unable to contain my excitement as I shook his hand ferociously. Everything I'd worked for that summer came to fruition in a room full of people who'd doubted me from the moment I walked through the door. I couldn't believe it, even as Randall dropped my hand and gripped my shoulder firmly with a proud smile.

My mind scanned reasons to decline, but came up empty. I was still completing my online M.S. Degree in

Publishing: Digital and Print Media from PSU and I loved Pittsburgh. Rye Publishing was one of the top publishing houses, and I had no other offers lined up. Nothing was keeping me from staying, except for the clawing notion that it meant more time away from someone really important to me. But if he felt for me the way he said he did, he would understand. He'd be happy for me.

And so I smiled, and accepted my first job offer — one I'd earned on my own.

"I don't even know what to say, Mr. Godsby. Thank you. And I'd be honored to join the Rye team full-time."

"Huzzah!" River joked, grabbing one of the flutes of champagne from Mona and handing it to me. Even *she* was smiling — and that was saying something. "A toast, to the new Rye Rookie."

"Cheers!" Everyone's voices rang out at once and we tipped our plastic flutes together. Then, it was business as usual, everyone slowly making their way back to their desks or meeting rooms.

"Does that happen every time someone is hired?"

River shrugged. "Every time they're promoted, yes."

A slow grin found its way to my face as I let that sink in. A promotion. I'd been promoted after just two months as an intern. River's hand reached up to squeeze my shoulder before he passed by me, and I stood there with my champagne, smiling like an idiot.

"You can get back to work now, rookie," Mona said, plopping down into her chair and tapping at her keyboard immediately. She cocked a brow and gave me a small smile of her own. "And congrats."

"Thanks, Mona."

I sort of danced my way back to my desk, full from the sandwich and the love from my new team. I had a job — a *real* job — and I'd earned it. Nothing could bring me down.

But when I sat back in my chair and grabbed my phone to text Mom, I remembered the phone call I'd be having in just a few short hours. With Jamie.

And I'd have to tell him I'm staying in the city.

• • •

I decided to pick up a nice bottle of whiskey on my way home.

I was celebrating, after all — even if a part of me didn't feel like it, knowing the phone conversation I'd be having soon. After the high recommendation from the liquor store owner, I ended up with a bottle of Whipper Snapper Project Q. It was an Australian whiskey, one I'd never tried or even heard of before, and I liked the name of it. It reminded me of what my dad's dad used to call me when I was younger, especially when I was being smart with him. I'd paid way too much for it, and like the bad ass I convinced myself I was, I poured it neat. Then, I sat down on my small couch with the nighttime view of Market Square and dialed Jamie's number.

I took my first sip as the phone rang, and though the whiskey burned, it was surprisingly smooth. I hissed a breath through my teeth, but knew that after that first glass, it'd be easy as water to drink.

"B?"

There was a hint of desperation in his voice, and it warmed my heart.

"Yeah, I'm here."

He blew out a breath, long and steady, and then he started speaking. "Okay, I just need you to sit there and listen to me for a minute, okay? I know you're scared of us, of what we've been in the past and what we might not be in the future. I know you're standing on your own for the first time and you're proud of that, hell I'm proud of that too, but I can stand with you."

"Jamie—"

"And I know long distance freaks you out, but we've made it through the summer practically *as* a long distance couple, even if we didn't title it that." I couldn't argue that point, but still — was it the fact that the pressure of a title wasn't there that allowed us to survive? "I've been thinking. Your internship is almost over, and I've been looking at some publishing places in Miami. A lot of them are hiring, and you have experience now. Your classes are online, B. You could come home, we could be together."

"Jamie, I—"

"No, just let me finish. I know this is a lot to ask. You don't owe me anything, and the fact that I'm asking you to uproot yourself and move back for me is selfish as fuck. But I realized last time you walked away from me, I didn't ask you anything at all. So this time, I'm putting it out there — I'm letting you know what I want. I want *you*. I want you to move back, hell to move *in*." He laughed, and I could feel his bright smile through the phone. It only tore my heart into yet another piece. "It doesn't have to be complicated. We can do this, B."

"I'm staying."

"Jenna's here, too. And your mom. And—"

"Jamie, I'm staying in Pittsburgh," I said louder. "They offered me a full-time job. Today."

Silence fell between us, and I picked up my glass slowly, taking another longer pull of the whiskey.

"Okay," he breathed the word out slowly. "That's okay. We can see each other once a month, take turns flying, and eventually we'll figure it out."

"It doesn't work like that," my voice broke with the words. "You have your dad's firm there. And I have my life here." Life was a little strong of a word, considering work *was* my life in Pittsburgh, but I'd moved to the city with a fire in my eyes and I was already making a name for myself. Thinking about complicating that with a long-distance relationship gave me hives, and hearing him say "eventually we'll figure it out" didn't help. What did that mean? We both knew he was never leaving his dad's firm, which meant that he expected me to "eventually figure it out" and move back home.

"That doesn't mean we can't have a life together, too."

I paused a beat, heart breaking a little at how wrong he was. "But it kind of does, Jamie. It all sounds so easy when you say it over the phone, but a long-distance relationship is hard. It's complicated and messy and neither of us needs that right now, not when we're both just getting started in our careers. It's just not the right time for us..." I shook my head. "It's never the right time."

There was a sigh on the other end, and I felt the time stretch between us before Jamie spoke again. When he did, his voice was lower, defeated, and the sound of it nearly made me drop my glass.

"That's not fair. You don't understand this, B — any of it. When you left Alder, you got to leave it all behind — the places we went, the memories we made. But I lived there. Without you. For three *years*." He paused. "And then, when I found you again, everything seemed right. The timing, the way we both felt. I finally got an answer from you, why you stayed away all those years, and I got it, B — I really did. I understood. You were broken from your father's death and you needed time and space. I gave that to you. Happily. I didn't know if I'd ever have you again but I didn't care because I knew what you needed from me."

My eyes welled as I thought of that time in my life. I remembered feeling so torn, wanting to stay at Alder and knowing that I couldn't. Jamie loved me enough back then to let me bring him down with me, and I'd never understand how he could still love me after.

"But now, you're telling me it's still not there — it's still not the right time. You couldn't be with me when you were broken, and now that you're standing on your own, you *still* can't be with me. So if I can't have you at your worst, and I can't have you at your best, then when do I get you, B? When does the timing line up for you to stop fighting what we have between us and just let me in?"

A sob cracked in my throat and I cleared it, sniffling as I took another drink. I didn't know what to say. In a way, he was right — it wasn't fair. But it also wasn't as easy as just pointing a finger to a time and place in my life and saying,

"There! That's the time I'll be ready." His nonchalance over it all rubbed me wrong, and I took another long pull of whiskey, realizing Jamie hadn't really ever seemed like he believed I'd make it and end up staying in Pittsburgh. He thought it was temporary, like me being in the city was inconveniencing him and *his* plans.

I loved Jamie, I always had, but we couldn't do long distance. I couldn't be the woman he needed me to be from thousands of miles away, when I had a job of my own and goals to fight for. I knew what he wanted, what he'd always wanted — a wife, a house full of kids. Maybe one day I'd want those things, too. But that day wasn't today.

And that's when I remembered what he asked me for that night we found each other again.

"What happened to one day?" I asked in a whisper.

It took a moment for him to answer. "Well, I need one day right now."

"And I can't give it to you, so where does that leave us?"

"I don't know."

I finished what was left in my glass and poured up another, the Whipper Snapper smoother than before just like I knew it'd be. It was sinking into my system while another, older Whiskey bled itself out.

I know you're probably furious with me in this moment. Hell, I'm furious with myself looking back on that night. But at that particular moment in my life, I thought I knew what was best. I thought I knew what would work and what wouldn't, what mattered and what didn't. I thought protecting myself from a potentially broken heart would be easier than trying to fight for love with distance in the mix. I'd walked away from Jamie before and it'd nearly killed me, but this time, I was stubborn — and I felt like it was him giving me the ultimatum. It was him ready to walk away from me, and I was just proud enough to let him if it meant standing my ground.

"Listen, I have a really big event coming up and tomorrow is going to be a long day…"

It was a sorry excuse, and Jamie knew it. The bigger part of me expected him to fight me on it, to demand I talk to him and figure this out, and I guess it should have been my sign that he was giving up on me. He was done waiting, done fighting someone who wasn't even blocking the punches anymore.

"Yeah, okay." He exhaled, and I felt that breath through the phone. I could almost smell him there with me, the oaky honey, similar to the whiskey I was drinking that night. "I just…" I waited for him to finish that sentence, but he never did, and it haunted me for nights to come after. "Goodnight, B."

"Night."

After we hung up, I sat there with my phone in my hands for a solid ten minutes, my eyes on the glass in my hand as I replayed our conversation. And that's when I realized it.

Jamie never congratulated me on my promotion.

I drank half the bottle before I finally turned in that night, and not even the expensive whiskey could silence my racing thoughts. I was stuck in the strangest place I'd ever been. I felt both solid in my decision and terrified

I'd just made the biggest mistake of my life, proud of my accomplishments yet ashamed of my stubbornness. But the truth was that summer, that year in my life — it was about me. I felt like I had all the time in the world, room for mistakes, room to grow. How could I have known how wrong I was?

I didn't call Jamie the next day, and he didn't call me. And so it went, for days, weeks, and months. It took too long for me to realize I'd dropped that beautiful bottle of whiskey. Too long to realize I'd broken it. By the time I figured it out, too long turned to too late, and I remembered all-too-well the other way Whiskey can burn.

FIFTEEN

The Angel's Share

I WAS ON FIRE.

I nailed the event at the end of my internship, which just seemed to propel me straight into my new full-time position. As much as I enjoyed my internship working under River, I was finally exactly where I wanted to be — finding new talent, building a client list, making connections in the publishing world. I was on my way to Literary Agent, and after that — I knew I'd be unstoppable.

There was something both freeing and absolutely suffocating about working hard and being rewarded. On the one hand, I was proud of myself. I'd figured out what I wanted in life, what I was good at, and I was making the right moves to set up a solid foundation for my career. Nothing made me happier than staying late at the office or coming in on a weekend if I saw the payout on the other end. Everyone at Rye Publishing knew who I was. To some, I was an inspiration. To others, a threat. And I loved being both.

But, on the other hand, work was literally everything in my life — which meant even if I tried to deny it, I was lonely. It wasn't that I was sad in that loneliness, but I felt it — like a ghost or a shadow in the corner of my apartment. It was always there, lurking, and when it got to be too much I found myself back in the office to avoid it. And so the cycle went.

Because work was my life, I ended up spending most of my time with River — which was dangerous in more ways than one. It was clear to me that he was curious, and not about my work ethic. But even though I'd let Jamie go, my heart still held onto him tight, and I did my best to make that clear to River. He hadn't made a move per se, but I saw the twitch of his fingers — he was ready, waiting, and I wondered when he'd strike.

I wondered what I'd do.

It was after eight o'clock one Friday night in November when the loneliness finally got to me. I was pouring over a new manuscript I'd curated from an up-and-coming fantasy author who was Indie up until that point but was now seeking representation. The book was amazing, I was completely immersed, at least until River tapped hard on the top of my cube.

"You know, that book will still be readable on Monday. Or even tomorrow — when you can read it on your couch and not hunched over in that shitty chair." I smiled, tossing the manuscript down on my desk and kicking back in my chair. I scrubbed two hands over my face before running them back over my curls. "You should call it a night."

"You're not my boss anymore, Riv. Haven't been for months." I winked, knowing he hated when I pointed that out. He always wanted me to work less, and that always made me work more. "You're just scared I'm going to make it to VP before you."

He laughed. "Honestly? At this point, I wouldn't be surprised if you did." Without warning, he stepped into my cube and jabbed his finger into the power button of my Mac, powering it down.

"Hey!"

"Seriously, come on. It's Friday night. Let's go get a drink." He held out his hand and I looked up at him, feeling the sparkle in his eye a little too close to a sensitive space still partly occupied.

I sighed. "You know, I am really tired actually. Maybe I should just go get some sleep."

He swallowed, and though I knew it wasn't the answer he wanted, he grabbed my hand and hoisted me up. "That works too. Just get the hell out of here."

"So bossy," I teased. His eyes lit up again, and this time I *definitely* felt the space spark around us. I cleared my throat, tossing the manuscript in my oversized purse and throwing it over my shoulder. "Walk me out?"

River didn't just walk me downstairs, but all the way to the entrance of my apartment building before he gave me a stiff hug goodbye and went to meet up with some of our coworkers at a little bar in Market Square. I rode the elevator up to my floor and moved through the motions that had become my new routine — drop shit at the door, kick shoes off, pour a glass of wine, hold the bottle in the other hand until I made it to my bedroom, where I changed into leggings and an oversized sweatshirt, then it was ass on the couch — my favorite place to be.

I sighed with relief as I tucked my legs beneath me and took a long sip of the red wine. It was dry, slightly sweet, and perfect. As I tossed my hair into a loose bun on top of my head, I laughed out loud. How pathetic. I'd been invited out to drinks with friends and I'd turned it down to sit by myself. I didn't even have a pet to cuddle with.

Flipping through the contacts on my phone, I dropped my finger on Mom's name and a picture of us at my graduation filled the screen. It'd been a while since we'd talked other than text, so I sat back, ready for a long conversation of catching up.

"Hi sweetie!" She yelled over the background noise.

"Mom?"

"Huh?"

"You there?"

A loud burst of laughter rang out and I heard Mom yell something before the noise disappeared. "Sorry, honey. Wayne and I are out at a new bar that opened downtown. What's up?"

Even my mom is cooler than I am.

"Oh, sorry. I was just calling to catch up."

"Aw, I miss you, honey! How's work?"

It was always the first question she asked me, and really it was the only thing she *knew* to ask about — work.

I sighed. "It's great. Kicking ass and taking names like always."

"That's my girl."

"I'll let you get back to Wayne. I love you."

"I love you, too. Is everything okay?"

Mom knew. She always knew. But tonight wasn't the night to unload on her. "Everything's okay, Mom. Give me a call tomorrow okay?"

"Okay honey. Talk then!" She ended the call quickly, and I chuckled, thinking how different she was from the mom who'd brought me up in high school. That woman never left the house except for work, and she rarely smiled. Wayne had sparked life back into my mom, and I loved him for it.

I poured up another glass of wine, realizing I'd finished my first one probably a little too quickly. Then, I dialed Jenna.

"Sup, betch."

"Please tell me I'm not interrupting your super fun Friday night out."

She scoffed. "Hardly."

"Good. My mom is already drunk and living it up and I'm wallowing in self-pity on the couch and looking for someone to whine to."

"Well," Jenna said on a breath, like she was adjusting her position. "Lucky for you, I just finished eating my weight in egg rolls and Ben & Jerry's and I'm only forty minutes into *Cruel Intentions*. The night is young."

"You're so beautiful."

"I know," she said around a mouthful of something — my bet was on the ice cream. "So, my pity party hat is strapped on. What are we celebrating?"

I clicked on my television for background noise, landing on MTV. "Oh you know, the usual. I miss the guy I basically told to fuck off and I have nothing to show for my current life outside of an extensive client list at work."

"Why is that a bad thing? You work your ass off and everyone sees it. I *wish* I had your work ethic. You're going to be making six figures by the time you're thirty."

"Yeah…" I traced the rim of my glass with my fingertip. "I mean, don't get me wrong, I love my job. I'm proud of what I've done."

"But everything sucks without Jamie."

I sighed. "Nailed it."

"Okay, before we go any further," Jenna said, and I heard her suck another spoonful of ice cream. "What do you need from me tonight? Do you want me to pet your hair and talk you off the ledge or do you want some tough bestie love that feels like an ass slap and a punch straight to the nose all at once?"

I took another, longer sip of wine, repeating her question in my mind. She'd been petting my hair and telling me what was easiest to hear for months, but for whatever reason, on that cold Friday night in November with the holidays just around the corner, I felt particularly homesick and lonely. I was ready to cry into my bottle of wine, to shed the emotions I felt bubbling up too high in my throat. And maybe, just maybe, I was ready to face the truth I'd been avoiding.

"Kick me in the teeth."

Jenna clapped her hands together on the other end of the line. "Okay, just remember you asked for this." She paused, shuffling around, and I imagined her sitting up straight like she usually did before we had our come-to-Jesus best friend talks.

I untucked my legs, stretching out on the couch and

pulling the throw blanket off the back to cover myself. "Mouthguard in place. Let's hear it."

"First off, you are your own worst enemy. You always have been. But this whole thing with Jamie showed me a whole new side of your warped sense of yourself and how you affect others."

"Okay, you have my attention. Explain."

"Well, you left Alder and never went back because you were so convinced that you were like poison or something. You thought he would drop out of school and lose everything he'd ever worked for because he wanted to love you while you were fucked up. But the reality is, if you would have gone back, Jamie probably would have brought you back to life sooner than you did on your own."

I frowned. "I don't think so. I was a mess back then. He had his own worries going on with his dad's firm and I didn't want to bring another source of stress into his life."

"Right. *You* didn't want to, but Jamie was happy to be the person you leaned on. He wanted to be. You just wouldn't let him. And then, you run into him out of some miracle at the literal exact moment in your life where you finally felt okay again. And yes, you moved. Yes, long distance sucks, but you know what? It's possible. I mean, do you *honestly* see yourself staying in Pittsburgh forever?"

"I don't know. Maybe," I said defensively. "The point is there's no way for us to know if the long distance thing will be permanent or temporary."

"Yes there is."

"How?"

KANDI STEINER

"You make the decision to have it be temporary, B. It's as easy as that. You look at what's important in your life, and if Jamie is a top priority, then you adjust everything else accordingly."

"He is important, but so is my career," I said, huffing. "I don't want to give up what I've finally figured out on my own for a boy."

"Oh please," she scoffed. "It's not like that and you know it. It's not like Jamie is asking you to stay at home with the kids and drop all your dreams. He's asking you to work with him, to be a team, to finally put him first now that the timing is right. I mean look, first he was dating me, then you were dating Ethan, then your dad passed, and then you moved away. Even still, after *all that*, you two somehow found your way back to each other. And now, the only thing keeping you from being together is *you*."

"You make it sound so simple."

"Because it is!" She laughed. "Babe, wake up. Jamie loves you. He put his heart on the line like no other guy I've ever seen in my *life*. Don't walk away from that because you think you're doing him some sort of favor. He knows you're not going to marry him and move back home right away. He knows you're not ready to have kids. It doesn't matter. He wants *you*, B. And even though you're trying to prove you don't feel the same for some stupid reason, we both know you do. Stop acting like not wanting him makes you strong. There's more courage in admitting you love someone and fighting for them than letting them go because it hurts less."

Suddenly, my wine tasted sour, and I sat the glass on my coffee table before laying back on the couch and covering my eyes with my forearm. Jenna's words didn't sink in slowly or jolt me like a shocking realization. No, the truth was everything she said I'd already known. Maybe I'd always known. So hearing her say them out loud only ripped the curtain down, the one I'd hung high to separate me from the ugly truth. Now, I was staring at it, right in the eyes, and it was just as terrifying as it had been when I'd covered it.

"I'm so fucking screwed," I cried, my voice breaking.

"You're not. You can still do something about it. But first, you need to figure out what it is that's always had you running from him."

I sniffed, letting my arm fall to the side and staring up at my ceiling. "I don't know how to love someone, Jenna. I just don't. I never saw it in my house, not with my parents. I never felt it with Ethan. I did with Jamie, and instantly — as soon as I realized I loved him — I was overwhelmed with panic and fear."

"Shit…" Jenna breathed. "It's your dad. You've got daddy issues."

"Wow, Jenna."

"No," she said quickly. "I'm sorry, I didn't mean it like that. I liked your dad, I was just as confused as you were when everything… when it all came out, you know? But it all makes sense now. You thought your mom loved your dad and then you found out what he did to her. And your dad was the first man you ever loved, and he hurt you — he practically killed you. You affiliate love with fear."

242

For a few moments I just breathed, thinking on what she'd said. It seemed too simple, too cliché, and yet at the same time it felt real.

"What do I do?"

Jenna paused, and I continued staring up at my ceiling, like the answer would fall down from the floor above.

"You call your boss and tell him you won't be in on Monday. Then, you book the earliest flight for tomorrow, you go shopping and get your hair done with your best friend, and you go get your man."

I laughed. "That's so dramatic."

"Love often is."

I pulled the blanket up over my shoulders and turned on my side, curling my legs to my chest. "What if he doesn't want to see me? We haven't talked since that night."

"Stop making excuses and book the damn flight. I'm hanging up now. See you tomorrow."

A sad laugh crept out of me. "I love you."

"You too. Text me your flight info."

"Okay."

"I'm serious."

"I know," I said, and she ended the phone call before I could thank her.

I was still terrified. I wasn't sure if I could do this, if I could do long distance, if I could be with Jamie and handle the pressure of a relationship along with the pressure at work. But if anything, Jenna had opened my eyes to the fact that I had been running from Jamie, and only for selfish reasons. I'd never shown him that he was important in my life, and he was. It was time I showed it.

And maybe love was scary, but with Jamie, it was amazing, too. It hurt worse to live without him, and I'd realized that now.

I emailed my boss, booked a flight, and then I finished my bottle of wine, all the while wishing it were Whiskey, instead. That was the night I convinced myself that I could take control of my life, of my relationship with Jamie, if only I made the decision to. Face your fear, and you can conquer anything — right? But what I neglected to realize was that even when it seems like everything has finally clicked into place, the biggest player in the game of life is timing — and you either have that player on your team, or you don't.

That weekend, I would learn quickly and painfully that timing was never on our side.

• • •

"Are you sure you don't want me to meet you there?"

I shook my head before realizing Jenna couldn't see me. "Nope, just touching up and then going inside. I want to do it on my own."

"Okay. I mean, not that I'm anxious to go and then be left behind when you guys go back to his place to bang all night but you can totally pull the best friend card if you need to."

I laughed, applying a fresh coat of dark burgundy lipstick. My gray eyes popped against the smoky shadow Jenna had showed me how to do and my lashes were long and dark. "I'll be okay."

"I know you will. Just be honest with him and then make up all night long."

"I like the picture you paint."

"Well shit, maybe I should just quit law school and be an artist."

I rolled my eyes. "Bye, Jenna."

Once I was alone in my mom's car, I let out a long, slow, shaky breath, staring at my reflection in the small visor mirror. My cheeks were hinted with a blush and my hair was styled with tight curls. I'd shopped all day with Jenna, and she was right — I felt more confident in a new pair of skin-tight leather leggings and deep v-neck blouse. I slid out of my sandals and pulled my heels from the passenger seat, putting them on one by one before bracing my hands on the steering wheel again. I let myself stall for thirty more seconds, then I grabbed my clutch and made my way inside.

I'd planned to show up at his house, but ended up running into his youngest sister at the mall when I was with Jenna. She'd told me he was going out tonight, to his favorite bar, celebrating after the hellish week they'd had at work. Busy season happened two times a year for them — February to May, and September through November. They'd survived, and I hoped me showing up would add to the celebration.

It was dark in the bar, and even though my stomach was tight with anticipation, I didn't seek Jamie out at first. Instead, I headed straight for the bar, sliding up on a barstool and flagging down the bartender. This was my first strategic move for two reasons: one, I needed libations to get through my nerves, and two, I was half-hoping Jamie would see me first. I was ready, I knew everything I wanted to say, but it would be easier if he had to make the walk across the bar to me. If he simply strutted up with that beautiful smile of his and asked, *"What are you doing here?"* with wonder in his eyes. Then, I could spill my heart like they do in the movies, and we'd spend the night the way Jenna imagined.

That's what I hoped for, but it wasn't what I got.

I did get a glass of Makers Mark on the rocks, a sweet bourbon that was easy to drink and made me feel a little less tightly wound. And then, I got hit on.

"Whiskey girl, huh?" a sweet voice asked. I turned, glass still at my lips, and found a strikingly beautiful woman on the bar stool next to me.

I nodded, smiling as I finished swallowing. "Yeah. You?"

She held up her bottle of Bud Light. "Nah, more of a cheap beer gal myself." She grinned wide, her sea-green eyes raking over me slowly. She reminded me a little of Mona with her long dark hair and exotic features, but Mona wore a constant look of distaste while this woman's smile was warm and inviting. "I'm Claire."

"B," I said, tipping my glass to her before taking another sip.

"Bee, huh? Like the bumble?"

I laughed. "Like the letter. It's just my first initial."

"Ah, makes sense now. Well, B, what brings you to this shit hole of a bar?"

The fist in my stomach gripped tighter. For a moment, I'd almost forgotten. "I'm here to see about a boy."

246

Disappointment settled in over her features, but she masked it with an easy smile. "Of course, should have known you'd be taken. Not going to lie, I was kind of counting my lucky stars that you slid up next to me looking all sweet, innocent, and lonely."

I laughed again, harder this time. "You're pretty bold."

"Beating around the bush is for pussies," she said with a wink, sipping from her beer. "Speaking of which, I have to say, totally thought you played on my team."

"Should I take that as a compliment?"

She shrugged, gathering her hair to one side of her neck. "Take it however you want."

I opened my mouth to respond, but my eyes caught on a large table across the bar behind Claire. It took a moment for them to adjust, but once they did, I couldn't find another breath, let alone another word.

Claire turned, following my gaze and turning back to me with raised eyebrows. "Disgustingly cute, aren't they?" She took another drink. "Try being around it twenty-four-seven. That's my best friend, Angel. She's been with this guy for — what? Maybe four months now? Pining over him for almost a year before that. He was all heartbroken over some chick he tried doing long distance with, but she was determined to break through that shit. Got to be honest, I told her to give it up, but eventually he took her up on a coffee date and the rest is history." She chuckled. "Gross, PDA history."

Claire was a talker, that much I figured out, and she kept going — on and on and on — but her words faded out as my heartbeat grew louder and louder between my ears. There he was, my Whiskey, but he'd never really been mine. That notion had never struck me quite as hard as it did in that moment I saw him with another woman in his lap, her arm around his shoulders and his around her waist as he looked up at her just like he used to look at me. Every now and then, she'd drop her lips to his, and his hand around her waist would tighten, along with the knot in my stomach. They were both smiling, laughing, *happy*.

And then I did the math. Four months would put them together in August, which either meant he'd moved on quickly or they'd been fucking around when we were still together. But we *weren't* together, not really, and that was the harshest zinger of all.

Acid rose in my throat and I pushed it back down with a long swig of Makers, turning in my seat to face the bar again.

"Whoa, you okay, sweets? Looking a little pale there," Claire said, cocking a brow.

I nodded, at least I think I did. I couldn't be sure. The music had morphed, slow, bass pounding along with my heart. I drained the rest of my drink, which only added to my nausea, then I stood abruptly, the bar stool screeching against the floor with the force. "Nice meeting you."

"You too?" She said it almost as a question, eying me as I grabbed my clutch and made to bolt for the door. But new high heels and rushing didn't mix with nerves, or anger, which I felt slowly bubbling, so I slipped, falling against the two guys who were seated right next to us. I mumbled an apology, pushing my way through the gathering crowd toward the door when I heard my name called over my shoulder. I ignored it, quickening my pace until I finally pushed through the exit. I inhaled a deep breath once the cool air hit my skin, nearly doubling over. For a second I stood, fumbling for my keys, and just as I steadied them and hit the unlock button on my car, I heard my name again.

"B?"

I couldn't catch a full breath, my chest squeezing with every attempt. I was going to pass out if I didn't calm down. I found my balance again before walking toward the parking lot, but glanced a look over my shoulder. "Oh, hey Jamie. Uh, yeah, I was just leaving though so—"

"Wait." He hooked a strong hand around my elbow and as soon as his skin touched mine, my entire body buzzed to life, just like it always did in the presence of Whiskey. I let him stop me, but I couldn't lift my eyes to his, so I stared at the hem of his shirt instead. "What are you doing here?"

There it was. There was the question I imagined him asking, only when I brought myself to look at him, his eyes weren't full of wonder — they were full of accusation. And that was all it took to tip my bubbling anger over the edge, the scalding liquid of it searing any rationality I had tried to hold onto.

"I'm here visiting my mom. I would ask you what *you're* doing, but I have eyes, so," I said, pulling my elbow from his grasp and motioning toward the bar with my tongue pressed hard against the inside of my cheek.

"What the hell is that supposed to mean?"

"Oh, I think you know *exactly* what it's supposed to mean," I seethed. *What was wrong with me?* The last thing

I wanted when I showed up tonight was a fight, but apparently the whiskey mixed with what I'd seen had lit a fire in my stomach that couldn't be put out easily. I folded my arms and stepped closer, causing Jamie to inhale a stiff breath at our proximity. "Tell me, did you fuck her the night before you asked me to talk? Did you feel guilty and desperate to lock me down before the pressure of long distance took you under?"

"*What?*" Jamie's nose flared and I felt every muscle in him coil with tension without even having to lay a finger on him. "What the fuck are you talking about?"

"I'm talking about the little pixie blonde who was just mauling your face," I answered. "Angel is her name, right?" Jamie blanched at that, and I smirked, feeling like I'd won when I knew I was the clear loser before I even walked into the bar. "Oh yeah, Claire? Her BFF? She filled me in on the whole situation when I spotted you two sucking face."

Jamie's shoulders were squared, like he was waiting for me to start swinging. I was almost to the point where I could, madness radiating off me like steam from a hot summer rain. I hated him. I hated myself. I wanted to run away as much as I wanted to pound my fists on his chest.

"And?" he finally challenged, stepping into my space this time. I sniffed, my eyes dipping away from his for a moment, but I didn't back away. "What, are you mad? Is that what you're trying to say? Because I'd be really fucking interested to hear why you think you have any right to be."

"Just tell me, okay? You cheated on me, didn't you? I was in Pittsburgh, and she was here, and it was easier with her, right?" I shook my head. "Why did you even make the big gesture? Why not just tell me?"

"You think I *ch*—?" He couldn't even get the entire sentence out. It died on his lips, killed by a sinister laugh and his hands rushing back through his hair. It was longer than the last time I'd seen it, just how I liked it. I wanted my hands in it, instead. I wanted his mouth on mine. Even now, even raging mad, I needed him. "Angel and I didn't start talking until October, not that that is any of your goddamn business. She asked me out countless times over the summer and I turned her down every single fucking time because of you. Not because it would have been cheating, since you made it perfectly clear that we were *not* a couple, but because I loved you, B."

This time I did flinch, and I stepped back quickly, suddenly uncomfortable from the heat I felt from his skin. But Jamie wasn't backing down, and he pushed into my space more, until my back was against the brick wall of the building and I had to look away.

"I fucking loved you, and you loved me, too. But you wouldn't be with me. Not when I asked, not when I *begged*, not when I proved to you that we could do it. You were the one who didn't—" Again, his words were cut short, and he dropped his gaze to our feet. I took the opportunity to look at him again, and his jaw ticked under the skin as his eyes slowly climbed back to mine. "You're wearing heels."

The heat in his gaze took a hard turn away from anger as those words left his mouth in a low, gravelly voice. It was primal now, and each breath he took felt connected to mine as I watched it leave his chest. The last time he commented on my heels, they ended up wrapped around his waist. Everything inside me craved that same connection, but the wine-stained lipstick smears from another woman on Jamie's lips annihilated that yearning like the snuffing of a flame.

"And you're wearing lipstick," I breathed, closing my eyes tight as the images of Angel on his lap assaulted my vision. I didn't want to fight anymore, I just wanted to leave.

It took a moment, but Jamie pushed himself off the wall, and I creaked my eyes open just in time to see him wipe at his bottom lip with his thumb. He shook his head, like he was disappointed — in himself or me, I couldn't be sure.

"Why are you really here?"

"I missed you," I answered honestly. I was always honest with Jamie, even when it hurt.

He cringed, two parallel lines forming between his brows as he pinched the bridge of his nose. "No, no you don't get to say that to me." He shook his head, dropping his hand as his eyes opened again. "I'm finally happy," he whispered, with a delirious chuckle. "Okay? Is that alright with you, B? Do I have your permission to be fucking happy?"

My jaw dropped, and I opened my mouth to argue but couldn't find the words before Jamie held up his hands to stop me.

"God, you are the most selfish woman I have ever met. Let me guess, you missed me, so you thought you could just get on a flight and I'd be here waiting for you, right? Because that's exactly what I did for three years in California, so why *wouldn't* you think that? But guess what? You wanted me to let you go so badly, and this time, I listened." His eyes were wide, wild, and he was shaking hard. "So no, you don't get to show up here and tell me you missed me. You don't get to—"

"Stop," I choked, pushing myself off the wall and walking as quickly as my heels would allow me toward my car. "Stop, Jamie."

He followed me. "What, too much for you to handle?"

"I hate you!" I spat, spinning in place and charging back toward him a few steps. "Go back inside, I'm sure *Angel* is waiting."

"Oh, she is." He grinned, walking with me a few steps more when I started back toward the car. "And I intend to make her wait. All night long. Remember how fun that always was? Making you wait until you couldn't stand it anymore?" His breath was hot on my neck even as we walked, and though my fists clenched in anger, my thighs clenched in memory. "Making you *squirm* under my hands, my mouth…"

"Fuck you, Jamie."

He laughed. "*Goddamnit*, you drive me crazy. You literally make me insane."

"Well good thing I'm leaving," I threw behind me, climbing into my car and hitting the lock button. Jamie was right outside my window as I sparked it to life.

"Yeah. Good thing. That does seem to be your specialty, doesn't it?"

I whipped toward him, found his eyes through the glass as he stared me down. His jaw was set, eyes covered by the shadows from the overhead lights in the parking lot. He was daring me to make the next move, but I was tired of playing the game. I flipped him off with a sweet smile, and then I peeled off, not chancing another look in my rearview.

Tears found me before I even realized they were threatening to fall. I swiped at them harshly, my hands shaking before a scream ripped through my throat. I hated him, I loved him, I hated myself for loving him. I hated myself for letting him go, for letting him find someone else. I was furious, but the truth was nearly everything he'd said about me was true. I was the one who didn't want us to be official, I was the one always leaving, and I was selfish.

I was *so* fucking selfish.

In that moment, for no longer than a split second, I realized I was more like my father than I thought.

I couldn't stay in that town another night, not knowing he was lying with Angel in his bed not even ten minutes away from me. Not knowing he was happy with another woman, and I was still selfish enough to wish he wasn't.

I packed my duffle bag as soon as I got back to Mom's house and caught a cab to the airport. With nothing more than a few texts to Mom and Jenna, I left South Florida with a new hole burned into my heart.

If I'd known back then about the Angel's tax, I would have laughed. They say every year a batch of whiskey goes without being bottled, each year it's aged, four percent of alcohol evaporates — and that's the Angel's share. It really was funny, then, that I'd neglected to bottle Jamie up for myself and so he'd been stolen by a woman named Angel.

I maybe could have laughed if I'd known that story back then, but then again, maybe not. Because the truth was it wasn't funny.

It wasn't funny at all.

SIXTEEN

Rehab

AFTER THAT, THINGS HAPPENED in threes.

Three days, I let myself mourn. In my head, I checked into an in-and-out version of rehab, housed at Casa a la B. As soon as my plane landed, I turned off my phone, stocked the house with wine, beer, vodka, everything *but* whiskey, along with copious amounts of junk food, and got down to business. I changed into my favorite pair of sweats and a loose sweater that hung off my shoulder and I didn't change into any other clothing until the seventy-two hours was up.

In those hours, I thought long and hard about a lot of things. I thought about work, about my current situation, about my family, about what point I was at in my life. At the forefront of my mind was Jamie and I — what we were, what we weren't. I listened to classical music mostly, took a lot of baths, gave myself room to think and cry and do whatever was necessary in the withdrawal process. I drank too much, ate very little even though I had plenty there, and at the end of it all, I came out with three very solid conclusions.

One, I was where I needed to be. I wasn't going to regret staying in Pittsburgh or taking the full-time job with Rye Publishing. I loved what I did, who I worked with, and how my future looked. I worked damn hard to make it to where I was. I knew going into my internship that the likelihood of me getting a full-time position was slim to none, and yet I'd impressed the shit out of them and landed a permanent spot. There were no regrets there. And, though I missed the surf, I really did love the city. I loved who I was becoming. Sure, I was lonely, but I had offers to go out — to make friends — I just had to start taking them. I could do that. It took me so long to figure out what I wanted to do with my life. Once I found it, I'd held tight to it, and now it was the only thing one hundred percent certain in my life.

Two, I was like my father. And that was okay. I had always said I was a combination of him and my mother, and it was true. I had his selfish tendencies, but they were balanced out by my mom's giving heart. I was angry with myself for leading with my father's half for the last several months, but I knew I couldn't change that. And in a way, I didn't want to. Everyone needs to be selfish at one point or another in their lives. Sometimes it's okay to put yourself first, and I didn't regret chasing my dream or standing on my own two feet. I only regretted losing someone I loved in the process. But now, it was about looking forward, and in my future I saw nights out with friends, a balance of work and fun, spending more time on the phone with my mom and less at my desk. Well, at least a *little* less.

Three, and perhaps the most difficult conclusion I came to was this: I had been blind. I thought I knew what Jamie and I were, what had developed between us — and in a way, I did — but in a larger way, I didn't. What I did know, I shied away from, afraid of consequences. Afraid of burning. You see, I realized that I loved him, I realized that he loved me, but that wasn't enough. Because what I *didn't* realize was that Jamie bruised my heart that first day we met, when he literally ran into me, and every time I'd seen him since then, it had been like jabbing that bruise with granite fingers. A self-inflicted wound. I liked the way it hurt with him, the way it stung, the way it wasn't perfect — and so did he. But I was done hurting myself. I was done hurting him, too.

I wasn't sober for even a single minute of my three-day bender, yet I emerged with a clear head and clean spirit.

That was, until the next round of threes hit.

It took three months for Jamie to try to call me. When he did, I ignored him twice, but my curiosity got the best of me on the third call and I picked up.

"B?"

That's all it took, him asking my name on a breath of desperation.

"I'm here, Jamie."

He breathed, either with a sigh of relief or uncertainty. "I am so, so sorry. God, I was such a fucking dick to you. I was monstrous. And you didn't deserve any of that."

"You're damn straight I didn't."

"I didn't know what to do when you showed up, okay? I was already drunk, I was confused, I was blindsided."

He paused, and I lifted the wine to my lips. I was going to wait. I was going to let him talk. "B, I can't... I don't know how to live in a life where you're not a part of it."

I gulped my wine a little too hard, fighting the urge to choke as I sat up straighter on my sofa. My eyes blurred with tears from the liquid going down the wrong pipe and I took a moment to gather myself, which left more time for Jamie to talk.

"I know things are different between us... I guess I was holding onto what we could have been at Alder or something, I don't know. I never meant to pressure you and I never meant to lose my shit on you, either. Sometimes you really do drive me crazy," he said with a chuckle and I smiled at that, because I knew the feeling. All too well. "But I need you, as a friend, B. I have to have you as a friend."

Friends.

My mind flashed back to the times we'd agreed on that very sentiment — and failed. Jamie Shaw and I couldn't be just *friends* — we didn't know how. Still, my stomach was tightening and curling in on itself as I sat on the phone with him. I missed him — so much — and here he was apologizing and asking me to stay in his life. I wanted him in mine. I knew it wasn't smart, I think I would have bet money right then and there that it would blow up in our faces, but I didn't care. Once again, even after my stint in rehab, I chose being selfish over being careful.

I sighed. "You never lost me, Jamie. You never could."

And it was true. I couldn't think of one scenario where he would lose me forever, because a piece of my soul was tied to that boy — and I had already lost so much of myself at that age, I refused to let go of what little I still held onto.

We talked on the phone for another three hours, and it took me all three to tell him I was sorry, too.

Three weeks after that, Mom and Wayne eloped. Then, they bought a boat, sold everything else, and decided to live on it. She told me all this over a nine-minute video chat, her and Wayne laughing like kids the entire time as they told me how crazy but *right* it felt. I couldn't have been happier for them, but it reminded me in a place far in the back of my mind just how lonely I was.

And so, I threw myself back into work and managed to finish out my online master's degree, but I made sure I scheduled in fun. I went out with the crew after work, happy hours and Pirate games whenever I could. I explored more of my city, even taking the time to go up on the Deumont Incline to see it from the best view. Jenna flew in for one week in March and it snowed, so we went sledding for the first time in our lives at a park just outside of the city. I still talked to Mom whenever I could — whenever she wasn't busy traveling with Wayne — which was rare, but I took any chance I could.

Three people were promoted before me, and in August, almost a year to the day since my first promotion, I made Literary Agent.

I already had an impressive list of clients, and they started growing rapidly once I had the official title and the means to get things done my own way without jumping through as many hoops. Commission was steadily building, changing my income in ways I wasn't expecting, and Randall knew me by name, which I couldn't say for everyone in our office. It seemed I had made just as many friends as I had enemies — which meant I was doing something right.

Everything was looking up. Jamie and I were actually succeeding at being friends. We didn't talk all the time, but we texted when we could, and called each other from time to time. That familiar ache and burn was still there when we talked, especially when he brought up Angel, but it wasn't as loud, and I was busy enough not to let myself dwell on it. Everything was fine.

Everything was *just* fine.

The phone rang three times on September 3rd, on a gray, cool day in the city. I watched the drizzle settle like fog over Market Square out my window as I answered.

He said only three words, but it was everything he *didn't* say that I heard loudest. Because you see, I was waiting for him to tell me why. *How.* I was waiting for him to tell me he was kidding, or that I'd misheard him. I was waiting for him to take it back, to rewind time, to let me figure out how I hadn't seen it coming. But he didn't say any of that. He said only three words.

"I'm getting married."

I ended up in a bar that night — the bar right under my apartment building. I flipped a manicured middle finger up to the voice in my head telling me I was stronger, that Jamie Shaw rehab had worked, that I had a program I could follow to find solace. It was all bullshit. Those three words hit me over and over and over again, each time with more force, each hit reminding me *just friends* was *just impossible*. So, I self-medicated.

A Love Letter to Whiskey

Three shots of Fireball.
And then River walked in.

SEVENTEEN
My Cup of Tea

"YOU'RE *FUNNY*," I SAID, smiling as I poked River in the chest.

He quirked one brow, amused, and lifted his gin and tonic slowly to his lips. "Am I now?"

I nodded. "Mm-hmm." Then, I sipped my own drink — my water — because clearly I had had enough. In fact, I couldn't even remember why I said River was funny. Did he make a joke? I wasn't sure.

I wasn't sloppy drunk, but I was definitely solidly buzzed. My feet were warm, smile loose, eyes hazy. I was still dressed in the yoga pants and loose t-shirt I'd been wearing in my apartment, and I didn't even feel a little ashamed about it.

I thought it would make me feel better to drink, to get out of the house, but it didn't. That fact didn't stop me from word vomiting to River in the hopes that it could change.

"Did I tell you he asked me to be his *Best Lady*?" I laughed, stirring the black straws in my glass of water, wondering if it would turn to vodka if I stirred long enough.

"You did."

"You know. Like the best man, like his number one. Except I'm a girl."

"Right."

"I said yes, of course," I added quickly. "Because we're so close, and I love him, but like... *really?*" I shook my head. "It feels weird."

"Feels to *me* like this guy really did a number on you," River mused, turning to face me more head on. His legs were so long, stretching out to rest on the heels of my own bar stool. I looked at him more closely that night, noting the light tone of his hair, the brightness of his eyes, the way his hair was always so put together.

"Yeah," I finally whispered.

"So, I'm going to go out on a ledge here but... is the guy you've been talking about Jamie?"

The fog in my head cleared a little at the mention of his name. Suddenly, my brain kicked into overtime, thinking over everything we'd talked about that night. What had I told him? How much did I spill? I traced back, remembering that I told him an ex was getting married, which was actually kind of a lie, but easier to explain. I told him we hadn't been split up but a year, which was true. I'd told him about us ending on bad terms at first, but reconciling, remaining friends, and then the phone call.

So, not much. But still, enough.

Enough for me to feel oddly protective of Jamie's name. I didn't want him to be known as an asshole, because he wasn't. In all actuality, *I* was the asshole. I also didn't like the fact that River remembered Jamie's name. Had he really seen it that many times on my phone? And what if Jamie ever flew up here to visit me — would River treat him badly knowing all I'd just divulged?

Nothing was making sense, but I somehow found the response I felt was right.

"Nah, you don't know him. Just an ex."

"That you were dating last summer as an intern?"

River's gaze was questioning. Not accusatory, not prodding, just curious.

"We never actually *dated*, technically. Like, if you want to talk titles and all. I don't know. New topic," I said, waving the bartender down to refill my water.

River's hand darted out and grabbed the bottom of my bar stool. He tugged me closer, our knees touching, and he leaned in close. "You've been talking about this guy all night, and now when we're getting down to the root of it, you want a change of subject. Talk to me."

His hand was on mine now, not invasive, just resting there. I swallowed. "I don't know how I feel about any of it yet. I really don't. I came straight here, drank way too much, and now I can't think straight." The bartender topped off my water and I took a drink quickly. "I'm sure the hangover tomorrow will be a bitch — in more ways than one."

River's thumb grazed mine then. "I know it hurts right now, and I'm not going to sit here and bullshit you like it's going to stop hurting tomorrow. Clearly you love this guy, enough to swallow your pride and be beside him on the most important day of his life."

I gulped. *The most important day of his life, and I would be a supporting actress.*

"But I want to be the first to tell you, since clearly you haven't heard it yet," he added, leaning in just a bit more. I smelled the gin on his breath, mixed with evergreen. He leveled his blue eyes with mine. "You are, by *far*, the most spectacular woman I have ever met. You're bright, driven, intelligent, funny, kind — I could go on all night, B. I really could. And there is not one doubt in my mind that there are good men out there who would give anything just to have a *chance* to prove to you what you're worth." He swallowed then, and my mouth fell open slightly at his words. They were so sincere, his voice so steady. "And the line forms behind me."

His hand slipped from mine up my arm then, treading boldly to frame my jaw before curving around the nape of my neck. His eyes were steady as they fell to my lips, but unsure. He was waiting for me to tell him it was okay, and that night, whether it was a good decision or not, I told him.

I leaned closer, twisted my hands in the starch fabric of his dress shirt, and pulled his lips to mine.

It was wrong — it was all wrong. His lips weren't as full as Jamie's, his tongue worked too quickly against mine, his hands were cautious and slow. He didn't smell like honey and spice, he smelled like paper and ink — which was beautiful, but he just wasn't Whiskey.

266

And that's when I realized, he didn't have to be.

I wrapped my arms around his neck, deepening our kiss, shedding any remaining thoughts of Jamie and Angel. Of the wedding. Of that night in general. We barely broke our kisses long enough to make it up the elevator to my apartment, and once we were inside, neither of us said another word.

River was frantic with me, like he couldn't believe we were in my bed, like he'd been waiting years to get this chance. I realized maybe he had. I'd caught on to his flirting, but I never realized he felt how he said he did in the bar. He didn't just want me, he noticed me — the best parts of me, and just that alone made him sexy in my eyes.

I tried hard not to, but I compared every move he made to Whiskey. The way he kissed my neck, the way his fingers felt inside me, the way he looked when he came. It was nice with River — fun, sweet, almost a little too intimate. That night, he wasn't my shot of whiskey, but he was my cup of tea — and maybe that's what I needed. A change in pace, a new addiction, a fresh taste on my tongue.

At least, that's what I told myself that night. I repeated it in my head until River stepped out early the next morning and I called into work. Just like I'd predicted, the hangover hit me like a wall of a wave.

I'd gotten wasted the night before, numbed myself with booze and the hands of another man. But now, in the orange dawn of the morning after, I felt everything I'd worked so hard not to.

Jamie was getting married.

He would never be my Jamie again.

I wasn't supposed to still love him.

But I did.

• • •

"Later, B," Mona said, shrugging on her chic leather jacket and pulling her long ponytail free from the neck of it. "Don't stay at work too late on your last night before vacation."

I stood up to stretch, rolling my eyes. "I hardly call this a vacation."

"Hey. It's like eighty degrees where you're going. It's thirty here. It's a vacation, even if all you do is sit outside the airport."

"I'll send you a postcard from Terminal A."

She narrowed her eyes but smiled. "Brat. Travel safe. See you next week."

I waved, reaching my hands up high and cracking my neck before sitting back down at my desk. It was only five-thirty, still early as far as I was concerned, and even though I didn't really have much left to tie up before I left, I wasn't ready to leave just yet.

The truth was, I had become the master of avoiding in the seven months that had passed since the night Jamie called me with his big news. I'd gone back to business as usual, keeping myself busy and my mind off the wedding. Of course there was the dress I had to buy for the occasion, and the planning I had to do as his "Best Lady", but other than the few things Angel left in my hands, I'd mostly avoided.

It wasn't that I didn't talk to Jamie, because I did, but I just didn't allow myself to dwell on anything once we were off the phone. That was made easier by the nights I spent with River in my bed.

He was so different from Jamie.

It wasn't that he was a good different, nor that he was a bad different — he just was. What we had was casual, and he never asked me to talk about it — to name it — to figure it out. We just worked like we always had, hung out in the same group like we always had, and occasionally, we fell into each other's sheets. That was it. It was simple, and it was exactly what I needed. I was avoiding, and he was letting me.

Still, I felt it in his demeanor. The longer we went on like that, the more he wanted to ask the questions I was glad he wasn't asking. I didn't know how much longer I had until he asked them. I didn't know what I would say when he did.

I managed to kill another hour before I turned on my *out of office* email and powered down my computer. I stood, stretching again, and jumped when River's hands snuck up behind me and grabbed my waist.

"About time you got out of here."

I looked around us as I spun to face him, making sure we were alone in the office. It wasn't that it'd be an issue if we were together, more that neither of us wanted the unnecessary attention. "You know this is early for me."

"Yeah, but tonight is an exception," he reminded me, locking his fingers at the small of my back. We didn't touch like this very often, opting more for the kind of touches that went with fucking for hours. But it was nice to be held that evening. River's brows dropped, and he pulled me a little closer. "You ready for your big trip?"

"I think so."

"You want to talk about it?"

Avoid avoid avoid.

"Nah, I think I'm good." River pursed his lips and I swatted at his chest playfully, putting some space between us. "I'm serious."

"Fine. Want to pass the hours between now and boarding time, then?" He licked his lower lip before settling with an easy grin. Any other night and I would have taken him up on the offer, but for some reason his insinuation made my skin crawl.

"I really need to pack, actually," I said, grabbing my purse off my desk. We started walking together toward the elevator as I continued. "And sleep. Because Lord knows I won't be getting much of that once my plane touches down."

River laughed as the elevator door slid open. He held his arm out as I stepped in and followed behind me. "That's true. Still kind of weird to me that you're throwing him his bachelor party."

"It's casual, just a night out at his favorite local bar. He didn't want anything big." I shrugged. "It's actually my first time being in a wedding, so this is all kind of new to me. I'm glad he made it easy."

"Yeah. Isn't the bride doing some big trip?"

I nodded as the elevator hit the bottom floor, and we stepped out into the lobby of our office building, both of us tugging our coats on as we walked into the crisp spring air. "She and her girls are flying to New Orleans for a bachelorette bash. We'll see if she shows up to the wedding with beads still around her neck."

River smirked, tucking his hands into his pockets. For a few moments we just walked in silence, enjoying the sounds of the city as the sun set behind the buildings. It was mid-March and chilly, but I loved it. Thinking back to the sweltering months in Florida and how we hardly had a winter, I didn't really mind that the cold liked to hang around Pittsburgh for a good portion of the year. I liked the dry, fresh feel of the air. It was promising.

"Just try not to think too much about work this weekend, okay?" River said as we reached my apartment building. "Relax, have some fun, and if it gets to be too much, you can call me."

"Okay." I hugged him quickly, planting a kiss on his cheek before ducking into my building. "Have a good weekend, Riv."

"I mean it, you can call me," he said again as I let the door swing closed behind me. I turned with a smile and waved one last time. River's blonde hair was mussed in the cool wind, and in his light gray pea coat, he looked straight out of a men's fashion magazine. I chewed my lip as I stepped into my elevator, wondering if spending the night with him would be such a bad thing after all. But I really did need to pack, and more than that, I needed to face my thoughts.

I'd been spending so much time avoiding, thinking that would make it all go away, but the truth was I would be on a plane the next day and then I'd be there — in South Florida — with Jamie. With his fiancé.

It was time to really think about how I felt about that.

I packed slowly, blasting the latest album from a local indie band River had introduced me to. I contemplated pouring up a glass of wine, but decided I'd rather have a clear head that night. So, I made a root beer float, instead. It reminded me of my dad a little, because it used to be his favorite dessert, but it was one of the comforting memories I had of my dad. Sometimes when I thought of him I felt pain, sometimes I felt a warm sort of sadness — and a root beer float brought me that second kind of feeling.

Once my bag was packed for the weekend and my outfit for the next day laid out, I stripped off my clothes, tied my hair up on my head, and sank down into the scalding water of a bubble bath.

I was on my second float now, and I scooped out a bite of vanilla ice cream as the bubbles piled higher around me, counting the freckles on my thighs as they disappeared under the foam. I hummed along to the lyrics of the music still pouring in from my bedroom speaker, and once the tub was full and my float was gone, I sat my glass on the ground beside the tub and slid down farther.

My toes played with the faucet, letting in little drops of water as my thoughts finally started to soak in along with the hot water.

Jamie was getting married.

I took a deep, cleansing breath, closing my eyes for a moment before blinking them open again.

It hurt. That was the first thing I realized — the first thing I admitted. Knowing Jamie was marrying another woman hurt. It was a regretful sort of pain, a twisting knot of *what if* mixed with the notion that it didn't matter. It wasn't just that he was marrying another woman, it was that he loved her. I'd never loved another man in my life, not even Ethan. It was only Jamie.

So it hurt.

I was going to miss him. That was the second thought that had sunk in. I knew his fiancé had put up with me this past year and a half, but I also could tell by the tone of her voice that she wasn't my biggest fan. Once they were married, I knew she'd pressure him more and more to distance himself from me. Hell, she was more understanding than I think I would be in her position. I wanted to hate her for being suspicious of me, but the truth was she should have been — and I wouldn't blame her if she didn't want Jamie being as close with me as he was.

The last thing that sank in was the most surprising, and I sat up a little straighter in the tub as it hit me.

I was happy for him.

It hurt, I was going to miss him, but he was happy — really, really happy — and that made me happy, too. I had always been selfish when it came to Jamie. I wanted him even when I couldn't have him, when I *could* have him but wasn't ready to. But now, because I still loved him, I was going to put his happiness before mine. I was going to deal with the pain, if only for just that weekend, because he needed me to.

He was my best friend.

I wasn't sure if that would ever change. I was scared it would, I felt that gnawing possibility deep in my core.

Without even thinking, I reached for my phone, toweling off my hands before finding Jamie's name and tapping out a message.

— **I'm scared, Jamie...** —

I stared at the screen with the blinking curser, waiting for me to finish the text. My chest felt thick, my breath hard to find, and before I did something stupid, I hit the backspace until the screen was blank again and dropped my phone back to the floor.

"It'll be okay," I whispered to myself, closing my eyes and resting my head against the back of the tub.

That night, I didn't sleep. I tossed and turned, mind racing with strange, fleeting dreams of Jamie and me. Finally, around four in the morning, I gave up trying to rest and turned on The Piano Guys, letting myself drown in everything Jamie. I let the memories wash in, forgot to breathe for a while, and reveled in the crushing weight of it all.

Thinking back on it now, I loved the way it felt that night. My heart was broken — completely, utterly shattered — and I liked the way that pain felt. It reminded me I was alive, filled me with hope that what we had was real — even if it had technically never truly existed. Jamie was never officially mine, but I had always been his — ever since the first taste.

Losing him hurt like hell, but in the end I still smiled, because at least I'd got to have him.

One more weekend with Whiskey, and then I'd have to let him go.

For good.

EIGHTEEN
The Shakes

AS SOON AS MY plane touched down, before I even made it to baggage claim, I grabbed a Venti Iced Americano from Starbucks. Not sleeping the night before an early flight and seeing Jamie for the first time in over a year had been a mistake, and I was feeling a strange mix of exhaustion and nerves. I figured why not add caffeine to the mix?

Sipping from the bright green straw as I took the escalator down to baggage claim, I focused on my breathing. I thought of the hot yoga class I'd taken with Mona a few months before and tried to channel that frame of mind, and it worked — at least until I opened my eyes again and saw him.

God, Whiskey had aged beautifully.

He was no longer the boy I knew. His features had shifted, even in that short year and a half we'd been apart. His jaw was always the first feature I noticed, and it was even more pronounced now, framing the smirk that rested on his lips as he held up a piece of notebook paper that said *JUST B* in big, sloppy handwriting. I smiled, and it made him grin wider, flashing white teeth and bright honey eyes. I stepped off the bottom step of the escalator and we each took three steps until we were standing face to face. He dropped the paper to his side, and we both took our time drinking the other in. His hair was short again, styled, almost like River's. He was dressed in dark jeans and a white v-neck t-shirt, but he wore a light-blue button-up over it. None of the buttons were fastened and it was cuffed at his elbows, showcasing toned forearms that told me without words that he was still surfing.

The barrel had aged him well, and even with the Angel's tax, he'd only gotten better over time. He was still just as potent, stinging my nostrils and making my mouth water. But now, his flavors had matured, his color had smoothed, and I knew without hesitation that if I was brave enough to try to taste him and he was stupid enough to let me, I'd never recover.

My eyes found his again and he let out a short laugh, opening his arms wide. "Come here."

I adjusted my carry-on bag on my shoulder and stepped into him, smelling the spicy oak of his shirt as he wrapped his arms all the way around me. Inhaling deep, I sighed into him, and I think we both felt it — like a piece of our soul had been found again. Like it was slowly melding itself back into place. "I told you not to come, I could have taken a cab."

"I guess I still haven't learned how to listen very well."

"You have learned how to dress, though," I said, my voice muffled in his shirt.

He chuckled, pulling back and grabbing my small bag from me. "And you learned how to walk in heels." His eyes dropped to my feet and one brow quirked. When he looked at me again, I swore I felt a heat behind his gaze.

I swallowed, tucking away a rogue strand of hair. "That's what happens when you dress business casual everyday."

"I know the feeling," he said, nodding toward the carousel with the bags from Pittsburgh. "I miss wearing basketball shorts or swim trunks ninety percent of the time."

"And I miss tank tops and sandals."

It was small talk. It was stupid. But we were treading lightly, testing the waters, feeling each other out.

Jamie grabbed my bag off the carousel, not letting me take it no matter how I argued, and then we were making our way to the parking lot. We didn't say much, a few sentences of small talk, Jamie telling me which way to turn to find where he'd parked. Once we reached his Jeep, he loaded my bags into the back and opened the passenger seat door for me.

"Welcome home, B," he said as I slid in. I wasn't sure if he meant South Florida or his Jeep.

The problem was, something had changed since the last time I'd been *home*. Mom was no longer here, Jenna was, but she was out of town, and Jamie's Jeep suddenly felt uncomfortable. I sat with my hands in my lap, trying not to be obvious about the way my eyes stuck on the evidence of another woman being in my spot. There was a hair-tie wrapped around the gear shift, a pair of women's running shorts in the back seat, a small picture of the two of them tucked into the corner of Jamie's dashboard. I didn't sink back and kick my shoes off, planting my heels on the dash in front of me. No, I sat rigid, hands folded in my lap, and looked out the window as Jamie drove me to my hotel.

"You okay over there?" he asked as we made a left turn.

I nodded. "Just tired. Long night."

Jamie didn't say anything else until he dropped me off at check in.

"You sure you don't want me to wait?"

He grabbed my bags from the back and sat them down in front of me. I watched as every muscle in his back moved with the gesture, and it took me a second to find an answer to his question. "No, it's fine. I think I need a quick nap," I lied. There was no way I was sleeping, but I didn't want to have to spend more time with Angel than was required.

"Okay," he conceded, though he looked a little disappointed. "Just remember we're doing the rehearsal 'dinner' kind of early since Angel and the girls have to catch a flight out for their bachelorette. Can you be at the country club at three?" He shifted, running a hand over the back of his head. "I would pick you up then, but I kind of have to be there earlier, and I know you want to sleep so…"

"I'll catch a cab over. Don't worry about me, Jamie Shaw," I teased, nudging him as I swung my carry on over my shoulder again. He seemed to relax a little then, and tucked his hands into his pockets.

"Never do."

He didn't make a move to leave at first. We stood, staring, our eyes saying more than our words as always.

Finally, he cleared his throat. "See you in a bit."

With that, he rounded the Jeep and I turned, rolling my bag behind me. After I checked in, I collapsed on the cool comforter of the bed and let out a long, slow breath.

Here we go.

• • •

"B!" Sylvia ran toward me as soon as I walked into the dining room where the rehearsal dinner was being held. The country club was small but grand, and even in the brand new rose-colored lace dress and nude pumps I was wearing, I felt underdressed. Sylvia hit me like a wall and I stumbled back with a smile as she hugged me. "You're here!"

"I am."

She pulled back, still holding my arms in her hands as she called out behind her. "Mom! Dad! B's here!"

Sylvia was Jamie's youngest sister, and the only one I'd really ever gotten close with. I'd met Santana a few times, mostly during holidays, but we'd never really connected the way Sylvia and I had. She still called me sometimes, and when I moved back from Alder, she helped Jenna keep me sane.

"So good to see you, sweetheart," Rhonda, Jamie's

mom said as she moved in next, kissing my cheeks. "Isn't it so great to see her, Wes?"

"It really is. How was your flight?" His dad asked next, throwing his arm over my shoulder to walk me over to the group gathered near a large table setting.

"A little bumpy getting out of the fog in Pittsburgh, but fine after that." I smiled at both of them, my heart warming. For some reason it meant a lot to me that they remembered me, that they were excited to see me, that they seemed to care about me being in their son's life.

Sylvia took my purse and dropped it at the table setting next to where she was sitting, grabbing my hand in a squeeze before scampering off again. And then, I realized it was quiet.

Everyone was staring at me. I wish I was exaggerating, but literally every eye was on me. I noticed Claire first, recognizing her from our short conversation in the bar the night I'd first seen Jamie and Angel together. Her eyes were narrowed, like it was clicking into place for her, and when I looked to the next person for relief, I didn't find it. Because the next person over was Angel.

It was the first time I was really seeing her, since I'd avoided photos on social media. She was beautiful, which annoyed me, with bright blonde, pixie-cut hair and fluorescent green eyes that popped against her tan skin. She was taller than me, even in the heels I was wearing, and I tried standing a little straighter to compensate. Her short white dress wrapped high around her neck where a chunky gold necklace sat, and everything about her screamed regal. She was put together, sophisticated — like she belonged in that country club.

And I certainly did not.

She kept her eyes on me, mouth pursed, and I scanned the rest of the crowd staring me down unapologetically. They must have been her family. I was starting to panic, my chest tight and sweat beading on my neck when Jamie stepped through the door with three other guys — the groomsmen.

They all came in laughing, and when the silence hit them, Jamie must have felt me. He turned from his buddy he'd been talking to and his eyes locked on mine immediately. "Well look who made it."

He was apparently oblivious to the death threats I was getting via eye laser beams because he crossed the room without a single hesitation, wrapped his arms around me, picked me up, and spun me twice before setting me back down. Then, he kissed my cheek, and threw his arm around my shoulder like his dad had.

"Looks like everyone is here now," he said to the group, who was still staring at me — more specifically, at Jamie's arm around me. "What's first on the agenda, my beautiful bride?"

That question seemed to jolt life back into the room, and a few of Angel's bridesmaids scurried off to grab provisions while Angel stepped forward. Her parents joined forces with Jamie's behind her, but she was too busy forcing a smile to hear what anyone was saying.

"You must be B," she said, lips as tight as the creases at her eyes. "I'm Angel. It's so nice to finally meet you." She thrust out her hand and I took it with an awkward smile. Jamie's arm was still around me.

"Man, this must be heaven," Jamie said, pulling her under the other arm. "My two favorite girls in one place. I'm the luckiest man alive."

Angel sneered a little before popping on her fake smile again, and I tried to ignore the sinking feeling in my chest at his words. Shrugging out from his grasp, I cleared my throat and pointed to the table. "Are we eating first, Angel? Or do you need any help getting everyone rallied for the walk-through?"

"Well aren't you a peach," she said, and it was the first time I noted a hint of twang in her voice. "We'll practice first, that way they have a little more time to finish the food. But don't worry, I got this." She winked up at Jamie and then put two delicate fingers between her lips and produced the loudest wolf whistle I'd ever heard. "People!"

The room stopped bustling as soon as she yelled, and my eyes widened along with Sylvia's.

"Let's do one quick walk-through outside before we sit down to eat. And I do mean quick. I also mean *once*, so pay attention to Bailey and then we'll have dinner and gifts." She turned to a short, plump woman in dress slacks and a light pink polo then, who I assumed was Bailey. She clapped her hands together and started ushering us all to our positions, and I stopped by my purse to pop two ibuprofen before making my way outside.

So far, it was just as bad as I thought it'd be.

My headache turned out not to be my biggest issue. In fact, it was nausea, and it hit me as soon as I saw the look on Jamie's face when Angel fake-walked down the aisle to him. Her bridesmaids were practically swooning out of their dresses because Jamie completely stole the show. He looked at her exactly like he should — like he couldn't believe he was lucky enough to have her, like there was no one else in the world for him.

I felt so sick by the time we sat down to eat that it was physically impossible to even try. So, I pushed the food around on my plate as much as I could and took microscopic bites between conversation with Sylvia and Jamie's parents. His older sister wouldn't be in until the day of the wedding, but I was actually okay with it because the four of us were cracking each other up at our end of the table. It felt sort of split, the families, instead of united by a marriage. Jamie sat on the other end with Angel, her family, and the bridesmaids, while I sat with his family on my left and the groomsmen across from us.

Jamie was clearly the life of the party at the other end, and I could tell just in those two short hours that Angel's family was smitten with him. Everyone was. Jamie was charming, he always had been, and I was pretty sure he could woo the panties off a nun if he really put his mind to it.

That didn't make me feel any better, though.

Still, from time to time, when my eyes would skirt their way to that end of the table, I'd find his staring right back at me. He watched me as he tipped back his small tumbler of whiskey, poured neat. He found me when everyone laughed around him, as if I was what was grounding him to the room, to the present moment. Every time he looked at me, my stomach reacted, and I hated myself for it.

I didn't know how to be Jamie's friend. That was clear now more than ever.

"Alright, you rowdy bunch, simmer down," Jamie said, standing with his whiskey firmly in hand. "The girls need to get to the airport, but before they go, we have a few gifts we'd like to give out."

Angel stood with him then, and they held each other close as the bridesmaids distributed gifts to the parents and siblings. They were classic — delicate necklaces for the moms, custom money holders for the dads, and small personalized gifts for each sibling. It was nice watching Jamie's parents open their gifts, especially seeing the tears well in Wesley's eyes as he clapped Jamie hard on the back in a man hug.

"Of course, we couldn't forget about our bridal party!" Angel added, her short blonde hair bouncing a little as she ducked under the table and retrieved additional gifts. She passed them down the table, and Sylvia handed me mine just as everyone else started tearing into their gifts.

For a moment I just watched them. I was nervous to open mine for some reason. Maybe because this was the first time I'd ever received a gift from Jamie, even if it was an obligatory one, or maybe because I was the only girl in his bridal party. When I saw the guys all pull out leather flasks with their names etched into the side, I breathed a sigh of relief. That was a neutral gift, one he could easily get for me.

I reached into the lavender bag that matched the wedding colors Angel had picked out and sifted through the tissue paper, but my hands found something hard and shaped like a hockey disc. I frowned, pulling it into my lap as everyone else continued to buzz about their own gifts. I looked up, but no one was looking at me.

Except Jamie.

He was smirking, waiting for me to see what he'd gotten me, and the nerves were instantly back because it damn sure wasn't a flask. There was a card stuck to the disc object that was still wrapped in tissue paper.

> *Thanks for always knowing exactly what I need.*
> *I couldn't do this without you. — Jamie*

My cheeks flushed, and I didn't chance another look to see if Jamie was still watching me. Carefully, I unfolded the tissue paper, and then, I snort-laughed.

Everyone's necks snapped in synchronicity, and once again, all attention was on me — exactly where I *didn't* want it at the moment, because I couldn't stop laughing. Tears glossed my eyes and I knew my face must have been the reddest shade as I tried to find my breath. Everyone was staring at me, but I was only looking at Jamie.

"What? What is it?" Impatient, Sylvia snatched the gift from my hands, breaking my eye contact with Jamie. She frowned. "*Devil Cat Board Wax*," she read, and I lost myself in another fit of giggles. This time, Jamie cracked up, too.

And the entire room turned to look at him.

He bent at the waist, holding up his hand not holding whiskey. "Sorry, inside joke."

Angel's eyes jetted to me then, and I almost felt my skin melt off my face from her glare. I probably should have reacted in a mature way by putting the gift away and turning the attention on her somehow, but in that moment, I didn't care what she thought. I smiled, caught Jamie's eyes once more, then Sylvia handed the wax back to me and I tucked it away.

In that moment, I realized he was still my Jamie — even if just a little bit.

When dinner was wrapped, the girls hugged and kissed everyone goodbye before making their way to the airport. The excitement radiated off them, and Jamie didn't seem nervous in the slightest that his bride-to-be was jetting off to one of the top party cities in the nation for a two-night bender before their big day.

Angel, on the other hand, had no problem showcasing her insecurity. Jamie was gathered where his parents and I had set up camp when she came rushing over, throwing her arms around him and kissing him in a way I was sure Wesley and Rhonda could have lived forever without seeing. She made sure I saw her tongue against his, her hands in his hair, his on the small of her back. When her eyes popped open, they were still kissing, and she narrowed them at me before pulling back.

"I'll miss you," she cooed, fixing his shirt. "Behave, okay?"

"Always." Jamie kissed her again, his a little more parent-friendly, and Angel gave me one last pointed look before joining her bridesmaids. They hooted and hollered as they left the room and then the two families set to work gathering up anything left behind.

As soon as she left, I could breathe a little easier. My hands found my ribs and I forced a breath against the tight fabric of my dress.

"You good?" Jamie asked.

"Yeah, just ready to get out of this dress," I said without thinking. I meant it exactly as I said it — I was ready for zipperless pants and a wireless bra — but when I turned to face him with a smile, there was that whiskey burn behind his irises.

"We should go out. The guys all have work tomorrow, but I took off. And it's early," he said, checking his watch. It wasn't even six yet, but I knew for sure that the last thing I should do is go out with Jamie alone.

"I'm actually still pretty beat," I whispered, clearing my throat to find a stronger voice for my next statement. "Probably going to stop by and see a few friends and then turn in early."

Jamie's face fell. "Oh, yeah. Okay." He shrugged his hands into his pockets and nodded to the gift bag hanging from my wrist. "So, you like the gift?"

I grinned then. "You're such an ass. Rory would have liked you."

He laughed, tucked me under his arm, and we walked out together. I turned down his offer for a ride back to the hotel, insisting he stay behind with his family and I'd catch a cab. I had lied, I didn't have any stops to make, anyone to see, and I went straight back to the hotel. I took a long, hot shower, dressed more comfortably, and kicked back on the bed with an audible sigh.

Flicking the television on, I debated calling River, but thought better of it. After an hour of watching *Family Guy*, I turned the TV off again and pushed a breath through flat lips.

It was nine o'clock.

On a Friday.

"This is pathetic," I murmured, hopping off the bed and sliding into my sandals. I didn't bother putting on makeup or changing, just grabbed my hotel key and purse and made my way downstairs.

I was suddenly craving whiskey.

• • •

Thank God for DoubleTree.

Those were the words I whispered under my breath as I munched on a free, hot cookie and drank Crown Royal black on the rocks at the hotel bar. I'd struck up a casual conversation with the bartender, Beuford, but for the most part I just sipped and snacked, watching the sports highlights on the television above the liquor bottles. I had no idea what any of it meant, the extent of my sports experience being the games I watched in high school and the four Pirate games I'd managed to make it to with the crew from work. Even then, I had no idea what was going on — I just cheered and booed along with everyone else.

It might have only been a touch less pathetic than lying in my hotel bed, but I felt good about my decision to mosey down to the bar. There were a few others around me, one man about my age at the end of the bar who was still dressed in business attire with a conference name tag hanging around his neck, two older couples conversing at a table behind me in the cushioned seating area, and from time to time, families would breeze past on their way out or to the pool. Just having the noise and other people around me made me feel better, and truthfully, it was about all the social interaction I could handle at that point.

The day had been hard.

I knew going into the weekend that it would be, but seeing Jamie with Angel had kicked me in the groin harder than I thought it would. It was easy to repeat the words to myself in a bathtub miles away — *Jamie is getting married* — but actually seeing him with his fiancé was a completely different story. It burned, it *seared*, it scarred.

Sighing, I took a long pull from my glass and ate the last of my cookie, brushing my fingers off just as the seat beside me was pulled out.

"That's more like it," Jamie said, and I paused mid-chew with the cookie still in my mouth. He eyed my glass, lowering down on the stool and waving a finger at the bartender. "I saw you nursing a glass of water at the rehearsal dinner."

I dry-swallowed the rest of the cookie and lifted my glass. "Yeah well, I wasn't in the mood to drink then."

"What changed your mind?"

"I'm sure you could guess."

The bartender placed a napkin in front of Jamie and he ordered his own Crown Black, poured neat, after confirming that's what I had in my glass. He took the first sip and sighed.

"You know, I'd like to say I'm surprised to see you here, but I guess I shouldn't be, huh?"

He shrugged. "You act like I don't know you." His hand was still wrapped loosely around his glass as he angled himself toward me. "I figured you'd get back here, realize it was early and you can't sleep after all, and end up here. I didn't know for sure," he added. "But I guess tonight, luck was on my side."

I picked up my glass and twirled it in my wrist, shifting the ice. "Guess so."

Jamie was staring at me in that way he always did, and for the first time in my life I wished he'd stop. "You're not okay, are you." It was a question, but he said it as a statement. "With all of this, I mean."

"I'm fine."

He sighed, running a hand through his hair and looking up at the basketball highlights on the screen before facing me again. "You don't have to do this, okay? You can leave, I can—"

"Don't be ridiculous, Jamie," I cut him off, forcing the most genuine smile I could muster. "What are you going to do? Refund me for the dress hanging in my room? For the flight here and back? Don't be dumb. Plus, I wouldn't miss this for anything. I love you," my voice cut off a little at the end of that profession, but I smoothed it over. "I want to be here. It's hard, and I'm always honest with you so I won't deny that, but I don't want to leave."

It wasn't a lie. Even if he told me I could leave and he'd pay me back for everything, I wouldn't. It hurt to be here, but it would hurt worse not to be — to be miles away wondering what he looked like, how they were together, what song they danced to, what color the stupid cake was. It was a sick sort of torture in a way, but I wanted to be with him — even if I couldn't be *with* him.

"Are you sure?" His brows bent and I reached out, squeezing his forearm.

"I'm sure." His eyes fell to my hand, and I retracted it, grabbing my drink again. Being around Jamie without being able to touch him was like drinking decaf coffee. It didn't satisfy. The buzz was within reach, yet completely unattainable at the same time. "Besides, you'll pay me back. One day I'll be the one getting married, and I'll expect you to be there."

He was still staring at his arm where my hand had been, and his jaw ticked a little then. He reached for his own drink, but his eyes stayed down. "I'm happy. I love her, B. I really do."

The knife twisted low, but I swallowed back the gasp. "I know."

"But I still love you, too." He lifted his eyes to mine then. "I don't know if that will ever change."

I didn't have to ask what he meant, because I knew. I felt it in everything that I was. Jamie Shaw was a part of me, and he would be forever. "I hope it doesn't."

He smiled, tentatively reaching his hand out to touch my cheek. I leaned into his palm and we both exhaled together, laughing softly.

"Ugh," Jamie said, thumbing my cheek bone before dropping his hand and shaking out his shoulders. "Okay, enough with the heavy. Catch me up on everything. How's work? Still kicking ass? Randall planning your next promotion?"

The conversation was easy from there. I filled him in on my life and he did the same for his. I wasn't shocked to hear his dad was already talking about Jamie's plan to partner at the firm, and my heart swelled with pride before a hard pinch hit it at the thought that Jamie was exactly where he always wanted to be. He was working at the firm, getting married, on his way to kids. It was all happening. I wasn't a part of it, and yet I was. We had always existed in the in-between, and I guessed we always would.

We laughed a lot that night, bullshitting and reminiscing on times past. He asked me if I had a boyfriend, in about seven creative ways, and I skirted the question each time, leaving whatever was happening between River and me completely off the table. We took what we needed from each other and that was all. The truth was, I didn't have time for a boyfriend — and I was okay with walking alone for a while.

"I guess I should probably let you sleep," Jamie said as I yawned, my third glass of whiskey now empty. He checked his watch and then studied me again, biting his lower lip. "You know, we should go surfing tomorrow."

"What?"

He nodded. "I mean, why not? We don't have any plans until the bachelor party tomorrow. The guys have to go pick up their tuxes after work and I'll be bored out of my mind and probably make myself sick with nerves if I'm alone all day."

"I think you're forgetting one key issue," I said, pausing to see if he'd fill in the blanks. When he didn't, I sighed. "I don't have a board anymore, remember?" Tucking my hands under my thighs against the leather barstool, I shrugged. "Mom sold everything when she and Wayne bought that boat — including my old lime green board."

"I know."

Jamie was just staring at me, goofy smile and glossy whiskey eyes. I quirked a brow. "Okay... so then you know I don't have a board for us to go surfing tomorrow. Unless I rent one, which sounds awful."

"You don't have to rent. You have a board."

He stood then, pulling out enough cash to pay for both of our tabs. I went to stop him, but my mind was too busy trying to wrap itself around what he was saying. "I don't understand."

He grabbed my wrists, tugging me forward off the barstool and wrapping me in a hug. He rested his chin on my head for a second, then pulled back with his hands still on my arms. "You didn't honestly think I'd let your mom sell your board to some random, did you?"

My mouth fell open, but Jamie didn't seem fazed at all, just tucked his wallet back in his pocket with an easy smile. "You bought my board?"

"Of course I did." He winked, and it took every last ounce of self-control I had to stop myself from springing forward. I wanted to kiss him, *hard.* I wanted him in my bed, his hands on me, my lips on him. No one loved me like Jamie did, and I hadn't yearned for one last night with him until that exact moment.

But he backed away, still facing me, taking three long strides with a cocky grin in place before he turned and called over his shoulder. "Pick you up at seven."

NINETEEN

Clean

I WAS FINALLY HOME.

Jamie sat on his board beside me, both of us straddling and waiting for the next wave. It was early, the sun struggling to rise in front of us, and the water was still chilly from the winter, but it was home. I traced the black designs on my board, stomach warm at the fact that Jamie had bought it from my mom. He'd stored it, kept it just in case I came back home. It seemed so little, but said so much.

"There's nothing like this," I whispered as a tame wave rolled under us. Jamie turned to face me, but I kept my eyes on the horizon. "There are so many amazing things to see, so many different cities and places, but nothing compares to the way you feel sitting on a board, waiting for a wave."

Jamie followed my gaze. "I know. It teaches you patience, reminds you how insignificant you really are while also somehow making you feel invincible, too."

"Like a soul cleanse or something."

He nodded. "It's not the same without you either, you know." His right foot brushed mine under the water. "It's weird. I surfed before I met you, I surfed all the time after you left Alder, and I still surf now that you're gone, but it just feels different when you're not here. Same board, same waves..." His voice trailed off. "Different vibes."

I smiled, squinting against the strengthening sun as I peered over at him. "Always such a charmer, Jamie Shaw." He blushed, and I swore it was the first time I'd ever seen it happen. "You're going to have to tone that down once you have a wedding band on your finger."

He laughed. "I think Angel will scare all the girls away without any help from me."

"No shit," I agreed quickly. "Like a pit bull in a sundress, that one."

"She loves me, and she's not afraid to go to bat for me if she has to," he said, and even though I didn't think he meant it to be a jab at me, it felt like one anyway. Jamie blew out a breath on a laugh then. "Holy shit, B. I'm getting married. *Tomorrow.*"

He lifted a brow at me, shaking his head as one of the brightest smiles I'd ever seen spread on his face. He really was so happy, and in that moment, I was, too.

"You ready?" I asked.

He stared at my hands on my board, thinking. "Yeah. I am. I really am."

When his eyes found mine again, they were tinged with just the smallest hint of sadness. I think he saw it mirrored in my own, and he kept my gaze there, not letting me look away. We both felt it in that moment, the reality of it all. He was gaining the woman he'd love for the rest of his life, but he was losing me in the process. Maybe not all the way, but we both knew it would never be the same after that weekend.

We didn't let ourselves mourn, though.

We surfed all morning, skin tight with sun and salt by the time we loaded up our boards and grabbed a quick bite to eat at one of the beach bars. We talked, we laughed, and for a few hours, it was just us. For all we knew, it'd be the last hours we'd ever have alone together, and we spent them wisely.

When we climbed back into his Jeep, I kicked off my sandals and propped my sandy feet on his dashboard, leaning back against the leather seat with a sigh. I closed my eyes, head dropping back against the headrest, and then I felt Jamie's hand on mine.

I turned my wrist, palm facing up to find his as his fingers wrapped around mine. Head still back, I turned to face him, cracking my eyes open slowly. For just a flash of a second, we were seventeen again, and I remembered that first night in his Jeep like it was happening in that moment. Jamie asked me something then, not with words but with a longing look. He wanted to say something, but it was stuck in his throat, and I knew it was better if he didn't say it out loud at all. So I squeezed his hand, and he gave me a tight smile before pulling his hand from mine and sparking the engine to life.

Looking back, we were stupid to think everything would work out. What did we expect, really? I'm not sure.

The truth was we were acknowledging the fact that he was getting married while simultaneously ignoring it, too. It was a dangerous dance, neither one of us leading, both of us waiting for a cue from the other that would never come.

Jamie decided on a whim that he wanted to go camping for his bachelor party instead of just going to the bar. It seemed like such a small thing, an impulse decision, a fun reroute in the weekend, but it ended up being the first domino that brought the rest down in a loud, beautifully chaotic crash.

And all we could do was watch it happen. In slow motion and lightning speed all at once.

• • •

Jamie had the strangest group of groomsmen.

As if having me as his "best man" wasn't already weird enough, he didn't have a single guy in his party who he'd known for longer than three years. Two of them were buddies from work, and the other was Angel's older brother. Don't get me wrong, he seemed close with all of them, but it was strange to me that he didn't have a more personal connection to the guys standing beside him on his big day. I realized then that Jamie was particular about whom he opened up to, who he let in, and I couldn't believe I'd never noticed that about him before.

The two guys from work were Ryan and Charlie, and they couldn't have been bigger opposites. Ryan was tall and lean, with strawberry blonde hair and more freckles on his cheeks than me. He was hilarious, always cracking jokes, and he and Jamie were like two peas in a circus pod when they were together. Charlie, on the other hand, was a dick. At least, that's how I perceived him. He was tall, too, but every inch of him was muscle. He had dark skin, dark hair, dark eyes, and he wore a constant frown. He never joined in on jokes with the other guys, and he seemed to always be scrutinizing me, like he was suspicious of me. Maybe he was, I couldn't be sure because he did everything he could to avoid talking to me. Jamie showed him a high level of respect, and I wondered if that grew out of work or personal experience, but didn't care enough to ask.

Angel's brother, Andrew, looked just like her. Blonde hair, tan skin, bright green eyes. He seemed a little suspicious of me just like Charlie, but he was nice to me, and actually talked to me more than the other two combined. He was nice, but I couldn't see a strong vibe between him and Jamie. I wondered if he was just in the party because Angel wanted him to be, but again, I didn't care enough to ask.

Still, oddball bunch that we were, we were having a blast. We'd packed Jamie's Jeep and Charlie's truck with camping gear, way too much food and an obnoxious amount of booze and headed out to the springs. I'd never set up a tent before, and to be honest we all kind of sucked at it, but we figured it out eventually, with the help of Bud Light, of course. It was so low key and casual after that, just the five of us hanging around a fire drinking and eating and laughing. We set up a table and played drinking games, which I hadn't played since college, and I found out that though my surfing skills hadn't waned

298

over the years, my ability to get a stupid white ping pong ball into a red plastic cup had.

It was an easy night, relaxed, and that's just what Jamie wanted. I loved him even more for that, for not wanting strippers and gambling and cigars. No one in the group seemed to care that we weren't out on the town, either. We were all content, and for a while, I relaxed. The weekend hadn't been so bad after all.

But it wasn't over yet.

"You know, most girls would have been annoying in this situation," Charlie said to me later that night when we were all sitting around the fire. Jamie was in the middle of telling Andrew a story and Ryan had already passed out in his tent.

"What do you mean?"

He shrugged, still not smiling. He *never* smiled. "I don't know. Some girls say they're 'one of the guys', but really that just means they fake interest in sports or cars or something else to seem cool and secretly hope they'll get pined after. I kind of expected you to be like that."

"And did I surprise you?"

"Kind of." He sniffed. "I mean, you clearly know nothing about sports, but you don't pretend to. You're just yourself. And it should be weird for you to be camping with a group of guys, but it's not. You're not flirting with any of us, you're not saying stupid shit." I thought he was going to continue, it sounded that way, but he just stopped talking, and I cracked a smile.

"So then why only kind of?"

Charlie drained the last of his beer, crushing the cup and tossing it into the bag we'd set aside for recycling.

"You may not be a fake chick trying to be one of the guys, but you are in love with Jamie." His hard eyes landed on me then and the smile fell from my lips. "You're keeping your cool on the surface, but I see it. You and Jamie are both playing with fire, and I don't want to be here when everything goes up in flames."

My heart was racing, and as much as I wanted to be pissed at his accusatory tone, I didn't blame him for it. "I wouldn't... I would never..."

He stood. "I don't doubt you. But you're also not the one I'm worried about." His eyes were on Jamie then, and Jamie's were on me. I looked back up at Charlie, and he cocked a brow. "You wouldn't make the first move, but what would you do if he did?"

I opened my mouth, but clamped it shut again because the question was rhetorical. Charlie didn't even wait for an answer.

"See you guys in the morning," he called over the fire, retreating into his tent before anyone responded.

"Yeah, I should probably turn in, too," Andrew said.

Jamie threw his arms up, spilling a little beer out of his cup with the motion. "Oh come on! It's not even one yet!"

"You get married tomorrow, remember champ?" Andrew said, smiling and clapping Jamie on the back as he stood. "We all have to be up and out of here pretty early."

Jamie laughed. "Yeah yeah, fine. Pansies."

Andrew flicked him off and I chuckled as he disappeared into his tent.

"What about you over there?" Jamie asked, eying me over the edge of his cup as he took a drink.

Charlie's words were in my head, and I almost told Jamie I was going to turn in, too. But he was clearly nervous about the next day, that's what I saw that the other guys had missed, and he wasn't ready to sleep. Everyone else had bailed, but I wasn't going to do that to him. Shaking off Charlie's warning, I moved to sit in the chair next to Jamie.

"Sleep is overrated."

He smiled, his glazed eyes holding mine. "You're the best, B."

"And don't you forget it." I cheers-ed his plastic cup with mine and we both drank, not needing to say anything else.

For a while we just talked, a little about the wedding and a lot about everything but. Somehow we ended up on our phones, taking turns showing each other stupid videos on YouTube and laughing until we cried. I'd just pulled up a video of a prank gone wrong that I knew Jamie would get a kick out of when nature called.

"Here, watch this," I said, shoving my phone into his hands and standing. "I have to find a bush to pee in."

He laughed. "Gross."

I curtsied, then skipped off behind the tents.

I had almost made it. I had almost escaped the weekend without much more than a bruised heart. But when I made my way back to the fire, Jamie held my phone in his hand, but he wasn't looking at it anymore. His elbows were on his knees, eyes on the flames, and I could see the wheels spinning. I slowed as I reached him, not even bothering to take my seat. I just stared at him, the dirt stains on his t-shirt, the way the firelight battled the shadows of the night on his face. It felt like an eternity stretched between us before he stood, holding my phone screen-side out toward me. "You kept my voicemails?"

I glanced at the screen, seeing my voicemail log, all filled with his name. I swallowed, taking the phone from him and clicking the screen light off before tucking it in my back pocket, my hand staying there. "Yes."

"You used to listen to them, those years when I was at Alder." It wasn't a question.

"Yes."

He nodded, swallowing. "Do you still listen to them?"

An ache zinged through my chest and I crossed my arms over it. "Sometimes."

Jamie lifted his eyes to me then, brows pinched together. "Why? You can call me, B. Anytime."

I laughed. "Yeah, I don't think your fiancé would have appreciated another woman calling you at two in the morning."

His eyes fell to my legs, and for a moment I thought he was going to argue with me, but he thought better of it. Up until that point, Jamie had been fooling himself. He thought he could marry Angel and keep me, too — but he couldn't. Not the way he wanted to. I didn't envy him, because I knew he loved her — I knew he cared for her. But he was a slave to the way he felt about me. I knew, because I was in the same shackles.

"We should get some sleep," he finally said.

"Yeah" I sighed, tucking my hair behind my ear before sliding past him toward my tent. "Night."

My shoulder brushed his bicep as I passed, and his hand shot out, wrapping around my wrist. I stilled, and he pulled me into him, wrapping his arms around my waist. At first I stood there, arms still by my side, but slowly, I trailed them up over his arms to latch my hands behind him. He buried his face into my neck, barely breathing, and the fire crackled next to us, giving the air the energy to keep us spellbound.

"Goodnight," he said, but he was still holding me. His hands gripped my waist, and a low groan rumbled in his throat. That one sound was directly linked to the heat that had settled in a pool low in my stomach and it sprung to life, filling me, clouding my head. Jamie angled just an inch, his lips grazing the skin of my neck, and I shivered. His breath was hot, laced with alcohol and the same honey sweetness I remembered so well. Just that one touch from his lips sent flashes of our nights together behind my eyes — his fingers inside me on the beach, his mouth on me in his kitchen, his eyes on me while I touched myself for him miles away in Pittsburgh. It all rushed in, and it was too much. My self-control was already a futile thing, and now it was virtually deceased.

"Jamie..."

As soon as his name left my lips, I regretted it — because I meant it as a warning, but it came out as a plea — and Jamie answered, effectively snapping the energy band that had been white hot and electric between us since I landed. His tongue dragged the length of my neck, teeth biting my jaw softly before his lips claimed mine. We both inhaled together, hearts racing as my arms tightened around his neck and his fingers bruised my hips.

I whimpered against his mouth, everything inside me screaming to stop while my hands pulled him closer. I was clawing at his back, dragging my nails through his hair, begging him not to stop when I should have been throwing him off. He kissed me just like he always had, full lips and expert tongue, hands strong and possessive.

My eyes shot open, scanning the tents, heart racing at the thought of one of the guys hearing us or worse — seeing us. As if he read my mind, Jamie backed me into his tent, breaking contact long enough to yank his shirt over his head and drop it next to his sleeping bag as he lowered me down. His hands were frantic as he spread my legs with his own, the friction of his shorts on mine stoking the fire we'd been trying so hard to extinguish before now. I couldn't catch a breath, my eyes hooded, brain clouded, heart heavy and aching with every drag of his teeth across my flesh.

He ran his hand down my thigh, hooking behind my knee and hiking my leg up high as he flexed into me harder. I moaned, eyes rolling back, self-control obliterated. His fingers slid around the back of my thigh and brushed under my shorts, running the length of my panties, and then my eyes shot open and I pressed two hands hard into his chest.

"I don't have the will to stop this, Jamie," I breathed. He fell down against my palms, mouth catching mine in a hungry kiss. I pushed back again, and he grinned, hips rolling into mine as I fought against the blood pounding hot and low. "You have to be the one to stop. I can't…"

My breaths were so loud, and they fueled Jamie's desire. He licked his lips, on his way down to kiss me again when I spoke louder.

"You're getting married."

He paused, hand stilling behind my thigh, eyes burning down into mine. I wanted to be a good person, I wanted to tell him to stop, to tell him it was wrong, but the truth was I wanted him. And I was going to let him make the choice.

"If you kiss me again, you could ruin everything." My chest heaved with every word. "If you kiss me again," I repeated, eyes locked on his. "I won't let you stop."

Jamie dipped a little lower, lips close to mine again, but he paused. His brows bent together, breath still hard on my skin, and I waited. I didn't tempt him further. I didn't buck my hips against him or run my nails down his back. I just waited, letting him think for a minute before he made his next move. When he sighed and dropped his grip on my leg, I let out the breath I'd been holding, closing my eyes so I didn't have to see realization dawn on his face.

He rolled off me, falling to the side, both of us on our backs and breathing like the oxygen burned.

"I'm sorry," he whispered, and I shook my head.

"Don't be. It's just lust, Jamie," I lied. He knew it was a lie, I knew it too, but Angel didn't deserve to be hurt just because we figured that out too late. He loved her, but he felt that same primal need for me that had always existed between us. It wouldn't be fair for me to let him throw away everything he'd built with her just because he wanted me one more time.

If he had kissed me even once more, I would have given up fighting. I would have given into him, and then we would have woken up the next day with hearts full of guilt. He would have been a cheater, and me a homewrecker. I sat up straight, needing distance, but Jamie reached out for me.

"Wait," he pleaded. "Can you... will you just stay? Just lie here with me."

I looked down at him, wondering if the battles inside his head were the same as mine. Nodding, I laid back down, and he pulled my back to his chest, breath slowly evening out until I knew he was asleep.

I shouldn't have said his name. I should have pulled away when he said goodnight, forced him to let go of me. I thought I was clean, thought I could handle the temptation, but I'd caved. I'd tasted him again, fed that carnal monster inside me, and it'd been the biggest mistake. Because now, I remembered so clearly how it felt to be with him, and I realized that even though I asked him to stop, I didn't really want him to.

But he had.

And tomorrow, he would marry another woman with me in the background.

I wasn't clean at all.

I wasn't sure I'd ever be.

TWENTY

Medicine

JAMIE'S TENT RUSTLING WOKE me early the next morning, daylight just barely breaking against the forest green fabric. I cracked my eyes open, meeting Charlie's hard eyes as he looked in at us. He tapped the back of his wrist, signaling to me that it was time to go. I nodded, and he frowned a little harder before dropping the curtain and leaving us alone.

My neck was stiff from sleeping on Jamie's arm, and I rolled slowly, cringing against the ache as I did. Jamie's eyes fluttered open when I moved, and I leaned up on my elbow, looking down on him as he gazed back up at me.

"Hey," I whispered.

He stretched a little, the sleeping bag pulling down to reveal his bare chest. "Hi."

The way Whiskey looked that morning nearly killed me. He watched me intently, eyes sleepy, hair mussed from my hands. It was the last morning he would wake up as my Jamie, and he wasn't really even that. He never had been, and yet he always was. We would never be together, and yet we'd never be apart. It was sick, it hurt like hell, and for some reason we both held onto the racking agony.

"Time to get you to the altar," I said softly, smile weak and shaded with words unsaid.

Jamie swallowed, nodding as he leaned up on the palm of his hand and ran the other through his hair. His eyes focused on the opening of his tent, still half-zipped from Charlie, and I let him take the time he needed. After a moment, he stood, swept his shirt off the floor of the tent, and stepped out without looking back at me.

He didn't look at me as we packed up the campsite, or as we drove back into town, or even as he dropped me off at my hotel. I told him I'd see him soon, and he simply nodded, shifting the Jeep back into gear and pulling away as I stood there with my bag on my shoulder.

I had two hours before I had to be at the club, so I took a long shower, letting the water scald my skin before it turned to ice. I was shivering when I finally shut it off, stepping out and staring at myself in the mirror as I wrapped a towel around my chest. Mascara ran under my eyes, my tight curls dripping water onto the swell of my breasts as I let my focus fall to the freckles on my cheeks.

It was time.

• • •

"Oh, thank God."

I had just stepped out of my cab, hand shielding the sun that was now high in the sky as an older gentleman rushed toward me. Another younger, rounder version of the man followed quickly behind him, both of them weighed down by large cameras and multiple bags.

"Are you with the Shaw wedding?"

"Yes?" I tucked my lipstick I'd been reapplying in the cab back into my clutch.

"Wonderful. We're supposed to be shooting the bride and bridesmaids getting ready, but no one is answering their phones, and the groomsmen are acting like security guards. They won't let us back to the dressing room area."

The man was wiry, and frankly too much for me in that moment, but he was sort of adorable, too. I held up my hands, calming him. "Okay, don't worry. I just got here, so give me a second to figure out where everyone is and then I'll get you where you need to go, okay?"

He nodded, sighing with relief. "Okay. Thank you."

I smiled, pushing past them into the country club. I didn't see anyone at first, not even Angel's family setting up decorations outside. I glanced briefly at the aisle out back as I passed through the main entrance and took a left toward where rehearsal had been. No one in sight.

But the closer I got to where dinner had been, the more my hairs stood on end. Something wasn't right. I heard faint yelling from down the hall, and I walked faster, nearly slamming into Charlie when he popped out of the rehearsal dinner room and landed a hand hard on my shoulder.

"You don't want to go back there."

There was definitely yelling happening, and Jamie was most certainly one of the voices. I tried to push past Charlie, but he strengthened his grip on my shoulder.

"I'm serious. Not your fight."

"What's going on? Where's Jamie? Why is no one setting up? The photographer is freaking out," I said, gesturing behind me. I saw Ryan and Andrew then, standing at the bar behind Charlie, both drinking what I was sure was hard liquor.

"B?"

I turned, and Sylvia gave me a sympathetic look before wrapping me in a hug.

"What's going on?" I asked, pulling back. Everyone knew something I didn't, and the uneasy feeling in my stomach bloomed even more.

Jamie's voice rose above the commotion in the room Charlie was blocking me from and we all turned just in time to see him rip the door open. It slammed back against the wall, propping itself open as he tore out of the room.

He didn't look at any of us as he pushed past Charlie, yanking on the tie around his neck until it was hanging loose. He kept walking, down the hall and out the front door without so much as a single word to any of us. I made to go after him and Sylvia pulled me back.

"Just let him go."

"What the hell is going on?" I asked, whipping around to face her again. She opened her mouth, but another voice spoke before her.

"You," Angel seethed, and my eyes adjusted to where she stood in the room behind Charlie. Her face was makeup-free, red and blotchy and shining with freshly shed tears as she stood. She was in a silky white robe that said "bride" in gemstones on the right breast, and she pointed one hard, shaky finger right at me. "This is all *your* fault!"

310

She kept screaming, but her mother popped up then, shutting the door before Angel could storm out after me. I looked to Charlie then, mouth open.

No. He wouldn't have…

"It's over," Sylvia said behind me, but I was still staring at Charlie. He seemed to be amused by my discomfort, and I realized I didn't know him at all. Of course he could have told her what he'd seen this morning, even if nothing had happened between Jamie and me. He didn't owe me anything, least of all loyalty. Sylvia said something else and it snapped me out of my thoughts.

"What?"

Her face crumpled. "She cheated on him. Last night."

The air was gone then, and I stared at her in disbelief. She cheated on *him*?

"I don't understand."

Sylvia blew out a breath. "I guess she saw Jamie post on Facebook that you guys had decided to go camping. It was a group shot of all of you, and his arm was around you, and it just set her off. She was drunk, all the girls fueled the fire and told her how wrong it was that he was going to be with another woman overnight. So they took her out, got her even more wasted, and she slept with one of the guys they met."

My mind was spinning. "I'm so lost. She saw a picture, so she cheated?"

Charlie butted in then. "She assumed if you guys were in the same place all night, you'd end up sleeping together." He frowned, crossing his arms, and I scowled right back at him.

311

"Yeah, well we didn't. And her trying to use our friendship and her own insecurities as an excuse to cheat is pathetic."

I expected him to argue with me, but the crease between his brows softened and he nodded. We may have *technically* slept together, but we didn't have sex, and I didn't want to explain myself to Charlie but it seemed I didn't have to.

Sylvia sniffed, and I turned to find her eyes glossy.

"He's got to be crushed," she said softly.

I sighed, rubbing her arm soothingly. "I'll go talk to him."

I was fuming now. I wanted to march through the door behind Charlie and rip Angel up by her pixie cut. She cheated on him, she betrayed his trust, she hurt him. But then my lips tingled where Jamie had kissed them not even twelve hours before, and I remembered that though she'd put the final nail in their coffin, Jamie wasn't completely innocent, either.

Neither was I.

"I just don't know how you come back from something like this," Sylvia added, wiping at her nose. My ribs crushed in a little tighter then, and I glanced behind her at the door Jamie had fled through.

"Me either."

• • •

Perception is reality.

To some, whiskey is a crutch. It's a drug, it leads to addiction, it dulls the senses and damages the mind.

312

To others, whiskey is medicine. A shot of bourbon can chase away what ails you, whether it be a sore throat or a broken heart.

That night, I realized that maybe I was Jamie's whiskey, too — and maybe we existed in both realities. Maybe we were bad for each other, but maybe we were good, too. As much as I hurt Jamie, as much as he hurt me, we were there for each other always — without hesitation, without expectation.

We were each other's drug as much as we were each others medicine. And in reality, they weren't really that different at all.

It wasn't as easy as I thought it would be to find him. I checked our spot at the beach, rang the doorbell at his house, and ran by all his favorite bars. I'd racked up over one-hundred dollars in cab fare by the time I found him, where I didn't expect him yet wasn't surprised to see him either. He was slumped over, still wearing dress slacks and shoes with that loose tie hanging around his neck at the DoubleTree bar where we'd spent my first night in town.

His hand was gripping a neat glass of whiskey as I took the seat beside him. The bartender nodded to me, pouring up the same Crown Royal Black I'd ordered the first night. He served it on ice, and even though I hadn't planned on ordering a drink, I sucked half of it down anyway.

Jamie looked miserable. He stared down at his glass, eyes bloodshot and glazed over. I debated reaching out, rubbing his back or squeezing his hand, but nothing felt right. So I waited for a while, just sitting beside him, drinking my medicine while he drank his.

I'd sat in so many comfortable silences with Jamie in my life, but that wasn't one of them. Every second of quiet felt like a needle prick to my lungs, making it harder and harder to breathe. I just wanted to comfort him, to help him feel okay, and I didn't know if I could. I wasn't sure how much time had passed when I finally spoke.

"You want to talk about it?"

It was such a lame question — cliché and overused. In reality, I think I already knew what my next move would be, but I buffered it first.

Jamie spun his empty glass. "No."

His voice was thick, and I simply nodded, already knowing that would be his answer. I wanted him to talk, to tell me everything running through his mind, but I knew that wasn't what he needed right then. What he needed was to escape, and I knew exactly how.

Fingering through my clutch, I fished out enough cash to cover both of our tabs, dropping it on the bar as I stood and drained the rest of my drink. My stomach flipped as I flicked down my spare hotel room key next. It landed right next to Jamie's hand, and I didn't wait for his reaction, just turned and walked casually to the elevators.

My heart raced as the elevator shot me up to my room, and my hands were already shaking when I slid my own key into the slot and let myself in. I tried to tell myself I didn't know for sure that he'd come, but it was a lie. I knew he would, and every inch of me sizzled in anticipation.

Jamie couldn't use his words that night, so I would have him use his hands.

Once I made it inside my room, I didn't know what to do. I paced, kicking off my heels before checking my

314

reflection in the bathroom mirror and splashing some water on my face. *I shouldn't do this*, I thought first. *WE shouldn't do this*. I thought the words, but I didn't believe them, because Jamie was all I wanted. I wanted him to want me. I wanted to heal him, to take his pain as my own, even if just for the night. I wanted him to know I was here, that I always would be.

I was patting my face dry with a towel when I heard the click of the door, and I froze, towel in hand. I looked up into the mirror, catching Jamie's reflection behind me as he dropped the plastic key card on the desk and stepped into the bathroom with me. The air around us buzzed to life, like gas just before the match is lit, and we both breathed it in, feeling the hum of it all.

I was still holding the towel, only my eyes peering over it at the broken man behind me. He moved slowly, eyes on my back as he closed the distance between us. Jamie had always been so strong, so tall and sure, but he looked small in that moment. He wasn't just broken, he was shattered, and he looked to me as if I held the broom and the glue.

His hands reached out for me first, and he dragged his fingertips from my elbows to my shoulders, sparking chills in his wake. He trailed them down next, along my ribs to my hips, where he grabbed on for life as his forehead fell to my shoulder. The light in the bathroom was dim, warm, and I watched in the mirror as Jamie winced in pain. I dropped the towel then, putting my hands over where his held me. He wrapped them tighter, squeezing me close, and for one brief moment, a tender sorrow filled both of us. A sorrow for what he'd lost — for what *we'd* lost — and for what the day had held.

When he'd dropped his head to my shoulder, he'd passed his weight to me, needing me to shoulder it with him. I took it as my own, and just as quickly as the moment had come, it passed. Jamie inhaled, dragging his lips along the slope of my shoulder as his eyes found mine in the mirror, a darker, pulsing heat filling them. He bit down at the apex and I arched into him, my hands reaching up and back for him. His rose with me, sliding under the low back of the dress I'd been wearing for the wedding that never happened. His hands, the ones I'd had on me the night before, the ones I'd stopped, cupped me under the thin fabric and I moaned, dropping my head back.

I didn't stop him this time.

Jamie caught the lobe of my ear in his mouth and sucked hard, another wave of goosebumps flooding my body. He slid the straps of my dress from each shoulder, one by one, and it dropped like a curtain to the floor, pooling around my bare feet. I hadn't been wearing a bra, and my panties were a sheer lavender scrap of lace. I lifted my head again, eyelids heavy as I found Jamie in the mirror.

I loved how Jamie always commanded my attention — whether in a crowded room or when we were alone. He waited, however long it took, for the right connection to hit between us before making any other moves. Then, Jamie bit hard on his lower lip, dipping one hand beneath the hem of my panties to brush my clit. My legs shook at the contact and Jamie retracted his hand just as quickly, spinning me before cupping me by the ass and hoisting me into his arms.

I locked my legs, lips fervent as they brushed the skin of his neck, his jaw, his mouth. Jamie carried me to the bed, dropping me down easily before pulling his tie over his head. Our breaths mingled together in a symphony as he worked at the buttons on his shirt while I watched, squirming below him, his eyes devouring me. I leaned up, balancing on my knees and working on his belt while he finished his shirt. Yanking the metal out of the loop easily, I unhooked and unzipped just as he ripped open the last button. His pants fell and he shrugged out of the white dress shirt, but I wasted no time. I palmed him through his briefs, evoking a raw groan that struck the match.

His first growl from my touch rocked the room, and I dipped my fingers into the band of his briefs, catching his mouth with mine as my hand wrapped around him, skin on skin. He thrust into my grip and I gasped into his mouth. It was too much, the sensation of it all. Years of waiting, of wanting, of wrong decisions and longing regrets. They all floated to the surface and yet drowned in the depths all at once.

Breaking our kiss, I pulled Jamie down hard, rolling until I sat on top of him. He leaned up, wrapping his arms all the way around me and grinding his hips into mine as he sucked his way down my neck. I rubbed my clit against the length of him before pushing a hand into his chest, forcing him into the sheets. Tonight, it was about Jamie — about him finding a release, or a numb, or whatever he needed. So I moved down his body, my mouth falling in line with my hands as they trailed their way to his briefs. My mouth paused there, hands working to roll them off as he lifted and maneuvered to help.

I looked up, eyes locked on his as I dragged the flat of my tongue from base to tip, and Jamie twisted his fists in the sheets, every muscle in his abdomen tightening at the sensation of my mouth wrapping around him. Every moment I got to have Jamie in my bed was incredible, but that night, tasting him like that, taking the weight of the day and replacing it with euphoria? That feeling was like a drug — a powerful, addicting drug. I bobbed slow at first, swirling my tongue and taking more of him each time until my lips touched his base, and every groan from him charged my desire. I held my breath against the gag when he flexed into me, balancing on my knees to use both hands next. They twisted in time with my mouth, and Jamie hissed in a breath through his teeth before reaching down to tug on my elbows.

He was done with foreplay.

I crawled back up, licking my lips as Jamie stared down at me panting. A part of me ached in that moment, not knowing what the next morning would bring, but I shook it off before it could fully land and make roots. Instead of thinking, I tightened my hand around him, stroking him once more before rolling off the bed and fishing a condom out of my purse. He was leaning up on his elbows, sculpted chest and biceps taut as he waited. I could have stared at him all night, my Jamie, my Whiskey. He was just so beautifully flawed, as if his scars and imperfections had been designed by the gods.

I braced my knees on either side of his thighs, eyes on his as I tore the package open with my teeth before rolling the condom on slowly.

For a moment it was just our breaths, loud and unsteady, impatient and wanting. I lifted, positioning him at my opening, and with as much restraint as I could manage, I lowered myself onto him, feeling him inside me again after years of being clean. I sank all the way down, and Jamie's hands were where my thighs met my hips, pulling me lower. We groaned together, the addiction flaring up like never before, and I rolled my body slow and controlled.

Jamie pulled me down, his arms holding me flush against him as he flexed into me. He pulled me into him like he was afraid I wasn't real, like he worried I'd disappear. He needed me close that night, and so we stayed like that, kisses hard and hot and demanding, bodies connected at every point. He'd roll up with me still sitting on his lap, one hand pulling my shoulder down as the other splayed at the small of my back. Then he was on top, hooking my leg until my ankle rested against his shoulder and he pushed even deeper inside. I loved the way he felt, the way he struggled to breathe as he slid inside me, over and over, reaching new depths, all the while lining our bodies at every possible point of contact. He couldn't get enough of me, and I never wanted to get enough of him. I never wanted to lose that primal need, that possessive desire that always existed between us.

When he flipped me onto my stomach, straddling my thighs and entering me from behind, our moans grew louder together. He rocked in hard once, twice, three times, and then he pressed his chest to my back, slowing his thrusts, each one causing my clit to rub against the sheets. He wrapped one hand around my throat, and the next pump delivered my climax. It took me under like a rip tide, rough and unapologetic, and I never wanted to breathe again. Not when Jamie came with me, not when he rolled to the side still inside me, molding himself to fit perfectly behind me. I held my breath and drowned happily in my vice.

At least until the morning came.

TWENTY-ONE
12 Step Program

I WAS HOT.

That was the first thought in my mind when I woke the next morning, kicking the covers off me as I stretched. My toes pointed, arms high above my head, and I squinted a little through the sunlight already streaming into the room. I'd forgotten to close the curtain last night, and I caught a glimpse of downtown out my window as my eyes adjusted.

And then I saw Jamie.

He was a silhouette against the city, sitting on the edge of the bed with his elbows resting on his knees. His back was hunched over, red marks from my nails visible in the morning light, and his head was down, dropped just below the curve of his shoulders. He was broken, and the sight of him was so achingly beautiful.

Pulling the sheets around me, I crawled to him, settling in behind him. The shin of my bent leg lined the bottom of his back and my other leg stretched beside his to the floor. I wrapped my arms around his abdomen, taking the sheet with me, and his stomach trembled a little at the light touch from my fingertips as I rested my cheek against his spine.

"How are you feeling?"

Jamie pushed a long, slow, weighted breath through his nose, lifting his head to stare out the window. "That's a loaded question."

I pressed my lips to his back, tasting the warm skin there, and waited.

"I feel a lot of things," he finally whispered after a while. "I feel *everything*."

"Talk it out with me," I pleaded, locking my fingers over his abdomen. Last night I'd let him escape, but today he needed to talk — he needed to digest. "Just start at the top of the list and work your way down."

Jamie cracked his neck, one of his lifelong tells, and one hand ran along my leg hanging beside his. He hooked a grip around the top of my calf and kept it, like holding onto me grounded him to this earth, to this moment.

"I'm fucking pissed," he said first, squeezing my leg. "And I'm hurt." His voice broke on that one, and I hugged him tighter. "The woman I was supposed to marry last night slept with another man without thinking twice about it."

I moved my lips from his back and flattened my cheek against it once more, listening to his heart through the back of his ribs as he continued.

"I'm sad, because all of it was for nothing — the planning, the stress of it all. My family is probably

322

heartbroken and hers, too." He paused. "And I feel guilty, because she wasn't all wrong — not completely. About me. About us," he said on a shaky breath. "I feel guilty because she was right. And I feel guilty because in a way, I also feel relieved."

Jamie moved then, lifting his arm and signaling me to climb under it. I dropped my bent leg to the floor and slid up, tucking myself into his chest as he wrapped his arm around me and pulled me closer. We both stared out at the city at first, and Jamie's hand lazily drew circles on my arm.

"I feel relieved because I loved her, but not as much as I love you."

I swallowed, and Jamie tilted my chin with his knuckles, kissing me with his eyes closed tight. When he pulled back, the saddest, softest smile met his lips. "I knew before you showed up, but when you did, I was helpless. I felt guilty as hell the other night when you stopped me, when you pointed out that I was being a shitty person for kissing you when I was about to get married, but I don't feel guilty today. Not for that, at least." He smirked, rubbing my jaw with the pad of his thumb. "I wasn't sorry the first time I kissed you, even when you weren't mine, and I'm not sorry I kissed you the other night, even when I wasn't yours. Because the truth is you've always been mine, and I'll always be yours, and that's just the way it is."

I leaned into his touch, smiling up at him, chest aching with everything he'd said. We hadn't been innocent, and neither had Angel. Where did that leave us? I couldn't be sure. "So what now?"

Jamie looked at me then, in that moment, in a way he'd never looked at me before. He shook his head, a small smile playing at the very corner of his lips as his hazel eyes watched me carefully. The green in them showed a little more in the light that morning, but the honey I'd always loved still dominated, and I couldn't look away.

"Be with me," he whispered.

With a sigh, I closed my eyes and nodded against his hand. When I opened my eyes again, he was grinning wide, and my heart nearly exploded. I felt it growing beneath my ribs, expanding, demanding more room to be felt.

"I hate to bring the moment down, but I think you have some things to take care of here before we make any other moves," I pointed out.

Jamie's smile fell and he nodded. "I know."

I didn't envy him, having to talk to the families, clear personal items out of each other's houses, deal with the venue and the professionals they'd hired. Would they get any of the money back? I doubted it. But then again, I wondered if Jamie cared. He'd said that though he felt guilty, he also felt relieved, and maybe his family would see that, too.

"Wait for me?" Jamie asked, turning to face me completely. Both of his hands slid to frame my face and his eyes searched mine.

I leaned in, answering with a kiss that said more than I could. The truth was in that moment, right there, I'd have waited forever.

But I never could have seen what would happen next.

324

Jamie made slow, sweet love to me once more before driving me to the airport. When we'd checked my bag, he pulled me into him, kissing me long and hard and needy without caring who was around us. I held on tight to him, too — and for some reason I couldn't explain, I felt an ending in that kiss. It was a period, a punctuation mark, and at the time I thought it was the end of that chapter. But later, I would mark it as the end of it all — the end of my addiction, my last taste of Whiskey, my final dance with fire.

Because when I pulled away, eyes bright and heart soaring, I asked Jamie to call me when he was ready.

And he never did.

• • •

I pounced back into Pittsburgh like a fuzzy, smiley kitten. Everything felt right when my feet hit the ground in my city, and I knew everything was finally going to work out. I just *knew* it. I felt it in every inch of my body, from my ears to my toes, and life had never been brighter than it was that Sunday. My lips were still swollen from Jamie, my heart full of his words — his promises — and the pit of anxiety I felt before I flew out Thursday had been replaced with a warm ball of relief.

While Jamie was back home handling what he needed to, I did the same.

I called things off with River, even though we weren't anything official, because it wasn't fair to him to let him think anything would come of it. As far as I was concerned, I was Jamie's now — hell, I always had been. I was all giggly over it, gushing to Jenna on the phone and even telling my mom, whom I barely ever talked to about my love life. She knew what I'd gone through being away from Jamie in college, but even that had been mostly endured on my own. There was a pep in my step, a light in my eyes, and everyone noticed.

River wasn't the only thing I had to handle, though. I threw myself into work, tying up loose ends and getting through my current projects so I could have a talk with Randall about slowing down a little. I told him I wanted to have more time for things that mattered a little more than work to me, and he smiled like a proud dad, telling me it was about time I stopped working so damn hard. He told me I was fantastic at what I did and slowing down a little wouldn't change that.

But as much as I knew I was prepared to do long distance with Jamie, I also wanted to have options, so I researched a few publishing houses in South Florida, not putting in any applications before talking to Jamie but doing the work to have the conversation, at least. I loved Pittsburgh, and I loved Rye Publishing — but I loved Jamie more. And I was finally at the point where I was willing to make whatever compromises I needed to for us to work. So that's how it was for the first few weeks — I handled my shit while Jamie handled his, and I waited for his call.

I waited.

And waited, and waited, and waited.

At first it was patient waiting. I still had things to take care of on my own, so I focused on those things, and on my thoughts and feelings for Jamie, soaking in them, giving them life. I loved him, he loved me, we wanted to be together, and so we would. It was the easiest, most simple time in our relationship, and I was happy to revel in it.

But then anxiety flared, massive and ugly, right in the middle of my chest. It was harder to breathe then, after a month of waiting, and I broke the silence first. I called him, hoping to just talk if not make plans, but he didn't answer. And he didn't call back.

"It's fine," Jenna assured me one night when I was pacing, feet burning a hole in my apartment floor. "He's got a lot going on, B. I mean seriously, his fiancé cheated on him. And all his feelings for you came rushing back *before* that even happened. He got ambushed with a shit storm and he's just trying to sort it all out. He told you to wait, so just… wait."

I'd listened to her, throwing myself into work because it was my go-to. Randall called me out on not slowing down at all, but I assured him I would soon — very soon — and I hoped in my heart that was the truth.

One day I was walking home from the office, balancing three manuscripts I planned to devour over the weekend, when my phone buzzed hard in my purse. I'd juggled the pages and my half-empty bottle of water, fumbling for my phone, praying I'd see Jamie's name. But when I finally fished it out, an unknown number was all that lit the screen — just another call from a telemarketer, or a bill collector with the wrong number, or someone trying to tell me who to vote for in next year's election. I sighed, hitting the ignore button and dropping it back into my purse before finishing the walk home.

Somewhere around the three-month mark, my anxiety blossomed into desperation and fear. I was barely sleeping, barely eating, and my work was suffering because of it. I was strung out, withdrawal sneaking in, and I tried calling him again. Three times. He didn't answer any of the calls, and on the third one, I caved and left a voicemail.

"Hey," I whispered before clearing my throat. "It's me. Listen," I paused then, staring out my giant window at Market Square. We were right in the middle of summer, and the city was buzzing with life everywhere but inside my apartment. "I know you had a lot to sort through. I know it's not as simple as sign a few papers, move her stuff out of your place and call me. I know that. I can't even imagine what you're going through, which is why I want you to call me anyway — regardless of if you're ready to see me yet. Let me help you through this, even if it's just as a friend." My voice shook a little with my next plea. "You need a friend, Jamie. Please, let me be your friend."

I hated asking that, because it wasn't what I wanted — I wanted more. I *needed* more. We'd tried being friends before, he'd asked me that very sentence time and time again. But having him as a friend was better than not having him at all, and I was starting to worry.

"Just call me, okay?"

I hung up then, dropping my phone to the armrest of my couch before numbly stripping off my clothes on the way to the bathroom. I took a long bath in the dark, only the faint light from my bedroom window sneaking through. I wondered what he was doing, what he was thinking. Was he hurting? Was he afraid? *Oh God*, was he with her again?

I shook my head against that final thought, convinced it couldn't be true, but there was really no way for me to know for sure.

Things declined quickly after that.

My fear transformed into anger and hurt, and those two emotions burrowed in between my ribs. Mom tried to talk me down at first, but once it'd been six months without a single word from Jamie, Jenna was firmly on my side. She was pissed, too — and that fueled my fire.

"Can you just… check on him?" I asked her one night.

"That sounds like a terrible idea, B."

I chewed the pad of my thumb, curling up on my sofa. "I know. I know it does, but I can't… I just need to know what's going on. Maybe he's traveling, you know? Maybe that's why he hasn't returned my calls."

"They have phones in other places in the world. And email."

Sighing, I planted my feet on the floor and ran a hand through my curls. "Please, Jenna."

She must have heard it, the desperation in my voice. It came back sometimes, drowning out the anger for a bit, and that night it was winning.

So Jenna checked on him, and it turned out to be the worst thing I could have asked her to do.

"I saw him," she told me the next night.

"And?"

She was quiet, and my stomach rolled.

"And… he looks fine. He was out at lunch with some work buddies. I saw him on his phone a few times… no girls or anything but, he looks okay. He looks… good."

The pain that tore through my chest with her words was a strange one. It felt like hot water, growing more intense in temperature as it leaked down deeper and deeper. I couldn't move away from it, couldn't cool it down, and it hurt as much as it fueled the anger that had been just below the surface.

I tried calling him one last time, on a night after I'd drowned myself in half a bottle of Jack Daniel's. I'd been stalking his social media, not finding anything new at all. He'd been tagged in a few random posts, funny memes and videos, but he hadn't posted a single photo, a single status, not even a single word. I wasn't sure if that made it worse or better.

He didn't answer when I called, just like I knew he wouldn't, and I thought really hard about leaving him the nastiest voicemail I could muster. I even let it click me over to voicemail, and I breathed into the receiver like a dragon, trying to tame myself yet falling short.

But I ended the call, staring down at my phone for all of four seconds before heaving it across my apartment. It hit the edge of my kitchen counter and splintered across the floor, and I cried.

He'd changed his mind.

Whiskey had made me promise I'd wait, and then he'd never come, stringing me along knowing my addiction was too strong for me to let him go. I'd fallen from the highest high to the lowest low, and now here I was, crumpled in a ball on the floor. I curled in on myself, rocking slightly, and let the tears come freely down my face.

I'd hit all the stages of grief before that night, touching on everything from denial to anger to depression. Now, I was rounding that base, heading home to acceptance. And I knew what had to happen once my feet hit the plate.

I let myself be broken for nearly another month before I started on my own twelve-step program. Step one was admitting that I was powerless over Whiskey — that my life had become unmanageable. He'd completely taken over, and maybe he'd had that hold on me for longer than I'd realized. Every time I thought I was okay without him, he'd show me I wasn't, and every time I thought I'd be better with him, he proved me wrong. It was a dangerous roller coaster ride and I was done. I wanted off. I wanted solid ground.

So I redefined everything about myself.

I'd checked into rehab once before, but it was a half-assed attempt. My heart hadn't been in it, I hadn't wanted to let him go. This time, I did. This time, I had a plan. This time, I'd given myself an intervention.

I was ready to grow up, tired of the games Jamie and I played. I wanted a real love, a real life, and I had to paint the way to get there. It killed me to let him go, and if I'm being honest — I knew I would never let him go completely. A part of him would always live in me, but I wanted that part of me subdued, buried beneath a brighter version of myself who could move on and live her life.

I looked back on all the damage we'd done — to ourselves, to those around us — and I mourned the time I'd lost fighting for someone who would never be mine. I'd been a fool, and now I was standing in the rubble of the life I'd wasted, drowning in both sorrow and a drive to build a new one.

I'd waited too long for Whiskey, and I refused to let him hold that power over me any longer.

And you know what? It actually *worked*. For the first time in my life, and with more pain and time than I'd hoped or even thought I could survive, I finally let him go. I deleted him off every social media network, wiped his number from my phone, packed all our pictures and memories away and started over fresh. I was *clean*. I'd moved on. I was happy. I was *free*.

Then, after almost two years without calling, Jamie just showed up.

TWENTY-TWO

Straight Up

TAYLOR SWIFT BLASTED THROUGH my apartment as I pranced around, hair tied up in a messy bun and half a bottle of wine already consumed. I sang the lyrics at the top of my lungs, sliding into the kitchen in my tube socks with packing tape in hand. The box I'd just packed full with dishes was padded and ready, so I closed the flaps and taped them shut, biting the cap of my Sharpie between my teeth as I scrawled *kitchen* across the cardboard. I smiled then, belting out a high note with the Sharpie as my microphone before dropping it back to the counter and tackling the next empty box.

There are rare, shining bright periods of our lives where everything seems almost too good to be true. All the pieces fall into place, effortlessly and beautifully, and we get to enjoy the final masterpiece with not one single worry. They're the kind of moments where we realize we're lucky to be alive, to be who we are, to be breathing the air around us. They're the kind of days that remind us why we had to suffer through the dark ones, why it's all worth it in the end.

That was the kind of day I was having.

It was pouring buckets outside, fall greeting the city with a cold, gray day, and yet I was emitting sunshine. I was drunk, a little sweaty, and a lot excited. Right on the heels of one of the worst years of my life, I'd happened to have had the best. Jenna had moved to Pittsburgh, I'd been promoted at work, and perhaps the most shocking of all? I'd found Mr. Right.

No, I'd found *the* Mr. Right.

Bradley Neil checked all my boxes. He was intelligent, witty, and sexy as hell. He'd built all his success on his own, chasing his dream of being his own boss and making it come true with his entrepreneurship. Brad was the founder and owner of an up-and-coming graphic design company, one he'd imagined into reality with hard work and creativity unlike anything I'd ever witnessed before. We met when Rye Publishing hired his company to completely remaster our logo and website. He'd caught my attention in the first meeting, reeled me in throughout the few weeks we worked together, and pulled me in hook, line, and sinker after the first date I agreed to.

From that moment on, it'd been like the sweetest fairytale.

Brad was a philanthropist, and I loved to give back with him. We'd volunteer in the community together, and in those times we learned more and more about each other. He told me he loved me after three months together. I said it back after four. After seven months, I met his family and

334

he met Mom and Wayne. And then after just eight months, he asked me to marry him, and I said yes without a single hesitation. I didn't think about how our relationship had been shorter than the one I had with my hair brush, or how it was probably absurd that we decided to only have a five-month engagement, or that I was practically insane for agreeing to move in with him even before we said "I do." And as much as you may hate me for it, I didn't think about Jamie — not one single time since the words "I love you" left my lips and met Brad's ears.

Oh, don't get me wrong. Jamie was there — he was always there. He still owned that monumental piece of my heart, of my soul, of my body. I felt him like a hummingbird right in the center of my chest, wings fluttering, blood buzzing. He was *always* there, but now, instead of focusing on that buzz, I'd dulled it with other, louder, more demanding sounds.

Because you see, it'd taken months of agony, of withdrawal, of anger and pain and depression and losing more of myself than I care to admit to finally emerge on the other side of my life with Jamie Shaw. Every minute hurt, until one day it was sort of a dull ache, and then with more passing time it weakened to only a pressure — that pressure in my chest. I'd completed my twelve-step program. I was clean. I wanted to *stay* clean.

So, no. As much as you may hate me for it, I wasn't thinking about Jamie. Not even a little bit.

In fact, I was so confident in my ability to *not* think about Jamie that I'd decided to drink for the first time in over a year. Part of my twelve-step program was giving up literal drinking, too. Every time I drank, I thought of Jamie. I wanted to call him or dwell on his memory. So, I gave up alcohol altogether — the literal and figurative versions, both.

But tonight I was celebrating, and so I'd popped a bottle of wine and though the old me could have pounded a bottle before feeling tipsy, the new me was drunk after half. But I was *happy* drunk — dancing, singing, packing. I felt it, a new chapter starting, a new day dawning.

I wasn't thinking about Jamie.

Not until the exact moment he showed up.

It was a soft knock at first, barely heard over the rain and music, and I was right in the middle of wrapping a wine glass in newspaper.

"Just a sec!" I called. I'd just tucked the glass into a box when a second, louder knock came. I huffed, wondering why they didn't just walk in anyway. I only ever had two visitors — Brad and Jenna — and both had keys. Clicking the pause button on my Taylor Swift jam sesh, I yelled louder. "I'm coming, I'm coming!"

I was still humming to the tune of *I Wish You Would*, hips swinging in my pale blue sleep shorts as I readjusted the bun on my head and pulled the door open without even checking the peephole. The air of it hit me with a whoosh, my smile bright and unsuspecting, and then I saw him.

Whiskey and water. A ghostly memory, a wound ripped fresh.

Did you know adding water to whiskey can actually enhance the flavor? It's true. Turns out, a little dilution can be good, but in this case, it was my worst enemy. Because there was Whiskey, and there was water, but there was no dilution — no, his flavors had only grown stronger, they'd only aged better, and I knew with a head full of wine that I was in deep trouble.

Jamie was completely soaked, long hair dripping into his eyes and rolling down the bridge of his nose, the angle of his jaw, landing on the flat of his heaving chest. His eyes hit mine like a blast of fire, hidden beneath furrowed brows, and the muscle over his jaw ticked twice as he clenched his jaw. I felt the anger rolling mercilessly off his hot skin and into my apartment. His right hand lifted, fingers closed tight over an off-white sheet of card stock with mine and Brad's names written in neat, gold cursive.

My eyes flicked to the wedding invitation and I swallowed, slowly finding him again. "Jamie," I breathed.

"No."

One word had never solicited such a guttural emotion from me before. I shuddered, tensing and waiting as Jamie clenched his fist around the invitation.

"*Fuck* no."

He pushed through the door then, moving past me quickly, leaving my arm slick with the water still falling off him. I stood in the doorway for a moment longer, closing my eyes and forcing three full breaths. *You can do this. You're clean. You are in control.* I set my shoulders and turned, closing the door behind me.

"By all means, let yourself in."

His back was to me, the ridges of it defined in the sticky, wet t-shirt he wore. He was shivering, and I wasn't sure if it was from the cold rain or his anger.

The longer I stared at him, the more I felt. Pain. Anger. Fear.

That last one was a new emotion, but it was the strongest. The truth was that even then, I knew what was coming. I could sense it. I was clean, but I hadn't been tested yet — and Jamie had picked the worst possible night to give me my final exam. I was drunk, I was high off emotions, I was *not* ready. And I was deathly afraid of the mistake I knew I'd make if he only pushed me hard enough.

Jamie faced my large window, looking out at the slanted rain as it drenched the city. He held up his hand once more, invitation thoroughly crinkled now in his clutches. "What the hell is this."

It was a question, but it wasn't asked like one — it was posed as an accusation, one I felt all the way to my core.

"I tried calling you…" My voice was quiet, weak, and I hated that because it wasn't a lie. I *had* called him — even after swearing I never would again. When Brad proposed, I knew I had to be the one to tell Jamie, even if he'd changed his mind about us. Even if he'd never called like he said he would. So, I tried getting in touch with him once more, but again, I failed.

Mom sent out the invitations last week.

Apparently his *mailbox* worked fine.

"Oh you did?" he asked then, spinning to face me. "And what exactly were you going to tell me? That you're getting *married*? Please tell me you're kidding, because I know that's not what you were going to call me to tell me. I *know* this invitation can't be real. This is all some big joke, right?"

Fear and sadness drained away and my defenses went up. Who the hell did he think he was? After two years of silence, he'd showed up demanding answers I wasn't sure he had a right to know. I crossed my arms, resting heavy on one hip. "*Excuse* me?" I scoffed. "No, Jamie, my fucking wedding is not a *joke*."

"So you're getting married?"

"Yes!"

Jamie's other hand flew to the invitation, ready to rip it to shreds, but he stopped himself, gritting his teeth before throwing the paper to the floor and running his hands through his soaked hair. He shook his head, and then one hand jutted out toward me. "How? *How*, B? After everything that... after we..."

"You never called!" I yelled, throwing my hands up in exhaustion. My apartment suddenly felt too quiet, only the pelting rain and our harsh words breaking the silence. "What was I supposed to do, Jamie?"

"Wait!" He cried the word out on a breath of desperation, face twisting with the emotion that had forced it out. "You were supposed to wait."

"For two *years*?"

"Yes!" Jamie stepped closer then and I flinched back. That reaction seemed to stun him, and he paused. "For as long as I needed."

"That's not fair," I cried. "I tried calling you, I tried calling everyone *around* you. You never called, you never wrote — you completely ghosted me."

"Oh, feels kind of shitty when you're on the other side of that, doesn't it?"

His words pummeled me, head snapping back with the figurative slap of them. It was the first time I thought of it that way. Jamie had waited for me — for three years, after I left Alder — and I'd never called him. I'd never given him any reason to wait. And yet still he had.

But I hadn't.

"That was different, that... I didn't promise you anything."

"Not then you didn't," he corrected me, just as a flash of lightning lit up the darkening sky behind him. "But just less than two years ago, you did. You promised me you'd wait."

"I love him!"

My voice broke with the admission, Brad's image assaulting me out of nowhere and reminding me why I couldn't have this conversation with Jamie. I'd promised myself to another man, one I loved madly, one who treated me right. One who was available — who always had been when it came to me.

"You do, huh?" he mused, nodding. He nodded over and over, small movements, teeth working the inside of his lower lip and nostrils flaring. Jamie looked around then, and it was as if he'd just realized he was in my apartment — for the first time. There were half-packed boxes littered everywhere. It was all there, proof I'd moved on without him, and I watched every second as it settled in. He turned back to me slowly after a moment, and his hazel eyes questioned me before his mouth did. "And do you love me?"

"No," I answered automatically. I'd trained myself for that one, all part of the twelve-step program. I'd repeated it, over and over. I didn't love him, I was only infatuated. I only wanted what I'd never had. I loved the high, the burn — that was all. That's what I told myself.

"No?" he asked. Jamie crossed the room then, and I circled the sofa, trading places with him. I felt like a cornered animal, except I wasn't scared — not even a little bit. The truth was I was excited. I was a fiend, right on the edge of a high I'd missed, a high I craved — and every nerve in my body was buzzing to life at the possibility. "You don't love me."

That time he said it as an incredulous statement, not a question.

"No."

My back hit the window he'd just been standing in front of and I had nowhere left to go. My hands pressed into the cold glass behind my thighs and Jamie moved slowly, closing in.

"You don't love me," he asked again when his breath was close enough for me to feel it on my lips. Rain tinged on the glass behind me, my heart pounded in my chest, and Jamie moved slow and easy, confident and possessive. He was there to take what was always his. "You don't want me, right now, right here?"

He whispered the last words, still damp hand running up my arm to cradle my neck, thumb lining my jaw.

I took a shaky breath, eyes fluttering closed, and said no again. At least, I thought I did, but I couldn't be sure. Every sound was morphed, every sense focused on the point of contact where Jamie's skin touched mine. My only goal in that moment was breathing, and it was damn hard to accomplish.

"Say it," he croaked, stepping even loser. The wet fabric of his shirt brushed my tank top, coating the lower part of my midriff just above my shorts hem. "Say you don't love me. Say you don't *want* me, and I'll go."

I cracked my eyes open then, and the vulnerability in Jamie's sliced me open. He was being honest. If I told him, right then and there, that I didn't want him — he would leave. I knew he would. It would have killed him, but he would have walked away. All I had to do was speak those four words and this could all be over.

I don't want you.

I said it in my mind first, testing the truthfulness of it, but when Jamie pushed farther into my space I knew I didn't have the time to think it over.

So the words flew from my lips.

"I don't want you."

Jamie stopped, his wet shirt still brushing against me as he breathed through the reality of what I'd said. His eyes flicked back and forth between mine, brows bent, heart unbelieving. He wasn't expecting that. Hell, *I* wasn't expecting that. It took him a moment to register. Then, slowly, he stepped back.

Chills broke along my skin where his body had been, the cool air of my apartment stinging like an ice cube. Jamie opened his mouth to speak but paused, clamping it shut again with a flex in his jaw. And then, just as he promised, he turned and walked away.

What happened in the next few moments was something unexplainable, something tangible and wrapped up in chemistry, because as soon as he took the first step away from me, my heart kicked into overdrive. It literally hit with a force that propelled me forward off the glass, and I opened my mouth with a ragged breath. He took another step and a white light invaded my vision. Another step, and my chest squeezed, ribs threatening to strangle my lungs.

My mind raced as I watched Jamie fulfill his promise. Panic ripped through me like a merciless rip tide, a thousand *what ifs* assaulting me like brutal waves. I tried to make sense of it all, but the wine clouded what grip on reality I still had, and when his hand landed on the doorknob, I kicked hard, emerging from the wave.

"Wait!"

Jamie's hand gripped the knob and his neck tilted, head down, like he was unsure if the word he'd heard was in his head or real. He turned slowly, and it was the last thing he took his time with, because as soon as he saw the tortured look on my face, he knew. He knew I wanted him. I always had.

I always would.

He crossed the room in five long strides. One, I took a breath. Two, I nearly cried. Three, I almost told him to stop. Four, I realized I never could. And five, lightning crashed behind me as Jamie's lips claimed mine.

My back hit the glass and my conscience hit the road, leaving me behind with a shake of its head. But Jamie's thumb grazed my bottom lip, and my tongue caught the saltiness of his skin.

That's all it took.

One taste, and every voice of reason was killed mid-sentence.

We both exhaled the moment our mouths met, hard and pleading, two years of pain and hurt and still-unresolved distance stoking the fire that had laid dormant for so long. Flames caught, and I gasped with the new oxygen, Jamie's wet body pushing into mine and pinning me against the window.

His hands ran down my arms, clasping hard around my wrists and pushing them over my head as his hips tilted forward. He kissed me like he'd never kissed me before, like he'd kissed me every day of his life, and like he'd never get the chance to kiss me again. Barrel-aged Whiskey and water mixed together, flavors exploding on my tongue with every sip. It was heaven. It was hell. It was wrong and right and I wished I'd never started yet I never wanted to stop. Loving Jamie was the sickest and sweetest oxymoron.

"You're not marrying him," Jamie growled against my lips, and though that sentence should have pained me with guilt, it only fueled my desire. I kept my wrists high as Jamie dropped his grasp, reaching for the hem of my tank top and ripping it up and over. My simple sports bra came off next, and then his hands found my wrists once more, tightening their grip. The cold, wet fabric of his shirt brushed my nipples and I moaned, arching off the glass and into him.

He dropped his mouth to my peak then, sucking the already tight skin, my hips bucking with the suction, wrists still pinned. Jamie's lips caught mine again, teeth nipping at the wine stains as he flipped my hands, forcing my palms against the glass over my head.

"Hold," he murmured against my mouth, and then he dropped to his knees.

Breaths expelled from my throat in bursts, chest heaving as I watched him hook his fingers beneath the band of my shorts. He slid them down to my ankles, fingertips searing my skin every inch of the way, and then he dipped one finger under the lace of my panties. We moaned together as he easily slid inside, and when Jamie's eyes caught mine, the stare was too intense. I dropped my head back against the window, fingers desperate for a grip the glass couldn't provide.

Jamie slid my panties down next, hands wrapping around the backs of my thighs as he planted one soft kiss against my center. I was completely exposed for him, save for the tube socks still on my feet.

"Fuck," I whispered, chest aching with want. He hooked his hand behind one knee and brought it to his shoulder, allowing him better access, and his tongue slid along my opening before circling my clit. He sucked hard, sliding two fingers inside me at the same time, and the leg holding me up shook. "Oh, *God*."

"Mmm," Jamie hummed against me, fingers deep and working with the rhythm of his mouth. The front of me was still wet from his shirt, my back slick with sweat against the glass, and my leg trembled as I balanced. He was so skilled, such an expert with his tongue, with my body. He knew me well — *too* well — and maybe that had always been my downfall. No one knew me like Jamie. No one ever would.

I was on the brink of coming when Jamie dropped my leg, crawling back up my body slowly, lips dragging against every inch of my skin as he did. My hands were still high on the glass and when Jamie saw, he smirked, eyes finding mine with a new heat. "Such a good girl."

He backed up, no longer touching me, and slowly, he peeled his wet t-shirt off and let it fall to the floor in a wet heap. His eyes were hooded, jaw jutted up and lip between his teeth as he unbuckled his belt. Jamie was practically fucking me with his eyes as his hands undressed himself, and I squirmed, aching and ready. He pulled a condom from his wallet before kicking off his jeans, and I swallowed, body remembering before my brain what it would feel like to have him inside me again. When he finally dropped his briefs, his erection sprang forward, and my mouth watered. He was so hard, all for me, and that fact obliterated any self-control I thought I had left.

I pushed forward, hands leaving their hold on the glass and reaching for him, instead. But Jamie caught my wrists, backing me into the glass and spinning me until my breasts and cheek were pressed into the glass. One hand held my wrists in place and the other dragged the wrapped condom down my arm, my ribs, the small of my back before he hooked my hips and pulled me back against him. His cock lined my ass and I whimpered, knowing just a few inches of movement could land him where I wanted him.

"Do you moan like that for him?" Jamie asked, the tip of his nose running the back of my neck. "Does he touch you like I do?" He sucked my skin between his teeth and his hand snaked around to find my clit. I should have been angry, I should have thrown him off and realized then

346

what I was doing. But I was blinded by lust, high for the first time in years, and his words only pushed me further into the addict state of mind.

Jamie pushed back, all contact lost, and I heard the rip of the condom wrapper. I breathed hard exactly five times before his hands pulled my hips into him, back arching, and he positioned himself at my opening. I turned my head, lips on the glass, breath fogging up against the rainy night — and then, he filled me, slowly, centimeter by centimeter, burning and stretching and murdering my attempt at rehab once again.

"God*damn*," he breathed, pulling out before gliding in again, this time a little harder, a little deeper. He repeated the motion, each time thrusting me into the glass, and I stared out at the rain-soaked city, wondering if it shielded us from the other high-rises or put us on a more prominent display. I didn't care. Let everyone watch, let everyone see my weakest and most euphoric moment.

Jamie's hands snaked into my hair and he tugged, pulling my hair tie loose, my throat exposed to the city as he rammed into me from behind. He sucked the lobe of my ear between his teeth and chills raced across my skin. Every touch was too much, every kiss too hot. He was consuming me, taking me under, my fight completely lost.

He was close, I could feel the tension in his muscles, the shortness in his breath, but he lifted me suddenly, breaking our contact and carrying me to the couch. I always loved how effortlessly he carried me, like I weighed nothing, like his strength was unstoppable. He touched me with such a gentle, yet firm demand. I felt safe with Jamie. Always.

He threw boxes off the couch, sitting on the middle cushion and pulling my thighs forward until I straddled him. My knees hit the cushion and I leaned forward, bracing on either side, and lowered myself down slowly. We moaned in unison, and Jamie's head fell back.

Which left him staring up at me.

For a moment, we moved slow, his eyes locked on mine, his hands wrapped around my waist. We breathed together, bodies slick with water and sweat, and I felt it. I felt every ounce of pain, of abandonment — all the emotions I'd fought into a closet over the last two years broke down the door and flooded out. Jamie's brows bent as one tear fell down my cheek and he caught it with his thumb, wiping it against my bottom lip before pulling my mouth to his. He kissed me with a promise I wasn't sure I was ready to hear, because in that moment, I wasn't thinking. I only wanted to feel. I wanted to burn.

You know, they say that Bill Wilson asked for whiskey as his dying wish. The man was *dying*, at the end of the line, and he wanted the one vice he'd been fighting all his life. Even the co-founder of Alcoholics Anonymous wanted whiskey on his deathbed.

And so I laid in mine, hand around the bottle, lips pressed to the rim, and I didn't regret a single minute of the night I sealed my fate.

Not one.

• • •

I regretted everything.

"Oh God."

Those were the first two words out of my mouth when I woke the next morning, lying in bed with Jamie, his arm across my stomach. My eyes adjusted to the light streaming in through the window, the sky a bright gray, and I counted the half-packed boxes. Boxes I would be moving. Moving into my fiancé's house.

My fiancé.

"Oh *God*."

I threw Jamie's arm off, scrambling to my feet with the sheet still wrapped around me. It twisted at my ankles and I fell, squeaking. Jamie popped up then, hair mussed, eyes still half-closed.

"Wha— you okay?"

Popping back up, I wrapped the sheet tighter, lifting the fabric from around my ankle and storming over to my closet. "No," I said firmly, closing the door to the closet behind me and dropping the sheet. I pulled on the first pair of jeans and shirt I found, still hopping into them as I spoke through the slits in the door. "No, Jamie, I am not fucking okay."

"What's going on?"

His voice was gravelly, thick with sleep, and it made me want to curl up with him. I kicked myself internally, huffing as I threw the door open, now fully dressed.

"Oh, I don't know. There's a naked man in my bed and it's not the one I'm engaged to."

Jamie scrubbed a hand down his face, watching me as I paced. "You're not getting married."

"What? Of course I am," I scoffed.

Jamie's eyes widened then, like my words were a shot of scalding espresso. "You can't be serious."

"Listen, last night was a—" I paused, waving my hands, still pacing.

"A what?" Jamie asked, standing. He was still naked, abs hard and rippling down to a V that pointed straight to the promise land. I tried not to stare, failed, and made a face when he didn't even attempt to cover himself. "A mistake?"

My brows bent together and I crossed my arms, meeting Jamie's eyes and regretting it immediately. Too many thoughts were flowing through me, each one combatting the one that preceded.

"Don't you fucking say it, B. Don't you say it was a mistake."

I cleared my throat, eyes on the window behind him. "I'm engaged," I croaked, and Jamie let out a loud growl, cursing and running both hands through his hair before storming into the living room. I followed, guilt swallowing me. All I could see was Brad's face, his smile, his trusting eyes. He would be so hurt if he found out what happened. The man who saved me from myself, and I repaid him by falling back into bed with the man who broke me in the first place.

So fucking stupid.

"I can't believe you did this to me!" I screamed as Jamie tugged on his briefs. He swiped his jeans off the floor next, angrily shoving one leg in before the other. "I was happy, I was *okay*, I let you go. And then you just show up here, after two *years* without a single word, and you—"

"You're not happy. You're *numb*. There's a difference."

My mouth popped open. "Don't tell me what I am,

350

Jamie Shaw! If you're so desperate to tell me something, how about telling me why you never called? Huh?"

"Does it really matter?" He threw back, pulling his shirt over his head. It was wrinkled from the rain, but he still looked mouthwatering in it. "You said you'd wait, and I said I'd come. Why did you give up? Why are you trying to push me away right now?"

"Because this isn't right! This," I said, motioning to my empty living room between us. "Isn't okay. We're toxic, Jamie. All we do is hurt each other, hurt the ones who love us, hurt *ourselves*." I was trembling, and Jamie noticed. He exhaled, moving toward me like he wanted to comfort me, but I held up a hand to stop him. "Don't."

Jamie paused, and for a moment we were both silent, the seriousness of the moment settling in around us like dust after a demolition.

"You want to know why I never called?" he asked, his voice low. "You think that will make you feel better? Because it won't."

I didn't answer, and Jamie sighed.

"B, I signed the wedding certificate the morning of the wedding. That was always the plan, sign the certificate before the day began so we wouldn't have to worry about it, and then we could put it away somewhere safe, and take it to the courthouse on Monday."

My stomach fell hearing about Angel. "Okay..."

"I signed it. Before I found out what she did." He sniffed, eyes connecting with mine. "After I left, she signed it, too. And that Monday, when I was trying to figure out my plan of attack to handle shit with her and get to you as fast as I could, she showed up at my house, claiming we were officially married. She went to the courthouse without me, B. We were legally married."

My heart stopped, for three long seconds, and started again with a kick. "Oh my God."

"Yeah," Jamie said, stepping closer. "At first, she begged for me to take her back, to make it work, but obviously, I refused. Then, she got her lawyer involved, and they said they'd go after me for everything because I'd been cheating on *her* with you." He laughed, shaking his head. "They had camera footage of us together in the hotel on what was supposed to be my wedding night with Angel."

My head was spinning, and I reached for the back of the couch, holding it to steady my shaking legs.

"If it was just my Jeep, or just my shitty house she wanted, I wouldn't have cared, B. But my father made me partner — officially. It was my wedding gift. And she wanted to take that, too. She wanted half of everything, if not more. She..." his voice trailed off, and I saw in his eyes that it was painful to even talk about any of this with me. "I got a lawyer. I had to block your number, my family, too. Until it was all resolved, any phone call or email or message on Facebook could have incriminated me. It didn't matter that she'd admitted to cheating the night before our wedding, because in the court's eyes, we'd still gotten married anyway. It was the biggest fucking mess, all of it, and I hated working with slimy lawyers and an even slimier ex. I hated *waiting*. But the only thing that kept me going was knowing that you were waiting, too. For me."

I tried to swallow, but came up dry. I had to sit. I fell to the arm of the couch, hand over my mouth.

"The day Angel finally gave up," he continued, his voice lower now, gruff and sad. "The day I received the finalization of our divorce? That was the same day I received your wedding invitation." He choked on a laugh. "Talk about sick irony."

I shook my head, too many times, temples pounding as my thoughts raced to catch up. "You should have called me. Somehow."

"I did! I called you from what I'm pretty positive is the only payphone still in existence, several times, and you never answered," Jamie shot back, chest heaving.

All the unknown numbers...

My temples throbbed again and I kneaded them with my forefingers, still shaking. "You thought I would wait, and I thought you changed your mind."

Jamie moved to me then, slowly, as if he was waiting for me to stop him. Then, he bent at the knee to meet me at eye-level. "I could never change my mind about you."

I pulled away from his nearness. It was too much. It burned, and not in the way I loved. "No. No, you should have found a way. You gave up too easily. You should have answered my call, or had your lawyer call me, or told Jenna, or fucking smoke signaled. This is too much. You abandoned me."

Words flew from my mouth, but none of it made sense. I felt everything crashing in at once, the universe laughing in the background. It had won again. Timing laughed with it.

"Stop doing this! Stop self-destructing, stop making this harder than it has to be," Jamie said, exhausted. "Maybe you're right, okay? Maybe I should have figured out a way to reach you, but I didn't, because you were supposed to wait. And none of that matters now, want to know why?" He touched my chin, lifting my eyes to his. "Because you still love me. And I love you."

I flew off the couch, running my hands through my hair before spinning to face him again. "No, it *does* matter. Because I'm getting married."

"No, you're not."

"Yes, I am!"

Jamie stood, jaw tight. "You're not marrying anyone but me."

I scoffed, and even as the laugh left my lips, his words sent a harsh yet warming zinger straight to my core. I loved hearing him say that, and hated myself for loving it.

"You can't do this. You can't walk in here, at the one time I finally have my life together, and make me rip it to shreds." The tears didn't slowly build and bubble over, they struck fast, glossing my eyes after one blink and sliding down my cheeks with the second one. "All we do is hurt. All we do is destroy, and one of us is always picking up the pieces, trying to move on or forget or not get our hopes up. It's sick. We're *toxic*." I was crying harder now, and once again Jamie reached for me, but I backed away. "And now, I risked everything I have to be with you last night, because I literally can't say no to you." I shook violently then. "I *cheated* on a man who didn't deserve it, on a man who wants to spend his life with me, on a man I

354

love, all because of my inability to let you go." I cried, tears streaming freely, hot and scarring down my cheeks. "Your love is poisoning me, Jamie!"

He cracked, something between a sob and a groan rumbling in his throat as his face twisted. Jamie crossed the room in three steps, shaking his head and mumbling *no* before pulling me into him. He held me tight, and I fought against another sob until he bent, his lips pressing into mine. I shoved him back hard.

"Stop it! Stop! You have to go, you have to *leave*, Jamie." My breaths were wild, voice too high-pitched.

Jamie stood there, staring at me, willing me with that damn stare of his to change my mind. When I didn't, he growled, punching a box of pans as he passed it and I jumped with the noise. I didn't watch him leave, didn't watch his back move through the door, didn't see his face when he whispered that he'd always love me, didn't hear the slam of the door behind him. All I heard was my heart, beating in my ears. All I saw was my hands, hitting the ground, tears falling to land next to them. All I felt was everything — every aching, shitty thing that had ever existed. Guilt, regret, love, lust, desperation, want, need, pain, fear, loss — all of it, all at once, like being caught inside a huge wave that broke just in front of me, swallowing me down into the depths of a dark, cold ocean of feelings I'd avoided for so long.

I don't know how long I stayed crumpled there on the floor, or how long I cried before my tears dried up along with my voice and I just laid there. My phone rang in the other room, but I didn't move. I soaked in my regret, in the horrific pain that only comes with a relapse, and I paid my penance.

I'd never hated myself more than in that moment.

• • •

I was still sore from Whiskey the night Brad and I finalized our wedding song.

And three months later, on the date that had been crumpled on an invitation between Jamie's hands in my apartment, I married Bradley Neil. I wore the white dress, he wore the black tux, we danced and ate cake and I smiled through it all. But it was a dead smile, a smile that never reached the corners of my lips, and I wondered if I'd ever smile again.

I wondered a lot of things.

I wondered if it was Jamie I saw escaping the back of the church when the priest asked him to speak now or forever hold his peace. Was that him, or had I just imagined it?

I wondered if the gaping hole where Jamie's warm buzz used to exist would ever close, if I'd ever get that part of myself back, or if it'd always belong to him.

I wondered if there would ever be a day, a single day in my entire life, where I would truly shake my addiction.

When I closed my eyes on my wedding night as Brad slipped between my thighs and thought of Jamie instead, I knew I never would. No matter what I said, no matter what I did, my addiction to Whiskey would always live on.

Whether I fed it or not.

TWENTY-THREE

A Love Letter to Whiskey

SO NOW, WE'RE ALL caught up.

It's crazy how fast the buzz comes back after you've been sober for so long.

I opened my door and felt tipsy just at the sight of him, eyes blurring and legs shaking. It used to take me at least a shot to get to this point, but my tolerance level had been weakened by distance and time, and just seeing him warmed my blood. I gripped the knob tighter, as if that'd help, but it was like trying to chug water after passing the point of no return.

Whiskey stood there, on my doorstep, just like he had one year before. Except this time, there was no rain, no anger, no wedding invitation – it was just us.

It was just him – the old friend, the easy smile, the twisted solace wrapped in a glittering bottle.

It was just me – the alcoholic, pretending like I didn't want to taste him, realizing too quickly that months of being clean didn't make me crave him any less.

I told you we couldn't start here.

And we can't end here, either.

It didn't really hurt to see him, didn't really heal, either. I had become so numb since my wedding day, so completely void of emotion. Jenna was worried about me, she wanted me to go talk to someone, and my mom was slowly shifting over to her side, too. I guessed I couldn't really blame them, not when I had self-destructed yet again, ending my marriage after less than five months. The truth was after Jamie left, I'd never been the same. I'd never recovered. I couldn't love Brad because I only had room to love Jamie, and I couldn't love Jamie because it hurt to do so. It was a mess, and I didn't know how to clean it, so I just walked away from it.

I'd moved out of Brad's place over a month ago, and yet boxes still sat stacked in my apartment, and wedding rings still glittered on my finger. I couldn't unpack, I couldn't move on, I couldn't admit to the fact that I'd ruined everything in my life. Work was the only place I wasn't struggling, and it was only because reading and writing and working were my escapes. I turned off my emotions there, and that's when I thrived.

"Can I come in?" Jamie asked. He looked nice, dressed in slacks and a salmon button up that was cuffed at his elbows. His hair was short again, face cleanly shaven, and I swore he'd aged ten years in the twelve months since I'd seen him.

I nodded, backing up and letting him inside. I wondered how he'd found me, if it had been Jenna or if he'd just tried my old apartment hoping I'd be there. I was lucky it was open when I moved out of Brad's. It felt like home, and at the same time, it was tainted with memories — especially of the last night I spent with Jamie.

I wish I could accurately describe what it felt like that day with him, but I was so numb. I had reached my all-time low, and I had no one to blame but myself. It was the moment before I could do anything to change it, the moment when the only thing I was capable of was breathing, and even that was just barely doable.

Jamie had his hands in his pockets, and he looked around my apartment, almost exactly how it had been the last time he'd seen it. When his soft eyes found mine, he offered a sad attempt at a smile. "Hi."

"Hi," I whispered back.

"You've lost weight," he said, and it wasn't a compliment. I'd always been thin, and I knew I didn't look healthy at the moment. But this was the game we played, wasn't it? We always commented on what had changed since the last time we'd seen each other, always ignoring what *hadn't* changed — which was the way we felt.

"And you've shaved."

Jamie rubbed at his jaw before tucking his hand back in his pocket. "I'm sorry I showed up unannounced. I had a work conference down at the Omni and I just… I just wanted to see you."

I swallowed, crossing my arms in the large sweater I was donning. "You want something to drink?" I asked, making my way into the kitchen. I almost reached for a bottle of whiskey, but shifted and grabbed a water from the fridge instead.

"I'm okay."

It was awkward, and it reminded me of when I'd ridden beside him in his Jeep the weekend he was supposed to marry Angel. We hadn't talked since he'd left, since I'd chosen Brad over him. I was mindlessly playing with the wedding rings still on my finger, rings I'd yet to take off even though I knew I should, and Jamie caught the motion with his eyes. His jaw clenched as he leaned against my kitchen island.

"So how are you?"

I almost laughed. How was I? Was it appropriate to tell him I was crazy, that I was depressed and broken and crippled by anxiety and what ifs? I knew it wasn't, I knew he didn't need my bullshit nor did he deserve it, so I forced a smile.

"I'm okay."

He nodded, and I took a moment to really study him — the edge of his jaw, the bulge of his biceps against the fabric of his shirt, the hint of sadness in his eyes as they fell to my wedding rings again. "Are you happy?"

I looked away, toward the window, where the city was cast in an orange glow with the setting sun. I couldn't answer that question without lying to him, so I changed the subject.

"Why are you here?"

Jamie followed my gaze, and we both looked out the window together. It felt like an eternity passed, like we watched the sun set and rise again before he spoke.

"It's been a long year."

His voice echoed in my empty apartment, gravelly and low.

I simply nodded.

"I had a lot of time to think about everything you said, and it killed me that I left the way I did without saying everything I wanted to say to you."

I closed my eyes, sucking my lips between my teeth and bracing myself. I wasn't ready to hear more from him, I wasn't prepared emotionally to do whatever it was he was about to ask me. But he wasn't there to ask for anything, he was there to end it. And in a way, that was worse.

"I want to stop hurting you," he started, and I opened my eyes then, catching his. "I never meant to, and I guess I can't really prove that, but I never meant to play all the games. I never wanted to hurt..." He swallowed, clearing the thickness from his throat with a small shake of his head. His eyes were on his feet then. "I want you to know that I love you, in every sense of the word." My heart fell to my feet and my hand clutched at the fabric of my sweater, twisting, holding on, bracing for the storm. "Things are and always have been very real between us."

My breaths came harder then, because I knew he was right. No matter how fucked up it all had been, it was also real. It was all so, so real.

"You're my best friend," he choked. I was so numb, like my head was submerged in an ice bath, and I couldn't even look at him any longer, so I fixed my gaze on the window again. Jamie stood straighter then. "And I'll always be somewhere for you, no matter the time, place, or circumstance."

A tear rolled swiftly and silently down the side of my face that Jamie couldn't see. I didn't wipe at it for fear I'd give it away.

He crossed the room, stepping into me, and I smelled the honey and oak I'd always loved. I closed my eyes and inhaled a breath I didn't let go of. Not when he kissed my forehead, not when he pressed a small box into my hand, not when he whispered, "Happy birthday," and not when he pushed back again, scent leaving me in a whoosh.

He walked slowly to the door, pausing with his hand on the knob. "I feel like goodbye isn't the right term, so I'll just say until the timing is right…"

I kept my eyes on the window, and only when he closed the door behind him did I breathe again.

I looked down at the small package in my hand, wrapped in brown paper and twine, and I cried.

• • •

I was officially twenty-eight.

It was such a strange birthday. I felt like I should have my shit together, and I clearly didn't. My career was about the only thing I had a handle on, and even that was questionable. I'd lost the man I loved my whole life, fucked up with Mr. Right and the guy who wanted to spend his life with me, and I lived in a small one-bedroom apartment alone.

Luckily, Jenna had showed up less than an hour after Jamie left.

"I don't care what you say, we're going to this stupid, cheesy eighties bar crawl. And you're going to wear this absurd dress with me and we're going to get totally wasted and bring in your twenty-eighth year in style."

Jenna was holding out a fluffy, lavender dress on a hanger to me, puffy shoulders and all. She sat heavy on one hip, typing away on her phone in her other hand, probably to her boyfriend, Dylan. They'd been dating almost since the exact day I started dating Brad. Their relationship proved to be stronger than ours, though, and I had a feeling he would be asking her a big question soon enough. It was sweet that she was here to celebrate my birthday, but celebrating was the last thing I felt like doing.

"I'd much rather opt for ice cream and wine in my pajamas."

Jenna scoffed. "Nope. Not happening. This is going to be your year, B. We have to kick it off the right way so the rest of the year follows suit."

"And an eighties bar crawl is the 'right way?'"

"Duh."

I chuckled, snatching the hideous dress from her hand as she smirked and waved me into my bedroom to change.

In her defense, we did end up having a pretty decent time. We danced and laughed and drank. We drank a *lot*. But by the end of the night, we ended up right back in my apartment. In fact, we ended up in my favorite place in the apartment — my bathtub. Still in our *Sixteen Candles*-ish dresses, tulle fluffed up all around us, and a bottle of Makers Mark that we passed back and forth. Jenna's playlist on her phone echoed off the walls of the bathroom and Jamie's gift sat unwrapped, cradled in the mess of our dresses between us.

"Okay, so are you drunk enough to open it yet?" Jenna finally asked around three in the morning.

I took another swig from the bottle, eyes a little hazy, and laughed. "I don't think that's a reachable point."

"What are you so afraid of?"

I shrugged, kicking the heels off my feet that hung out of the tub. Jenna followed suit, and we swung our bare feet as I passed the bottle back to her. "It's not that I'm scared. I just don't know what good it will do opening it."

"You're not curious?"

"Of course I am."

Jenna huffed. "So open the damn thing. I'm dying over here."

She tossed the box into my lap and I picked it up with shaking fingers, thumbing at the twine and wondering what it could be. It was light, and it rattled with each move of my hands. "I don't know how I'll feel after I open this," I admitted, turning to Jenna then. Jamie had only ever given me one gift before then, and it was a funny one, an inside joke, but this felt heavier.

"Well that's why I'm here," Jenna said with a smile. "To help you figure it out."

She squeezed my leg through the puffy fabric of my dress and my hands gripped the box tighter. I chewed my lip, unsure, but my fingers were already peeling away at the twine and paper. It was strange, the way my heart raced the same way it always had in the presence of Whiskey. Maybe it was the Makers, maybe it was the unknown gift, or maybe it was my body waking up, realizing before even I did that twenty-eight really would be a year of change.

When the paper was shed, I let it fall beside us, popping open the lid of a small, navy blue box. There was tissue paper inside, wrapped around something, and I was still shaking slightly as I peeled it back.

"Oh my God," I whispered when the tissue was gone. Jenna leaned in closer as I rubbed the cool metal of a simple charm keychain.

There were six charms, and one small note.

Even if you must move on,
please don't ever let us go.

I read the note over and over, eyes misting before I thumbed through the charms. There was no explanation needed for them.

It was a keychain, which reminded me of our drives, so many of them over the years. The nights we laughed, nights we hurt, nights we just existed as a boy and a girl. His passenger seat would always be mine, and this keychain proved it.

The first charm I noticed was a music note. Classical music, our rare and kind of weird relatable preference. I thought of the playlists we'd had over the years, of The Piano Guys, of music that didn't need words the same way Jamie and I never did.

Next was a surfboard, followed by a cat. I laughed at that one, wondering if that story had really meant more to him than I ever knew. Then, there was a bottle of whiskey. It looked similar to Jack Daniel's, and memories of the bon fire at Alder flooded my mind at first before I realized it was also our first shot together. In my kitchen, all those years ago, when the addiction hadn't yet been discovered and yet we had both felt it playing just below the surface.

So many times we'd been burned, and yet every time we wanted more.

The last two I focused on made my chest ache. One was a simple silver airplane, and I thought about the distance between us over the last several years. Between Florida and California, and then Florida and Pennsylvania, and always in our minds. Distance and time had always dictated so much for us, and for the first time in my life, I was starting to wonder why I let it. The very last charm was a flat, rose gold heart. I didn't have to think hard on that one. His heart belonged to me, just like mine would always belong to him.

"You okay?" Jenna asked after a moment. I was so silent and still, save for the slight movement of my thumbs over the charms.

"He loves me," I whispered. I'd known it all along, I'd heard it a million times, yet it was the first time it actually hit me. "Even after all this, Jenna. He *loves* me."

She nodded, leaning her head on my shoulder and passing me the bottle of whiskey. "I think he always has, babe."

I sniffed, not wanting to cry because I wasn't sad. I really wasn't. I was relieved, and hopeful — even if unrightfully so.

"What am I supposed to do? All we do is hurt each other. How do I know we'll ever be able to make it? How do I trust him with a heart he's broken so many times?"

Jenna thought while I thumbed through the charms again, thoughts racing.

366

"What's your biggest fear with it all? You know as well as I do that if you give your heart to him, really give it to him, he'd never do anything to hurt you. If anything, it should be *him* who's afraid — and clearly he's not. So what's the real issue?"

I chewed my bottom lip, answers to her question swirling in my head. "It's just, look at the path of destruction we've laid. He cheated, I cheated... twice." I cringed with the admission. "We've hurt others around us, and we've never *really* been together. It's always been about not being able to have each other. What if it's just about wanting what we can't have? What if that's all part of the allure? It just feels wrong, and in the eyes of most sane people, it is. We're built on lust and bad decisions."

"But are you?" Jenna challenged, sitting up again. She turned to face me, tucking her feet inside the tub. "No, you and Jamie never had it easy. And yes, you hurt a lot of people along the way. But at the end of the day, it's your life, B. You have to live with it, no one else. So you can't think about the people around you, how you've hurt them or what they think of you. It's up to *you* to be happy because no one else is going to do it for you." She smiled then, blue eyes bright in my dim bathroom. "Whatever you choose, make sure it makes you happy."

"That sounds a little selfish."

Jenna shrugged. "Yeah well, sometimes selfish and smart are synonymous."

It was like surviving an explosion. For over a year, my ears had been ringing, eyes adjusting to the smoke, and now, all of a sudden, everything had cleared. I'd let myself be ruled by fear and anger, pain and sadness, but

● ● ●

The next morning, while Jenna was still fast asleep in my bed, I sat down at my laptop, and I started writing.

I started writing my love letter to Whiskey.

I started writing the book you're reading now.

The honest, hard to read and even harder to write account of my eleven-year addiction to Whiskey.

I know I've put you, as a reader, through a lot. Maybe through too much. I wouldn't blame you if you hated me right now, because the truth is there are more than a few times in my life where I made the wrong decision. I am flawed, and though I know it was hard to read, I'm not sorry for telling the truth. I'm not ashamed of my path. In a way, I think it's about figuring out who we are through the mistakes we make.

I know who I am. And I know who I need.

So, Whiskey, if you're reading this, I hope now you understand. We've always blamed timing, but the timing has always been right — we just never listened.

Up until this point, I've never fought hard enough. But if you give me the chance, I'll fight every single day of our lives together. I'll go to battle for you, and I'll win the war in the end.

You asked me for one day, but one day never came. You asked me to choose you, and I never did. You asked me to be with you, and I never was.

But now, it's our time.

One day is here, and I choose you. I've never been anyone else's but yours, and I never want that to change.

Now, you just have to choose me, too.

I'm sorry that up until now, I saw you as something I should quit instead of something I should fight for.

My heart is, always has been, and always will be yours.

By the time I finish this, by the time you maybe, *hopefully* read it, you'll be on the cusp of your thirtieth birthday. I don't know where you are, I don't know who you're with, but I hope you remember. I hope you remember our drives. I hope you remember our days on the water, our nights in the sand, our wasted time and the minutes we cherished. More than anything, I hope you remember the pact you made to a wide-eyed girl eleven years ago.

I've hurt you. You've hurt me. I don't deserve you, and you've always deserved me. You don't have to forgive me, you don't have to leave the past behind, but I'm asking you to, anyway.

This is my love letter to you… everything I have is in these pages. Now the pen is in your hand.

Come find me, Whiskey.

I'll be waiting.

The End.

EPILOGUE

Last Drop

THE SURF IS GOING to be perfect today.

It's just barely past eight in the morning, and I'm sitting in my favorite spot in the entire world — Jamie's passenger seat. Our boards are strapped in on top of the Jeep, two half-empty iced-coffees sitting between us, and the wind whips our hair around as we cruise down to the beach.

It always burns a little, sitting in this seat, thinking of what could have been. I've tried to let those thoughts go over the years, but it's not as easy as it seems.

It's not easy not to think about the years that passed that I could have been his, or about the nights we both spent alone that we could have spent together. It hurts to think about, and yet I can't *not* think about it all. I think sometimes life is about embracing what hurts, because pain is one of the most vivid emotions we can feel. Pain reminds us that we *are* alive, and I'll always appreciate that stinging reminder.

Jamie's hair is longer, just the way I like it, and he wears an easy grin as we drive. Barrel-aged Whiskey looks even better in the bright morning light, the amber notes in his eyes shining. He's talking about the surf report and where to eat lunch, but a ray of sun hits the wedding band on his left hand as he shifts positions on the steering wheel, and suddenly my mind is far away.

He did finally get married, just a few months after his thirtieth birthday.

I swallow, chest aching a bit as I think about the lucky woman who will get to live out the rest of her life as his wife. She and I don't really get along, but I'm sure that's no surprise to you.

She doesn't deserve Jamie, though I guess no one ever will in my eyes. Honestly, I think his wife is selfish. I think she's a little lost, a little broken, and a little too fond of making mistakes. Sometimes it hurts when I see them together, but I don't let myself focus on the bad, because the truth is she makes him happy. It may not make sense to me, but it doesn't have to — because he loves her.

And that's enough for me.

I kick my sandals off, propping my feet on the warm dashboard in Jamie's Jeep just as a familiar melody comes over the speakers. *The Piano Guys* always take me back to the first time I sat beside Jamie, and it must do the same for him because he stops talking, hand reaching for my thigh. He gives it a gentle squeeze and every cell in my body buzzes to life at the touch.

I lay my head back against the seat and tilt my head to look up at him — my Jamie, my Whiskey. He's looking at me in the way he always has, the way I hope he always will, and I wonder if he'll ever be able to touch me without me feeling that same familiar, aching burn.

But that's the thing about whiskey, isn't it?

It's strong, to the very last drop.

I face the windshield again just as we park, the waves rolling in ahead of us, sunshine blazing hot on our shoulders. I inhale the salty breeze, letting go of the breath slowly, breathing in the moment. Sometimes I feel like we have to rush, but then I remember that time isn't our enemy the way I always thought. Turns out, time is our friend — the friend we never listened to, but we're learning how to more and more every day. The friend who might have always known a little more about us than we did.

You see, I may not always like his wife, and she may be far from perfect...

But I'm so happy she's me

Love,

Whiskey

"Timing is a hell of a thing. In the end,
that's what it all comes down to.
The potency of an attraction or the
purity of a connection mean very little
if you're on separate journeys. You and I were
a perfect fit, we were, there was just
too much distance between us to see it."

— SEPARATE JOURNEYS | Beau Taplin

PROLOGUE
The Beginning of the End

"ARE YOU FUCKING KIDDING me?"

I stood there on B's doorstep, just like I had two times before.

The first time, I had her wet, crinkled-up wedding invitation in my hand and the fury of every Greek god rolling through me as I stared at her in disbelief, ready to remind her that she was damn sure *not* marrying anyone — not unless it was me.

The second time, I was resigned, heartbroken, a shell of who I once was as I finally admitted to myself that she was never mine at all.

I let her go that day.

She was married — or so I thought. She had a new life to start. She'd told me, right to my face, how badly I'd hurt her, how much loving me brought her pain. And I admitted to that. I apologized for it, and I meant every word. I begged her with one last gift not to forget us, even as she moved on, and then... I left.

That was the last time I saw her.

And then, two years later, I saw her fucking book.

I didn't read much — not anything outside of the surfing magazines I subscribed to, anyway. But I was walking past a bookstore in downtown Miami when I saw the window display, dozens and dozens of copies of that black and white book with those golden letters on the front.

I'd walked past that bookstore for years. It was between my father's office and the bar we frequented every Friday for happy hour.

Hundreds of times, I'd likely walked past that exact display without noticing it. Maybe hundreds of times. I didn't know how long ago the book had been published, or how long it had been a bestseller, and to this day, I have no idea what made me *finally* look at that window as I strolled past. Perhaps it was the universe, ready to fuck with me again after leaving me to suffer alone for a while.

It wasn't the title that made me stop.

It was the name.

Brecks Kennedy.

I'm not sure how long I stood there gaping at the window, blinking over and over, trying to convince myself I wasn't seeing what I thought I was. When I finally came to, I ran inside and all but threw my credit card at the poor cashier, immediately rushing back to my apartment and devouring the whole thing in one night.

One long, sleepless, agonizing night.

She'd lied to me.

Okay, maybe *lie* was a strong word — but she'd let me believe she was still married that day I showed up to let her go. She had that ring on her finger, and I just assumed...

Looking back now, I can see all the signs I missed in my depressed daze. Because that first time I'd shown up with her wedding invitation, half her apartment was in boxes. She was *moving*. Out. Or rather *in* with her soon-to-be husband.

So why was she still in her apartment when I went back those months later?

I should have realized it, but I didn't. The only thing I could process at that time in my life was letting her go.

And damn it if I didn't fail miserably — even when I told her that's what I was doing.

She wrote a book for me.

She wrote a book for me.

For me. *About* me.

About *us*.

Now, my third time standing in this doorway and looking into her apartment, the light shining through her floor-to-ceiling windows overlooking Pittsburgh, I felt everything I'd tried to deny myself for nearly two years.

I felt the rush of her eyes meeting mine, the possession that always rolled through me when she was in my presence, the magnet — strong as ever — pulling me into her before she could even register that it was me.

"Jamie," she breathed, and the sound of my name on her lips nearly unraveled me, nearly erased any questions I had or any urgency to know what the fuck that book meant. The way she said my name always tested my willpower, and at that moment, I nearly gave in, nearly pushed through that door and slammed her into the wall and took what I knew was always mine.

But I managed a breath, holding up the tattered book I'd read a dozen times in the last week.

"What the hell is this?"

If you're reading this, dear reader, then I know you've read B's story. I know you had to go through the same torture I did — perhaps even more so, since you lived out those thirteen years in the matter of approximately three-hundred-and-sixty-two pages.

You deserve to know what happened next.

You deserve a happy ending — at least, as *happy* as masochists such as ourselves can provide.

But, before I can tell you the end of *her* side of the story, I need to at least tell you some of *my* side.

So, again, we can't start here.

We have to go back.

Way back.

To the very first drop...

ONE

Assassin

SHE WAS RIGHT ABOUT one thing.

The first day I met B, she did, in fact, fall flat on her face.

It was particularly hot that day in south Florida, sweat rolling down my back in consistent streams as I ran the path I'd frequented since I was a freshman. Primarily in the fall, that path that circled a little suburbia lake was part of my morning ritual. Basketball season was in full effect, which meant running in the mornings and staying well after practice in the afternoons to work on my lay ups and free-throw shots.

If you couldn't tell already by B's recount of our love story, I'm persistent when it comes to what I'm passionate about.

I can still remember every singular moment of that first taste of each other, from the way my sneakers sounded hitting the paved trail to the steady rhythm of my breath as I ran. It seemed like the universe slowed down time when I looked up from my feet and saw them — Jenna and B — running side by side before B pulled out a little in front.

She thinks I didn't see the exact moment when she noticed me, but it was impossible to miss.

I felt her eyes on me like warm hands, like an embrace from an old friend and a kiss from a stranger all at once.

Those slate gray eyes pierced me right through the chest, enough that I pressed my lips together against the sting of them. I smirked a little when those eyes wandered the length of me, and I gave myself permission to do the same — taking in her wild and unruly hair, the freckles speckling her cheeks, the lean, athletic build of her body, her toned little stomach peeking out between the band of her black shorts and white tank top. I remember her legs more than anything, how she was so short, and yet they seemed to stretch on for days, and my eyes caught on her neon pink sneakers for just a moment before I snapped my focus back to her eyes.

Or, it *would* have been her eyes, if she hadn't turned around to mouth something to Jenna.

Keep in mind that I was as stupid boy back then, so while *now* I would have realized the plan of attack should have been to slow to a walk and try to talk to them as they flew past, back then, my peanut brain thought it made more sense to *accidentally* run into her.

I'd drastically underestimated how much of a punch that little thing could pack when she slammed into me.

Or how much of a backboard *I* was, since I sent her flying straight to the ground.

Still, the plan *did* work in a way. Because though she was on her ass, she was looking up at me — those peculiar gray eyes — and when I smiled down at her, offering my hand to help her up, I knew she felt it, too.

I didn't know what *it* was, to be clear. I knew it was something — new, unfamiliar, exciting. But again, I had teenage boy brain.

Which is exactly why everything happened the way it did in those next few minutes, setting off a domino effect of bad timing and things — *people* — getting in our way.

B slipped her hand into mine, feather-light and un-sure, her eyes as wide as silver dollars.

"You okay?" I asked, subtly checking her for bruises or bleeding. I wanted her to answer before I tried to help her stand.

But she didn't respond.

She didn't so much as breathe as she looked at me, which I know *now* was because she was apparently stunned by my handsomeness — her words, not mine. But at the time, I read that little quirk of her brow and lack of response as rejection.

I read it as her not being interested, not even a little bit.

I read it as my mere presence offending her.

I read it wrong.

"Oh my God, are you fucking blind?!"

Jenna was the first to speak to me, and then she promptly shoved me away from B, stealing her hand from mine and hoisting her up.

B was still a little off-kilter when Jenna turned on me, those little blue eyes of hers narrowed. "How about you brush that long ass hair out of your eyes and watch where you're going, huh, champ?"

Jenna crossed her arms then, popping her hip to the side, and that's when I noticed *her*.

Tan and curvy, long blonde hair, a spicy attitude rolling off her in heat waves that both terrified and amused me. She cocked her brow at me when I didn't answer, and so I arched mine right back.

And for just a split second, Jenna's shield yielded, and I saw the faintest blush on her cheeks.

"Hi," I said, reaching out for Jenna's hand this time. "I'm Jamie."

"Well, *Jamie*, maybe you should make an appointment with the eye doctor before you run over another innocent jogger. And you owe Brecks an apology."

Jenna nodded toward B, who cringed and shrank away from me.

Again — at the time, I read this as her being so disgusted by me that she physically grimaced. I didn't know the story of why she hated her name, that it was hearing *Brecks* as her introduction that had her nose crinkling like that.

I smirked at Jenna first, and then tried that smile on B as I said, "I'm sorry. I should have been watching where I was going."

With that last word, I arched my brows a bit, because B and I *both* knew it wasn't me who had been turned around mouthing something to my friend and not watching the running path.

But then again, *she* didn't know I'd run into her on purpose...

"It's fine," B murmured, her cheeks tinging pink.

I tilted my head then because that blush threw me off. I wondered if I'd read the situation all wrong, if maybe she *was* interested. I tried to find the answer to that question in her eyes, but then Jenna cleared her throat, and my attention snapped back to her.

So, you see, B was right about a few things when she told you about the first time we met. But she was wrong about one very, crucial point.

I didn't see Jenna first.

I saw her.

I just didn't think she saw *me*.

• • •

Trying to explain what happened in the following months is like trying to understand the concept of how large the universe is.

Dating Jenna was easy. We just… *fit*.

She was the captain of the cheerleading squad and I was on the basketball team. We looked good together. We *felt* good together. And as a teenage boy, there was nothing more I could ask for than to have one of the hottest girls in school as my girlfriend — and to get *all* the perks that went along with that.

And yet… I still wanted more.

More meaning B.

She came with dating Jenna, part of the package, and at first, I assumed I'd have to win her over since I was relatively certain she hated me after that first interaction on the running trail.

What B didn't tell you in her side of the story is that she was rather prickly with me in those first couple of weeks. Any time I would show up to walk Jenna to her next class, or we'd hang out by my Jeep after school, B would find an excuse to leave.

But not before throwing me a dirty look for good measure.

I thought she hated me, thought I wasn't good enough for her best friend, maybe, or that I smelled or something.

It wasn't until that evening on our surfboards — a happy accident that I later realized was one of the biggest moments of my adolescent life — that I wondered if that was just how B was.

Reserved. Careful. Hesitant to trust.

When she told me about her name, about why she never wanted anyone to call her by it, I understood why.

My attraction to B didn't strike me like lightning. It didn't hit suddenly and all at once. It bled into my skin, my muscles, my bones, my *soul* like an assassin in the dead of night.

It was slow, and calculated, powerful and deceiving.

And once it had its hands on me, I was forever in its grip.

We both knew we were walking a dangerous line. I felt it in the way she looked at me, the way she flushed when my knee touched hers at the football games, the way she couldn't bear to watch when Jenna was in my arms.

And like the selfish little hormonal prick I was, I didn't want to stop it.

I knew with just a few words I could shut it down. I knew I could stop giving her rides to school, I could stop sitting with her at the games, I could stop surfing with her, riding around town with her, finding every excuse possible to be with her.

I could… but then again, I couldn't.

She was, in every sense of the word, my addiction.

But it wasn't until Christmas Eve that I realized she was my salvation, too.

There was a demon slowly being born in the hollow of my chest that fall semester — my *last* fall semester in high school. I'd been able to mute it by throwing myself into basketball, spending time with Jenna, and pretending like I didn't have deeper feelings for B.

But when Jenna left for Colorado that Christmas break, and basketball practice was put on hold until after the holiday, I couldn't ignore it any longer.

It sucked me down into a dark, bottomless ocean, cutting off every breath I tried to take. It pelted me with every question, worry, and fear I'd been so artfully avoiding.

I was graduating high school. I was leaving Florida. I was moving on to the next chapter of my life.

And I was fucking petrified.

It was after midnight when I reached for my phone more out of panic and desperation than anything else, and I didn't know *then* why B was the first person I thought of, but I know now.

- Are you awake? -

My heart was in my throat as I waited for her to answer, staring at the open text screen in the otherwise dark of my bedroom. I'd kicked the covers off, laying spread eagle in my bed in just my boxers as I waited for her to answer.

- Indeed I am. -

The breath of relief that flooded out of me was unlike anything I'd ever known — more so than hitting a shot at the buzzer.

I should have known then I was playing with fire.

- Take a drive with me? -

- Sure. -

I jumped out of bed so fast, I tripped on the sheets tangled around my ankles, thumping hard to the floor. But I was up in the next heartbeat, hurriedly yanking on a hoodie and basketball shorts and grabbing my keys.

Fifteen minutes later, B was in my passenger seat, her bare feet on my dash.

I didn't realize it then, the comfort just that alone brought me. That seat beside me? It belonged to her — literally *and* metaphorically. And when she was there, everything felt okay.

I had the music turned up far too loud, trying and failing to drown out my thoughts. William Joseph's "Standing the Storm" spilled from the speakers as I drove us through town. It was quiet that night, barely any other cars on the road, because every normal person not suffering from a panic attack was home in bed waiting on Santa Claus.

It was an hour of me sighing and shifting around and gripping the wheel so tight my knuckles hurt before B reached forward and turned down the music.

"Did I ever tell you about why I hate cats?"

I frowned, thinking I'd misheard her as my head snapped back. But when I realized I'd heard correctly, the faintest smile found my lips. "Oh, this ought to be good."

"See, I had a cat once," she said, sitting up straighter and tucking her feet under her thighs. I still remember how... *comfortable* she looked in that moment. She wore an oversized sweatshirt and tiny little shorts, her toes painted a bright purple.

That moment, right there, was the first time I felt the urge to hold her.

"Her name was Aurora," she continued, snapping me back to her story. "Like the princess, but we called her Rory. Only she wasn't a princess. Like, at all. She was actually the devil."

A loud laugh boomed out of my throat.

"She refused to shit in her litter box. I'm serious — refused. She would shit right outside of it, instead. And because I'd begged my mom for the damn cat, guess who got stuck picking up after her?" She poked both thumbs into her chest. "This girl. But that wasn't the worst of it."

God, why is she so fucking cute it hurts?

"Should I pull over for this?" I asked.

"This is serious, Jamie Shaw!" She smacked my bicep, and damn it if I didn't love the way she looked when I teased her.

"Anyway," she continued. "So, Rory would always find small ways to torture me. Like she would eat her string toys and then throw up on my favorite clothes. Or wait until I was in the deepest part of sleep and jump onto my bed, meowing like an alley cat right up in my ear."

"I think I like this Rory."

She glared at me like she wasn't afraid to hit me right in the balls if I kept pushing her, which only made me grin wider.

"You think you're hilarious, don't you? Do you just sit around and laugh at your own jokes? Do you write them down and re-read them at night?"

That earned her a real laugh from me.

"As I was saying," she said, giving me another look before she continued. "She was a little brat. But for some weird reason, she always loved to be in the bathroom with me when I took my baths."

"You take baths?"

The question flew out before I could stop it, because now, all I was thinking about was B, naked, bubbles covering everything but her head and knees.

"You're seriously missing the point of this story!"

"There's a point to this story?" I teased, trying to ignore that I was *still* thinking about her in a bathtub.

B huffed, but couldn't hide the way I was making her smile.

I loved that.

God, it was like a hit of cocaine.

"Yes!" she screamed with a bit of a laugh. "The point is, I thought that was our bonding time. Rory would weave around my legs while I undressed, and she'd hang out on the side of the tub the entire time I was in the bath, meowing occasionally, pawing at the water. It was kind of cute."

"So you bridged your relationship with your cat during bath time?"

"Ah, well see, one would think that. But, one night, that little demon hopped onto the counter and just stared at me. I couldn't figure out why, but she just wouldn't stop staring. She kept inching her paw up, setting it back down, inching it up, setting it down. And finally, I realized what she was going to do — and she knew I did — because as soon as realization dawned, Rory smiled at me — swear to God — and flipped the light off in the bathroom."

The image had me doubling over, fighting through my laughter to keep my eyes on the road.

"I'm terrified of the dark, Jamie! It was awful! And so I jumped up, scrambling to find a towel so I could turn the light back on. But because I'm a genius, I yanked on the shower curtain to help me stand up, but that only took it down, and me along with it. I fell straight to the floor, but I broke my fall with my hands instead of my face."

"Luckily."

"Oh," she chided. "Yeah. So lucky. Except guess where Rory's litter box was?"

My eyes widened, and I turned to her with realization striking like a hot iron. "No!"

"Ohhh yeah. My left hand landed right smack in the middle of a steaming pile of poo. And Rory laughed inside that little manic head of hers as she watched the whole show."

I was thankful we pulled up to a red light then, because I was laughing so hard I had this old man wheeze thing going on.

"This seriously has to be made up."

"I only wish I was that creative."

We both laughed, and the tension that had been hanging around me since the start of Christmas break had thawed a bit. When the light turned green, I sighed, taking it slower than before as I continued our cruise.

"So. Baths, huh?"

I couldn't help myself.

Fucking masochist — as if you didn't know that by now.

B nodded, untucking her legs and resting her feet on the dash again. "Yep. I do my best thinking submerged in a tub of hot water. Bubbles are an added bonus."

She winked.

I tried *really* hard not to get a boner.

"Baths are to you as driving is to me."

"Mm-hmm," she agreed. "Which brings us to the purple elephant in the car." She leaned her head back, eyeing me as the smile slipped from my face. "Care to tell me the reason we're driving around this dead ass town in the middle of the night?"

My stomach tightened at the question, at the way it felt for someone to point a flashlight into my darkness and demand to know what's there.

"I don't know, B," I said after a moment. "I just... ever since school let out, I can't stop thinking about how fast everything is changing. I mean, it's Christmas, my last Christmas home with my family. In six months, I'll no longer be in high school. In eight, I'll no longer be in Florida. It feels like my entire life I've been aching to grow up and move on, and now that it's all here, I'm dreading it."

My rib cage squeezed in on my lungs.

"It's too soon," I croaked. "I'm not ready. I'm... scared."

I took a sharp left turn toward the beach, knowing then that I needed it. I needed the sand between my toes,

394

the sea breeze in my hair, the sound of the waves to sooth my thoughts.

"It's okay to be scared," B whispered.

"Is it?" I challenged, parking the Jeep in a free spot in front of a beach bar.

I rolled down my window to check the parking meter, making sure I didn't need to pay, and when I verified it was free this time of night, I sighed, resting my elbow on the window panel.

"I've always been so sure of everything. Confident. And here I am at one of the most exciting times of my life and I feel like hiding."

Admitting it aloud felt like trying to eat mud.

B rolled her window down, too, so I cut the engine. Immediately, the distant sound of waves rolling in against the shore behind the bar filtered in, and I swear we both visibly relaxed, the way you do when you get home after a long day.

"I think it's normal, to feel both excited and terrified of the future," B said after a while. "And I'd be willing to bet every senior goes through what you are right now. You're excited to get out of high school, but also sad, because as much as it's sucked, it's been fun, too. I mean, look at you — you're this big basketball star and you're playing your last season, your hot little girlfriend is a junior, so you know she's not coming with you, and you're going from a familiar city and state to one you've only visited before now."

My stomach soured at the mention of Jenna.

Because I realized in that moment, I hadn't really thought of her. Not like I should have been. I didn't think of her when I texted B, or the entire past hour I'd had her in my car. And when I voiced my fears... leaving her wasn't one of them.

That had to be a bad sign.

"What I'm saying is, it's okay to feel what you're feeling," B continued. "I'd be more concerned if you weren't scared."

For a minute we were silent, and I ran both hands back through my hair.

"What if I fail? What if I hate college and all the pressure and I just crack?"

"You won't."

"But what if I do?"

"You won't, Jamie," she said again, leaning over the console. She said it with such conviction, such honest belief that it made my eyes water.

She wouldn't speak again until I looked at her, and when I did, my next breath was a fiery one — smoky and difficult to consume. Her gray eyes shone in the bit of moonlight creeping in through the windshield, her curls soft and frizzy and wild, and I wanted to trace the constellations the freckles on her cheeks made, just like the stars in the sky.

"Over the past few months, I've learned a lot about you," she said. "I know that when you want something — *truly* want it — there's no chance in hell you'll ever give up on it. Like when you wanted me to go watch one of your stupid basketball games, even though you knew how much I hated it and you found new ways to pester me every day until I finally gave in."

396

She laughed a little at that, trying to lighten the mood. What she didn't realize was that in that moment, staring into her moonlit eyes, I was having an epiphany.

And when she cleared her throat and leaned in a little closer, I nearly passed out from the strength it took to keep from kissing her.

"I know how much your family means to you, how much the firm means to you, and since you never play fair," she teased, "you don't have to worry about not succeeding."

I tried to smile, tried to shake off every thought that was assaulting me then — which no longer included anything about high school or college. But B reached out, her hand gently resting on top of mine, and I let out a shaky breath through my nose as I focused on that point of contact.

"In all seriousness, you're not going to fail. Because that's not who you are. And I think once your feet hit California, you're going to buzz to life with the energy there and use that to drive you forward. And you're going to drink too much and stay up too late, but you're also going to study hard and work harder, and one day you'll be back here, running the firm, with the wife and kids you've always wanted."

I didn't miss the way her eyes flicked down at that, and it made me wish more than anything that I could jump inside her head and know if she felt what I was feeling, too.

"And I'm going to be sitting right here saying, 'I told you so.'"

I angled myself toward her, then, unable to resist the pull of gravity any longer. And with that slight adjustment, we were just inches away from something that would ruin us both. I knew it. I know now that *she* knew it.

I looked at her lips, and I wanted to taste them so badly, I didn't care what the consequences were.

"I hope you're right," I finally whispered.

I swallowed, turning my hand where hers hovered over it. I wanted to hold her. I wanted to lace my fingers with hers and feel what we could be if we gave in to that moment.

But she backed away quickly, forcing a smile and a playful wink. "Always am."

It was like a rubber band snapping, a painful little sting to knock me back to reality. I think I smiled at her. I think I looked out the window. I know for sure I turned on a new playlist, mostly because if I didn't have something to distract me, I was going to do something stupid.

It was almost dawn when I turned the Jeep on without asking if B was ready to go home. Regardless of her answer, I knew we both needed to get back.

When we pulled into her driveway, I let the Jeep idle, wishing the universe could give me just a few more hours of darkness.

B reached for the door handle, and the need to keep her with me even just a little bit longer won.

"Can I ask you something?"

She paused, nodding.

"What happened to Rory?"

She gave a sleepy smile. "My grandma came and stayed with us not too long after the bathroom incident, and she and Rory fell in love. I suggested she take her, and I'd barely gotten the sentence out before Grandma was loading her up in the car."

I returned her smile, eyes searching hers, looking for an answer to a question I hadn't been bold enough to ask.

"Can I ask you something now?" she whispered.

"You can always ask me anything."

You would have thought those words were a bucket of ice water for how B's demeanor shifted with them.

"If Jenna wasn't out of town, would you have texted her tonight instead?"

I frowned, heart picking up its pace in my chest.

No.

That was the answer that roared inside me, my soul begging me to just tell her the truth. But the better part of me knew that wouldn't be right.

Maybe I also knew that once we crossed that line, there would be no going back.

And I didn't know if that was really what I wanted.

I cared about Jenna. I was intimate with Jenna in a way I hadn't been with any other girl before. I didn't want to hurt her.

And I didn't want to mislead B until I knew for sure.

Words were lead in my stomach, too dense and heavy to lift.

"Don't make me answer that," I breathed.

I watched her for a reaction, for a tell to let me know if she wanted me to say yes, or no, or if she felt what I was feeling. But she was stone cold, her poker face impeccable.

Nodding, her lips spread into a quick smile, but it slipped just as quickly as it'd appeared. "Goodnight, Jamie."

With that, she opened the door and closed it as quietly as she could. I waited until she successfully snuck in through her bedroom window, and then I drove away.

My mind raced even more once she was out of my car, but the subject matter had dramatically shifted. I spent every moment of that drive home reminding myself that I cared about Jenna, but that didn't mean I couldn't care for B, too. And of course, I felt attracted to her, because she was gorgeous and fun and… different. But that didn't make me a bad person. And it didn't mean I had to fuck everything up to act on impulse.

But it wasn't until I brushed my teeth and climbed into my bed, the morning light shining through my blinds, that I realized what I felt.

I scrambled for my phone, taking it off the charger long enough to type out the text.

— **Thanks for tonight… You're my best friend, B.** —

She didn't answer, but somehow I knew she felt the same.

And so, we slipped back into our normal — me dating her best friend, her dating her surfboard, and both of us convincing ourselves that friendship was all that existed between us.

T W O

The Fact

I WASN'T SURPRISED WHEN Jenna broke up with me.

Maybe I should have been. Maybe, if I only saw our relationship from the outside the way B did, I would have been shocked. Maybe if I experienced it through Jenna's perspective, the doting attention I gave her, and how I couldn't keep my hands off her, I would have found it hard to believe.

But the truth was, after Christmas Eve?

I was never the same.

I was with Jenna, in every way a boyfriend can be. We spent all our waking hours together, held hands in the hallway, filled our weekends with dates whenever one of us didn't have practice.

I was with Jenna.

But I wasn't *with* Jenna.

Because in my head, I was always with B.

I could deny it all day long, play the part of just being her friend when anyone else was around, but the sick truth

401

was that I couldn't get the girl off my mind. I tried spending less time with her, but that only made the thoughts louder and more demanding. And when I *did* spend time with her, I found a million more reasons to feel the way I did.

It was sick, and selfish, and not fair to Jenna.

Which was why when she broke up with me, I wasn't surprised — but still, I *was* hurt.

There's nothing like that first heartbreak. We can all think back to ours — middle school, high school, maybe after. The first time you thought you had your whole future in front of you with someone, and then very suddenly, realized you didn't have shit.

That's what I mourned when Jenna broke up with me.

I saw our relationship playing out like my mom and dad's did. I saw high school sweethearts turning into husband and wife. I saw a house full of kids. I saw going to the same college and building a life together.

I even thought, eventually, I'd drop my fascination with B.

But when Jenna broke up with me, and the first thing I wanted to do was drive straight to B's house, I knew I was in big, *big* trouble.

First and foremost, I didn't want to hurt Jenna. I also didn't want to hurt B. And by running to her in that moment, I would have done both. I would have put B in a difficult position, choosing between being loyal to her best friend and being there for me, and I would have made Jenna question our relationship, question what she meant to me.

Especially because I knew damn sure that I would have made a move on B.

I was in too vulnerable a space, and I wanted so desperately to let B fill the void. I knew she would have, too. I knew if I showed up, ran my hands back through that curly hair of hers and tugged until she looked up at me, I know she would have let me kiss her.

So, I stayed away.

I didn't so much as text B, let alone call her or go to her place. I threw myself into the last month of school I had left, spending time with the guys on the basketball team and getting everything ready to move to California.

I stayed away.

Until I didn't.

I can't explain the mood that slipped over me the night of graduation. Maybe it was a mixture of anxiety and immense relief, a dizzying cocktail of pride and fear. I wasn't really worried about going to college anymore — mostly because I knew it was happening, plain and simple, so I might as well embrace it. I *also* wasn't super sad about graduating. I knew I'd miss high school, but in a sense... I was ready to leave.

So, after my gown and graduation cap had been put away in my room, I told my parents I was going out to celebrate, dodging my youngest sister and her plea to join me.

I picked up a few guys from the team in the Jeep, their 7-Eleven cups filled with something more than the orange soda it looked like. I played it calm, cool, and collected the whole drive to B's, but there was a storm brewing inside me, thunder rolling and lightning crackling enough to make the hairs on my arms stand up.

I'd been inside B's house a few times, chatted with her mom while B got ready to surf or picked out her outfit for the football game, but I'd never seen it like that. Every inch was packed, people dancing and playing drinking games, smoking and laughing, making out and hooking up. The music was so damn loud you had to scream to hear anything, and it was so unbearably hot that I wanted to strip my clothes off as soon as we walked all the way inside.

Of course, B beat me to it.

I'll never forget that moment, walking into the crowded house and seeing her through said crowd like a fucking vision. She looked around like she was trying to solve a math equation, and then with a shrug, she crossed her arms over her midriff to grab the hem of her V-neck, lavender shirt.

And she peeled it off slowly, the damp fabric sticking to her skin, revealing nothing but a thin, white tank top beneath.

I knew without asking for confirmation that she wasn't wearing a bra.

I couldn't take my eyes off her, not even when I knew I should. And thanks to the two shots in a row the guys made me take as soon as I parked the Jeep down the road, I had the viewing pleasure through buzzed eyes.

I kept my gaze on her, feeling that electric rush after depriving myself of her company for so long.

As if she felt me, too — she snapped her head in my direction.

And then she promptly dropped her drink.

Our eyes met across the room, hers wide and caught off guard, while mine were hooded and shameless. She flushed under the intensity of the gaze, muttering something to Jenna before she tore her eyes away from mine and started stacking cups for a new drinking game.

But no sooner than she'd started fussing with the cups, she dropped them just the same and bolted back toward the hallway that I knew led to her room.

God, I wanted to chase her.

I spent the next five minutes thinking about what would happen if I did. I talked to classmates and took pictures and lined up shots, all the while imagining surprising B in her room, locking the door behind me, and then promptly pinning her against it and kissing her the way she deserved to be kissed.

I somehow managed not to follow the urge, though, deciding to wait until she came back out. When she did, her hair had been wrangled into a bun, and she'd painted her lips a deep crimson.

She ran straight into the kitchen, opening a cabinet and hanging her hands on her hips as she stared up at something on the top shelf.

I muttered an excuse of needing to pee to the guys on the team I was hanging out with, and then made my way across the house to where she was now climbing up on the counter.

My hands were on her hips before I could convince myself it was a bad idea.

"Here," I said, speaking right into the shell of her ear. "Let me help."

I held onto her tightly as I lifted her, easily placing her on the counter so she could reach the top of the cabinet. For a moment, she just stayed there, frozen, and I didn't move my hands where they gripped her slick skin.

Once she had what she was looking for — a blender, it turned out — I helped her down.

Slowly.

And I'd be a lying sonofabitch if I said I didn't enjoy every inch of her body rubbing against mine on the way down, particularly when her ass rubbed right along the shaft of my cock.

I groaned at the sensation, at the carnal need it evoked in me, and I held onto her even after she was on the ground. It wasn't until she turned to face me that I forced a breath and told myself to calm the fuck down.

Those sweet, innocent gray eyes lifted to mine.

"Hi, Jamie."

I smirked. "Hi."

She flushed, clearing her throat and glancing down at where I still held onto her hips.

I didn't budge.

Finally, she slipped out of my grasp, plugging the blender in and immediately reaching into the freezer for ice. I watched silently as she gathered the other ingredients to make a frozen margarita, and then I made my way to the counter, leaning up against it and folding my arms.

I studied her as she worked on the cocktail, noting how her tank top stuck to her in wet patches, how her shorts were small enough to show the bottom crease of her ass, how long and lean and toned her legs were. I especially noted how long and dark her lashes were, how those crimson lips were pouty and begging to be tasted.

"You're wearing makeup," I mused, watching as B dumped ice cubes into the blender and covered them in tequila.

"And you're wearing dress shoes."

I looked down at the brown oxfords on my feet, chuckling before I lifted my gaze back to hers.

And then, I said fuck it.

I couldn't go another minute without her in my arms.

"We should dance."

"Wh—"

She couldn't protest before I grabbed her wrist and twirled her out across the kitchen, tugging her back into me just the same. I held her close then, swaying like there was classical music playing instead of rap.

B just giggled, breaking free after another spin and retreating back to the blender.

"You're drunk, Jamie Shaw."

"And are you, B Kennedy?"

She clicked the blend button, speaking a little louder over the noise. "I'm getting there."

She eyed me then, pinning her bottom lip between her teeth as she assessed me.

"What have you been drinking, anyway?"

"Whiskey," I answered.

She chuckled. "Of course. I should have guessed."

"What's that supposed to mean?"

She shrugged, using a spoon to break up a large ice chunk before replacing the top on the blender and turning it on again. "Just makes sense. You're practically whiskey on legs, anyway. The color of your hair, your eyes, the way you smell — it's like your spirit drink."

"I remind you of whiskey?"

I didn't know why that made me happy, made me smile, made my chest swell a little bit. I liked the thought of being her vice. I liked the thought of her looking at me and thinking of sweet, burning temptation.

"In every sense of the word," she murmured.

She fell quiet, keeping her eyes off mine.

"We should do a shot."

I was already grabbing the bottle of Jack Daniel's and filling two shots before she could protest. I slid the one into her hand and lifted the other.

"I'm making a tequila drink," she pointed out. "Mixing will probably screw me in the long run."

"Nah, you'll be fine."

"I don't know, Jamie…"

"Oh, come on," I challenged, taking a small step toward her. I had to fight not to step all the way into her, to press my chest to hers and take her hips in my hands again. "Don't you want a little whiskey on your lips?"

Her eyes snapped up to mine, a warning and a curious question all at once.

She knew what I was asking.

She just didn't dare to answer.

I cocked a brow, waiting, and after a long pause, she lifted her shot glass, too.

"To bad decisions."

My grin doubled, and I kept my eyes on hers as I shot the whiskey back and watched her do the same.

408

Our fingers brushed when we sat our glasses on the counter again, and then her tongue jetted out to chase the last bit of golden whiskey clinging to her painted lips.

I imagined that tongue so many other places, imagined those lips wrapped around me and those eyes cast up at me just like they were now.

I met her gaze again, and I knew she knew as much as I did that everything had changed.

But I left her alone.

At least, until the party ended.

• • •

I stuck around well after everyone else that night, helping B clean up the mess our classmates had made the best I could.

Which was to say — not very much.

"I have to call out," she said, hands on her hips as she surveyed the ruined carpets, the stains on the walls, the beat-down furniture.

I ran a hand through my hair. "When does your mom get home?"

"Late tomorrow night." She looked at her phone. "Or should I say, late tonight."

"You've got time. It's not too bad," I tried to lie. Her deadpan stare told me I failed. "Okay, so the carpet is shot, but everything else is fixable."

"My TV remote is missing."

"Replaceable."

"There's a mustache made out of spitting tobacco on my face in one of the only family pictures we have."

409

I tucked my hands into the pockets of my dress pants. "Yeah, you're kind of screwed."

"I told you what would happen if I mixed alcohol," she teased, and I loved the way her sleepy, still slightly buzzed smile lit up that bleak moment.

"Let's get out of here for a while."

"Are you crazy? I need to clean. I need to..." She waved her hands around. "Do something. About all of this."

"You've already admitted that you're screwed, B. What you can do is only going to take a few hours, so why not send out tonight with a bang?"

She chewed her lip as she debated, and the way her eyes flicked between mine, I knew there were warning bells sounding in her head.

Luckily, she didn't listen to them.

"What do you have in mind?"

• • •

Thirty minutes later, Chad Lawson's *The Piano* album played on my phone speakers, B and I spread out on a blanket on the beach. I'd slid our cab driver an extra ten bucks to take us through the only drive-thru open in town, and so we unwrapped our breakfast burritos while the sun struggled to rise over the water.

I'd grabbed us a Vitamin Water, knowing we both needed to hydrate, and I took a long pull before passing it to B.

"Think this will save us from a hangover?" she asked, taking a sip before passing the bottle back to me.

"I think it's one of my more brilliant ideas. What cures a hangover better than greasy eggs, Vitamin Water, and the beach?"

"So modest," she teased, but then she took her first bite, and I took great satisfaction in the melty goodness cleaning her of her sarcasm. "Homahgawd."

She groaned, taking another bite as I watched her, amused.

"You're welcome."

She smiled back at me, and then we fell into that comfortable silence we so easily did, our eyes on the water as the sky slowly turned from blue to purple.

B was still in those tiny shorts and that damp tank top, and she shivered, the morning breeze cool and refreshing, and so far from the hellish heat that had existed in her house all night.

"Here," I said, unbuttoning my dress shirt. I yanked my tie off before shaking one arm out and then the other. I didn't miss the way her eyes were stuck on my chest, my abdomen, as I draped my shirt over her shoulders.

When she sighed, I swallowed at the sight of her wearing my clothes, at the way the wind blew tendrils of her hair out of the bun she'd fixed it in.

"Thank you," she said. "So, you excited to get out of here? Ready to cause trouble at UC San Diego?"

I shrugged. "Yes and no. Remember our talk over Christmas break?"

She nodded.

"I'm still feeling a bit of all that. Don't get me wrong, I'm excited for this next chapter and all that, but it's still a little scary."

So much for the macho shit I'd felt earlier.

Maybe it was being there on the beach. More specifically, there with *her*. It was our place. This was where we could be exactly who we were — no walls, no secrets.

"It'd be weird if you weren't scared," she said.

I tried to smile, but it fell flat — because as I watched her dig into her burrito like an animal, I realized I wanted her more than I wanted anything or anyone.

But still, I couldn't have her.

I didn't know what I was thinking. What? Was I going to take her to the beach, lie her down in the sand and make love to her, and then just leave her? Throw up a peace sign and say, "Sorry, baby. College calls?"

My chest pinched at the thought because I knew it would kill her.

Hell, it would kill *me*.

She wouldn't graduate for another year. I couldn't reasonably ask her to wait for me, and yet that selfish plea was ready to roll off my lips.

Luckily, she spoke first.

"You've been avoiding me."

She didn't look at me, just watched the sun slowly rising over the horizon.

"Not just you."

"I know," she said, but I saw the hurt in her eyes when she continued. "I just thought maybe you'd call me. Or want to go for a drive. Or…"

She didn't finish that sentence, but it gutted me just the same.

"I wanted to," I said, leaning back on my hands. "I don't know. Jenna hit me at a time that was already so hard for me, you know?" I frowned at the lie, because I hated telling it, but it was easier than admitting the truth — that I'd stayed away for fear of not being able to control how much I wanted her. "My parents were high school sweethearts."

I knew without looking at her that those words hurt. She didn't want to think of me having a life with Jenna any more than I wanted to think about having a life without B.

"It's okay that Jenna wasn't the one."

"I know," I said quickly, and I decided to tell at least *some* truths. "I think I always knew. She was fun, we clicked, had some great times together. But there was something missing."

I turned to face her then, but she kept her eyes on the waves, refusing to meet my gaze.

"You'll find someone," she said softly, eyes still on the waves.

And that's when my stupid idea clicked into place.

I sat up straight. "Well, I don't like leaving my life to chance. So, I have a proposition. If you're game, that is."

She finally looked at me, cocking a brow. "Why do I feel like I should run right now?"

I laughed to hide how hard my heart was beating.

"I say we make a pact."

"A pact?"

I nodded. "If neither of us are married by the time we're thirty, we marry each other."

"Oh my God," she scoffed, leaning up to mirror me with an incredulous look on her too-beautiful-for-this-world face. "That is so stupid, Jamie. It's also the plot line for every cheesy Rom-Com ever."

413

I shrugged, wiping the sand from my hands before I looked out at the water. "Sounds like someone is scared."

"I'm not scared. It's dumb."

"Mm-hmm."

"I'm going to be married by thirty, Jamie. And you're definitely going to be locked down by then."

"So then you have nothing to worry about," I challenged, pinning her with my gaze again. I shot my hand out for hers. "If we're not married in twelve years, you become Mrs. Shaw."

She eyed my hand like it was poison. "That's not fair. You turn thirty before me."

I shrugged. "My pact, my terms. Do we have a deal?"

Her dark eyebrows bent together as she stared at my hand, and then with a roll of her eyes and a dramatic huff, she grabbed it and shook firmly three times.

"Fine. But this is dumb, and pointless."

I smiled a winner's smile.

"You're so weird," she added when I dropped her hand.

"Yeah, but you love me anyway."

I knew she loved me — just as certainly as I knew I loved her. Maybe we weren't ready to say it yet — not seriously, anyway. But we both knew.

I soaked up every moment of that last day with B, not wanting to let her go, not wanting to leave her behind. But I took solace in the pact we'd made, stupidly believing it actually mattered, that we could make a promise at seventeen and eighteen and somehow keep it as the adults we didn't even know we'd become in twelve years' time.

But I also knew that in one year, my little surfer girl would find her way to California. There was no way she wouldn't, not with her mind made up.

And so I'd go to California, get through freshman year, and wait for her.

For when we could finally be together.

THREE

Sorry, Not Sorry

IT WAS OVER A year later before I saw B again.

My life had completely changed — as it often does when you go to college. I was already through my freshman year, excited about getting into more major-specific courses as a sophomore, and *thoroughly* enjoying student activities on and off campus… if you catch my drift.

It was move-in week, the Alder campus crawling with students and parents unloading U-Hauls and heaving boxes across campus to the dorms. I was already moved in and settled, and so I spent the pleasantly warm afternoon on the basketball court, flirting with freshmen as they walked past.

Everything in my life finally felt on track.

I loved Alder — which I'd been accepted into last minute, thanks to my uncle knowing someone who knew someone in the admissions office. Truthfully, I hadn't worked hard in high school to impress on my college applications, so I'd been waitlisted, at first. I was fine going to UC San Diego, even though my dad and uncle graduated from Alder.

But my uncle wasn't having it.

And once he pulled the strings and got me in, I realized why he was so adamant about it.

Alder was every new adult's wet dream. The campus was gorgeous, close to the beach, and one of the only universities that allowed alcohol on the grounds. I was on an intramural basketball team, never had a class that was more than forty students, and my professors knew me by name. Add that to the fact that you actually had your own *room* in your dorm, as opposed to sharing bunk beds with a stranger, and I was sold.

Fortunately, my roommate my first year had been so cool, we'd decided to room together again. He was entirely too smart for me, and far more motivated to become someone than I was, but I liked his spirit — and the girls he brought around.

I don't want to say I'd forgotten about B because that would be a lie. I obsessed over her all summer after graduation, and it wasn't until I was a couple months into my freshman year that the obsession subsided. But even after, she was always there, like a buzzing presence in the back of my mind, in the barrel of my chest. I felt her. I longed for her.

I waited for her.

And when the universe was finally ready to reward me for my patience, it delivered her right to me.

Sweat dripped down from my hair into my eyes as I walked across campus, basketball tucked under my arm

417

and shirt sticking to my skin. I chuckled to myself at the mixture of personalities as freshmen scurried about, their parents fretting behind them.

To get to my dorm, I had to walk right by the rows of tables set up to help freshmen find their dorms or sign up for clubs or get connected to tutors, and I weaved through the anxious crowd with an amused smile.

I saw her hair first.

Those lush, wild curls flowed in the gentle breeze, the sun peeking out from behind the clouds and shining a ray of light right on those freckles I could probably chart by memory, if I tried. Her legs stretched on for miles in the white shorts she wore — modest, but short enough to make me stare a little longer than was appropriate. One look at the baby blue tank top she wore with it told me she'd somehow toned up even more, and I wondered how much of the summer she'd spent on her board.

My heart was a bass drum as I watched her, not believing my eyes. I knew she wanted to go to school in California, but I never guessed she'd end up *here*.

She was smiling softly, looking around as she adjusted the JanSport bag on her shoulder and the student in an Alder University polo searched for her dorm information. My feet moved me toward her automatically, even though I had no idea what I was going to say or do once I got to her.

I knew only one thing for sure.

I needed her in my arms.

Tucking the basketball I had under a nearby bench, I made my way toward where she stood, chest tight with anticipation.

The student helping her was a girl I recognized — Melanie Baroque. She was a sophomore now, like me, and one of those girls who loved to be involved in every aspect of campus life that she could be. She was perky and sweet, and when I'd taken her back to my dorm after a basketball game last fall, I'd learned she was also eager to please.

Melanie snapped her fingers as I approached the table behind B. "Ah! Found it!" She plucked a folder out of the stack in front of her, checking its contents before looking back up to B. "Brecks, right?"

My stomach soured at the sound of the name, the one so tainted for my surfer girl, and I saw the way it affected her. B's smile slipped, her shoulders deflating, but she forced a breath and opened her mouth to answer.

I beat her to it.

"It's B," I said.

I saw her freeze, her body stiff as she turned to face me. She looked as if she'd seen a ghost, her eyes wide, lips slightly parted. Her eyes trailed every inch of me, and need surged inside me at the blush that found her cheeks as she did. When her eyes met mine again, I slid up beside her, crooked smile in place as I held her gaze.

"Just B."

B was still frozen in place, her eyes drinking me in, and I noted how hard it was for her to swallow, to speak.

"You cut your hair," she finally breathed.

I chuckled, and I couldn't help myself from reaching out to touch her, my fingers gliding along her cheek before I tapped her nose. "And you got a nose ring."

She smiled, still in a trance as she watched me, and I knew she wasn't paying a lick of attention to Melanie

419

as she gave her her dorm information. With a smirk, I reached over the table to take the envelope and keys from Melanie with a wink.

"Good to see you, Jamie. How have you been?" she asked, batting her lashes at me.

"Oh, you know, same old same. I think I got this," I told her, holding up the envelope. "Take care, Melanie."

I ignored the way Melanie tried to tell me she still wanted me with that look of hers, steering B away from the table and toward a clearing in the crowd.

"I take it you two know each other?" she asked, nodding back to where Melanie was still staring at me.

I shrugged. "You could say that."

The tease worked, and B rolled her eyes so hard I was pretty sure she saw brain matter.

I laughed — the most genuine, heartfelt laugh I'd had in a long time — pure joy at her being close enough to breathe the same air as me overwhelming. When I finally stopped, I just shook my head, looking at her like a miracle before I opened my arms wide.

"Come here."

"Ew," she said automatically, shaking her head and walking the other way. "You're sweatier than two rats fucking in a gym sock."

"Oh, come on," I teased from behind her, already following. "It's just a little perspiration."

And then, I swooped in, wrapping my arms around her and hugging her to my chest as I spun her around. She squealed, laughing and flailing until I finally relented and set her feet back on solid ground.

"Why are you so sweaty?" she asked on a laugh. "And why are you here?"

"I just finished playing basketball out at the courts. And I go to school here. Which, I guess that makes two of us now," I added, holding up the envelope from Campus Housing.

She snatched it from my grip and flipped through the contents, holding out her hand for the keys, next.

"I didn't know you went here," she said, but her blush betrayed her.

"Sure," I said. "It's okay that you're stalking me, B. Maybe I kind of like it."

"You wish," she replied, nose still in the papers. "Seriously though, you were supposed to be at UC. What happened?"

"Remember my uncle I told you about? The one who had connections at a university in California?"

She nodded, and I spread my arms open wide as if to gesture to the campus as a whole.

"You're looking at the same university my dad and uncle graduated from, both with their degrees in Accounting. At first, my application was waitlisted, but my uncle knows a few of the guys on the Admissions Board, and he worked some magic."

"And now here you are," she said, peeking up at me through her lashes. I loved that feeling of having her eyes on me, of knowing her stomach was in knots being this close to me again.

"Here I am," I repeated.

She shook her head, dipping her gaze back to the envelope. Every cell in my being buzzed with her near, the unyielding brightness of all the possibilities blinding me.

"So, you made it to California after all," I mused.

She looked up then, her eyes mischievous and alluring. I wasn't even sure she knew when she did that, when she looked at me in a way that made my balls tingle and my mouth dry with the urge to touch her. She played innocent, but her gaze told me something else.

"I guess I did," she breathed.

We were selfish in that next moment, eyes devouring each other, and I was already planning the rest of our day, the rest of our night, the rest of our *lives*. A million images flashed before me — campus bonfire parties, late nights studying in the library, early mornings surfing the waves, lazy afternoons tangled in the sheets...

But it was all wiped away in an instant because my roommate appeared out of nowhere, grabbing B from behind and spinning her around just the same way I had.

My first instinct was to punch him, *hard*, right in the nose. It was a guttural response, one I couldn't control if I tried, and as soon as he dropped her back to the ground, I surged forward with the intent to do just that.

Until he spoke.

"Oh my God, I almost forgot how beautiful you are," Ethan said.

Then, he dipped her back like a fucking prince in a movie, kissing her the way I'd always dreamed of doing.

My stomach dropped at the sight, at the way she melted for him, the way he looked at her like she was his world

422

once she was upright again. His hands framed her face, revering her, and they smiled at each other like they were in love.

I was going to be sick.

I cleared my throat when they didn't stop the stupid love-sick stare after a long pause, and that seemed to jerk Ethan back to the present moment. He perked up, tucking B under his arm like he'd done it a hundred times before.

Like he owned her.

My fists curled at my sides.

"And I see you met my roommate!"

B's eyes widened, and she turned to me with a dozen questions dancing in her gaze, but I just clenched my jaw and slowly put the sickening pieces together.

Ethan had gone to Florida for the summer. He told me he met a girl. He told me he was in love. He told me she was coming here. He told me he'd found his First Lady — since the prick wanted to be President one day.

He told me all about her.

But he never told me her name.

"Jamie is your roommate?" B squeaked.

"Yeah," he answered, pointing his finger between the two of us. "Y'all know each other?"

All those possibilities I'd fantasized about disappeared into a wisp of smoke, and I felt it — the stone I hardened into in that moment as I answered, "We went to high school together."

B swallowed. "Yeah. He dated my best friend back in the day."

The words *best friend* gutted me, and I ground my teeth together.

423

"Huh!" Ethan mused, grin still in place. "What a small world!"

My nose flared as I looked at B, at Ethan, at where their hands were weaved together. And I realized I was quite literally going to be sick.

"I was just heading back to the dorm to shower," I said. "I'll see you later, Ethan."

"Later, bro."

I allowed myself one final glance at B, and then I jogged off, retrieving my basketball from under the bench before I ran the rest of the way across campus to our dorm.

When I got there, I ran straight to the toilet and surrendered my lunch.

Along with every dream I'd had of B ever being mine.

• • •

To my credit, I did *try* to stay away from B after that.

I knew from experience that my moral compass went haywire in the presence of that girl, so I made sure to be out of the dorm when she was there with Ethan, and I occupied my time with other girls, trying to pretend like they could fill the void B left in me.

It wasn't until that party when B showed up in her tiny, hot pink swimsuit with her breasts pushed up to her fucking chin that I realized I didn't *want* to stay away — and I had to find a way to be with her without ruining my friendship with Ethan.

So, I decided I would be her friend.

I could be *just* her friend, I told myself. I could hang out with her without crossing any lines, without putting her in a sticky situation with her boyfriend, without torturing myself. The fact that I truly believed this makes me laugh now, but at the time, I convinced myself thoroughly enough that I started calling her to hang out.

And when she tried to ignore me, I showed up after her shift at work and decided I wouldn't take no for an answer.

You know how that day went, the way it felt to have her in my passenger seat again as we drove around San Diego. I introduced her to the city, all the while reveling in the way it felt to just *be* with her again.

This is worth it, I realized. *I'll take her in any way I can.*

I thought, maybe, I really could drop my infatuation with her and settle just being her friend. But when we were in the snake garden at UC San Diego, that ridiculous attempt at lying to myself was shattered.

I still remember the way she looked in that moment, the two of us shielded by high bushes and flowers as she flushed at the mere mention of the word *sex*. It had started off with me just teasing her about her romance books, but then, teasing transformed into carnal need.

I *had* to know what got her off, what made her unravel.

More than that — I had to know how Ethan was failing her, if only for my own selfish pleasure.

"He's fine. Good…" she said, not able to look at me as she finally conceded to my plea for her to tell me how Ethan was in the sack. "I just, I wish it was more… exciting. He's so sweet, gentle, and that's nice but…"

Her words faded, cheeks burning an even deeper red than before.

425

"There's no real passion. There's no urgency. I'm all for sweet nothings whispered in my ear, but sometimes I just want to be thrown onto the bed, you know? Ravaged. Like he can't fathom the thought of taking his hands off me."

She said every word in this breathy, unintentionally sexy voice. It was likely because she was afraid someone would overhear us, but it struck me to the core, awakening a primal need in me. I replayed her words on a fiery loop in my head.

Thrown onto the bed…

Ravaged…

Like he can't fathom taking his hands off me…

If only she knew how intently I felt those very things, how I would shred her clothes and bury myself inside her if she just said the word.

Clouds shifted overhead, the sun beaming on us as B finally brought her gaze to mine. I struggled to keep my breathing steady, to keep my hands at my sides, to not slide those hands into her hair and crush my mouth to hers in that very moment — Ethan be damned.

Somehow, I controlled myself. And I could only utter three stupid words.

"I get that."

After I dropped her off back at her dorm with a promise to take her for her first California surf the next morning, I raced back to my dorm, ignoring Ethan when I got home and locking myself inside the bathroom.

My pants and briefs were on the floor in an instant, my throbbing cock in my hand as I ran the water as hot as

KANDI STEINER

I could stand. With one hand braced on the cool tile wall and the other stroking me, I imagined B in that shower with me, imagined her wet curls and water dripping off her lips as I made her moan my name. I could picture everything — the way she'd close her eyes, the shape of her mouth opening for me, the lean muscles of her stomach leading down to the apex of her thighs.

I came with a groan, resisting the urge to let her name roll off my lips in the process.

That night, I tossed and turned in a fitful sleep until my alarm went off, and I jumped up far too briskly for it being that early in the morning.

I couldn't wait to see her.

I couldn't wait to be on our boards, to have her to myself, to fantasize a little longer.

Friends, my ass...

When I got to her dorm, I called her, knowing just from her voice that she was barely awake. And when she answered the door, I was tested on every level possible.

B stood there in nothing but a tiny pair of navy blue boy shorts, the trim of them white and hugging her brown skin, and an even smaller cropped white t-shirt. She didn't wear a bra beneath it, and her nipples pebbled from the cool morning air washing over her, goosebumps breaking along the length of her stomach, her arms, her thighs...

She reached for me without saying a word, grabbing my hand like it belonged in hers, and she tugged me inside.

My heart hammered in my chest, cock twitching at the sight of her ass cheeks peeking out of the bottom of her boy shorts as she toted me back to her room. She shut the door behind us, crawled right into bed, and pulled me with her.

My pulse was a kick drum in my ears. I thought that was it. I thought she wanted me, too. I thought she'd dragged me in there before the sun could rise so we could commit that sin we'd been fighting in complete darkness.

She pulled the covers up over us, turning so that she faced the wall and her small body curved into mine. Her ass rubbed against my hard-on, and I sucked in a stiff breath at the warmth, at the way she rolled her hips happily and let out a content sigh.

And that's when I realized.

She wasn't even awake.

Of course, she was *awake* — enough to walk and open doors and climb back into bed, at least. But she was essentially sleep walking, probably so tired from our day before that she didn't realize what she was doing in her exhaustion.

I sighed, allowing myself a few stolen moments before I said anything. I ran my hands through her hair, willed my cock to settle as I savored the warmth of her tangled up with me.

Finally, when I had composed myself, I whispered in her ear.

"B, WAKE UP."

"Mmmm," she murmured, swatting behind her like she was trying to find her alarm clock. She hit me, instead, her hand tugging at my t-shirt. "Sleep."

I chuckled. "Come on. We should get going if we want to catch the morning surf."

I felt the moment she really woke up — the way she stiffened, the way her pulse quickened to a gallop. I didn't have to see her face to know her eyes had popped open wide when she hastily retracted her hand from me and threw the covers off.

"How did you get in here?" she whisper-screamed, grabbing her phone to read the time.

"You let me in, goofball. I called you."

"What?" She scrolled through her phone, and I assumed she saw her call log, because she frowned even more. "I'm so confused."

I sat up on the edge of the bed — mostly to put space between us, now that I could see those damn boy shorts again. "You let me in. Then, you grabbed my hand and pulled me back here before crawling back into bed."

"Oh my God." She smacked her forehead and I laughed.

"Relax. You're just tired. We can do this another time if you want to rest."

"No," she said quickly, scooting past me off the bed. She grabbed a swimsuit out of one of her drawers and then headed for the bathroom. "Give me a sec to change."

"You don't have to, we can—"

"I want to. I've been here almost two months now and still haven't surfed. And that's one of the biggest reasons I wanted to come to California, anyway."

I tried…

I tried to get her to stay…

I tried to get us out of this…

At least, that's what I told myself.

With a nod, I stood. "Alright, then. Go get dressed. I'm parked in the G Lot."

I grabbed her board and headed for my Jeep, and I gave myself a stern talking to while I waited for B.

"She is not yours. You cannot have her. Let it go. Let *her* go."

When she bounced across the lot to my Jeep with a blazing smile on her face, I knew it was futile.

We got her a wet suit when we made it to the beach, and then as the sun stretched and bid us good morning, we paddled out for my little surfer girl to catch her first wave. It felt like home, sitting next to her on my board as we talked and waited for the next wave, and we existed there — just the two of us — all morning and afternoon.

It was around two when she said she needed to get back to campus. I'd teased her about not being prepared for the Cali waves, only to be told shut the fuck up immediately by her delivering news that she had a date with Ethan.

I did my best to school my emotions when she told me, and we surfed one last wave before packing it in.

As we made the hike back up the boardwalk to the Jeep, we were both silent. But I felt it, already, the devil himself stirring inside me. I knew before it happened that I was about to do something stupid. I just didn't know how to stop it.

I loaded our boards, throwing on a t-shirt and trying not to watch as B stripped out of her wet suit and slipped on an oversized sweater, instead. She still shivered a bit as she gazed out at the water, at the sun making its descent over the ocean. Her hair blew all around her, like a golden halo.

I slid up beside her, resting my elbows on the rail next to hers.

"I can't believe we're in California," she breathed.

I smiled. "Together."

She squinted against the sun when she turned to look at me, her gray eyes almost blue in that light. "Thank you for today, Jamie. Yesterday, too."

"We're just getting started," I said.

We stood there a moment, both of us silent.

Kiss her, the devil whispered.

But I fought him off a little longer.

"By the way, I have to ask. How come you left the push-up bra at home? I was kind of looking forward to seeing you try to surf in it," I teased.

She glared, nudging me with a smile playing at the corner of her lips. "It was a pool party, okay? I needed something a little more showy than my surf tops that make me look like a boy." She glanced down at her chest then, as if she couldn't see that she had *plenty* of cleavage for any straight man to appreciate.

"Oh, so you were putting on a show that night, huh?"

"Well, you see, someone had been ignoring me," she teased back. "So I needed to find a way to get some attention."

She scrunched up her nose, sticking her tongue out a bit at me, and I wanted to laugh. *God*, I wished I could have just laughed and got in the Jeep and held that *just friends* façade in place.

But I couldn't. I couldn't smile. I couldn't do anything but look at her with longing bursting from my chest.

"You don't look like a boy, for the record," I said.

She laughed, and the sound undid me.

I stepped closer, finally giving in to what I wanted. My hand slid into her salty hair, and she stopped laughing. She stopped *breathing*, and so did I.

"And I wasn't ignoring you. I was avoiding you. I was trying to stay away." I swallowed, searching her eyes before my gaze fell to her lips.

Kiss her.

My other hand slipped into her hair, too, framing her face.

Kiss her.

"I was trying to stop myself from doing this."

I pulled her into me, claiming her lips with my own, and the devil cheered.

We both held our breath, the kiss so powerful it felt like the whole universe shifted with it. I half expected her to shove me away.

But she didn't.

She pressed up onto her toes, wanting more, her hands fisting in my shirt, and mine gripping her hair tight as we both exhaled together. I became an animal at the sound of it, at knowing she wanted it, too. I sucked her plump bottom lip between my teeth with a groan, letting it go only to kiss her even harder, to slide my tongue along the seam of her lips until she let me inside.

Her legs trembled, and I held onto her tighter, letting her know she could trust me, that I had her, that it was okay.

Except it *wasn't* okay.

Because I was kissing my roommate's girlfriend.

And she was cheating.

The realization struck me like lightning, and I broke our kiss, pressing my forehead to hers on a curse. We were both panting, still dancing on that line, both desperately wanting to climb over it, and yet knowing we shouldn't.

"Jamie, I—"

"Have a boyfriend. I know."

I fought the urge to curse again as I let her go, and as soon as I did, I had to turn away from her, *walk* away from her. My hands raked through my hair, and then I rested them on top of my head, staring at the parking lot feeling like a fool.

"Goddamnit," I whispered. "I'm sorry."

I closed my eyes against the emotion surging through me. I couldn't look at her. I couldn't face what I'd just made her do.

"We should go," she whispered after what felt like the longest moment of my life, and she slipped into my passenger seat without waiting for me to respond.

It took me a while to get the nerve to get in that Jeep with her, and when I did, I started the ignition without looking at her. I couldn't turn on a playlist, either.

Every song reminded me of her.

So, I let the wind be our soundtrack, and we drove back toward campus in silence.

Until her phone rang.

B frowned at the screen, swallowing hard before she answered with a weak voice.

"Hey, babe."

I gripped the steering wheel tighter, accidentally pressing too hard on the gas. I didn't realize I'd done so until I passed a speed limit sign and noted that I was twenty over.

I slowed down, listening.

"On my way now," B said. "Listen, I'm really exhausted, could we maybe go to dinner another night?"

My chest ached with guilt, and when I chanced a glance at B, her eyes were welling with tears as Ethan spoke.

"I miss you, too," she croaked after a minute. "Give me an hour and then you can head over."

She ended the call as I pulled onto campus, and when I parked the Jeep in G Lot, she immediately reached for the door handle.

I hit the lock button before she could pull it.

"I'm sorry, B."

She closed her eyes, freeing one solo tear that I wished desperately to wipe away, but I kept my hands on the wheel.

"Ethan is a great guy and he cares about you, and I know you care about him, too. And what I did today was selfish. It was foolish."

I ruined it. I fucked everything up.

I lost her.

I didn't know if that moment was the last I'd ever have with her, but just in case it was, I had to make sure she knew.

"I'm not sorry I kissed you," I said.

434

Her eyes widened a bit, hesitantly finding mine.

"But I'm sorry I did it when you weren't mine to kiss."

Her bottom lip quivered, her eyes searching mine for the longest time. And then, with a broken voice, she said, "I'm sorry, too. I think maybe this was a bad idea."

"No," I argued, my heart lurching in my chest. I let the wheel go then, turning to face her. "Listen, I promise, I won't pull that shit again. But please, don't push me away. We can still be friends, B. I don't want to lose you."

I pleaded as much as I could with my eyes, hoping she could see me — the *real* me — the me only she knew.

"Please, let me be your friend."

She looked at me like she didn't know if she could trust me or not, and I couldn't blame her, not after what I'd done. But I held her gaze steady, letting her know I meant every word.

"Okay," she finally said.

I let out a sigh of relief.

"But we can't…. I can't…" She waved her hand behind her, back toward the direction of the beach, and I nodded.

"I know."

She nodded, too. "Help me with my board?"

I was a wreck after that, especially when I got back to the dorm just in time to watch Ethan shower and get ready for his date with B. He was all smiles, a lovesick puppy as he rambled on about how great she was, like I didn't already know.

When he was gone, all I could think about was that he was with her. That he might be touching her, kissing her, tasting her…

I punched a hole through my wall, growling like a beast and realizing I would have to fix it before he got home. At least it gave me a project, something to keep my mind off them being together, off *her*.

Of course, it didn't work.

Nothing did.

I laid awake that night, staring at my ceiling with a fist-size hole in my chest.

I thought it would be okay. I thought we could take a few steps back and be fine.

But Ethan wasn't stupid. He smelled the threat I imposed, and I couldn't even blame the motherfucker when he told B to stay away from me. I knew he'd asked her, without either of them telling me, because we went from hanging out every week, to her ignoring me in a snap of his fingers.

I respected it.

I obeyed it.

Until my world came crashing down, and I knew the only one who could save me was her.

FOUR

Us and Other People

"IT'S GOING TO BE alright, son," my dad tried to assure me on that cold February morning, but I could tell from how rough his voice was that it was a lie. Or, at the very least, an assurance he couldn't make with full faith. "You just focus on school, okay? I don't want you worrying about this."

I ran a hand back through my hair, trying to digest it all. "How am I not supposed to worry?"

"Your dad has a handle on the situation," Mom chimed in, and again — her voice gave her away.

I swallowed, nodding, trying to believe them.

"Recessions happen. It's natural for our clients to cut back where they can, and sadly, we're usually one of the first places they think to cut. Besides, if they're not making money…"

"They don't need our firm," I finished for Dad.

"Everything will right itself. It always does," Mom said, and I could imagine the warning look she was giving my father even though I couldn't see her face. "We've been through worse, and we survived."

Barely, I wanted to say, but I kept my mouth shut.

"Go have fun!" Mom continued. "You're a college student, which means your only responsibility is to keep your grades up and earn that degree, okay? Besides, didn't you say B is there with you?"

My chest caved in on itself then, and I wished I hadn't told them. My parents loved B almost as much as I did, and now that she'd been ignoring me, it was just another splash of salt in my wound.

"Mm-hmm," I managed.

"You should call her. Make her take you out and take your mind off things. She always knows how to make you smile."

Thanks for the sucker punch to the gut, Mom.

After we exchanged *I love you's* and promises to talk soon, we ended the call, and I sat there on the edge of my bed with my head hanging between my shoulders.

I needed to move. I needed out of my head.

Changing quickly, I grabbed my ball and headed out to the courts, wasting away the morning as I ran drills and sweated it out. I skipped class and didn't even care. Still, when morning rolled into afternoon and the evening creeped in, I knew once it got dark, I'd be in hell with my thoughts if I didn't think of a way to combat them.

And the only person I wanted in that moment was B.

I pulled up her name on my phone, rolling my lips together and knowing it was a bad idea. She'd made it clear without telling me a word that she needed space — likely for the health of her relationship with Ethan.

I should have respected it.

I should have found a different way to handle my shit.

But my heart ached for her so fiercely, I couldn't deny it.

— **Where are you? I'm coming to pick you up.** —

My stomach rolled as I sent the text, and I threw my phone on the bed, trying not to look at it again until it buzzed with her reply.

— **I'm with Ethan doing campaign stuff. Rain check?** —

I cursed.

The part of me who was more mature, more respectful, told me to leave it alone.

But just seeing his name made the part of me that was so damn possessive of her win out.

— **Aren't you almost done for the day? I can wait. Just take a drive with me.** —

I saw the little bubbles bouncing that indicated she was typing something. They appeared and disappeared several times before they were gone all together.

She was ignoring me.

Take it as a sign, Jamie. Leave her alone. She doesn't want to see you.

I tried putting on a movie. I tried studying. I even debated texting one of the dozens of numbers I had in my phone for girls I *knew* wouldn't ignore my request for attention.

But I couldn't shake the thought of being with B, of having her in my passenger seat and telling her what was going on. I didn't know if she had any more cat stories up her sleeve, but I knew one thing for sure:

If I was whiskey, then she was the barrel that held me, that helped me age, that made me better.

I needed *her*.

And nothing else would do.

I picked up my phone before I could overthink it, calling her. She didn't answer, so I called again, and again, and again.

After the sixth time, I cursed, typing out a text that was as desperate as I felt.

— I need you, B. Please. —

My heart was in my throat as I watched those little bubbles bouncing again. But this time…

— See you in twenty. Lot G. —

I was out the door in two minutes flat.

• • •

I shivered a bit as I stood against my Jeep waiting for B, even in my Alder hoodie and sweatpants. My hair was still a little damp from my shower earlier, and likely a fucking mess from how much I'd run my hands through it since then.

I had my eyes on my shoes, thoughts racing, until I heard the soft taps of her sneakers against the pavement. I looked up, my heart stopping in my chest when I laid eyes on her after so long.

She stopped, like she felt it, too, and I drank her in.

B wore sweatpants, too, and an oversized sweater that hung off her shoulder. She didn't have a stitch of make-up on, but her skin glowed like the sun, her eyes bright and showing me without her saying a word that she was scared of me.

Of being close to me.

Of what she might do if the opportunity was right.

Her hair was resting on her shoulders in tight, ringlet curls, still slightly wet. She opened her mouth like she wanted to say something, but then she closed it again, waiting.

I frowned, more emotions than I fully understood at that age rushing through me as I took in the sight of her, as I realized what just seeing her did to me.

It made me burn, it made me fucking *wild* with jealousy, and somehow, it made me feel like everything would be okay, too.

I pushed off the side of my Jeep before I really realized what I was doing, and then she was in my arms.

She inhaled a stiff breath as I wrapped her up, dropping my head to the crown of hers and squeezing her tight. She was hesitant, but then her arms snaked around me, too, and she held me just the same.

I couldn't get her close enough.

Every second that I held her, relief bled into me like a warm summer breeze. I inhaled the scent of her shampoo, citrusy and sweet, wishing I could just hold her like that forever.

"Jamie," she breathed, trying to pull away.

"Not yet," I pleaded.

She paused, but nodded against my chest, and I held her for a moment more before pressing a selfish kiss to her forehead. I let her go then, climbing into the Jeep as she took up her usual spot in my passenger seat.

André Gagnon blasted from my speakers as I threw the Jeep in drive and drove us off campus. I knew where I wanted to take her, but first, I just wanted to drive.

I kept silent, my eyes on the road. My body hummed with the need to talk to her, to tell her what was going on. I cracked my neck a few times on the drive, tapping my thumb on the steering wheel, my knuckles white where I gripped it. I didn't relax until B kicked her boots off and propped her fuzzy sock-covered feet up on my dash.

Seeing her like that had me loosing a sigh, the tension in my shoulders ebbing.

Two hours passed on that drive, both of us silent and listening to the music. Finally, we drove slowly through Mission Valley and Pacific Beach before winding up through Bird Rock toward La Jolla. We both rolled our windows down, B hanging her hand out the window and surfing the air waves as the heat still blasted high enough to keep us both from freezing.

I pulled into a parking space, cutting the engine and hopping out without a word. I grabbed the large bag I'd packed from my trunk, and then I started walking.

B didn't even ask where we were, she just followed.

I wound us through a few small houses and a grove before walking onto a small, secluded beach. It was a hidden spot, public — though, from how close it was to the elaborate houses on its edge, most people assumed it was private property.

I pulled a thick blanket out of the bag I'd packed, laying it out on the beach before I took a seat. I glanced back up at B, pulling out a second blanket for her to cover up with and patting the spot next to me.

She peeled off her boots and plopped down beside me, and I covered us both with the blanket, our shared warmth easing the bite of the cool wind.

"What would you do if everything you had planned for your future went up in flames and there was nothing you could do about it?"

B was leaning back on her hands, her eyes on the ocean, and she shifted a bit. "Find a new future, I suppose."

"What if there wasn't one?"

She hugged her thighs to her chest then, resting her cheek on her knees as she turned to look at me.

God, the way that girl looked at me.

Her eyes shone in the moonlight, and those gray pools were an ocean all their own. "What's going on, Jamie?"

I swallowed. "Things have been hard, you know? I mean, we're in college, but we're not too dumb to see how the economy is suffering right now. But I never thought it would directly affect me. I think we're at that age where we just feel invincible, like nothing can touch us, but it can." I shook my head, picking at the strings on the edge of our blanket. "My dad's firm is going under. It's going fast. And I'm here, in California, in fucking college, powerless to do anything to save it, yet depending on it all the same."

Her hand moved for mine so quickly, so naturally, like that's right where it belonged.

I turned my palm up to meet hers, lacing our fingers together, holding on tight like she was the gravity that held me steady.

"How bad is it?"

"Bad," I croaked.

She leaned her head on my shoulder, that citrus scent finding me once again.

"But is there a chance it'll be okay?"

I shrugged. "I guess there's always a chance."

"So focus on that," she said. "Jamie, your father built that firm. It's been a part of him since he was twenty-six years old. He's put blood, sweat, and tears into it. Do you think a little recession is going to kill his dream? His baby?"

I frowned, considering her point.

"No way," she answered for me. "Because the Shaw's are fighters. When you see something you want — truly want — you go after it. All of you. And your dad is going to find a way to keep the firm alive. There is no other option for him."

"It's not that simple," I argued. "There's less of a need for high-end accountants when businesses are tanking. The few clients they have left are seeking out cheaper options, if not battling their own demise."

"Okay, but this recession isn't going to last forever. If your dad can just hold on—"

"And what if he doesn't, B?"

I turned to her then, hating how frustrated I sounded — but it was exactly how I felt. And I knew I didn't have to hide that, not with her.

"What then?"

"Then he starts over, Jamie." She sat up straighter to face me, too. "And so do you. And you figure it out. Because that's what life's about. It's about paddling out and fighting the waves until you find the perfect one to ride home on."

"I don't know if I could start over," I admitted, my heart cracking with the thought of it.

B moved until she sat in front of me, wanting all of my attention.

Like she didn't already have it.

Like it wouldn't always belong to her.

"Don't you remember what I told you Christmas Eve when we were in high school?"

My frown ebbed, and I nodded.

"I meant it then, I mean it even more now. You're only a sophomore in college, and already you've done two internships and started preparing for your Certified Public Accountant examination, which you don't even need to think about until grad school. You're acing your classes and building a network by attending all those fancy events downtown. You're doing it, Jamie. You're making your own dreams come true, just like your dad did. This recession will pass, and you'll come out on top no matter what because that's just who you are."

The more she spoke, the more my heart calmed, the beat of it finding a steady rhythm.

How is it this girl believes in me this much?

"You're right," I said with a determined sigh. "I can do this."

"You can," she said, squeezing my hands in hers.

That squeeze hit me somewhere so deep, the light couldn't reach.

"I'm not going to lie and say that I'm not scared," I added. "But I believe you when you say I can do it. I believe you when you say it will be okay."

"Good. Because I'm right, like, ninety-seven percent of the time."

I gave her a small smile.

"I think I'm going to go home this summer, try to help my dad turn it around."

"You should. It'd be a great experience for you, and I know your dad would love having you around."

"Would you come with me?"

The words flew out of my mouth before I could think better of them. I meant them — *God*, I meant them — but I knew by the way her eyes widened that I was stupid for voicing them out loud.

She pulled her hands away from mine, and my nose flared at the loss.

"I don't know what my plans are for the summer yet. But you'll be fine without me."

"You've been pulling back lately," I whispered.

She shook her head, staring at her hands in her lap.

"You have. Don't lie to me."

"I never could."

"So then tell me what's going on."

She sighed. "Ethan feels threatened by you, I think."

I tried to act surprised — but really, it was just affirmation of what I already knew.

"That's the wrong word," she backtracked. "He just... I don't know. He feels like he has to compete with you. And I hate that I made him feel that way. I just need to

446

focus on my relationship with him, and I can't do that if he sees me spending all my time with another man."

"But we're us," I reminded her. "It's *always* been us."

"Has it?" she argued, looking up at me through her dark lashes.

The boldness of that question shocked me still.

"Seems to me like it's always been us and other people."

I swallowed, tracing the edges of the shadows battling with the moonlight on her face.

She was right.

First, it was Jenna. Now, Ethan.

But I was tired of letting other people stand in our way.

"It's just us right now," I said, voice low.

"Jamie…"

"You said you could never lie to me," I whispered, heart pounding in my chest as the air seemed to come alive around us, like the earth couldn't help but buzz with anticipation, too.

"I couldn't."

"So then tell me, B," I said, reaching out for her. I grabbed her wrists in my hands, gentle — yet firm — and tugged her closer. "Is it Ethan scared of you being alone with me, or is it *you* who's afraid?"

The muscles of my jaw were tight and strained as I watched her, those wide eyes, those parted lips…

Answer me, I pleaded with my gaze.

"Both."

Her admission was soft, but it stroked the fire already burning inside me.

I licked my lips. "Why?"

"Because I don't trust myself when I'm with you."

I squeezed my eyes tight at finally hearing it, at knowing she felt the same. I blew out a hard breath through my nose, my right hand dropping hers and running up her arm before sliding to her neck. I felt along every inch of her skin, breathing smoke the whole way.

When my eyes opened again, it was like seeing her for the first time.

I leaned in closer, and B backed away, farther and farther until she was on her ass and I was on my knees in front of her, invading her space.

"Would you be mad if I kissed you right now?"

"Yes," she breathed, the lie thinly veiled.

"Then I hope you'll forgive me later."

I closed the distance then, catching her rebuttal with a sweep of my tongue against hers. She gasped at the touch, pushing up on her knees to meet me, and I groaned at the way that gasp elicited something primal deep inside me.

My hands slid under her sweater, gripping onto her waist and holding on for dear life. And my theory that her saying she'd be mad if I kissed her was a lie was proven when she started tugging at my hoodie, her fingers clutching the fabric and pulling me closer.

I broke our kiss, trailing my teeth and tongue down the length of her neck, loving the taste of her. My hands moved up of their own volition, and when my thumbs brushed the lacy bottom of her bra, B hissed.

My cock twitched in my sweatpants, eager and impatient, and when I traced the edges of her bra and she arched into the touch, I had to fight against every urge in my body to keep moving slow.

I spun her away from me, holding her hips steady as she lost her balance. I wanted her facing the waves. I wanted the ocean — *our* ocean — to have a front-row view to me driving my little surfer girl wild.

She leaned back into me, and I kissed her neck, biting down softly as our conversation in the snake garden came flashing back to me.

"Is this the passion you've been missing? The urgency?" I asked, smirking at the chills that broke on her skin, and I sucked her earlobe into my mouth. I hooked my thumbs under her bra, realizing taking it off would take too long, and I'd waited long enough to touch her.

I pushed it up enough to let her breasts spring free, and they were the perfect size, fitting into my palms like they were always meant to be there.

I hummed my approval as I rolled each nipple, pinching softly. B arched into me, her ass rubbing against my hard-on and making my next breath hard to grasp.

"Because I can't fathom taking my hands off you right now," I told her, remembering that was what she wanted, what she needed.

If only she knew I'd felt that way about her for years.

I snaked a hand into her hair, tugging back until I could capture her mouth with mine. I wanted to consume every moan she let out, wanted to taste it and savor it and commit it to memory. She moaned even louder when my other hand slid down her lean stomach, and I dipped under the band of her boy shorts and sweatpants in one swift push, smirking when she bucked against the touch.

She writhed and whimpered when I dove my hand down deeper before pulling it out again, back up to her breasts. I wanted to tease her, but my girl was impatient, too.

She grabbed my hand and forced it back down.

I smiled against her mouth, biting her bottom lip and granting her wish.

The moment I slipped my fingers between her thighs, we both moaned.

"Oh *fuck*," I breathed, cock aching at how wet she was. I slid my finger between her lips, pressing the middle one just an inch inside her. Her hands reached back for me, her nails digging into my legs as I withdrew that finger and pressed it in again, a little deeper.

I took my time, slowly moving my finger in and out, deeper and deeper each time. When I added a second finger, B broke our kiss, crying out and leaning into me even more.

"Shhh," I warned, the hand I had holding her hair moved to her mouth, instead. She bit down on my fingers, and I didn't have time to tease her about it before she slid her hand between my thighs and firmly gripped my cock through my sweatpants.

I groaned, thrusting into her small hand as my head fell back. I wanted more. I *needed* more.

I let go of her long enough to rip my shirt overhead, and B turned, panting at the sight of me before she stripped her clothes off just the same. We watched each other, breathing erratic and fiery as layer after layer was shed, joining the blanket under us in the sand.

When we were both naked, we stared at each other, chests heaving and eyes wild. Her mouth parted at the sight of my cock, and I fought against the urge to smirk at her reaction.

When our eyes met, we crashed into each other once more.

Her hands swept into my hair as I lowered her down, sliding between her legs and reaching behind me until I felt the blanket. I pulled it up over where our hips met, and with the movement, my shaft slid along her wetness, splitting her lips open just enough for her to coat me.

A rumble of curses flew through me, and I was two seconds away from plummeting into her when I realized.

We didn't have a condom.

I slowed my kisses, heart hammering at the loss, at not thinking ahead. But I didn't expect this. I didn't plan for it.

"We need to slow down," I breathed.

"Like hell we do."

I smirked against her lips, but kissed her slower still. "I don't have a…"

I pulled back, nearly crying at the sight of her spread out under me like that, at being so close and yet…

"We don't have protection."

B's eyes widened a bit, searching mine, but then she swallowed. "It's okay."

My heart skipped.

B bucked her hips up, digging her heels into my ass and inching us closer again. "I'm on birth control. And I'm clean. Are you?"

"Yes," I cursed, because the fact that I was about to be inside her without a single barrier between us was enough for me to know I was about to be fucked for life.

I dropped my forehead to hers, savoring the way her nails dug into my shoulders.

I should stop this, a distant voice warned.

But then, B breathed my name, wrapping her hands around my neck and pulling my lips to hers once more.

"I can forgive you for kissing me," she said. "But I can't forgive you if you stop right now."

And that was it.

That was the last shred of dignity I held onto, the last bit of morality I glimpsed before I groaned, kissed her hard, and flexed my hips, filling her fast and eager and all at once.

We both gasped, open mouths against each other, chills cascading down every inch of us. I withdrew, slower this time, before pressing inside even deeper.

"*God*, B," I hissed. "I've dreamed of what this would feel like, taking you, feeling you wrapped around me. But it doesn't even compare. I can't…" I shook my head, words lost, especially when she wrapped her legs around me even tighter. "I'll never—"

"I know," she said.

This was the moment that changed everything.

We felt it in our bones, in our soul, in every point of contact where our slick skin connected. There would be no going back from this, and yet, there was no other option *but* this either.

Being inside her was coming home.

But it was also jumping off a jagged cliff into a shallow pond.

I think I knew, even then, that that night was all I'd have with her. I took my time, savoring every taste and touch and kiss and moan. I wanted to fill every void Ethan had left in her, wanted to fuck her so thoroughly that none of her romance novels would ever live up to what she experienced in real life with me.

I was branding her, and I wanted her to feel every burning skin cell as I did.

When she came, her moans soft and sweet, her hands fisting in the blanket and swirling the sand beneath it, I took a mental snapshot, never wanting to forget what it felt like when that girl came apart at my touch.

And then I found my release, too — wicked and all consuming.

I never wanted to stop kissing her, once we both came down. I wanted to lie there in that blanket, on that beach, on that *night* forevermore.

I knew now that I'd had her, *truly* had her, that meant I could lose her, too.

And that loss was one I knew I wouldn't survive.

FIVE

The Games We Play

THE NEXT NIGHT WENT so differently from what I imagined, my head was spinning.

Friday was a wash. I didn't even have time to sleep after I dropped B off before I had to get ready for my first class. After talking to B, I heard my parents' voices ringing in my head about focusing on what I could control — which, right now, was staying on top of my grades and graduating with my degree.

Even as tired as I was, I resisted the urge to skip class. If this was all I had control over, I would do it right.

My phone was long dead before I got back to my dorm after that night with B, so I put it on the charger and left it there for the day, haphazardly tossing my textbooks and laptop into my bag before dragging myself out the door.

Little did I know how that small decision would fuck everything up.

I thought I'd be back to my dorm by noon, that I'd go to my first class and then go straight back to get a nap.

I planned on texting B then, if not going to her dorm to surprise her, but I forgot about the group project meeting I had right after class.

Look, I *know* from B's point of view, it looked like I was up to shady shit that next morning. But the girl B saw me with my arm around was Tina, a sweet girl from my economics class whom I liked giving a hard time. She had a boyfriend at another college, and I was a shameless flirt, and I just loved to tease her. She always teased me back and played into my antics, which is exactly what B saw when we walked out of that coffee shop.

I didn't see *her* at all.

After that meeting, I went straight back to my dorm and face planted on the bed, exhausted. And I slept through the night.

That next day, I saw the missed text from B. All it said was *hey*, and as simple of a text as it was, it made me smile and bite my lip and think about all the ways I'd had her the night before.

But texting her back wouldn't do.

I had to see her.

I took a long, hot shower, hating that I was washing away her scent along with the grime of the last forty-eight hours. The only solace I found was that I'd have her in my arms again soon.

Of course, that solace was quickly chased by guilt, because I knew we'd have to make a plan to tell Ethan about us — and no matter how we broke that news, it wasn't going to be pretty.

Still, I believed in us, in what we had, and I knew we'd get through anything together.

Ethan and his campaign partner, Shayla, were camped out in our dorm living room working on God knows what when I walked into the kitchen to get a glass of water. I chugged it all at once before refilling, and then sat in one of the chairs, watching them work and chatting with Ethan.

The guilt nearly ate me alive, sitting there with him as he smiled and prattled on about his campaign while I thought of the news I had to break to him. It was too much to stomach, and I'd just made an excuse about needing to run across campus for something, ready to bolt to B's dorm, when she flew through the door.

"I brought tacos!" she announced, kicking the door closed behind her and holding up two bags.

My heart stopped at the sight of her, and I couldn't help the smile that bloomed, no matter how I knew I needed to be careful.

Of course, that smile slipped as soon as she ignored me completely and looked right at Ethan, instead.

"You didn't," he said.

B nodded, setting the bags down on the kitchen counter before waving hello to Shayla. "I did."

Look at me, I willed her.

But she kept her eyes on him.

Ethan picked himself up from the floor and rushed over to her, wrapping her in his arms and greeting her with a long, slow, heated kiss.

My nostrils flared, fingers curling into fists.

"Marry me," he murmured against her lips.

And then, she giggled, swatting him away playfully like nothing had changed.

It took everything I had to sit there and watch it, to force a breath, to swallow, to not jump out of my chair and land my fist right in Ethan's nose for kissing my girl.

Because she *was* mine — whether he knew it or not.

"I'll get this all set up," B said, gesturing to the taco bags. "Whatcha working on?"

"Just going through inventory, figuring out next week's plan so we can have some fun and not think about this election tonight at the party."

"Amen!" Shayla yelled.

B tried to smile, but it was weak, and then she stepped closer to Ethan. "Do you have a second to talk? I... I need to tell you something."

My heart stopped.

Fuck.

Thoughts raced through my mind faster than I could keep up with.

She regrets it. She's going to tell him and beg for forgiveness. She doesn't want me. It's all over.

But then I frowned, because that didn't make sense — not after last night. Not after *everything*.

Ethan grabbed her arms, concerned. "Is everything okay, babe?"

"Yeah, I'm fine," she said. "I just, there's just something we need to talk about."

"Okay," he said, and then he glanced back at Shayla. "Would it be okay if we talked later tonight? We're really trying to get all this done before the party. I mean, that is, if you're sure you're okay and it can wait?"

I knew I should pretend to do something on my phone, or leave the room, or do *anything* other than sit there and stare at them, but I couldn't move.

"Yeah, sure. Yeah, it can wait." She smiled. "Go get back to it. I'll make everyone a plate and then come help."

"Thank you," he whispered, kissing her cheek once more before jogging back over to take a seat on the floor next to Shayla. They bent their heads together, pointing at something on her screen and talking numbers.

And finally, B looked at me.

My jaw tightened, possessiveness and a love so deep I couldn't fully reach it consuming me as I tried to read her expression. She was sad, that much I could garner. But there was something else there.

I couldn't figure it out before she tore her gaze from mine.

And then I realized I didn't give a fuck if Ethan found out this way — I had to know what was going on.

In the next breath, I was up out of my chair and standing behind her in the kitchen.

"What are you doing?"

She jumped a little, but didn't turn to look at me as she retrieved a stack of plates from the cabinets.

"Making tacos. Want some?"

"Don't play dumb, you've never been good at it."

"Because you know me so well."

"I do," I said loudly, not caring who heard, and I grabbed her wrist before she could reach for the taco shell and keep pretending like she didn't see me.

We both glanced up at Ethan and Shayla, but they were deep in their own conversation over the laptop.

"I do fucking know you," I said again, lowering my voice this time. "What's wrong?"

"Nothing."

"B," I pleaded, but she tugged her wrist from my grip.

"Nothing. I'm fine."

"You're fine," I deadpanned.

She sighed, piling the first shell with grilled chicken before dropping it to a plate and facing me.

She was absolute stone when she answered, "Yep. Are you going to help me with these or not? Because otherwise you're kind of in the way right now."

Okay, *now* I was past confused.

I was pissed.

And I wanted to know *exactly* what the hell she was doing.

I let out a sharp laugh. "That's fine, I don't mind being in the way. Seems to be my favorite place to be, actually."

B glared at me.

"What's gotten into you?" I asked, wondering where my soft surfer girl from the night before was now. "Did I do something?"

"Why would you think that?"

I scoffed, crossing my arms before I stepped into her space. "Oh, I don't know, less than thirty hours ago you were forcing my hand between your thighs, and now you won't even look at me? Yeah, maybe that."

"Shhh!" she whisper-screamed, eyes wide as she glanced at Ethan before her glare found me again. "Stop. It was a mistake."

Her words hit me like a slap to the face, and my neck snapped back with the force.

"A mistake," I repeated.

"We were both vulnerable, it was a heavy moment. Shit happens."

"Shit hap—"

I couldn't even finish the sentence. Bile rose in my throat as I threw my hands up, raking them through my hair before clasping them to rest on my head.

This isn't her.

This isn't what she means.

I forced a calming breath, knowing this was a wall she was putting up, and I had to be careful trying to climb it, lest she add another ten feet to it before I got the chance to climb over the top of it.

I let my hands fall to my sides again. "What are you even saying right now? Do you hear yourself?" I asked her, my brows folding in ward. "Do you *see* yourself? You're shaking, B."

Her bottom lip trembled with that, and I tried to reach for her, tried to find that connection that I knew would get her back to her right self.

But she backed away, hitting the counter in an effort to stay away from me.

"I see just fine, thank you. Well enough to see that whatever happened the other night clearly didn't stop you from shacking up with Tina yesterday."

Her eyes were hard when they met mine, and I balked, confused.

"What? Tina?"

"It's fine, Jamie. I saw you two together, but it's okay. What happened with us... it didn't mean anything to me either."

460

My heart thundered in my chest.

It didn't mean anything.

"So we're cool," she finished. "Like I said, shit happens."

B went back to plating the tacos like the conversation was done.

Like *we* were done.

Part of me was absolutely gutted. I felt like she'd taken a rusty blade and shoved it right between my ribs into my lungs, depriving me of a clean breath.

It hurt.

God, it hurt to hear her say those words.

But it also pissed me the fuck off.

Because I knew, even then, that she was lying.

"Wow," I finally breathed, shaking my head as I moved in closer. I invaded her space, noting how she stiffened when my breath hit her ear. "I don't know what you *think* you saw, but if this is really how you feel, I'm glad your twisted little mind made this shit up to make you feel better about it."

With that, I pushed off the counter and stormed to my room, slamming the door behind me.

• • •

I was still seeing red when I made it to the bonfire later that night, alcohol already swimming deep and warm in my system. I'd started drinking as soon as B left our dorm that afternoon, and I hadn't stopped since.

But I'd taken my time getting to the party, debating going at all since I knew she'd be there. Call me a masochist or the most lovesick sonofabitch to ever live, but even after what she'd said, even after how she'd acted — I had to see her.

A sick part of me hoped I could get her alone, that I could somehow get her to talk to me. And maybe the beer gave me confidence that her hearing me out would change everything.

Regardless, all of my plans went out the window when I finally got to the party.

Because Jenna was there.

And suddenly, a new plan had formed.

"Well, I'll be damned," Jenna said, staring at me like she'd seen a ghost as I approached her and B at one of the benches on the other side of the fire.

I'd spotted B's hair from across the party, chest tightening, but I never stopped moving toward her. It wasn't until I was halfway to her that I realized who she was with.

"Jamie?!" Jenna cried, shaking her head and laughing as she launched herself into my arms. She was so much like the girl I'd dated in high school, and yet she carried herself differently, enough for me to know that college had changed her, too.

B ignored me just like she had earlier, sipping her flask with her eyes focused somewhere else.

"What the hell? What are you doing here?" Jenna asked me when I released her.

I laughed. "What do you mean? I go to school here."

Jenna's jaw dropped, and she turned from me to B. "What? Oh my God, B, how did you never tell me Jamie went to the same school as you?"

It was my turn to look at her, and *fuck* did it hurt when I did. I could tell just by one glance that she was far from okay. Her eyes were bloodshot, glazed, her skin pallid.

But she had that little jaw of hers set, still determined to play whatever game she was playing.

I smiled. "She never told you, huh?"

B just shrugged, absentmindedly playing with her hair. "I figured you saw on social media or something."

"Yeah, right," Jenna said on a giggle. "This asshole deleted me after he broke my heart."

I cocked a brow, noting the wicked smile on Jenna's lips. I'd seen it a thousand times before, knew it like the back of my hand.

She was flirting.

And one little glance at B told me it was driving her insane.

I let my eyes sweep over Jenna, and while she was still as gorgeous as ever, I only did it to get under B's skin.

Because if she wanted to play this fucking game, she'd learn soon enough that I wasn't one to lose.

"I seem to remember being on the other side of that heartbreak," I mused.

B shot to her feet suddenly, looping her arm through Jenna's before she could respond. "We should make the rounds, I want to introduce you to everyone."

But Jenna didn't take her eyes off me. "Yeah, in a minute. I think Jamie needs a drink."

I *did* need a refill, but I looked at B, hoping she would stop this before we had to go any further. When she didn't say anything, I sighed, looking back at Jenna with a smile.

"That I do. Escort me?" I asked, holding out my arm.

Jenna dropped B without a second thought, looping her arm through mine, instead. "Of course."

And that was just the beginning of our sick little game that night.

B couldn't keep her eyes off me and Jenna for the next half hour, though she didn't move to join us. She just watched us from her perch, drinking angrily from her flask and pretending like she didn't care. It was driving me mad, whatever it was that she was doing, but I didn't know how to reach her other than to play along.

Jenna was easy to talk to — she always had been. It was part of the reason we'd dated for as long as we had. She filled me in on how college in New York was going while I told her about my life in California, and we reminisced on old times, laughing at the stories we swapped.

All the while, I felt B's eyes on me, and I wished for her to come and pull me away.

Time passed in a buzzed blur, and Jenna and I eventually found our way to the fire pit where Ethan and Shayla were.

Just in time to watch B stumble over and sit in Ethan's lap.

My tongue was sandpaper as I watched him grip her hip in his hand, pulling her closer, holding onto her like she was his. Technically, in that moment, she was.

But I knew the truth.

B had always belonged to me.

She always would.

"Hey," he whispered.

"Hey," she said back with a smile.

I tore my eyes away from them, focusing on Jenna. Her words were something along the sounds of Charlie Brown's teacher, though, as I kept my peripheral vision on B, grinding my teeth when Ethan grabbed her chin and kissed her.

I tried to focus on what Jenna was talking about, tried to focus on anything but what Ethan and B were doing, what they were talking about, but it was useless.

Fortunately, B made the first move.

"We should play a game," she said to the group.

Jenna clapped her hands together. "Oh! Yes! How about Never Have I Ever?"

"Classic choice, bestie," B said, and I knew from the way she sloshed some of her beer out of her cup when lifting it that she was drunk. *Too* drunk.

Her eyes held promises for a dangerous night ahead.

"We're a little old for games, don't you think?" I said, and I meant it in more ways than one as I stared at B.

She just shrugged. "You don't have to play. Tina just showed up, why don't you go get her a drink and leave us kids alone?"

I had to fight from rolling my eyes.

Jenna quirked a brow at me. "Girlfriend?"

B was smiling all sweet and innocent at me, like she'd caught me in some trap. But she was a fool, and as childish as it was, I wanted to make her feel like one.

"No. B has some weird obsession with my Economics project partner and can't let it go."

B rolled her eyes. "Whatever. Stay or go, I don't care. Ethan, you go first."

I knew then that Ethan wasn't okay — likely with the amount of alcohol his girlfriend had consumed. He was always worried about his reputation, about how the campus perceived him — especially since he was running for president. "Okay. Never have I ever had a one-night stand."

Jenna and I drank without hesitating, and I winked at her over my cup. But when I finished drinking, my eyes found B.

She hadn't lifted hers.

"Not drinking, B?"

"Nope," she said, and then hurriedly tried to change the subject. "Your turn."

"You've never had a one-night stand?" I pushed, leaning my elbows on my knees. I cocked a brow at her, challenging.

"I was her first," Ethan said. My stomach soured, rolling even more when he pulled her into him and kissed her cheek before saying, "Her only."

B kissed him quickly, but I knew she was feeling just as sick as I was.

"How sweet," Jenna cooed.

"Yeah. So sweet," I deadpanned, but I couldn't cool the angry fire raging inside me at the sight of them. B thought he was so perfect, that he was some tender little bunny that could never hurt anything or anyone.

She didn't know the way he talked about her when he first met her, before *I* knew who it was he'd met.

He'd called me after their first night partying at PSU and told me he found his fuck buddy for the summer, that she was a virgin, and he couldn't wait to defile her. He'd joked about it and, being the asshole that I was, I'd joked about it, too.

Because I didn't know it was her.

But now, everything had changed, and it was time to call him on his shit.

I was fucking tired of the games.

"So, my turn, huh?" I snipped. "Hmmm… Never have I ever had a threesome."

B smiled at Jenna, for reasons unbeknownst to me until I read her side of the story, but that smile didn't stay in place long once she realized Ethan was taking a drink.

"Wait, seriously?"

Ethan cringed. "I was a freshman, I thought it was cool at the time. It didn't mean anything."

"Oh," B said. And I saw it, the moment she realized he could lie to her, that he could keep something from her.

That he wasn't the saint she'd made him out to be.

"Are you mad?" Ethan asked.

B's eyes found mine, and she glared, like she knew what I was trying to do.

I just smiled back.

"Of course not," she said. "It was before me. No big deal."

She smiled, letting Ethan kiss her neck as she took another drink.

"Your turn," she said to Jenna.

The game went on, and honestly, I lost focus with how hard I was trying not to storm over to B and rip her out of Ethan's lap. I wanted to throw her over my shoulder like a fucking caveman and take her back to my dorm. I wanted to demand she stop this shit and talk to me like a fucking adult.

I did laugh a bit to myself when Shayla said she'd never had sex on the beach, which promptly made B choke on her beer before racing off to refill it just to escape the situation.

All night long, B played her game, grinding on Ethan in front of me like I didn't know what she was doing. I just let Jenna hold my attention, let her think I was just as interested as she was in rekindling what we had for one night of fun. Truthfully, I was about five minutes away from saying I needed to piss and then escaping the party altogether.

I was exhausted — both from lack of sleep and the utter fucking ridiculousness of the game.

But I couldn't leave B, not with her continuing to drink when she'd clearly had enough. I was worried about her. I wanted to peel her away from the party, too. I wanted to get her alone.

I just didn't know how.

I was in a daze, half-listening to Jenna when I realized there was some sort of commotion going on across the bonfire.

My eyes landed on B just in time to see B rip her arm out of Ethan's grip, her brows furrowed, eyes menacing.

"What, afraid I'll damage your perfect reputation before election?"

Shit.

Jenna and I exchanged a look, and I stood without her saying a word, knowing I needed to step in and save B from herself.

"It was embarrassing to kiss me earlier, guess it'd really be embarrassing if I took my clothes off," she said as I made my way over. And then, she stripped her sweater off, revealing a thin tank top underneath.

I cursed.

"Okay, come on. We're leaving," Ethan said, trying to grab her.

"You can go if you want. I'm not ready to leave."

"That wasn't a request."

"And mine wasn't a suggestion."

"Damnit, Brecks!"

I stopped mid-stride, heart beating in my ears at the sound of that name that didn't feel like a name at all. And I saw all the blood drain from B's face, saw her eyes widen and well up with tears.

"You're not getting in that pool," Ethan said, oblivious to what he'd just done. "End of story."

B stared at him like she wasn't sure if she wanted to murder him right then and there, or run away before she started crying in front of everyone.

"B..." I said softly, holding out my hands for her. "Come on. I'll walk you back to your dorm."

It was like she snapped out of a daze when she looked at me, but she scowled just as quickly.

"I can walk myself," she spat.

She swiped her sweater and boots off the ground, already storming toward the parking lot as Ethan just stood there.

I waited for him to go after her, and when he didn't, I shook my head.

"You know she doesn't go by that name," I said, voice low and more menacing than I intended. "And you know damn well why, too."

Ethan shook his head. "I didn't mean to upset her. But come on, you saw her. She—"

"Is drunk. Yes, I know. Which is even more reason why you should be taking care of her, not being a fucking asshole."

Ethan narrowed his eyes then. "Bro, what the fuck."

But I had already turned away from him, jogging after the girl he was stupid enough to let go.

"Go away, Jamie," B threw over her shoulder at me when I caught up to her, the darkness of the parking lot falling over us.

I gritted my teeth.

"What? Nothing to say now?"

"I said *go away*."

"Oh, come on," I challenged, hot on her heels. "You've been doing your damnedest to get my attention all night. Well, you've got it."

She scoffed. "Contrary to your belief that the world revolves around you, Jamie, you were the last thing on my mind tonight."

"Bullshit."

She spun to face me then, seething. "Just leave me alone! Go back to Jenna and give her the Tour de Jamie's Bedroom. I've heard it's *quite* the tourist spot on campus."

And that did it.

I'd had e*fucking*nough.

"Damnit, B!" I yelled, slamming my palm against a nearby truck. "What the hell do you want from me? You give yourself to me after all this time, and then treat me like scum the next fucking day, saying it was a mistake and didn't matter to you."

My chest heaved, emotion surging through me like a tidal wave.

"But then, you act like a goddamn fool when you see me with your best friend?"

I stepped into her then, desperate for her to see.

"You think I slept with Tina? I didn't. She's in my class, nothing more. You think that night didn't matter to me? It did. It's all I've thought about since," I confessed, my voice breaking.

B swallowed, her lips trembling as I moved in even closer.

"You think it doesn't kill me to see Ethan's hands on you? It does. It fucking *murders* me."

I panted, shaking my head.

"You think what happened between us wasn't real? It was." My eyes fell to her lips then, those plump, trembling lips that belonged to me. "And it still is."

I descended on her, catching her gasp with a hard kiss as I pressed her into the truck. She relented only a moment before her hands found my chest and she shoved, hard.

I stumbled back, the two of us watching each other with heaving chests like wild fucking animals.

And then, she launched for me.

Her mouth found mine, eager and desperate, and she clutched at my sweater as I lifted her. I pinned her against the truck, kissing down her neck, sucking on her collarbone, branding every piece of skin she had just in case she ever thought to forget again. When I found the swell of her breast over her tank top, she hissed, moaning and leaning into the touch.

"Stop," she breathed, and I groaned at the game, at how hot it was even now. My hand dipped under her tank top and B whimpered, breathing hard into my mouth as I slid my tongue inside her mouth.

But then, she shoved me back again.

"Stop!"

I swallowed.

"We can't do this."

"Why not?" I panted.

"B?"

I whipped around to find Jenna staring at us, her eyes narrowed and somehow wild at the same time.

She crossed her arms, gaze bouncing between the two of us. "What the fuck is going on?"

I let out a long breath through my nose, suppressing a curse.

"Come on, Jenna," B said. "Let's go."

And then, she grabbed Jenna's hand and left me there.

Had I known then what I know now, what would happen next, I would have stopped her. I would have told Jenna to fuck off and carried B back to *my* bed. I would have spent every last precious minute with her between my sheets before our world came crashing down.

But I didn't know.

I thought she needed space. I thought I was doing the right thing by letting her go.

The next morning, I learned just how cruel life could be.

• • •

Jenna was the one who called me.

She was frantic, telling me between sniffs and sobs of her own what had happened to B's dad the following afternoon. I was already getting dressed, already pulling on my sneakers as she continued.

"Where is she?"

"I don't know," Jenna said. "Her mom called her this morning, and for a long time she just laid in bed and cried. Then, she asked me to start packing her things. She... she grabbed her board and called a cab until she found one who would take her with it."

"I'll find her."

It was a promise, and I ended the call, already jogging for my Jeep.

My mind raced the entire drive to the beach, thinking about the last two days and all the shit that suddenly seemed so small, so insignificant. I would have laughed at the stupid games we played the night before if it didn't make me sick to think about.

I think I knew, even then, that she was going to break my heart.

Relief found me when I saw her standing on the beach at the very first spot I took her surfing. She had her board tucked under her arm, her hair whipping in the wind as a storm blew in, and she stood there at the water's edge, waiting.

I walked to her slowly, not really sure what I wanted to say, what I *could* say to make it okay.

Her dad was dead.

He was gone. And while that would have sucked in *any* situation, the fact that their relationship had been so fucked since she found out what he did to her mom certainly made it worse.

My body hummed to life when I got close to her, and I marveled at the way the sunlight shone on her skin before it disappeared behind a dark cloud.

"You can't go out there," I said.

Even from the angle behind her, I saw her bottom lip quiver, but she hiked her board up higher, sniffing. "I'll be fine."

"It's about to storm, and it's getting dark."

She didn't respond, so I eased in, careful not to startle her as I grabbed the other side of her board. I tugged gently, and she gripped it tighter at first, but then she released, her shoulders slumping as she let me take it from her.

I set it in the sand gently, turning back to her as her glossy eyes watched the waves.

For a while, I just stood there with her, our eyes on the ocean as the wind whipped our hair. My heart ached, and with the surge of it, I reached for her — just barely — my pinky brushing hers.

She closed her eyes, and then she slid her palm into mine, and we both held on tight.

"Jenna called me. She… she told me what happened."

Her thumb rubbed mine as another deep roll of thunder met us.

"Talk to me," I begged, voice soft and weak.

Her nose flared, lips trembling. "I don't know what to say."

"Don't worry about it making sense, just talk. Just… get it out."

She nodded, again and again, rolling her lips together as silent tears ran down her cheeks. I wasn't even sure if she realized they were there. She didn't move to swipe them away, just let them fall.

"I'm supposed to hate him," she finally whispered. "I was named after the freckles on his cheeks, the same ones on mine, and I'm supposed to hate him. He raped my mom," she choked, the tears coming more fierce with that.

I squeezed her hand.

"And I never knew. I never knew that the hands that taught me how to ride a bike were the same ones that held my mom down the night I was conceived. I never knew the eyes that cried with tender joy the day I lost my first tooth were the same ones that watched my mom beg for him to stop hurting her."

She shook her head, and I knew every word was excruciating for her to say. I just held onto her, letting her know she wasn't alone.

"He was always there. He was the one to buy me my first notebook and pen and tell me to write. He was the one who took me on a shopping spree the day my childhood best friend moved away. He was always there." She covered her mouth, squeezing her eyes shut. "And then he wasn't, because I pushed him away, because I was supposed to. I haven't talked to him since the day I graduated high school. I ignored his phone calls. I told him not to come to Christmas dinner for the first time in my life." She squeezed her eyes shut even harder. "I didn't talk to him, Jamie. And now I'll never talk to him again."

I reached for her, crushing her to my chest as she relented to the sobs assaulting her. I held her tight as the first drops of rain found us.

"It's okay to love him," I told her, another deep roll of thunder echoing.

"No, it's not," she breathed, and then she lifted her glossy gray eyes to look up at me. "Just like it's not okay to love you."

My nose flared, emotion strangling me as I angled her face up even more, cradling her neck in my hand. "You love me?"

She nodded, biting her lip as she released more tears.

"Why is that not okay?"

"Because," she whispered, shaking her head as she gripped my shirt. "I can't be with you right now, Jamie. I'm going home tomorrow for the funeral and I just... I can't promise you anything. I can't..."

Her voice faded, and I swear my chest split open, because even though I hated it, I understood exactly what she was saying.

In that moment, I didn't have any other choice but to love her through the darkest time of her life.

And I knew right there on that beach that I wouldn't get to do it the way I wanted to.

I felt her pushing me away, felt her isolating herself, felt her need to get away from me and Alder and *everything* until she sorted through what she was feeling.

It gutted me.

But I wanted her to know I was still with her.

I lifted my other hand, cradling her face and searching her eyes.

If she was leaving, I needed her to know the truth.

"Is it okay that I love you back?"

She let out a soft whimper of a cry, but I cut it short, pressing my lips to hers and fighting against the overwhelming urge to cry that hit me once we sealed that kiss. Everything in my body warned me of the hurt that was about to come, but I ignored it, wanting nothing more but to savor whatever I had left with her.

"Stay with me tonight," I whispered against her lips.

She nodded, letting me pull her into me, and she gave herself to me one last time.

I spent that entire night making sure she felt safe, and warm, and loved. I kissed her like I'd never have the chance again, and in my gut, I really thought I wouldn't.

She left that next day, and she never came back.

She never called. She never texted.

She never answered when I tried to reach her, every birthday and every anniversary of her father's death.

Life went on without her, the cruel bastard that it is. I wished it would have stopped. I wished a fucking semi truck would have taken me out and ended the misery.

But slowly, time stretched on. I went to school, but I stopped dating. I played basketball, but I stopped surfing.

I graduated.

I moved back home.

I moved *on* — at least, as much as I could.

I convinced myself I would be alright without her.

But the day the universe decided to put us in the same place again, I realized just how naïve I'd been.

SIX

Tonight and One Day

IT WAS ONE OF those times in life when everything feels right.

The night I walked into that little dive bar just a few blocks from the office, I was floating on a cloud of possibility. I'd just been notified that I passed my CPA exam, and my father had officially offered me a position at his firm. Half the partners, and another half-dozen accountants were out with me to celebrate, and I had this permanent smile on my face, this permanent feeling that I was on the cusp of something big.

All my life, I'd had this pretty little dream for my future. I wanted to go to the same university as my dad, get my CPA, join the firm, work my way up, and eventually become partner. Along with that, I wanted to find the woman of my dreams, marry her, and fill a house with babies.

It was the cliché American dream, and I got shit for it from all my friends growing up. They'd call me soft and a pussy and everything else they could think of to try to make fun of what I wanted. But I never wavered. I knew from a young age what I wanted, and I wouldn't stop until I got it.

That night, passing that exam and getting my official job offer? It felt like checking off a giant box. It felt like stepping into the next chapter.

It felt like the future I'd always wanted was *right* there, brushing my fingertips.

If it sounds like I'd moved on and found a life without B — it's because I had.

Don't get me wrong, that girl had a permanent place in my heart. I was an absolute fucking wreck for a solid year after she left, and the longer we went without a single word between us, the more my heart broke.

But as time went on, I grew to realize I couldn't hold on to hope for something that *could* have been. I had no choice but to move forward — even if I had to do it with her still hanging onto my heart.

I still called her, twice every year, once on her birthday and once on the anniversary of her father's death. She never answered, and because she'd gone ghost on all social media, I had no idea where she was or what she was doing.

I knew she had the same phone number, though, her sweet voice telling me each time that I'd reached her, and to leave a message after the tone.

Three years. Three years of wondering, of longing, of letting her go and yet never truly being able to. Three years of missed calls and unanswered voicemails. Three years of being clean.

And then I walked into that bar.

And I saw her.

It was her hair I noticed first — because any time I saw a woman who had hair even *close* to B's, it called my attention, and I'd stare until the woman turned around, and I was disappointed yet again to find it wasn't her.

But this time, over the top of her head, I spotted Jenna.

And her mouth was hanging open like a frog trying to catch flies.

My heart thundered in my chest as she murmured something to B, and then she whipped around, her gray eyes slamming into me like a hurricane.

All the noise — the music, the laughter, the sound of glasses clinking together — it all faded away the moment her eyes met mine. The guys I was with were already making their way to the bar, clapping me on the shoulder and telling me how drunk they were going to get me, but I just stood there, smiling, full disbelief washing over me as I took in the sight of her.

Her hair was longer than it had ever been, full and curly, but falling down past her shoulders now. I knew without being an even inch closer that she'd been surfing, because her skin had that permanent summer glow, her freckles more pronounced than ever. Those lips of hers that always bewitched me were parted in that moment, and I swear, just the sight of them open like that made my pulse tick up a notch.

I was moving toward her before I realized it, my legs and feet and *heart* not able to resist the magnetism between us.

I saw the breath B took, the way it hitched in her throat, the way she couldn't look away from me either as I made my way across the bar. She turned in her barstool, allowing me proper access to the rest of her, and I took in the tiny, strapless top she wore, how it hugged her breasts and proudly displayed her collarbone, her neck, her toned midriff. I knew without her even standing yet that those jeans were painted on, tight and tempting, and when I caught sight of the tall, black high heels on her feet, I sucked in a hot breath.

She crossed her legs, dangling one of those heels like lure, and I let her reel me in until I was standing right in front of her.

I tucked my hands into my pockets, not even a little ashamed as my eyes roamed over her again. I couldn't stare long enough. I couldn't get enough of her to last me another minute, let alone a lifetime.

"You changed your hair," I finally mused, taking my time as I dragged my gaze up the length of her and met her eyes.

"And you got a tattoo," she said, her voice warmer and sweeter than I even remembered.

I glanced down at the bit of my tattoo peeking out from where I'd shoved the sleeves of my dress shirt up to my elbows, smirking, but then my eyes were on her again.

It was a long moment of the two of us just staring, smiling, drinking each other in.

Then, I shook my head. "You have two seconds to get off that barstool and into my arms before I drag you off it."

She blushed, not able to fight her smile as she slowly stood. Just like I assumed, those jeans were painted on tight, and the moment she was standing, I took her in my arms.

Her sweet scent invaded every sense, my body humming back to life like it'd been a caterpillar locked in a cocoon until that very moment. I spread my wings, wrapping them around her and letting out a content sigh at the way it felt to stretch, to feel her warmth against me, to hold her familiar shape in my arms once more.

And then, in a whoosh, everything came back.

It was suddenly too loud, bar patrons laughing, music blasting, glassware clinking all around us. But I held onto her tight, not believing she was actually there, and sure as hell not willing to release her until I knew for sure she wouldn't disappear in a whisper of smoke once I did.

"Oh, hey, Jamie, nice to see you, too," Jenna snarked from her seat.

I regretfully loosened my grip around B, but she didn't sit, just reached for her beer and stood there next to me like she, too, was afraid I'd disappear if she moved too far away.

"Hi, Jenna," I said, appeasing her. She gave me a knowing smirk before I turned back to B. "So, celebrating tonight?"

She had a graduation cap on her head, and I flicked the edge of it, chuckling at her embarrassed groan.

"Yes. I got a piece of paper that says I'm great at pulling all-nighters and regurgitating textbook notes."

I smiled. "Congrats."

"And she got into grad school," Jenna added. "In Pittsburgh."

"Pittsburgh?" I echoed, and though I tried to play it cool, I knew I couldn't hide the way my brows shot into my hairline, the way my heart accelerated at the thought of her leaving when I'd just found her again. I frowned at B. "What's my surfer girl going to do in a city like that?"

She visibly swooned at the question, her eyes widening before she blushed and looked down at the label on her beer bottle. She peeled a little more of it back, shrugging.

"And you?" Jenna asked. "What are you doing back in Florida?"

"I'm celebrating, too, actually," I told her. "Passed my CPA exam and accepted a job offer from my dad."

B's head snapped back up at that, and I saw it in her eyes before she spoke — pride and awe. She was one of the few people in my life whom I ever opened up to, so she knew what a big deal this was for me.

"Really?" she asked on a breath. "Wow, that's amazing. I'm so happy for you."

"Thanks."

I couldn't take my eyes off her. And I realized then that I didn't want to share this moment with Jenna, or the other girl at the table with them, or all the guys who'd come out to celebrate with me tonight.

The universe whispered to me that my time with her was short, and that I'd better not waste it.

"Want to get out of here?"

B swallowed, her eyes heating for a moment before she played it off with a smile. "You know I hate clichés."

I shrugged. "I also know you'll make an exception for me."

"Oh? Do you now?" B shot a brow up into her hairline, an amused smile playing on her lips.

I tucked my hands into my pockets again, confident.
"I do."

B watched me for a long moment, debating, and when
she bit down slightly on her bottom lip, I sucked in a hot
breath I knew I couldn't let go of or I'd take her right there
for everyone to see.

"Oh, for God's sake, go," Jenna said. "Go before he
gets me pregnant with that fucking look of his."

B covered her laugh with her hand, and I didn't hide
my smirk as she grabbed her purse and apologized to her
other friend at the table.

Then, her eyes were on me again.

"Lead the way."

• • •

"I can't believe you traded in ScarJo," B said after we'd
driven around town for a while, her hand running down
the length of the leather seat she sat in.

Even though it wasn't the old Jeep, she somehow
made the new one feel just the same — like it was home.
She had her heels kicked off and her feet on my dash, her
long hair blowing in the wind, that same young, carefree
smile on her face.

Except now, that smile was tinged with something a
little dark, a little sad, a little all-encompassing. It was the
kind of smile you earned from living for a while, the kind
that came from having gone through hard-enough times

that you truly understood how few and far between the good ones were. You knew to appreciate them.

And you also knew they couldn't last.

I chuckled. "Yeah, well, ScarJo started getting cranky in her old age. I held onto her until about two months ago before giving in and upgrading."

"Oh, I'm sure it was so hard to do," B teased.

She was making a joke about how nice the new Jeep was, but for some reason, the way she said it made me defensive — like she should have known how hard it would be for me to give up the old Jeep, knowing everything that had happened inside it.

I sniffed. "Yeah, well, there were a lot of memories in that Jeep. I didn't want to let her go, not until I had to."

She quieted at that, and all the fun from the evening was sucked out the window, riding away on a breeze. I was done catching up and talking about the surf.

I needed answers.

"You never came back," I whispered.

She grimaced, pulling her feet off the dash and tucking them under her legs, instead. "I know."

"And you never answered my calls. You never called me back. You never…"

I grit my teeth, gripping the steering wheel hard as I worked to gain my composure. It was an effort not to punch something, not to want to scream at her and kiss her breathless at the same time.

"I know," was all she said.

We pulled up to a red light, and B let her head fall back against the headrest, turning to look at me as the red light reflected on her skin.

"Nothing I say is going to make you feel better, Jamie. I have excuses, I have reasons why I pushed you away, but none of them will make up for the fact that it was shitty of me to do. I was young, I was hurting, and I didn't know how to handle my new reality. I ran away from you, from California, because I thought it was the right thing to do. And in a way, I'm glad I did, because I needed to heal. But in a way, I hate myself for how I left you."

I clenched my jaw hearing those words off her lips — that she left me. Maybe I hadn't admitted that to myself yet.

"My dad's death changed me, Jamie," she croaked, covering my hand with hers. I sucked in a breath at that warmth. "And what I did to Ethan, it was against every moral code I had, and I hated myself for losing control, for loving you when I was supposed to be loving him. It was just…"

She closed her eyes, and I realized then how hard that time of her life had been — not just because of her dad, but because of us, too. I sighed, turning my hand so I could take hers in my grasp.

"I was fucked up," she whispered after a moment. "And I needed time."

The light turned green, and I moved my eyes to the road once more, but B kept her hand over mine as I shifted gears.

"And now?" I asked.

B was silent a moment more.

"Now, I'm sitting in your Jeep, and nothing has changed, yet everything has."

I nodded, frowning, not knowing what that meant. Everything *had* changed. Three years had turned both of us into entirely new people.

And yet…

B sucked in a breath before continuing. "And I'm wondering how much longer you'll fight the urge to kiss me before you finally give in.

My eyes snapped to hers then, not sure I heard her correctly.

"Because I leave in less than forty-eight hours, Jamie," she whispered, her shoulders deflating with desperation and longing. "And I need you to kiss me before I board that plane."

I didn't expect it.

I didn't expect her to tell me out right, without playing games or making me read into what she *wasn't* saying.

She wanted me.

She *needed* me.

I took a sharp turn, cracking my neck as my heart thudded hard in my ribcage.

"I'm taking you to my place. Now," I said. "If you didn't mean even a word of what you just said, you have roughly seven minutes to take it back. After that, you're not allowed to say another word, not even my name, because I'm going to fuck you speechless."

I turned, waiting for her to argue, for her to tell me we shouldn't. I was testing her, challenging her, daring her to fight. Because that was the last warning I would give before I took her.

A Love Letter to Whiskey

And this time, I would take a bigger piece of her when I did, and I wouldn't give it back — no matter what happened after tonight.

B only licked her lips and uttered two words that were my undoing.

"Drive faster."

• • •

Warning bells sounded loud in my ears as I slammed my front door closed behind B, immediately pinning her against it and tossing my keys when I did. She wrapped her legs around me, her high heels digging into my ass as I crushed my mouth to hers.

That first kiss, that first taste of her after so long was enough to make me come right then and there. Just her lips on mine, her tongue, her whimper at the touch set my soul on fire.

Someone could have pushed me off her in that moment and told me the heartbreak that would come later, and I still would have shoved them aside and taken her, anyway.

There *was* no walking away. Not then, not ever.

I stripped her top off like the scrap of fabric it was, groaning when I realized she didn't have a bra on underneath. Her dark nipples pebbled, peaks rising, and I would have sucked each one between my teeth had she not moaned my name next.

"Jamie," she begged.

"Shh," I warned, meaning what I said in the Jeep.

488

I didn't want her to say a fucking word — not until she was coming and screaming my name.

There was a little hate flowing between us as I carried her into my kitchen, but it was the kind of hate that was just across the thin line between it and all-consuming love. I hated her for what she'd done to me, for how she'd left me, for the time she'd denied us. But I also loved her so fiercely that it didn't matter what she did to me — I'd still want her.

How fucking sick it was, and yet, how perfectly right it felt.

I dropped her to the ground in front of my kitchen counter. "Take these off," I rasped, tugging at her jeans before my hands were on my own pants, making quick work of the button and zipper. My eyes snapped to her heels next. "Leave *those* on."

The side of B's mouth curled up into an impressed smile, like she was about to devour the man I'd grown into in her absence. She took her sweet ass time with her jeans, her breasts bobbing, nipples teasing me with every move she made until her jeans were around her ankles. She stepped out of her heels long enough to shake them off, and then she stepped right back in.

And there she stood, her perfect body illuminated by the light in my kitchen, wearing nothing but a scrap of black lace around her hips and those tall ass high heels.

"Good girl," I mused, stripping out of my boxers next. I palmed my aching erection as my eyes trailed over her, and I could have pumped myself three times right then and come on that beautiful canvas she was presenting me with.

But when she reached for her panties, it snapped me back to the fact that I had only precious time with her — and I didn't intend to waste it.

"Leave them," I said, shaking my head. "Turn around."

I kept stroking myself as she spun, looking over her shoulder at me with those big, stormy eyes. I used my free hand to sweep her hair to the side, holding it tight as I kissed along her exposed neck.

God, the way she tasted, the way she writhed and panted and surrendered herself to me. It was the most intoxicating drug of my life — the addiction I knew I'd never be free of.

I released her long enough to grab her hands and guide her down, bending her at the waist and wrapping her fingers along the other side of the kitchen island. The view was nothing short of a masterpiece, her back arched, spine drawing a direct line down to her plump little ass that was poked out and waiting for me. I kissed all the way down her back and bit that juicy apple with a growl as B gasped.

I stood then, trailing my hand along her ass before I gave it a swift little pop that made the meat jiggle. B jumped, surprised, but then she gave me a satisfying moan of approval.

I held her hip with one hand, the other sliding along the lace of her G-string until my fingers slipped between her soaked lips. She was just as turned on as I was, and I slipped two fingers inside her, loving the way she writhed with the impact.

"Fuck," I rasped, withdrawing my fingers before I slid them in again.

This pussy is mine.

I felt the possession like a curse consuming my entire body, and with a growl, I tapped the insides of her thighs. "Open."

She obeyed, and when her legs were spread enough to allow me the access I needed, I dropped to my knees, sliding her thong out of the way so I could run my tongue along the slick slit of her. I licked all the way to her clit, moving her legs apart even more so I could suck it the way I wanted to. She trembled so hard I thought she'd fall, and I chuckled a bit as I backed up, licking all along her lips before I repeated the cycle.

B arched more, wanting my mouth on her clit, and I gave her what she needed, circling and providing the right friction I knew she needed to chase her release. Her legs quaked and her knuckles went white where they held onto my counter.

But before she could come, I released her, standing.

I thought B might actually cry when she looked back at me, but I just smirked and wiped my mouth. "Don't move."

I swiped my pants off the floor, digging into the pocket for my wallet. I had a condom stashed in there just in case, and I threw my pants down again once I had it, making my way back to B.

She was trying to stand, but I pressed my hand into her back before she could, flattening her against the counter once more. Then, I was right behind her, my shaft settling in the sweet spot between her ass cheeks.

We both groaned.

I ripped the condom wrapper open, covering myself with the latex before teasing her with my crown. I ran it down the length of her ass, slipping it between her wet lips and lining it up at her entrance as she arched, begging me to fill her.

But I just left it there, waiting and ready, as I bent down and grabbed as much of her hair as I could hold in a tight fist.

"All this fucking hair," I cursed, sucking her earlobe between my teeth.

She gasped as I tugged, her back arching, gaze drifting up to the light above us.

And then I filled her, mercilessly, burying myself in her deep enough that she'd never forget who she belonged to.

I paused when I was all the way in her, both of us shaking with the feel of it, and I dropped my forehead to her back. "God, I've been fantasizing about my hands in your hair like this all night. And these fucking heels," I moaned, standing straight. I still had her hair twisted in my fingers, so she arched with me as I slammed into her again.

I fucked her like I hated her, like she was everything I loathed, and like I'd die if I didn't destroy every last inch of her. When my hands finally fell from her hair to grab her hips, I picked up my pace, loving how she cried out and moaned and begged for more.

My little surfer girl, she knew how to ride the waves.

I slowed after a while, wanting to take my time, to savor the way she stretched and opened for me with every new thrust. The way she was pressed up against the counter, her clit rubbed against the granite, and I felt her widening her legs and maneuvering her hips so she could catch more of that sweet friction.

My girl wanted to come.

But I wasn't ready.

"Not yet," I warned, and then I spun her, dipping down to pull her into my arms as I rushed us down the hall toward my bedroom. We were a mess of angry kisses and clawing hands as I did, and B whimpered as I laid her down on top of my comforter, like even a second of separation might kill her.

She challenged me with her gaze as she backed up to the pillows, and I chased that beautiful body, settling between her legs and capturing her mouth with mine. Her shoulders hit my headboard and I spread her thighs with my own before dropping my hips and slipping into her again.

I filled her to the hilt, the backboard aiding me, and we both shuddered at the connection.

"Goddamn, B," I growled, shaking where I suspended myself above her. She dug those damn heels into my ass and I hissed, biting her neck in return. I flexed my hips in and out, just a little, keeping that connection between my pelvis and her clit. Those little thrusts were just what she needed and I knew it.

She came with a cry so loud I felt like we were in a fucking porno, my name rolling off her lips like a plea and a curse all at once.

I smirked against her lips when she finished, slowing my pace between her legs. Then, I hooked one of them under the knee, hiking it up high until her ankle rested on my shoulder. I kissed the thin skin there, my eyes locked on hers.

She was so fucking perfect. So beautiful and sexy and addicting and *mine*.

I felt her deeper in this position, her heat swallowing me up every time I thrust forward. And she kept those steel eyes on me, begging me to come with her, to spill inside her.

And so I did.

I shook with the release, with the kind of climax only B could provide. It wasn't the empty, hollow one I'd found countless times in other women. It was my whole body shaking, brain going numb, her nails digging into my soul and leaving a permanent mark right beside the one she'd left three years ago.

There was nothing in the world like fucking B, and maybe the universe knew it. Maybe it knew if it gave me more than just a few times in those years we fought against timing, it would have driven me mad with jealousy if anyone so much as looked at her after knowing what she felt like. Maybe there were beings at work that knew, like with any addiction, that I had to be strong enough to control myself before I could surrender to the high.

I collapsed on top of her, panting as she trailed her nails along my back. I shivered under the touch, kissing her neck before I pressed up to balance on my elbows above her.

"Well, damn."

She giggled as I kissed her nose. "My thoughts exactly."

"You have to be mine after that," I breathed, and in that moment, it was as obvious as the fact that the sky was blue and water was wet. She was mine. *Finally*, she was mine.

But then her smile dropped.

"I can't."

"Fuck that," I argued, and I thought it was a game. I thought we were playing. "You can. You are."

"I'm leaving Sunday night, Jamie," she said, breaking our train of kisses to look me in the eyes.

I hated the seriousness I found there.

I let out a breath, frowning. The universe was a cruel sonofabitch to let us find each other right before she was about to leave.

But I couldn't let her go yet.

"So be mine for the weekend."

B's shoulders sagged. "I can't. I have plans with my family. This is it... this is all I have."

This is all I have.

She was honest. She was telling me long before all the pain that would come next exactly what she could give me and what she couldn't.

But I couldn't accept it.

"Why can't we be long distance?"

She laughed at that, wrapping her arms around my neck. "Because that's a guaranteed way to get our hearts broken."

It was me who deflated then — because I realized I'd already been broken. For three years, I'd been broken.

She was the only thing that made me feel whole.

"But I'm not running from you anymore, Jamie," she said when she saw the dejected look on my face.

I studied hers, hoping like hell there wasn't an ounce of a lie in those words she'd just spoken. "Does that mean you'll answer my calls?"

She smiled, nodding. "Just… let's not try to put a name on this. On us."

I released an aggravated breath, but as I searched her eyes, I realized I'd take her in any way I could — even if the thought of not claiming her with my name on her skin and a big neon sign flashing above her that said JAMIE'S PROPERTY made me see red. "Alright, then," I conceded. "I need you to give me two things."

B arched a brow, waiting.

I licked my lips. "Tonight, and one day."

"Tonight," she echoed. "And one day."

I nodded. "I have to have both."

There was no other option for me. She *would* be mine, one way or another, and I was willing to wait.

But I had to have her word.

Her eyes searched mine for a long while before she nodded, pulling me down to kiss her once more. And that connection made me grow hard inside her, body aching for more, ready to seal the deal all night long if that's what it took.

I only had until the morning, anyway.

No sense in wasting the night with sleep.

I took B in every way I could that night. I tasted her until she came on my tongue, saw stars when she tasted me just the same. We showered and then fucked again. Ate

496

and then fucked again. Slept for approximately twenty minutes and then fucked again.

Everything felt right.

Even knowing she was leaving, even knowing she didn't want to put a title on us, I stupidly believed that we'd made it. We'd survived those three long years apart. She'd healed and I'd grown, and now, we'd be together.

I was so focused on making her fit into *my* plan, I didn't bother to think about what *her* plan was. I didn't think about compromise, about her wanting a career — even though I knew my girl, how determined she was, how she'd always been a go-getter and thirsty for a life of her own.

I assumed she'd want me more than anything else, that she'd give up who she was and walk away from her goals just to have me.

And that turned out to be the biggest mistake of my life.

SEVEN
Touched by an Angel

"DAMN," I SAID WHEN the video chat connected, dropping my keys on the counter as I smiled at B's view from her apartment. Pittsburgh spread out in front of the floor-to-ceiling windows like an endless sea of stars. "Look at you, big city girl."

"Pretty, right?"

B gave me a tour of the entire place as I kicked back on my bed, muscles sore and skin salty from a good surf session. Hearing her voice on the phone felt like someone standing on my chest. It was hard to breathe, knowing I'd had her and let her slip through my fingers again.

We'd been talking every day and night since the one we spent together in my apartment, but it wasn't the same as having her here. The way she talked about her new internship at Rye Publishing, I knew she was happy. That girl had been writing since I'd known her, but had always been too shy to show it off. Still, she was knowledgeable,

498

talented, and I knew it wouldn't be long before the big wigs at that publishing house realized how valuable she was.

She was right where she should be.

Except that she wasn't with me.

And somehow, that just never seemed right.

"Alright, I know you're dying to show me the bathtub," I said after she gave me a view of her bedroom.

"Of course. Had to save the best for last." The camera was shaky as she walked into the bathroom, revealing a claw-foot tub of her dreams. "Ta-da!"

"*Oooohhh, ahhhh,*" I teased.

"Isn't it gorgeous?" she asked, scanning the tub from one inch to the other with the camera before she turned the water on. "Totally worth the extra five-hundred bucks a month."

"You're right. I'd pay at least a thousand."

"Glad we're on the same page."

I smirked, one arm under my head as I watched the screen. But when B turned to face the mirror, my breath cut short.

Fuck.

She stood there in her bathroom butt ass naked, her hair slightly kinked like she'd worn it up all day, makeup still in place from being at the office. Her hair was pulled over her shoulders, covering her breasts, and the mirror cut off at the bottom of her belly button, leaving my imagination to run wild wondering if she was freshly shaved between her legs, or if she had a little landing strip, one I'd love to trace with my fingertip.

"Jesus," I breathed as my eyes drank her in. "You really did save the best for last."

B flushed, playing with her hair. She wanted me to take control, and though I could only do so much this far away, I knew how to give her what she wanted.

"Pull your hair back," I told her.

She swept her hair into one fist, pulling it behind her back and revealing her slight breasts, the nipples peaked as the room steamed around her.

"Now I really wish I was there."

I scanned her slowly, my cock growing hard and straining against my swim trunks. I scrubbed a hand over my face before I ripped at the strings of them, tugging until they were off my hips.

"What are you doing?" she asked sweetly, but she knew *exactly* what I was doing.

"I'm going to make you feel good," I said. "Get in the tub."

I flung my shorts to the side as she slipped into the water.

"Do you want to see what you do to me?"

She nodded, and I flipped the view on my camera, giving her a view of my abs, my hard cock as I took it in one hand and squeezed. I groaned at the feel of it, wishing it was her hand instead as I stroked myself and watched her eyes on the screen.

"Fuck, Jamie," she whispered, sinking deeper into the water. She grabbed one of her breasts, massaging it as I ran my hand over my shaft again.

"Pretend that hand is mine," I instructed. "Touch yourself the way I would if I were there."

B bit her lip, dragging her hand down into the water and letting the camera follow. It was hard to see through the water, but I knew her hand slipped between her thighs, that her fingers rubbed her clit as she arched into the touch with a deep moan.

It was sweet torture, watching her play with herself as I rubbed out my own release. We took our time, panting and moaning and sweating before we both came. I cleaned up while B drained the tub, and then we both crawled into bed, halfway across the country from each other, but it somehow felt like she was right there.

"Be with me," I whispered.

"I am with you."

"No, I mean, really be with me. Be my girlfriend."

Her sated smile slipped, eyebrows furrowing.

"Why do we have to put a title on it? Can't we just... I don't know. We're friends, Jamie. Best friends. I love talking to you, I miss you, I like making you feel good."

She blushed, and I tried not to curse at the way she'd called us *friends*.

"Exactly, so why does it freak you out so much to be official?"

"It's not that it freaks me out," she tried to explain. "It's just that this is the first time in my life that I've ever been completely on my own, Jamie. I need to just be myself for a while. You know how the last few years have been for me."

I had to fight not to scoff at that, because I *didn't* know. She'd refused to let me in. She'd shoved me out of her life, and had I not walked into that bar that night, I'm not sure she would have ever let me back in.

"Let's just exist, and let it go where it will go. No sense in putting pressure on either of us right now."

I swallowed, heat claiming my chest. "Are you hooking up with other guys?"

"What?" B balked, shaking her head. "No, of course not. I don't even know any other guys out here."

"That's not the point."

"I know, but I'm just saying."

I gritted my teeth. "Would you be okay if I hooked up with other girls?"

Her face paled, and I knew before she answered that she would hate it just as much as I would. "Yeah. I mean, I guess. I get it. You have needs."

Liar.

"Again, that's not the point." I sighed, running my hand through my hair. I didn't know how to make her understand. "I know it sounds stupid, but when I lost you three years ago, I told myself I'd never let that happen again. It's important to me to be with you, B. But I can't be if you don't let me."

B was quiet a moment.

"I'm not going anywhere," she finally said with a smile. "But I can't give you my all right now. I'm here to work, to get my graduate degree, and to find the rest of myself that's still floating just out of reach. I want you, I do," she promised. "Just give me some time to figure out my new surroundings, okay?"

My heart broke with that, because I wanted her to have her dream just as much as I wanted to have *her*. I knew it was important to her.

I just hated that I wasn't top of the list.

"Whatever you need, I'll give it to you," I promised.

But it was me who was the liar that time.

• • •

The summer flew by in a wicked heat stroke, it seemed. And I tried to stand by my promise, all the while feeling like a disease was festering in the pit of my stomach.

On the good days, B and I would watch movies together from afar, or talk on the phone all night and I'd pretend it was enough. She even came to visit me for a weekend — though, even then, I had to share her with her mom and her mom's new boyfriend, Wayne. Still, I cherished any time I had with her.

But it always left me wanting more.

And soon, the bad days began to outweigh the good ones.

I couldn't understand why she was fighting it, fighting *me*, why she wouldn't be mine the way I wanted her to be. I was young, selfish, and I didn't understand how hard B had worked her entire life for the opportunity she had at Rye Publishing.

I also didn't understand how important it was for her to be building a life on her own after everything she'd been through. That city, that job, they were just the beginning. This was her stepping into her independence, making it through a tumultuous childhood and excruciating period of grief.

I'd been so privileged with my own childhood and family, I just didn't understand.

"Maybe it's time for you to ask for what you want," my youngest sister, Sylvia, told me one night.

We were sitting on the beach, the wind on our face as I poured my heart out to her. Although, Santana was closer in age to me, Sylvia and I had just always understood each other in a way my other sister and I never did. Santana lived in New York now, but Sylvia was living at home with Mom and Dad for now, and I selfishly loved still having her close.

"I have. She knows."

Sylvia shook her head. "I don't mean tell her what you want and then accept when she says no. I mean, tell her that you *need* something more concrete than what you have now, or you need to walk away. Because, Jamie, this in-between you're stranded in?" Sylvia shook her head. "It's killing you."

She was right. Over the summer, I'd found it harder and harder to eat right and treat my body well. I was drinking way more than I should have been, and never finding a restful night of sleep.

It was a special kind of hell, and yet the thought of walking away from B made me double over with a fierce stomachache.

"What if I ask her to be with me, and she says no again?"

Sylvia sighed. "Then you let her go."

I mulled over that conversation for days before I finally got the guts to tell B we needed to talk. I hated sending that text, knowing it would likely have her wheels spinning, but there was no other way around it.

I couldn't pretend anymore.

As you know already from reading her side of our story, timing was never kind to us. And while, in that moment, I felt completely valid in everything I felt and was asking of her, I see now how selfish I was, how I couldn't see past what was right in front of me to the potential future we could have together.

She wasn't asking me for anything but time and space, but giving it to her felt impossible.

She called me on the night she found out she'd been promoted at Rye Publishing. Of course, I didn't know that yet, and so with my sister's words in my ear, I begged B one last time to give me what I needed.

"I just need you to sit there and listen to me for a minute, okay?" I told her when she called. I was pacing my living room, heart thundering unsteadily. "I know you're scared of us, of what we've been in the past and what we might not be in the future. I know you're standing on your own for the first time and you're proud of that, hell I'm proud of that too, but I can stand with you."

"Jamie—"

"And I know long distance freaks you out," I continued, because I knew if I let her stop me, I'd lose my nerve. "But we've made it through the summer practically as a long-distance couple, even if we didn't title it that."

I took a breath, knowing that that fact alone strengthened us. We'd been through so much already. I had no doubt we could survive anything.

"I've been thinking," I told her. "Your internship is almost over, and I've been looking at some publishing places in Miami. A lot of them are hiring, and you have experience now. Your classes are online, B. You could come home, we could be together."

"Jamie, I—"

"No, just let me finish," I pleaded, glancing at my laptop on the kitchen table. I had tabs and tabs of publishing jobs open within an hour of where I lived, a document with all the links ready to send her the moment she said yes. "I know this is a lot to ask. You don't owe me anything, and the fact that I'm asking you to uproot yourself and move back for me is selfish as fuck. But I realized last time you walked away from me I didn't ask you anything at all."

That sentence hit me harder when I voiced it out loud, because as much as I wanted to be angry with her for those three years of silence, I'd *let* her walk away. I hadn't told her that I needed her, that I wanted to be with her through it. Maybe if I had, things would have been different...

"So this time, I'm putting it out there," I said. "I'm letting you know what I want. I want you. I want you to move back, hell, to move *in*." I laughed, something between insanity and love flowing through me like a tidal wave. "It doesn't have to be complicated. We can do this, B."

"I'm staying."

"Jenna's here, too. And your mom. And—"

"Jamie, I'm staying in Pittsburgh," she said louder. "They offered me a full-time job. Today."

I paused at the top of a breath, the air filling my lungs, until what felt like a needle prick had me deflating like a helium balloon. I sank in on myself, frowning, sure I didn't hear her right.

She was staying.

She got a job.

She was staying.

"Okay," I finally said. "That's okay. We can see each other once a month, take turns flying, and eventually we'll figure it out."

"It doesn't work like that," B said, her voice breaking a bit.

My heart cracked.

"You have your dad's firm there. And I have my life here."

I swallowed against the emotion threatening to suffocate me. "That doesn't mean we can't have a life together, too."

I wished I could see her, then. I wished I was right there in her apartment with her, holding her, looking into her eyes when I told her I believed in us.

"But it kind of does, Jamie," she said after a moment. "It all sounds so easy when you say it over the phone, but a long-distance relationship is hard. It's complicated and messy, and neither of us needs that right now, not when we're both just getting started in our careers. It's just not the right time for us... it's never the right time."

I shook my head, over and over, disbelief strangling me. How could she push me away like this? How could she ignore everything I was saying, dig her heels in so deep on the fact that we couldn't make it long distance without even trying?

"That's not fair. You don't understand this, B — any of it," I said. "When you left Alder, you got to leave it all behind — the places we went, the memories we made. But I lived there. Without you. For three years." I paused, my chest heaving. "And then, when I found you again, everything seemed right. The timing, the way we both felt. I finally got an answer from you, why you stayed away all those years, and I got it, B — I really did. I understood. You were broken from your father's death and you needed time and space. I gave that to you. Happily. I didn't know if I'd ever have you again, but I didn't care because I knew what you needed from me."

Tears welled in my eyes, my nose flaring at the memory of what it felt like to think I'd lost her forever.

I didn't know if I'd survive that again.

"But now, you're telling me it's still not there — it's still not the right time. You couldn't be with me when you were broken, and now that you're standing on your own, you still can't be with me. So if I can't have you at your worst, and I can't have you at your best, then when do I get you, B? When does the timing line up for you to stop fighting what we have between us and just let me in?"

B let out a sob at that, and it damn near broke me, because I hated that I was hurting her. But goddamnit, she'd been hurting *me*. And I couldn't take it anymore.

"What happened to one day?" she asked softly.

I swallowed. "Well, I need one day right now."

"And I can't give it to you, so where does that leave us?"

I chewed my cheek, shaking my head, not willing to admit it yet. "I don't know."

B was silent for a long while, the truth of it all sitting between us like a bomb ready to explode.

508

"Listen, I have a really big event coming up and tomorrow is going to be a long day…"

I closed my eyes at the sorry excuse, letting one cooling breath flow through me.

This is it, I thought. *This is the end.*

"Yeah, okay." I let out a breath, and my heart clamored in my chest, begging me to try one more time. "I just…"

But I stopped there because what else could I say?

"Goodnight, B," I said, instead.

When she ended the call, I dropped to my knees, and I cried.

• • •

I let her go after that.

It killed me to do it, but it killed me even more to try to hold onto someone who wasn't holding onto me.

The first few weeks were the worst. I couldn't eat, couldn't sleep, couldn't keep myself from pulling up her number and staring at it. I never gave in, though. I never called.

But what hurt me more than anything was that *she* never called either.

I had regrets in those first three weeks. I regretted the way I came at her, regretted that I didn't congratulate her on getting hired when she'd worked so hard for it, regretted that I'd had that conversation over the phone instead of flying to her.

But soon, those regrets became too much to hold, so I let them go, too.

Santana flew in from New York after about two months of me moping, and together, she and Sylvia got me out of my funk. They made me hit the gym with them for a week straight, took me out surfing, got me back out and around friends, and by the time Santana flew back to the Empire State, I felt like I could finally start over.

That was the precise moment Angel walked into my life.

Angel Connelly was a spicy little thing. By the looks of her, you would have thought she was as innocent as her name. She was petite, with short blonde hair and bright blue eyes. She had a bit of a southern accent that gave her this shining charm, but the more you got to know her, the more you realized she'd fight like a pit bull if it came down to it. She was passionate about her job, yoga, and church — not necessarily in that order — and when she wanted something, she didn't give up until she got it.

It didn't take long for me to realize she wanted me.

Angel worked in the same building where my dad's office was. She was in advertising, and we stumbled into each other in an elevator ride down to the lobby one night after work. This was back in June, back when the only woman I could *see* was B.

Angel tried to shoot her shot, but I turned her down, telling her I had a girlfriend.

It was *technically* a lie, but I'd assumed it wouldn't be that way for long.

Even after that, though, Angel and her friends would somehow end up at the same bars as me and the guys after the work week, and I got to know a little more about her each time. She was friendly, funny, nice. I liked her.

And when B broke my heart, Angel was there to pick up the pieces.

After my sisters pulled me out of my funk, I was trying to focus on me, working out and surfing and trying to impress my dad enough to offer me partnership at the firm. I stayed late at work one night, and when I finally rode the elevator down at almost nine o'clock at night, I ran into her — she'd been staying late, too.

She asked if I wanted to grab a drink.

And even though B flooded my mind in that exact moment, even though my stomach coiled at the thought of spending time with another woman, and even though I knew I didn't have much of myself left to give... I said yes.

It surprised me, how much fun I had with her that night. Angel was a storyteller, and she kept me laughing and enthralled until almost two in the morning. I walked her home, gave her a kiss on the cheek, and she typed her number into my phone.

I called her the very next morning and asked her on a proper date.

I knew part of letting B go meant getting back out into the dating world. And since I hadn't really *ever* dated, in the sense of having a steady girlfriend and not just a woman in my bed, I was excited about the possibility.

It was all part of my plan, after all — the degree, the job, the wife, the kids. How did I expect to get the latter half of that dream if I didn't start dating?

It was easy with Angel. We were complete opposites, which meant there was never a shortage of date ideas. I tried to teach her how to surf, which she failed at miserably, and she took me to a hot yoga class that I almost passed out in. I made her watch horror films that had her clinging to my side, and she made me watch reality TV shows that I pretended to find cheesy and dramatic, when secretly, I kind of liked them, too.

Days turned into weeks and weeks into months, until we were on the cusp of the holiday season. That was when I made things official with Angel, and for the first time since Jenna, I had a girlfriend.

It was a warm night in November, standard for South Florida, when B crashed back into my life without a warning.

Angel and I were out at a little hipster bar with her best friend, Claire, and some of the guys I worked with. After a long week at work, we reveled in letting go, the alcohol buzzing through us as Angel sat in my lap and kissed me far too inappropriately for the public eye.

I didn't stop her though.

I loved the way she made me feel, how I never had to question that she wanted me, that she cared about me, that I was the first thing she thought of when she woke up, and the last thing before she fell asleep. She spoiled me with her attention, with her affection, and I drank up every drop of it like a kitten lapping warm milk.

I had her wrapped up in my arms, my tongue halfway down her throat when there was a crashing sound somewhere near the bar. We broke away from each other, looking toward the source of the noise, and that's when I saw it.

All that fucking hair.

I didn't even need a second look. I knew it was her.

"B?" I called.

But she pushed through the door without even a look in my direction.

Angel frowned when I stood, scooting her off my lap. "What's wrong?"

"I... I just need some fresh air. I'll be right back."

"Want me to come with you?"

"No," I answered quickly, and then I sighed, turning and grabbing her face between my hands. I kissed her sweetly. "I just need a sec. Be right back."

Angel frowned again, but nodded, and let me go.

I all but ran out the door, catching up to B just as she reached her mom's old car. She fumbled with the keys in her hands before shakily hitting the unlock button, the car lights flashing with a little *beep-beep*.

"B?"

My heart stopped at the sight of her, at the way she froze when she heard my voice. She was breathing heavily, but threw me a glance over her shoulder, trying to force a smile.

"Oh, hey, Jamie. Uh, yeah, I was just leaving though so—"

"Wait."

I hooked my arm around her elbow, turning her to face me, but she wouldn't look at me. She looked like she was one second away from crying.

I frowned. "What are you doing here?"

She closed her eyes, shaking her head slightly before she finally looked at me.

When she did, you'd have thought I'd killed her dog.

"I'm here visiting my mom. I would ask you what you're doing, but I have eyes, so," she snipped, her tongue pressed into her cheek as she ripped out of my grasp and gestured toward the bar.

I balked.

Did she actually have the audacity to be upset that I was with someone? After nearly *four months* of no contact from her? After what she last said to me?

My brows bent even more. "What the hell is that supposed to mean?"

"Oh, I think you know exactly what it's supposed to mean," she seethed, folding her arms over her chest as she stepped into my space. "Tell me, did you fuck her the night before you asked me to talk? Did you feel guilty and desperate to lock me down before the pressure of long distance took you under?"

"What?" My nose flared, anger and disbelief battling inside me.

Now that I've read her side of the story, I know that Claire lied to her about the timing with me and Angel — which was typical Claire, to be honest. But at the time? I just thought she was crazy.

"What the fuck are you talking about?"

"I'm talking about the little pixie blonde who was just mauling your face," B spat. "Angel is her name, right?"

Hearing Angel's name on her lips shocked me, and I couldn't say anything back, couldn't *do* anything but blanch.

"Oh yeah, Claire? Her BFF? She filled me in on the whole situation when I spotted you two sucking face."

That wiped the shock from me, and I squared my shoulders, ready for the fight.

"And?" I asked, stepping right back into her space like she'd stepped into mine. "What, are you mad? Is that what you're trying to say? Because I'd be really fucking interested to hear why you think you have any right to be."

"Just tell me, okay? You cheated on me, didn't you? I was in Pittsburgh, and she was here, and it was easier with her, right?" B shook her head. "Why did you even make the big gesture? Why not just tell me?"

"You think I ch—?"

I couldn't even finish the sentence. I stared at her like the mad woman she was before a laugh cut through me — not because *anything* was actually funny, but because I couldn't believe the words I was hearing. I dragged my hands through my hair, shaking my head.

"Angel and I didn't start talking until October, not that that is any of your goddamn business. She asked me out countless times over the summer, and I turned her down every single fucking time because of *you*. Not because it would have been cheating, since you made it perfectly clear that we were not a couple, but because I loved you, B."

She flinched at that, just the way my heart cracked with the admission. But when she tried to back away, I kept moving toward her, pressing in and in until her back hit the brick wall of the bar.

"I fucking loved you, and you loved me, too," I seethed. I saw nothing but red in that moment. I hated her, and yet I loved her still. I wanted to grab her arms and shake her just as much as I wanted to pin her against that wall and fuck her until she admitted she was mine.

She was the source of my insanity, but I still craved her any time she was near.

"But you wouldn't be with me. Not when I asked, not when I begged, not when I proved to you that we could do it. You were the one who didn't—"

I shook my head, dropping my gaze to the ground to try to catch my composure. I was losing it, and I hated myself for it. I was finally happy. I was finally *clean*, and I didn't want to go back to the dark place she'd left me in four months ago.

But when I looked down, I saw those goddamn black stilettos on her feet, and my mind flashed back to the last time I'd had them wrapped around me, those heels digging into my ass as I railed her.

My jaw clenched. "You're wearing heels."

I met B's gaze with a heated one of my own, and I swear to God, we were both less than half a second away from shredding each other's clothes. I inched forward, ready to pin her, ready to kiss that stupid angry look off her face.

But then she scoffed.

"And you're wearing lipstick."

She closed her eyes then, as if suddenly, she'd been drained of every argument she had.

My heart ached in my chest as I pushed off the wall, away from her, and I wiped at my mouth, cursing under my breath when I saw Angel's wine-colored lipstick on my thumb.

"Why are you really here?" I asked her, dejected.

"I missed you."

Her words hit me like ice picks to the throat, stealing my breath with them.

I cringed against the pain, pinching the bridge of my nose as I closed my eyes.

"No," I said, firm and loud. "No, you don't get to say that to me."

I shook my head, meeting her pitiful gaze again with my body screaming for me to get away from her, like she was a flame and I was too close, seconds away from being burned.

"I'm finally happy," I croaked, almost laughing. "Okay? Is that alright with you, B? Do I have your permission to be fucking happy?"

B's mouth popped open, like it shocked her, but before she could say anything, I beat her to it.

Turned out, I had *plenty* to say after four months of silence.

"God, you are the most selfish woman I have ever met," I said, shaking my head at her. "Let me guess, you missed me, so you thought you could just get on a flight and I'd be here waiting for you, right? Because that's exactly what I did for three years in California, so why wouldn't you think that? But guess what? You wanted me to let you go so badly, and this time, I listened."

I was shaking — *bad* — and there was no use trying to hide it. Even though I meant every word I said, I was still like an addict being served a shot of vodka. Trying to deny her, to say no when all I wanted was to bury myself inside her was like trying not to breathe.

"So, no, you don't get to show up here and tell me you missed me. You don't get to—"

"Stop," she choked, her eyes welling, and in a flash, she pushed off the wall and stormed past me. "Stop, Jamie."

I was hot on her heels.

"What, too much for you to handle?"

"I hate you!" she screamed, turning back toward me and advancing a few steps. "Go back inside, I'm sure *Angel* is waiting."

"Oh, she is," I mocked, still on her heels as she turned around and stormed toward her mom's car. "And I intend to make her wait. All night long. Remember how fun that always was? Making you wait until you couldn't stand it anymore?" I saw the way I still affected her, and I wanted her to hurt. I wanted her to feel the pain I'd been living in. "Making you squirm under my hands, my mouth…"

"Fuck you, Jamie."

I laughed, then, feeling as crazy as that laugh made me sound. "Goddamnit, you drive me crazy. You literally make me insane."

"Well, good thing I'm leaving," she spat, and then she climbed into the car, slammed the door, and fired the engine up.

I stood right outside her window, chest heaving.

How dare she. How dare she show up now, as if I was just supposed to wait, as if I only matter when it's convenient for her.

And yet, I didn't want her to leave either.

"Yeah. Good thing. That does seem to be your specialty, doesn't it?" I clipped.

She whipped around to face me through the window, her eyes wide, chest rising and falling in a rapid rhythm.

Stay, I willed her.

Fight back.

Fight for me.

My jaw was tight as I watched her, waiting.

But after a moment, she just flipped me the bird with a sweet smile and peeled off like I didn't matter to her, like I wasn't worth the energy.

And I let her go.

I felt like I was walking underwater when I made my way back inside the bar, and Angel seemed to know something had happened, but she didn't press me. She just gave me a long, sweet kiss, and then grabbed my hand and said, "Let's go home."

It took a while, but eventually, I broke down and called B to apologize for how I'd acted that night. Though I'd meant every word, I knew I shouldn't have been as much of a dick to her as I was.

But more selfishly, I didn't know how to live without her in my life.

We found a sort of weird friendship, but mostly, she lived out her life in Pittsburgh while I lived out mine in our hometown.

Time.

How do you even measure time?

It seemed to slip through my fingers after that, and I lost myself in the way Angel made me feel — loved, complete, whole.

Maybe I was still dreaming the day I dropped to one knee and asked her to marry me.

Maybe I was in a daze when I asked B to be by my side on my wedding day.

All I knew was that while I was fully ready to step into a new life with Angel at my side, I couldn't quite let go of the woman who'd always been in that place.

But when B came back into town, I realized I'd have to.

I couldn't have Angel and keep B — not the way I wanted to.

Still, even that week before the big day, I dreamed about it.

And it wasn't Angel who walked down the aisle to me in those dreams.

It was stormy gray eyes and wild and unruly curls, freckles and warm brown skin.

It was B.

It always would be.

E I G H T

The Waiting Game

THE SECOND SHE APPEARED at the top of that escalator at the airport, I knew I was playing with fire.

It'd been over a year since the last time I'd seen her, since I'd screamed at her and dared her to fight me. She'd grown into a woman in that time, it seemed — her body leaner than before, cheeks more hollow, neck elongated, eyes holding a bit more history.

She locked those gray eyes on me as she rode down, gaze never wavering, and I wondered if her heart was pounding as hard as mine, if she felt that same magnetic pull that had always been there.

When she made it to the bottom, her eyes fell to the sign in my hand — the one that read *Just B.* She smiled, but then stood there, unsure.

I opened my arms, welcoming her home.

"Come here," I said.

Even with her carryon bag slung over her shoulder, the second she was in my arms, I closed my eyes and in-

521

haled a warm, comforting breath. All the nerves from the wedding, all the worry over seeing B for the first time in such a long time, it all disappeared the moment we connected.

Of course, it flooded right back the second we pulled apart.

B had more control than I did. She insisted I drop her off at her hotel, that we not hang out before the rehearsal dinner. And after, when all my friends went to bed because they had work in the morning and I begged her to hang out with me, she declined.

Of course, that didn't stop me from showing up at her hotel bar.

I knew her better than she gave me credit for, and I knew whether she admitted it or not, that she had to feel some type of way being back in town for my wedding. I savored those stolen moments with her, the time spent catching up at the bar, the morning surf the next day, the rides around town in my Jeep.

But under that joy of being with her sat a sticky residue reminding me I was closer and closer to getting married.

That I was closer and closer to marrying someone who wasn't B.

The emotions I felt with her near confused me at first, maybe because I truly thought I could slip into some sort of *actual* friendship with her now that I was serious with Angel. But the more time we spent together, the more I realized that longing for B was still there, deep in my chest, and it was excruciating to deny myself the pleasure of submitting to it.

As shitty as it was to admit, I was glad Angel had her bachelorette party in New Orleans. I was glad to have those last days before my wedding with B.

One last hit.

One last high before I committed to being clean.

The night before the wedding, when my groomsmen humored me in camping at the springs, I finally started to accept it. I watched B joking with the guys around the fire, thought of how my whole life would change in mere hours, and had this weird, sort of *sad* awakening.

It's okay that she won't be in my life the way I thought she would, I convinced myself. *Because she's still my best friend. And I won't lose her — ever.*

All my groomsmen wussed out far too early that night, retreating into their tents to sleep, and warning me I should do the same. But I was wired, my nerves a mess and my mind racing. I was far from ready to sleep.

Fortunately, B stayed up with me.

It was easy, there by the fire, catching up and talking a little about the past, about the present, about the future. I loved to listen to her go on and on about the books she'd read, about the promising authors she worked with. I teased her about becoming one herself someday.

And no, the irony of that now is not lost on me.

Eventually, we ended up on our phones, watching stupid YouTube videos as was a frequent past time for us when we were younger. We watched some of the old classics before showing each other new finds, and before long, we were laughing so hard tears pricked our eyes.

"Here, watch this," B said, shoving her phone into my hand. "I have to find a bush to pee in."

I laughed. "Gross."

With a mocking curtsy, she skipped off behind the tents, and I turned my attention to her phone.

She'd pulled up a video of a lip sync battle with some of my favorite celebrities, and I laughed as I watched it play out. But then a notification came through for a missed call and a voicemail, making the video pause.

I frowned, clicking the notification. It was a call from Jenna, and I debated calling her back just to fuck with her. I hadn't talked to her since that night I ran into her and B at the bar after I passed my CPA exam.

Because the service was so shitty out at the campsite, the call didn't come through at all — just the voicemail.

My thumb hovered over Jenna's name to call her back, but then, I saw it.

My name.

Not just once, not just twice, but line after line of voice-mails in her log with my name next to them.

My heart stopped, ears ringing as I tapped the first one I saw.

Hey, B, it's me. I, uh…

There were muffled noises then, and the memory came flashing back, how I was sitting on the beach watching the sun set, my board next to me. I remember wishing so badly she was next to me, too.

I just wanted to wish you a happy birthday. Twenty-one today. That's a big one. I wish you were here so I could take you out for a proper celebration.

I tried to laugh, and even now, I remember how that fake laugh had brought tears to my eyes.

524

Please, B. Call me back. Please.

My throat burned as the voicemail ended, and I stared at the fire, listening as the branches and leaves rustled under B's feet on her way back to me. I didn't even bother to hide the screen. I waited until she stopped, and then I stood, turning to face her, and holding the screen so she could see.

"You kept my voicemails?"

B swallowed, her eyes flicking to the phone and back to me before she swiped the device from my hands and hastily shoved it in her pocket. "Yes."

"You used to listen to them, those years when I was at Alder."

B looked like she wanted to disappear. "Yes."

I nodded, swallowing, trying to process what that meant. "Do you still listen to them?"

"Sometimes," she confessed.

That confession was like a block of cement slamming into my ribcage.

"Why?" I asked, pained. "You can call me, B. Anytime."

She laughed. "Yeah, I don't think your fiancée would have appreciated another woman calling you at two in the morning."

The mention of Angel seemed to shock me back to the present moment, and I sighed, tearing my eyes from hers as I digested it all.

She kept my voicemails.

She still listened to them.

She... *God*, what did that mean?

I realized with a powerful split of my heart that it didn't matter. Because in less than twenty-four hours, I was getting married. I was marrying a woman who cared for me, who loved me, who had done nothing but treat me right from the moment she first met me.

And B was right. Marrying Angel meant my relationship with B would change. There was no way it couldn't.

My shoulders slumped with the realization.

"We should get some sleep," I finally said.

"Yeah," B said. She tucked her hair behind one ear before trying to slip by me to her tent. "'Night."

But her shoulder brushed my arm as she passed, and without even deciding to do it, my hand shot out and wrapped around her wrist, stopping her.

And I pulled her into me.

She was stiff, at first, but slowly, her hands trailed up my arms, hooking behind my neck as she hugged me in return.

My nose burned. My eyes stung. I felt every painful, raw emotion there was to feel in that moment as the fire crackled behind us.

"Goodnight," I said, but I held her still.

My hands roamed, finding her waist and squeezing, and I couldn't fight the low groan that came from my throat.

I still want her.

I still need her.

I angled my mouth, just an inch, but it was enough that my lips brushed her salty neck. B shivered at the touch, and I tried to pull away. Truly, I *tried*.

I just couldn't.

"Jamie…"

My name was both a warning and a plea not to stop when it slipped between her perfect lips, and maybe it was the alcohol, or maybe it was just that undeniable force between us, but I dragged my tongue along her neck, biting the edge of her jaw.

And then, I kissed her.

We both inhaled at the touch, my hands gripping her hips even harder as she tightened her grip around my neck. She pulled me into her, and I held her steady.

A soft whimper slipped from her next, like she knew just as much as I did that we should stop but didn't have the fight in her to actually do it. Her nails ripped at my back, dragged through my hair, begged me not to stop.

And so, I didn't.

I was two seconds away from fucking her right there by the fire when her eyes shot open, and when she scanned the tents containing all the groomsmen around us, it snapped some sense into me.

I backed her into my tent, only removing my hands from her long enough to yank my shirt off before I lowered her down into my sleeping bag. We were all longing breaths and moans, brains fuzzy and hands chaotic as I spread her legs with my own.

My erection rubbed along the seam of her shorts, and we both groaned as I ran a hand down her thigh, hooking behind her knee and hiking her leg up so I could flex into her harder. We weren't even naked yet, and I was ninety percent certain I could come right then and there.

B moaned, the sound like a symphony, and she let her head fall back, allowing me access to her neck.

I slipped my fingers around the back of her thigh, brushing the lining of her shorts before I found her panties. I felt how wet she was, how much she wanted me, too, and it obliterated any self-control I had left.

I pressed one fingertip between her lips.

And then B pressed her hands hard into my chest, breaking our kiss with a loud exhale.

"I don't have the will to stop this, Jamie," she breathed.

I was so desperate for her, I didn't give her the chance to say another word. I pressed against those palms on my chest, and claimed her mouth once more.

She pushed again, and I grinned.

I loved the game.

Pretend you don't want me. Pretend you're not soaking wet for me.

I caught her with another hungry kiss, rolling my hips against hers before she broke our kiss again. "You have to be the one to stop. I can't…"

She was breathing so hard she could barely speak, and it only edged me on. I licked my lips, ready to kiss her silent again when she found her voice and knocked me back to the cold, hard ground with three simple words.

"You're getting married."

That stopped me.

I paused where I hovered over her, panting, eyes searching hers like I couldn't believe she'd just said what she had. I waited, hoping she'd take it back, that she'd wrap those arms around my neck again and pull me down into her.

Sin with me, I begged.

Don't stop this now.

"If you kiss me again, you could ruin everything," she said, chest heaving, eyes already filling with tears. "If you kiss me again... I won't let you stop."

Automatically, my head dipped, lips on track for hers. I didn't *want* to stop. I didn't give a fuck about what I ruined.

Except when something I couldn't name stopped me right before my lips connected with B's, I realized that wasn't entirely true.

Angel's sweet face flittered through the steamy haze. I saw her sky-blue eyes, her dazzling smile, the way her cheeks would shade red when I made her laugh.

My heart cracked.

What the fuck am I doing?

I sighed, releasing my grip on B's thigh before I rolled off of her, and we both stared up at the tent ceiling with our breaths labored and shallow.

I almost cheated on my fiancée. I almost threw it all away. I almost...

My jaw clenched, and I shook my head, shame rolling in and fiercely replacing the carnal need that was just coursing through me.

"I'm sorry," I whispered.

B immediately shook her head. "Don't be. It's just lust, Jamie."

A lie. A lie in my honor, but a lie, no less. She and I both knew it had always been more than lust between us. It was love, pure and passionate, unyielding even after all this time, after all we'd put each other through.

But just as I loved her, I loved Angel.

Angel, who had chosen me, too.

Angel, who wouldn't hook up with me and then just leave, telling me a hook-up was all we could be.

B would never be mine, not the way I wanted her to be. She didn't have that in her to give.

It broke my heart. It killed me. But it was the truth.

B sat up, ready to flee the tent, but I stopped her.

"Wait," I pleaded. "Can you... will you just stay? Just lie here with me."

Her brows folded together, but she nodded, letting me take her in my arms and hold her as she laid back down.

For most of the night, I laid awake, committing the feel and smell of her to memory.

This was it.

And I fully accepted it. I said my last goodbyes with gentle kisses pressed to her hair throughout the night, with silent tears soaking my pillow, with my heart aching fiercely in my chest.

Then, the next day, I found out Angel had cheated on me.

And everything I thought I knew went up in flames.

• • •

I felt like a fool.

Not in the cute, humorous way. Not in the way you might feel slightly embarrassed to yank on a door that clearly says *push*.

No, I felt like a blind, naïve, wool-pulled-over-his-head, rose-color-glasses-wearing fool.

KANDI STEINER

I was thankful, at least, that Angel had had the balls to tell me what she'd done. Although, I still think the only reason she did is because her best friend, Claire, warned her that *she'd* tell me if Angel didn't.

I didn't care to hear her excuses, especially not when she tried to blame *me* for her infidelity. Seeing a picture of B with me and the rest of the groomsmen, she just assumed that because my arm was around her, I was fucking her, too.

And so, Angel tried to beat me to the punch, I guess.

It was childish, and selfish, and so fucking unbelievable that my lip visibly curled any time I remembered how pitiful she was, sobbing as she told me the story.

She'd thrown our life together away over pure jealousy and false accusations.

Well…

Somewhat false.

I supposed I couldn't blame her for seeing what everyone else saw, what B and I *knew* deep down — which was that we'd always have feelings for each other, no matter who else came into our lives.

And if I were being honest with myself, I wasn't completely innocent. Before B stopped me, I'd been seconds away from doing just what Angel assumed I would do.

Stopped us.

I grimaced at the thought of it all, stomach roiling as I took another sip of whiskey. My head was hung low between my shoulders, the noises from the hotel bar muted around me.

After I'd discovered the news, I couldn't be around anyone — least of all B when she showed up and watched

531

me storm out of the venue, questions in her eyes. I didn't want to answer them, not hers or anyone else's.

And so I got in my Jeep, and I drove.

I drove and drove until the sun set and long after. Finally, I pulled into the DoubleTree parking lot where B was staying, and I parked myself at the bar.

I knew she'd eventually find me, and when she did, she just pulled up the seat next to me and sat down, ordering a drink for herself.

I didn't know what to say, so I just sat there beside her, drinking and drowning in my misery.

"You want to talk about it?" she asked after a long while.

I spun my empty glass on the bar. "No."

She nodded like she already knew the answer before she asked.

Then, she reached into her clutch, throwing cash on the bar to cover our tabs just like I had a couple nights before. She stood. She drained her drink.

And then she flicked down a hotel room key card on the bar in front of me.

The key to *her* room.

I knew it without her saying it, and she assumed as much, leaving me there without a word otherwise.

I stared at the key, at my empty glass, at my fingers drumming an unsteady rhythm on the bar. Part of me wondered if I should just call a cab and go home, sleep it off, call B in the morning and talk to her when I had a right mind about me.

But the bigger part of me buzzed to life at the invitation, at the thought of her knowing that — in that moment — I couldn't use my words.

But I needed her all the same.

My heart beat on like a kick drum as I took the elevator up to her floor, and I slipped the card into the slot, a soft *click* before the light went green.

I opened the door, pushed inside, and found B standing in front of the bathroom mirror, her face freshly washed, a towel in her hands.

I dropped the key on the desk by the door, walking into the bathroom with her. She didn't turn, just watched my eyes in the mirror, chest still like she wasn't breathing at all.

The air crackled to life like the fire had last night, like it wasn't air at all but thick, buzzing electricity.

At first, it wasn't even that lust-filled need I felt for her. Burying myself inside her or making her moan my name wasn't what went to the top of my mind.

I just… *needed* her. I needed my best friend. I needed to hold her and be held, to know someone understood, that someone knew how broken I was in that moment.

That someone wouldn't leave me to figure it out on my own.

I slowly closed the space between us, reaching out and dragging my fingertips from her elbows up to her shoulders. She shivered a bit as I dragged them down next, tracing her hips before I held onto them tight.

My forehead dropped to her shoulder, and I winced against the pain that radiated through me with that touch.

It hurt to hold her after all the ways we'd hurt each other. It hurt to know in another universe, I would be married to a spiteful woman, having lost my chance with B forever.

It hurt that I fell in love with someone who could hurt me so easily, without even considering, and that I was willing to give B up for her.

Because I thought it was the right thing to do.

Because I thought B didn't want me the way I wanted her.

But she did. I knew, right then in that moment, that maybe for the first time in our lives, we were on the same page.

B dropped the towel, placing her hands over where mine held her waist. I squeezed her tighter then, wrapping her up, and I sighed at how she was so willing to bear the weight of my pain with me.

I held her that way for a long, meaningful moment.

And then, I gave in to the other need coursing through me.

Her scent filled my nose as I ran my lips along the slope of her shoulder, my eyes on hers in the mirror. I bit down gently at the apex, rewarded with an arch of her back and her hands reaching behind her. She wanted more of me, and so I obliged.

My hands slid under her dress, cupping her full ass as she moaned and let her head fall back against me. Gone were the warning bells and soft voices telling us to stop.

In that moment, it was just us.

No one else mattered.

We gave ourselves to each other that night, in every possible way. With every touch, every kiss, every thrust, we surrendered.

No more games. No more pretending. No more wasted time.

And the next morning, when the sunlight streamed in through the windows, we swore it out loud.

"Be with me," I whispered against her lips.

And she nodded, knowing there was no other way.

Still, it had been her to point out the obvious, that I had some things to handle here before we could figure out what came next. I didn't know if I'd move to Pittsburgh, if she'd move here, or if we'd live somewhere else entirely. I didn't know if it would take a few days to sort through the mess with Angel, or a few months.

All I knew was that none of that mattered, because at the end of it all, I got to have B.

I asked her to wait for me, and she'd agreed. I just needed a little time to get everything together.

At least, that's what I'd thought.

• • •

I blinked, staring at the paper Angel held between us, a victorious smile on her face.

And then, I lunged for her.

A roar ripped from my throat, and she flinched, but fortunately for *her*, my father was there, and he held me back from doing anything truly stupid.

"What the fuck is *wrong* with you?!"

Angel's eyes filled with tears, and it made me even more angry. "Baby, I made a mistake. But it didn't matter. It was one night. I don't even know the guy's *name*."

"Like that makes it any better," I spat.

She sighed. "It was a mistake, but it doesn't have to cost us our future. The venue and all the vendors are willing to work with us. We can just pick a new date to do the wedding. We can—"

"Are you insane?" I laughed at her. "I'm not marrying you, Angel."

"Technically, you already did," she pointed out, nodding to the marriage license between us.

I ground my teeth as my father squeezed my shoulder, telling me to sit down.

Angel had shown up to my parents' house the Monday after the wedding — the same Monday that I'd gone to tell Mom and Dad and my sisters what happened between me and B. Not surprisingly, they were all thrilled, even if they were a bit pissed about all the money they'd shelled out for the wedding.

I had their support, though, and I knew with that, the rest would be easy.

Angel and *her* family were next on my list to handle, but she showed up first.

With a signed, notarized copy of the marriage license she'd turned into the court that morning.

"I don't give a fuck," I told her. "We'll go get it annulled. *Today*."

"I won't agree to that. And since you willingly signed it the morning of our wedding, I doubt they'll believe you weren't aware of what you were doing."

"You fucking *cheated* on me, Angel!"

She flinched at that, swallowing. "Your word against mine."

That made my father frown, his fury the substance mine was born of. "Now listen here, young lady, this is absolutely uncalled for. You and Jamie clearly did not get married after what happened. We need to go make this right."

"I *am* making it right," she spat at him. "Your son is my husband, and whatever transpired between us is in the past." Her eyes met mine then. "Please, Jamie. I want to make things right. I want us to have the future together that we always wanted."

"And I want you to jump off the nearest cliff."

My dad squeezed my shoulder again in warning, but I saw his lips quirk up just a bit.

Angel's face flattened. "Fine. You want to play hard ball? Then, let's play." She stood then, her chair making a screeching noise against my parents' dining room floor. "My lawyer is already well aware of our situation. And with all my bridesmaids willing to swear in court that I was so drunk I only *thought* I cheated and confessed to you not in my right mind, when really they'd all carried me home and put me to bed? You don't have a leg to stand on."

I frowned. "Claire wouldn't."

"Oh, she would. And," Angel said, leaning over the table. "I know *exactly* where you were the night of our wedding, and who you were with."

I clenched my jaw, not admitting it even when she stared me down.

"Lucky for me, there are cameras in that hotel lobby bar, and if we had to go to court over this, I'm *sure* I could obtain the footage from that night if I needed to."

"And do *what*, exactly?"

"Show proof that it was *you* cheating on me."

Fury flamed in me, and I felt it going through my father, too.

"We can either work this out like adults and be together the way we were supposed to be before that home wrecking whore showed up here," Angel said, standing. "*Or*, you can get a lawyer and divorce me like you want. But with this little piece of evidence on my side, just know I'm coming for half of everything you own." Her eyes met my dad's then. "Including the firm."

I stilled. My father stilled. Everything was so damn still.

Ice water trickled through my veins, my worst nightmare that I hadn't even considered coming to fruition right in front of me.

"Take a few days to think on it," she said calmly. "And call me when you come to your senses."

My dad and I both sat there frozen as she left the house, and then Mom, Sylvia, and Santana rushed in, their faces paling at the sight of us.

I snapped out of my daze, reaching into my pocket for my phone. I had to call B. I had to talk to her. I had to—

"No," Dad said, grabbing my phone before I could unlock it. "Not yet. Not until we talk to Jim."

Jim.

Our family lawyer.

538

My stomach somersaulted as I turned to look at my father, who wore an expression like he'd just seen exactly how his death would play out and when it would happen.

"You really think she has a leg to stand on, Dad?"

He frowned, looking at my mom first before he found my gaze again.

He didn't have to answer for me to know.

And so, the most hellish two years of my life began. I couldn't so much as send a letter to B without it raising flags, without it being something that could be used against me in court. My lawyer tried his best to keep me positive, to make me believe him when he said it wouldn't be long before it would all be over with.

I snuck phone calls to B from the only payphone in town, maybe still in existence, but she never answered. Leaving a voicemail was too risky — especially since Angel's lawyer could request access to B's phone record if she got crazy enough.

And taking this case alone, I knew she was crazy.

So, I tried my best to just work and bide my time, to get the green light from my lawyer and the damn divorce *done* so I could finally call B. No, *fly* to her, take her in my arms, and know she'd never be out of them again for as long as I lived.

She said she'd wait for me, I assured myself on the hard nights.

B was always a woman of her word, and I knew no matter what — even if she was angry with me, even if she had questions, even if I'd hurt her with my silence... she would wait.

But the day the divorce was finally finalized, I got an invitation in the mail.

To her wedding.

NINE

You're Not Marrying

Anyone But Me

EVERYONE TRIED TO STOP me.

My parents. My sisters. My friends at the office. Hell, even *Ethan* — who had bigger fish to fry as a lawyer out in California — took the time to tell me it was a stupid idea to fly to Pittsburgh and track B down.

I didn't care.

Rationality had been obliterated, emotions taking the wheel, and they steered me onto a one-way flight to Steel City.

She had her address as the return address on the invitation she sent, so it was easy to track her down after I checked into a hotel and dropped my bag. I didn't plan to stay there longer than one night. I *planned* for B to fall into my arms, to tell me the wedding was a joke, to finally fucking *be* with me.

Finding her apartment building was easy. Getting upstairs without her knowing... well, that proved a bit trickier. Luckily, the doorman was easily persuaded with a fake story about how I was her long-lost half-brother and I was there to surprise her. He rang me right up after that and wished me luck.

Maybe part of him felt sorry for me since I was completely soaked from the rain. I was also shivering — more from nerves and anger than from the cold, but he took pity.

I held that wedding invitation crumpled in my fist the whole elevator ride up to her floor, my ears ringing. And when I finally stood in front of her door, I didn't pause to think about what I would say when she answered it.

I knocked, hard, and when she didn't immediately answer, I knocked three more times.

"I'm coming, I'm coming," I heard her annoyingly say from inside.

And then the door flew open, and there she stood — my surfer girl, in tiny sleep shorts, a tank top thin enough for me to see her nipples peak at the sight of me through her sports bra, and tube socks.

Her hair was tied up in a curly mess of a bun on top of her head, her face makeup-free, freckles pronounced under the low lighting of her apartment. She gaped at me, those plush lips in a soft *O*, and I just stared at her, chest heaving, torn between the urge to demand answers or to cave completely and pull her into me.

Seeing her killed me as much as it brought me back to life. I just wanted her in my arms. I wanted to feel her again. I wanted her to tell me everything would be okay.

But the wet invitation in my hand screamed otherwise.

I lifted my hand, nose flaring as B's gaze fell to the invitation crumpled in my grasp.

She swallowed. "Jamie…"

"No."

She shuddered as I fisted the invitation into a wadded mess.

"*Fuck* no."

I didn't wait for her to invite me. I pushed past her into the apartment, pacing.

"By all means, let yourself in," she deadpanned.

I kept my back to her, eyes on the large window overlooking the city. Again, the urge to say *fuck it* and just run to her, bury my face in her neck, wrap my arms around her… it was so fierce, I had to will a long, soothing breath to stop myself.

Finally, with my back still to her, I lifted the invitation again.

"What the hell is this?"

Silence.

And then…

"I tried calling you…"

Her voice was weak, and I couldn't stop the low laugh that slipped from me as I spun to face her.

"Oh, you did? And what exactly were you going to tell me?" I pressed. "That you're getting married? Please tell me you're kidding, because I know that's not what you were going to call to tell me. I know this invitation can't be real. This is all some big joke, right?"

I saw it, the moment the surprise of me showing up on her doorstep faded, and pure anger seeped in, instead. "Excuse me?" She scoffed. "No, Jamie, my fucking wedding is not a joke."

"So you're getting married?"

"Yes!"

My other hand flew for the invitation, and I was ready to rip it in half, over and over, until it was confetti on her fucking floor. But I stopped myself, gritting my teeth before I threw the invitation on the ground just to get it away from me.

I ran my hands through my sopping wet hair, shaking my head before I threw a hand out to her.

"How? How, B? After everything that... after we..."

"You never called!" she yelled, throwing her hands up as the rain poured harder and harder outside. Thunder rumbled. "What was I supposed to do, Jamie?"

"Wait!" I cried, my voice breaking with an edge of desperation I hadn't realized I felt until that exact moment.

It can't be real.

I swallowed, voice softer now. "You were supposed to wait."

B cracked, but then asked, "For two years?"

"Yes!" I answered quickly, stepping toward her.

She flew back just the same, like I was poison, like she'd die if I touched her.

It made me stop in my tracks, heart aching at the sight.

"For as long as I needed," I tried.

"That's not fair," she said, her eyes watering. "I tried calling you, I tried calling everyone around you. You never called, you never wrote — you completely ghosted me."

"Oh, feels kind of shitty when you're on the other side of that, doesn't it?"

Her head snapped back with the accusation, and I wished I hadn't said it as soon as it came from my mouth.

But her having the audacity to complain about being *ghosted* after what she did to me at Alder was too much for me to stomach.

"That was different," she whispered. "That… I didn't promise you anything."

"Not then you didn't," I said as lightning cracked in the sky, lighting up the entire apartment. "But just less than two years ago, you did. You promised me you'd wait."

"I love him!"

The declaration slammed into me like a train.

"You do, huh?" I mused, nodding.

That nod seemed to echo, over and over, because I couldn't process those words. She *loved* him? Who even *was* he? And how? How in less than two years could she forget about me, about *us*, and love someone else?

My nostrils flared, teeth working the inside of my cheeks as I considered it. I thought about just walking out right then and there. I figured that was it, she loved him and therefore there was no chance.

Except I had loved Angel.

But it didn't change the fact that I loved B more.

Silence stretched between us as I looked around, finally realizing all the boxes that were half-packed all around her apartment.

They were moving in together.

She had moved on.

But still, I wasn't ready to let go.

I turned to face her again. "And do you love me?"

"No."

"No?" I asked, moving toward her.

She circled the sofa, trading places with me so that it was her closest to the windows now. I felt like a wolf descending on its prey, but I didn't believe her, and I was going to call her bluff.

"You don't love me."

"No."

Her back hit the window, hands pressing into the glass at her hip as I moved in on her.

"You don't love me," I asked again, mouth close enough to hers that I could taste her if I really wanted to, if I didn't want to wait for her to tell me she wanted it, too.

I was there to take what had always been mine, and she knew it.

"You don't want me, right now, right here?" I asked, my voice singing to her along with the rain against the window. I ran my hand up her arm to cradle her neck, running my thumb along the line of her jaw.

She shook at the touch, her eyelids fluttering closed, but she said it again. That stupid word.

"*No.*"

Bullshit.

"Say it," I demanded, stepping even more into her. My wet shirt soaked her tank top as I pressed against her, my body already humming to life at the contact. "Say you don't love me. Say you don't want me, and I'll go."

She cracked her eyes open, and those gray irises reflected the stormy weather as she searched my gaze. The anger and possession I felt resided a bit, and my shoulders slumped, grip easing on her.

As much as it would kill me, I meant what I said. If she didn't want me, if she didn't love me anymore, I'd go.

But she did. She loved me, and she wanted me, and I didn't care what had transpired between us over the past several years. I knew I'd hurt her. I knew these past two years had been an extra torturous hell. But I could explain that all away. We could fix it — *all* of it.

I just needed her to say the words.

Instead, she said the last thing I expected.

"I don't want you."

My breath hitched, and I frowned, searching her gaze like I wasn't sure I'd heard her correctly.

But she stared back at me, unwavering, chin held high.

I couldn't admit it to myself, not even after hearing her say the words.

Still, I managed to push away from her as my heart screamed in protest. It begged me to ask again, to not let her go.

But what else could I do?

I love you. I always will.

I needed to tell her, but when I opened my mouth, I realized it didn't matter.

She already knew it.

And it still didn't change a thing.

So, I clenched my jaw, and then, just like I promised, I turned and walked away.

The steps I took across her apartment toward her door felt like a walk down death row. My shoulders slumped, chest aching, head pounding at the loss I couldn't even truly understand. It was too big to wrap my mind around.

But this was it. She was getting married.

And not to me.

The door handle was cold when I reached for it, and then thunder grumbled through the apartment as B cried out.

"Wait!"

I paused, unsure if I'd really heard it or just wished for it so badly my mind was playing tricks on me.

I tilted my head, turning slowly.

And then I saw it.

She wore the look I'd seen since we were teenagers, the longing, heartbreakingly sad look that told me she loved me — even when she wished she didn't.

And she wanted me, too.

My control snapped like a dry piece of pasta.

I crossed the room in five long strides, B's breathing picking up more and more with every step. Her eyes stayed locked on mine, her hands against the window, and she opened her mouth to say something when I finally reached her, but I silenced whatever it was with a hard, passionate kiss.

Lightning flashed, and B gasped into my mouth before I ran the pad of my thumb along her bottom lip, savoring the way it felt to taste her again.

When her tongue chased my thumb, licking it, I groaned, and crashed my mouth onto hers once more.

Two years of pain and longing and anxiety dripped off me like rain as I pushed B against the window. I couldn't get close enough, couldn't find enough contact as I grabbed her wrists and pinned them over her head.

"You're not marrying him," I growled against her lips, and like a good girl, B kept her hands suspended above her head as I grabbed the bottom of her tank top and peeled it up and over. I made quick work of her sports bra next, groaning at the sight of her after so long. And then, my hands were on her wrists again, and I dropped my mouth to suck one perfect nipple between my lips.

She bucked against the touch, writhing, and I grinned as I moved up to kiss her again before I turned her palms until they were flat against the window.

"Hold," I told her.

And then I fell to my knees.

My little surfer girl panted and heaved as she watched me hook my fingers in her sleep shorts and strip them down to her ankles. I dipped one finger under her lacy panties with my eyes on her, and we moaned together as I slid that finger inside her, feeling how wet and ready she was.

B dropped her head back against the window as I fingered her, and then I wrapped my hands around the back of her thighs, holding her steady as I planted a feather-light kiss on her clit.

"Fuck," she whispered, and I grinned against her mound before hooking my hand behind one of her knees. I brought it to my shoulder, careful to balance her as I ran my tongue along her slit before flicking her sensitive bud.

Her legs shook violently when I pressed two fingers inside her, tongue still lashing right where I knew she loved it.

"Oh, God."

"Mmm," I hummed, and she trembled again at the vibration. I sucked and licked and tasted her like a savage beast, like I hadn't eaten in weeks, and she was a four-course meal.

She was close to coming when I crawled back up her body, kissing her with the taste of her pussy still fresh in my mouth. I grinned when I saw she'd kept her hands right where I told her to.

"Such a good girl."

I backed up then, stripping my wet shirt off before I slowly unbuckled my belt. I kept my eyes on her, raking over every blessed inch of her toned body as I undressed. And when I dropped my briefs, my hard-on springing to attention, B lost control.

She pushed off the glass, desperate to touch me, but I caught her wrists again and spun her.

Pressing her chest into the glass, I held her wrists in place with one hand and dragged the wrapped condom I'd slipped out of my jeans along her arm, her ribs, the small of her back. My bare cock slipped between the supple cheeks of her ass, and she whimpered.

"Do you moan like that for him?" I asked, running the tip of my nose along the back of her neck. "Does he touch you like I do?"

I sucked her earlobe between my teeth as I ran one hand down the front of her, circling her clit just enough to make her shake for me.

Fuck.

I couldn't wait any longer.

I pushed back from the window, ripping the condom open and sheathing myself quickly before my hands were on her hips again. She arched her back for me, and

I slipped my crown between her lips, both of us holding our breath.

A flex, slow and steady, and I filled her.

B moaned as she stretched open for me, as her knees quaked and her pussy throbbed.

"Goddamn," I breathed, withdrawing before I pressed in again — a little harder, a little deeper. The way I had her pressed against the window, anyone looking at our building would see us. They'd see her dark nipples flattened against the glass, her cheek, mouth open as she panted for me. They'd see me pounding her from behind, taking back what had always belonged to me.

I ran my hand up her spine before fisting her hair and tugging, arching her neck for me so I could kiss and bite along that sensitive skin. I kept my steady pace, orgasm building with every thrust inside her. She was so fucking wet, so tight, so *mine* that it drove me insane.

When I was close, I withdrew, carrying her to the couch. I dropped her long enough to throw the boxes on the cushions off onto the floor, and then I sat in the middle, reaching for her hips and pulling her toward me.

B straddled me just like she knew I wanted — her perfect tits in my face, knees on either side of my thighs as she sat down on my cock. We cursed, my head falling back as she dug her nails into my shoulders.

When I opened my eyes and saw her, the lust faded — only for a second — as I realized the magnitude of that moment.

B felt it, too. She slowed, and for a while, it was nothing but our steady breathing as she rode me, smooth and steady. I held her with a knot in my throat, with my heart on my sleeve, with every ounce of pain and abandonment being soothed with every thrust.

B's eyes watered quickly, and then a tear slipped free, one I caught with my thumb. I frowned, wiping that tear across her bottom lip before I pulled her down into me. I wrapped my arms around her, holding her tight, my lips eager and promising against hers as she rode out her release.

It's okay, I hoped that kiss told her. *I'm here now. Everything is okay.*

I believed that. With all my heart, I believed it.

But when the morning light came, everything was *far* from okay.

• • •

"Oh God."

B stirred under me, her heavy breathing dragging me from a groggy sleep. I blinked, but before I could even register what was happening, B said it again — louder, and with more fear.

"Oh *God*."

She threw my arm off her, scrambling to her feet with the sheet wrapped around her. It twisted around her ankles and she fell, popping back up with a squeak as I shot up in bed.

"Wha— you okay?"

She wrapped the sheet around her tighter, running to her closet. "No," she cursed, shutting the closet door. "No, Jamie, I am not fucking okay."

"What's going on?"

She threw the door open a second later, dressed in shorts and a t-shirt now.

"Oh, I don't know. There's a naked man in my bed, and it's not the one I'm engaged to."

It was early, that much I knew. We hadn't had much sleep, that much I made *sure* of. And now, I had no idea what the fuck she was talking about.

I scrubbed a hand over my face. "You're not getting married."

"What? Of course, I am," she scoffed.

Her words hit me like a bucket of ice water, and I snapped my eyes open, locking them on hers. "You can't be serious."

"Listen, last night was a—"

She paused, and my heart stopped before kicking back to life with a vengeance.

"A what?" I dared her, standing. I didn't care that I was naked. In fact, I loved the way she couldn't help but trail the length of me, the way I knew she wanted me — even as she tried to pretend she didn't. "A *mistake*?"

She frowned, folding her arms over herself as she shrank back.

"Don't you fucking say it, B. Don't you say it was a mistake."

She cleared her throat, looking out the window behind me.

"I'm engaged," she croaked.

I growled, slinging a string of curse words as I ran both hands through my hair. I stormed to the living room with B on my heels, and I swiped my briefs off the floor, anger rolling off me in plumes.

"I can't believe you did this to me!" she screamed as I tugged on my jeans next. "I was happy, I was okay, I let you go. And then you just show up here, after two years without a single word, and you—"

"You're not happy. You're numb. There's a difference."

Her mouth popped open. "Don't tell me what I am, Jamie Shaw! If you're so desperate to tell me something, how about telling me why you never called? Huh?"

I closed my eyes, disbelief that this was her reaction after last night striking me silent. I was so tired of fighting. I was so fucking tired of all the goddamn games.

"Does it really matter?" I asked, tugging on my still-damp shirt. "You said you'd wait, and I said I'd come. Why did you give up? Why are you trying to push me away right now?"

"Because this isn't right! This," she said, motioning between us. "Isn't okay. We're toxic, Jamie. All we do is hurt each other, hurt the ones who love us, hurt ourselves."

She trembled so hard I heard it in her voice, and it fucking broke me to see her hurt like that. It always had.

I let out a breath, moving toward her, ready to take her in my arms and soothe the pain. But she held up a hand to stop me.

"Don't."

I paused, swallowing.

"You want to know why I never called?" I finally asked, voice low. "You think that will make you feel better? Because it won't."

She didn't answer.

I sighed, because I knew her knowing the truth would only make her hurt more. She wanted to believe that I'd forgotten about her, about us, that I'd moved on and was living out my life pretending she never existed.

In that narrative, I was the bad guy. She could get married to someone new without a single ounce of regret.

But the truth?

The truth would kill her.

"B, I signed the wedding certificate the morning of the wedding," I said, resigned. "That was always the plan, sign the certificate before the day began so we wouldn't have to worry about it, and then we could put it away somewhere safe, and take it to the courthouse on Monday."

She swallowed. "Okay…"

"I signed it. Before I found out what she did." I sniffed, eyes flicking between hers. "After I left, she signed it, too. And that Monday, when I was trying to figure out my plan of attack to handle shit with her and get to you as fast as I could, she showed up at my house, claiming we were officially married. She went to the courthouse without me, B. We were legally married."

She blinked. "Oh my God."

"Yeah," I said, stepping closer. "At first, she begged for me to take her back, to make it work, but obviously, I refused. Then, she got her lawyer involved, and they said they'd go after me for everything because I'd been cheating on her with you." I laughed — not because it was funny, but because I wanted to fucking *murder* Angel just thinking about it, and needed to laugh to save myself from doing just that. "They had camera footage of us together in the hotel on what was supposed to be my wedding night with Angel."

B paled, her hands reaching out for the back of the couch to steady herself.

"If it was just my Jeep, or just my shitty house she wanted, I wouldn't have cared, B. But my father made me partner — officially. It was my wedding gift. And she wanted to take that, too. She wanted half of everything, if not more. She…"

My voice gave out, and I took a breath, shaking my head before I continued.

"I got a lawyer. I had to block your number, my family, too. Until it was all resolved, any phone call or email or message on Facebook could have incriminated me. It didn't matter that she'd admitted to cheating the night before our wedding, because in the court's eyes, we'd still gotten married anyway. It was the biggest fucking mess, all of it, and I hated working with slimy lawyers, and an even slimier ex. I hated waiting. But the only thing that kept me going was knowing that you were waiting, too. For me."

B stumbled to the arm of the couch, sitting on it as one hand covered her mouth.

"The day Angel finally gave up," I said softly. "The day I received the finalization of our divorce? That was the same day I received your wedding invitation." The laugh that came from my throat nearly choked me. "Talk about sick irony."

B was still for a long moment, and then she just shook her head, over and over and over.

"You should have called me. Somehow."

"I did! I called you from what I'm pretty positive is the only payphone still in existence, several times, and you never answered," I shot back, chest heaving.

B shook even more as she pressed her fingertips to her temple, massaging. "You thought I would wait, and I thought you changed your mind."

I thought she'd stop me when I moved toward her again, but when she didn't, I bent to my knees, waiting until she looked me in the eyes.

"I could never change my mind about you."

She closed her eyes with a quivering lip like I'd struck her.

"No," she said, pulling away. "No, you should have found a way. You gave up too easily. You should have answered my call, or had your lawyer call me, or told Jenna, or fucking smoke-signaled. This is too much. You abandoned me."

"Stop doing this! Stop self-destructing, stop making this harder than it has to be," I begged, exhausted. "Maybe you're right, okay? Maybe I should have figured out a way to reach you, but I didn't, because you were supposed to wait. And none of that matters now, want to know why?" I touched her chin, lifting her eyes to meet mine. "Because you still love me. And I love you."

She flew off the couch, away from my touch, running her hands through her messy hair. "No, it *does* matter. Because I'm getting married."

"No, you're not."

"Yes, I am!"

557

I stood, jaw tight. "You're not marrying anyone but me."

My words shocked her for only a moment before she scoffed.

"You can't do this. You can't walk in here, at the one time I finally have my life together, and make me rip it to shreds." Tears assaulted her, falling so quickly she couldn't bat them away fast enough. "All we do is hurt. All we do is destroy, and one of us is always picking up the pieces, trying to move on or forget or not get our hopes up. It's sick. We're toxic."

She cried so hard she could barely breathe, and again, when I tried to comfort her, she ripped away from my touch.

"And now, I risked everything I have to be with you last night, because I literally can't say no to you. I cheated on a man who didn't deserve it, on a man who wants to spend his life with me, on a man I love, all because of my inability to let you go."

She cried and cried, looking at me like I was the fucking devil.

"Your love is poisoning me, Jamie!"

A violent sob lurched through me, face twisting with emotion as I crossed the room. I had to hold her. I had to make her see that our love wasn't poison — it was our saving grace.

I shook my head, pulling her into me, holding her as tightly as I could as another sob wrecked me. I bent, pressing my lips to hers, but she shoved me back.

"Stop it! *Stop*! You have to go, you have to leave, Jamie."

She breathed wildly, tears streaming down her face.

Please.

Please, don't do this.

Please, don't let me leave. Don't make me leave.

Hold me.

Kiss me.

Be with me.

Ask me to stay tonight.

Ask me to stay forever.

I begged her, though I didn't say a word. She felt every word I didn't say as we stood there in her apartment, breathing fire, ice in our veins.

But she didn't budge.

I growled, punching a box as I passed by it. It was full of pans, and it clamored to the floor, but I didn't care. I stormed out of that apartment, out of that building, out of that city with my heart splintered into jagged, paper-thin shards.

And that was it.

That was *really* it.

I snuck into the church the day she married Brad, stomaching only the first five minutes before I had to leave. I just had to see it for myself, had to know that she really meant it, that she loved him and we were truly over.

Watching her walk down the aisle to him was all the gut-wrenching proof I needed.

I only flew to see her once more after that, to apologize for what I'd done, for how I'd tested her before her wedding when she'd already made promises to another man. It wasn't fair. And she was right.

I *was* poison.

So, with one final parting gift, and a promise that I would *always* be there for her should she ever need me, I pressed a kiss to her forehead.

And I let her go.

Let *us* go.

Until the day I saw her goddamn book in the bookstore window.

TEN

Worst Ending Ever

AND THERE YOU HAVE it.

We're all caught up.

"Are you fucking kidding me?" I asked B, and even then, even with a mixture of love and curiosity and fucking *rage* searing through me, I wanted nothing more than to kiss those lips of hers that were parted in shock at the sight of me.

"Jamie," she breathed, and the sound of my name on her lips nearly unraveled me, nearly erased any questions I had or any urgency to know what the fuck that book meant. The way she said my name always tested my willpower, and at that moment, I nearly gave in, nearly pushed through that door and slammed her into the wall and took what I knew was always mine.

But I managed a breath, holding up the tattered book I'd read a dozen times in the last week.

"What the hell is this?"

Her eyes watered, lips rolling together. "It's... well, it's a lot of things." She frowned then, opening her door wider. "Come in so I can explain."

"Explain now."

She smiled a bit, her shoulders relaxing.

And then, her hand reached out for mine, wrapping around where I held the book. That first touch, that first feel of her skin over mine made me shudder.

"Please," she begged. "Come inside."

With a deep breath, I nodded, letting her guide me into her apartment. So much had changed since the last time I'd been in it, which now I could only think about while simultaneously kicking myself for not seeing. How had I missed all those boxes still there? How did I not think to ask why she was living in this apartment when she should have been all moved in with Brad?

The signs were so obvious, and yet I was so fucking heartbroken I couldn't see past the torrential rain pouring down over my entire life.

"Do you want anything to drink?" B asked, and then she chuckled, gesturing to an electric kettle. "And by *anything*, I mean tea or water? Afraid I don't have anything stronger."

My heart was unsteady and weak in my chest as I watched her move about the kitchen, something possessive clinging to my ribcage. But somehow, just seeing her, just hearing her voice calmed me — even without the answers I so desperately needed.

"No whiskey?" I teased.

Her eyes were sad for a moment before they found mine. "Not since the last time I saw you."

My façade cracked, and I shook my head, looking at the book in my hand for a long moment before I let it fall to her kitchen counter with a *thwap*.

"What is this, B?"

She chewed her cheek, pouring herself a small cup of tea before she leaned a hip against the counter, her hands wrapped around the steaming mug. "It's an apology. And an explanation. It's a love letter, just like the title says." She paused. "It's our story."

Our story.

I swallowed at how my pulse ticked up at those words.

"Our story," I repeated, looking at the book and then back at her. "It has the worst fucking ending I've ever read."

A surprised laugh slipped through B then. "Well... I guess that's because I was kind of hoping that *wouldn't* be the end." Her smile fell then. "I was thinking maybe we could write an epilogue."

"*Come find me*," I said, repeating the last words written in that torturous book — the words I'd read and dissected a hundred times. "*I'll be waiting.*" I shook my head. "Why did you wait? Why didn't you just come find *me*?"

That question shocked her still, her eyes widening, throat constricting with a thick swallow.

"I wanted you to have the space to really decide if you could forgive me, if you could read my side of everything that happened between us and understand why I did everything I did. I..." She paused. "I didn't want to just show up at your door and lure you in the way I knew I could — the way we've *always* been able to with each other. I wanted you to know that this time, it's real. This time, there's nothing or no one standing in the way." She shrugged, her brows folding together. "Like I said in the end... I wanted you to choose me, too."

"Choose you," I repeated, laughing as I ran a hand over my mouth. Then, I let out a growl, shaking my head as I turned back to her. "Goddamnit, woman. I've *always* chosen you. There has never *been* another choice for me. You. You, and only you. That's the choice."

B looked like she was on the verge of crying, like my words were knives between her ribs. But still, she smiled, looking down at her tea with flushed cheeks before her eyes found mine again. "If that's the truth, then why haven't you kissed me yet?"

The air buzzed around us, all those years of heart-break and anger humming in time with the passion and love that had always existed. Half of me wanted to flip her couch and punch a hole in her wall and shake her like a damn rag doll.

But the other half of me, the stronger half, just wanted to stop wasting fucking time.

She barely had time to set her tea down before I crashed into her, wrapping her in my arms and crushing my mouth to hers. She whimpered when I did, melting into me, and distantly I realized I was crying. Tears wet my cheeks as a sob ripped through me, but I kissed her harder, held her tighter, swept her off her feet and blindly stumbled back to where I remembered her bedroom to be.

"You evil woman," I rasped against her lips when I dropped her into the sheets. "You psychotic, infuriating, *perfect* fucking woman."

564

B laughed a little against my bruising kisses as I laid her down, crawling over her until I pinned her into the mattress.

"I can't tell if you love me or want to murder me," she mused.

"Both," I answered honestly, and I kissed her before she could laugh again, rolling my hips to silence her tease.

"I'm sorry," she whispered, making me stop as she framed my face in her hands. Her eyes welled with tears as they flicked between mine. "I'm so sorry, Jamie."

"I thought I lost you," I confessed, the words strangling me.

B just smiled. "Silly boy. Don't you know by now that you never could?"

I dropped my forehead to hers. "Even now, even with you under me, with you in my arms... it doesn't feel real. It's like a dream."

"Or a nightmare, since it's us," she teased.

I looked at her then. "I mean it. Jokes aside, B... I let you go. I thought it was really over. I thought... and then I saw your book, and now I'm here, and I just... *fuck*," I cursed, shaking my head. "I can't lose you again. I can't—"

"You won't," she promised, holding my face in her hands as she searched my eyes. "This is real, Jamie. It's me and you now."

"Forever."

"Forever," she echoed, and then my lips claimed hers, slow and on the wings of a shaky exhale.

Every kiss came slower than the first, our lips warm and smooth against each other as we carefully undressed.

I pushed up on my knees long enough to strip my shirt overhead, to help her out of her plaid pajama shorts and tank top. I marveled at her body with every layer shed, remembering what it looked like nine years ago, and counting every lucky star in the galaxy that I got to appreciate it all these years later.

"Marry me," I whispered against her lips when we were both undressed, slipping between her thighs as I made the request.

She gasped at the feel of me, of my shaft sliding into her wetness, stopping just at the brink of entry. "Yes."

"Tomorrow. No, today."

She laughed, tucking her hips so that the crown of me slipped just a centimeter more inside her. It took all my restraint to focus on her answer instead of on how badly I wanted to be buried inside her.

"Today. Tomorrow. And every day after," she whispered, kissing me long and hard. Then, her nails dragged down my back, over my ass, digging into the flesh. "Now, *fuck me*, Jamie Shaw. Remind me what it's like to be yours."

I groaned, my hands slipping under her shoulders and holding on tight as I flexed and filled her. She arched and moaned with the connection, opening for me even more as I withdrew and pumped in again.

"More," she begged, and I hissed, pushing back onto my knees and hiking her ankles up on my shoulders. I wrapped my hands around her thighs, flexing into her and finding more depth just like she'd asked.

Her hands fisted in the sheets, back arching, tits bouncing as I picked up my pace.

She came within seconds, and I wasn't even a little ashamed when I did, too.

"Fuck," I cursed, falling down onto her. Her legs went limp, and she chuckled, kissing my slick shoulder as her fingertips drew lines on my back.

"Again?" she asked.

"Again," I echoed, and then I was kissing her, flipping us until she was on top as we slipped into round two.

ELEVEN

Happy Ever After

IF YOU DIDN'T PICK up on it from reading her book, B is a little bit of a masochist.

I blame that fact for why she couldn't write a *real* epilogue to save her life. That tiny, barely a page, torturous thing she gave you and called an epilogue was just cruel, which is exactly why I wanted to write to tell you what happened in-between.

I wasn't kidding about wanting to get married that day. However, I found it impossible to leave B's bed once I had her naked, and we spent — quite literally — *all* day and night making up for lost time.

We were both sore and exhausted and blissfully sated by the time we finally fell asleep late that night. The next morning, in the early purple light of dawn, I woke B with gentle kisses over her left ring finger knuckle.

Her eyes fluttered open.

"Marry me," I whispered.

She nodded, and then after one more round — because how could we not — we started planning.

I was content to just go to the courthouse that day and *demand* they waive the three-day waiting period so we could be married by the time the sun set that evening. But B talked me out of it, using her bewitching kisses to convince me we should do a proper celebration and ceremony.

So, we applied for our license, waited the three days, and then jumped on a plane to California.

California was our place. It was where we were young and reckless together, where we finally caved in and submitted to our true feelings — even if it wasn't the best timing. It was also where we surfed our first real waves together, where we realized that no matter what happened, we'd always be there for each other, someway, somehow.

"Do you think we're crazy?" I asked my sister, Sylvia, on the evening of the wedding as she fixed my bow tie.

She smiled. "Absolutely." Her eyes found mine. "But I also think you're meant for each other."

"Mom and Dad didn't even seem surprised when I told them."

"None of us were." Sylvia finished up my tie and then grabbed the lapels of my tux. "*We* all already knew it would be you two in the end. We were just waiting for you dummies to figure it out."

The ceremony was small and intimate — just my parents, my sisters, B's mom and Wayne, and of course, Jenna.

It was golden hour on the west coast, the sun slowly making its descent over the water as my father clapped my shoulder from where he stood beside me. My eyes were on the sand around my shoes, my heart racing out of my chest. And then he bent to whisper, "Here she comes."

With a steadying breath, I lifted my gaze, and there she was.

B walked barefoot through the sand toward me with golden rays of light illuminating her hair like a halo. She wore a white, lacy dress that was shorter in the front and longer, flowier in the back. It showed off those immaculate legs of hers, and the lace tapered her waist, the slim spaghetti straps highlighting her sleek collarbone, elegant neck, and lean arms.

I mapped those freckles on her cheeks as she flushed and walked slowly toward me. They were more pronounced after surfing for a few days, her sun-kissed skin a warm brown, but it was her smile that I couldn't stop staring at.

She smiled like it was the happiest day of her entire life, like she'd been just waiting and counting down the time to *this* very moment.

And I felt the same.

I didn't realize how tight my chest was, how constricted my throat was, how my nerves were making me tremble until my stare crawled up, up, up to meet her eyes.

Her metallic, stormy gray eyes.

As soon as our gaze met, I was hit with flash after flash of memories.

I saw the first time we met, how she looked up at me from where she'd fallen down with one lone curl hanging over her eyes. I saw her tired eyes that night on the beach before I left for college. I saw her laughing in a cat café and surfing the barrel of a wave. I saw her crying at the loss of her father, saw her laughing as we watched a movie from afar when she was in Pittsburgh, saw betrayal and hurt when she saw me with Angel for the first time.

So many incredible moments.

So many painful ones, too.

My eyes watered with each one, and B must have known what I was feeling, because her bottom lip quivered, and she pressed a hand over her heart as if to soothe it.

Maybe she was feeling it, too.

Maybe she was realizing in that exact same moment I was that all the heartbreak had been worth it.

Sounds snapped back to me when B was close, and I realized not only was *I* crying, but so was everyone else seated around our makeshift ceremony location. There wasn't a dry eye on that beach, and when B made it close enough for me to reach out and take her hands in mine, I said *screw the rules* and kissed her right then and there.

"I think you're supposed to wait until the end of the ceremony to do that," she breathed against my lips with a smile when I released her.

I shook my head, lining her jaw with my thumb as I counted all the lucky stars that brought her into my life.

"I've waited long enough."

• • •

One year later, we bought our first house together near Newport Beach, California.

I wondered if the universe had decided we'd been through enough hell in our teens and twenties that it decided to give us a break in our thirties, because everything just kind of fell together for us once we were married.

While we debated B moving back home to South Florida or me moving to Pittsburgh, we knew in our hearts that we wanted to start our lives somewhere new and fresh. California was what called to us most.

Like I said — it was our place.

B started looking for publishing houses that had branches in Los Angeles, thinking she'd have to start over.

When her boss found out, he lost his mind.

Turned out, B had earned their trust and respect. So much so that the thought of losing her drove them to put their thinking caps on and figure out a way to keep her.

And so, B became the first film rights representative for Rye Publishing, opening a small branch for them on the outskirts of L.A.

As for me? I was in the same boat. I thought I'd have to start at the bottom of a new accounting firm, work my way up again. And I was fully prepared to do it.

Until my dad handed me the keys to a small office space he purchased in Huntington Beach.

"It's time to start a new legacy," he'd told me, and just like that, I was in charge of our first expansion of the firm.

I was exhausted from unloading our U-Haul, back aching as I lowered myself to the laminate floor with a groan. I propped myself up against the wall, wincing as I tried to get comfortable.

B chuckled when she saw me. "You alright there, old man?"

I smirked, but before she could walk past me with that little attitude of hers, I reached out and captured her wrist in my hand.

"Get down here and I'll show you *old man*."

She laughed as I pulled her into my lap, and when she was seated, her arms wrapped around my neck like they belonged there always. I pulled her in for a long kiss, and then we sat there on the floor of our new house, boxes stacked all around us.

"So, we can get a big sectional and put it there," B said, shifting in my lap so she could point out where she wanted the couch. "Mount the TV on the wall. I definitely want a record player. We can put it back in that little corner."

She smiled, and I watched her tap her chin as she looked around pensively.

"We can clear out some space in the garage to put our surfboards and hang all our equipment. You can build a locker for us, can't you?"

"Whatever you want."

She smirked at me. "*Whatever* I want? That's a dangerous statement."

"It is. Sadly, I'm powerless when it comes to saying no to you."

"Hmmm," she mused, snuggling up closer to me. "Is that so?"

I kissed her nose in answer.

"Well, in that case, I want a bench built for under the big window upstairs," she told me. "And I want to line the walls around it with so many books I'd never be able to read them all."

I laughed.

"And… I want a rocking chair."

"A rocking chair, huh?" I asked, surprised. "For the porch?"

She shook her head, suddenly shy as she looked at her finger and trailed it down the front of my shirt. "For the nursery."

She peeked up at me through her lashes as I frowned, confused.

"The nursery? We don't have a…"

I didn't finish the sentence.

My heart thumped loud in my ears as B swallowed, her eyes searching mine, and she covered my hand as she moved it to rest on her stomach.

I let out a shaky breath, looking down at where I held her before my questioning gaze met hers, and I couldn't swallow, couldn't speak, couldn't *breathe* as I watched a small smile bloom on her lips.

"I'm pregnant, Jamie."

The words hung suspended between us, and I blinked, over and over, not sure I heard her correctly.

And then I lost it.

I crushed B to my chest, wrapping her up so tight she laughed and made a joke about not being able to breathe. But I couldn't let her go, couldn't do anything but hold her tighter as I fought the urge to cry.

She was pregnant.

She was pregnant with *my* child.

It was unlike anything I'd ever felt before, that realization, like being touched by an angel and thrown off a cliff at the same time.

"You look terrified," B joked.

"I am."

She laughed. "But wait, isn't this what you've always wanted?" She grabbed my hand again, placing it on her stomach. "A wife, a house, and now... fill that house with kids?"

B smiled at me, waiting for me to tell her she was right. And maybe, had this been eighteen-year-old me, I would have.

But I knew the truth now.

"No," I breathed, and B frowned, tilting her head to one side as I slid my hand along her cheek and into her hair.

"No?"

I shook my head, pressing a long, slow kiss to her lips before I whispered, "The only thing I've always wanted, B, is you."

EPILOGUE
Seven Years Later

GOOD MORNING, MY BEAUTIFUL *wife. And Happy Mother's Day.*

Today is all about you, my dear, and so I've taken the kids and run far, far away to give you peace. That being said, I know today is the last day I should be asking anything of you — especially since you run everything in this household, as well as the agency, day after day — but I have an assignment for you.

It's your turn to read my book.

Of course, it's not nearly as long as yours — you've always had a way with words that I never did. I also didn't have a whole publishing house at my disposal, so I hope you don't mind the streaky ink from my work printer, or the mess of staples holding this thing together. But I got to read your side of our love story.

Now, I want you to read mine.

There's a bottle of bubble bath by the tub, or a bath bomb if you prefer, and your favorite tea is ready to brew. Lunch will be delivered right to the door, and I'll be back around three.

Go soak, read, and relax.

And tonight, it's just you, me, the piano guys, and a blanket on the beach.

Don't worry — the kids will be with Sylvia and Drew.

And we don't get them back until the morning... if you catch my drift.

I'm going to spoil you even more than usual today, my little surfer girl, and worship every inch of that body of yours. But first, I want you to read my side of our crazy, stupid, perfect story.

I want you to understand how madly in love with you I am, and have been — since the first moment I laid eyes on you.

You were wrong, by the way.

It was you I saw first.

Love,
Whiskey

BONUS
Content

Just B,

This is our first Valentine's Day together. Like, actually together. But it's not our first Valentine's Day.

Our first one was when I was 18 and you were 17. I gave your best friend a box of chocolates and a huge stuffed bear, but I gave you my heart, and just like I suspected, you never gave it back.

Then there was the time you were Ethan's Valentine. He bought you a tennis bracelet, one I saw you wear only twice, but what I remember most was when you took it off that next morning to go surfing with me.

Let's not forget the three years we both spent alone, because even when you didn't answer, my heart only called to you.

When I was Angel's, when you were Bradley's, when we were young and stupid and fought so hard not to give in. When it was nothing we needed and everything we wanted. When it was right, and when it was wrong. All those years, every February 14th, you were my Valentine.

You wrote me the best love letter that's ever existed, but I have a lifetime to pay you back, letter by letter, note by note.

This is number one.

Love,
Whiskey

• • •

**Letter to readers, originally
made for Bookified Designs:**

August 9th, 2019
Newport Beach, California

Hey Whiskey Girl,

It's been so long since we last corresponded — almost three years, to be exact. I hope all is well on your side of the world, and that you've been reading a mountain of five-star romances since we last met.

I'm sending you a wet hug from the sunny shores of Newport, California. B is out in the water, floating on top of her surfboard and waiting for the next wave to roll in. I always love to see her like this — hair wild and curly, freckles dotting her cheeks, lips a little chapped from the sun. If you can believe it, she's gotten even more beautiful with age — and somehow, more skillful in the waves, too.

So, just in case the ending of her book left you wondering... yes, that beautiful, stubborn, impossible woman is my wife.

As for me, I'm on the shore, soaking up the afternoon rays and watching Zoe build a sandcastle.

Oh, did we not tell you about Zoe?

She was born just two years after that book you read — the one that told the tortorous love story B and I made together. Zoe has her mother's hair, and those adorable freckles, and she's even got a hint of her smile — though, B would argue that Zoe's smile favors mine. And that little girl also has my eyes — the honey whiskey ones, as B would say.

We moved out here to Newport when we decided we couldn't be farther than a thirty-minute drive to the surf. And if I thought catching waves with the woman I loved was the best thing in the world, I never could have imagined what it would feel like to build a life with her.

It's the most addicting thing.

I know we put you through hell. I know reading our storyw as hard, that it made you scream, and cry, and throw your Kindle... which is why I wanted to update you, to let you know that all that pain, all that burn... well, it was worth it.

We're all doing just fine.

And we can't wait to tell you more.

Until next time, stay golden — just like whiskey.

Jamie Shaw

KANDI STEINER

• • •

A Note From Lauren Sweet, narrator of the
A Love Letter to Whiskey audiobook:

I've narrated more than 225 romance audiobooks. I've narrated amazing stories of love of all kinds, all ages, and all body sizes. There've been harems and werewolves and second chances, and I have lost my virginity more times than I can count. Even with all that, I can honestly say that A Love Letter to Whiskey stood out.

I remember leaving the booth every day feeling totally gutted in the best way possible. It was an experience of putting all my emotions on the table, because that's what Whiskey asked of me. Some books reach deep inside you and demand you pay attention. They grab hold of you and don't let you go. Not until you've consumed every last drop.

As an audiobook narrator, I love books that challenge me to use all of myself. I love books that delve deep into the human experience, that make your gut churn because you know they're talking about something so real that it scares you. I love a good happy ending, but I also love the dark, underside of things. Whiskey does all that.

It reminds me of my favorite Shakespeare sonnet, number 147:

> *My love is as a fever longing still,*
> *For that which longer nurseth the disease*

There was something deeply poetic and darkly rich about Whiskey, with writing that got past the barriers of your head and straight to your heart. I'm honored to have been able to lend my voice to it.

I hope you love it as much as I did.

Lauren Sweet

• • •

Fun Facts from the Author:

The yellow house on Scenic Drive that B lives in during high school was based on the house *I* lived in when I was in high school. And yes, it was bright yellow with red shutters on the windows, and it was right on Scenic Drive.

Pittsburgh became a star in this book after I visited for the Black & Gold Author Event hosted by Southern Belle Book Blog. I fell in love with the city and knew I wanted to set a story there.

B's love of taking baths is inspired by my own, and how much comfort I find in them when I'm going through a particularly tough time in my life.

While most of my novels take months to write and edit, A Love Letter to Whiskey flew out of me in nine short weeks. And this was while I was still working a full-time job 45 hours a week. It completely consumed me, and I couldn't sleep until I'd written for these two crazy characters.

When I first wrote the scene of Jamie and B surfing in California, I had them both in swimsuits. It was one of my beta readers who informed me (someone who had never been to Cali

ornia at the time) that the Pacific ocean is a lot colder than the Atlantic over here in Florida. Turns out, surfing in a skimpy bikini isn't the best choice, and so I re-wrote the scene with B discovering how different the surf was on the other coast.

Jamie and B's love for The Piano Guys stemmed from my own obsession with them in college. They were my favorite to study to, and it opened my eyes to how much I actually really love classical music. Since then, I've expanded my knowledge of the genre and still write to it to this day!

There were two scenes that I physically cried during writing: the scene when Jamie and B fight in her apartment after hooking up when she's engaged, and the scene where they fight in the parking lot after B tries to surprise Jamie and finds him with Angel. Those scenes just played out so viscerally in my mind and I couldn't help but get swept up in the emotion.

My favorite scene in the book is a tie between the fight scene in the parking lot and the bonfire scene at Alder, just because they were so young and emotions were so high. I loved that angsty feeling!

I swore I'd never write a longer ending or anything from Jamie's POV... and apparently, I lied. ;)

ACKNOWLEDGEMENTS

A book is never truly written by just one person, and I had the A-team on this project. I have so many people to thank, but first (mostly to save you from having to read this novella), I want to address you — the reader. Man... that was a rough one, wasn't it? I know I put you through a lot of emotions with A Love Letter to Whiskey — some that you probably loved, and some that you probably wanted to kill me for. I just want you to know that I love you, and I am so thankful that you let me take you on this journey — even if it wasn't the easiest. Please, don't ever stop reading. And don't ever stop taking a chance on Indie. OH, and come find me on the internet, because I love to hang out with my readers. You can start by joining the Kandiland (https://www.facebook.com/profile.php?id=1408360979440689) group on Facebook.

Hey Staci Hart — WE DID IT! Can you believe it? We actually wrote books together... at the same time... and survived! And, it was the best experience ever. I don't want to remember what it was like to do this without you, and I hope I never have to again. I love you more than whiskey sours. #SteinHarts #BestieRelease

This book would have been an absolute train wreck without the help of Sasha Whittington and Monique Boone. Thank you for not only being two of my best friends, but also being the most kick ass beta readers ever. I know it was hard, reading in chunks, letting me leave you at the WORST possible places, but it was worth it in the end. You helped me see what I couldn't, and for that I'm grateful. I love you both!

Becca Hensley Mysoor, GOD I love you. Thank you for always being there to send me encouraging hearts and gifs and just for spreading light into the world. My life is brighter with you in it. I love you.

Thank you, Brittainy C. Cherry, for loving my words and me, too. Writing with you is such a privilege and an honor. You are quite possibly the most beautiful soul to ever exist. Thank God we found each other.

I can't forget about my Buddy Brew coffee buddy — Kathryn Andrews. You are just... the absolute SWEETEST person. Thank you for making me laugh, celebrating my successes, and helping me through the rough days. I love writing with you, and I hope we can make this a ritual that lasts much longer than just one book.

Karla Sorensen and Ilsa Madden-Mills, thank you for propping me up like two bad ass, gold-plated crutches. Writing this book was HARD, and each of you helped me in your own ways along the road. I appreciate you more than I can say in words.

Momma, I always write the sweetest acknowledgement for you. This time, I want to thank you for teaching me how to drink like a champ. Those whiskey references came in handy, after all. ;)

To Beau Taplin, thank you for inspiring me with your words and for letting me quote my all-time favorite poem in this story. It set the tone, and I'm thankful to have your blessing.

Oh, Kellee Fabre. You have been here since the very beginning and Lord help me if you ever decide you're over my shit. LOL! Thank you for threatening me EXTRA hard this time around. Your (scary) but loving messages make my life.

To the rest of the beta team: Monique Buntin, Ashlei Davison, Jess Vogel, Maegan Abel, Kristen Novo, Tina Lynne, Patricia Leibowitz (QUEEN MINTNESS), Sara Butler, and Sahar Bagheri. WHEW. I wasn't kidding when I said I had the A-Team on this one. You guys seriously KILLED this beta read. You brought the best feedback and for that I'm thankful. You ALSO brought a lot of emotions, with voice messages, texts, phone calls, and snotty-faced photos. Thanks for tapping into this world with me and loving it as much as I do. I'm so thankful for every single one of you.

To Elaine York, my incredible editor and formatter. I may breathe life into my stories, but you breathe freshness and beauty, and I am so thankful I found you. Your encouraging editor notes made my heart flutter. Please don't ever leave me!

Half of you probably wouldn't have purchased this book without the beautiful photography from Lauren Perry of Perrywinkle Photography. I am simply amazed by your talent and your soul, Lauren, and I hope we can work together for many years to come.

Erin Spencer, where do I even start with you? Thank you for promoting me like your life depends on it. And, thank you for your voice messages while you read ALLTW. I've never gasped out loud in the grocery store before, but I guess there's a first time for everything. ;) Our friendship is one of my very faves. I love you!

To my "Writing Little" Cassie Graham, thank you for checking in on me while I wrote ALLTW and always having nothing but sweet things to say about my writing.

We've been together since the very beginning, too, and I know we'll last until the very end.

Angie Doyle McKeon, my BUMBLE BEE! I cannot tell you how happy I am to see a message from you in my inbox, whether it's book related or not. Thank you for coming into my life and please say you'll stay forever. I adore you!

Shout out to Jessica McBee for chasing your dreams so hard you made me want to get up and chase mine. You inspire me as much as I do you, my dear, and I love your soul. Thanks for being a friend.

A huge thank you goes to the team at Give Me Books for taking me on for promo. You guys teaming up with Southern Belle Book Blog was like riding a magical unicorn down a rainbow road.

To the two groups that keep me going — Tribe and Kandiland. I am... just completely flabbergasted that I have somehow surrounded myself with the most uplifting women (and man — lookin' at you, Chase!) in the entire world. You push me when I feel like quitting, hold me when I can't catch my breath, and pop champagne when it's time to celebrate. Thank you for always being there.

And, as always, thank you, God, for blessing me with a writer's heart and a dreamer's soul. I pray He will always keep me humble, thankful, and kind.

MORE FROM
Kandi Steiner

The Becker Brothers Series
On the Rocks (book 1)
Neat (book 2)
Manhattan (book 3)
Old Fashioned (book 4)
Four brothers finding love in a small Tennessee town that revolves around a whiskey distillery with a dark past — including the mysterious death of their father.

The Best Kept Secrets Series
(AN AMAZON TOP 10 BESTSELLER)
What He Doesn't Know (book 1)
What He Always Knew (book 2)
What He Never Knew (book 3)
Charlie's marriage is dying. She's perfectly content to go down in the flames, until her first love shows back up and reminds her the other way love can burn.

Close Quarters
A summer yachting the Mediterranean sounded like heaven to Jasmine after finishing her undergrad degree. But her boyfriend's billionaire boss always gets what he wants. And this time, he wants her.

Make Me Hate You
Jasmine has been avoiding her best friend's brother for years, but when they're both in the same house for a wedding, she can't resist him — no matter how she tries.

The Wrong Game
(AN AMAZON TOP 10 BESTSELLER)
Gemma's plan is simple: invite a new guy to each home game using her season tickets for the Chicago Bears. It's the perfect way to avoid getting emotionally attached and also get some action. But after Zach gets his chance to be her practice round, he decides one game just isn't enough. A sexy, fun sports romance.

The Right Player
She's avoiding love at all costs. He wants nothing more than to lock her down. Sexy, hilarious and swoon-worthy, The Right Player is the perfect read for sports romance lovers.

On the Way to You
It was only supposed to be a road trip, but when Cooper discovers the journal of the boy driving the getaway car, everything changes. An emotional, angsty road trip romance.

A Love Letter to Whiskey
(AN AMAZON TOP 10 BESTSELLER)
An angsty, emotional romance between two lovers fighting the curse of bad timing.

Weightless
Young Natalie finds self-love and romance with her personal trainer, along with a slew of secrets that tie them together in ways she never thought possible.

Revelry
Recently divorced, Wren searches for clarity in a summer cabin outside of Seattle, where she makes an unforgettable connection with the broody, small town recluse next door.

Say Yes
Harley is studying art abroad in Florence, Italy. Trying to break free of her perfectionism, she steps outside one night determined to Say Yes to anything that comes her way. Of course, she didn't expect to run into Liam Benson...

The Christmas Blanket
Stuck in a cabin with my ex-husband waiting out a blizzard? Not exactly what I had pictured when I planned a surprise visit home for the holidays...

Black Number Four
A college, Greek-life romance of a hot young poker star and the boy sent to take her down.

The Palm South University Series
Rush (http://www.kandisteiner.com/newsletter) (book 1) FREE if you sign up for my newsletter!
Anchor, PSU #2
Pledge, PSU #3
Legacy, PSU #4
Ritual, PSU #5
Hazed, PSU #6
Greek, PSU #7
#1 NYT Bestselling Author Rachel Van Dyken says, "If Gossip Girl and Riverdale had a love child, it would be PSU." This angsty college series will be your next guilty addiction.

Tag Chaser
She made a bet that she could stop chasing military men, which seemed easy — until her knight in shining armor and latest client at work showed up in Army ACUs.

Song Chaser
Tanner and Kellee are perfect for each other. They frequent the same bars, love the same music, and have the same desire to rip each other's clothes off. Only problem? Tanner is still in love with his best friend.

ABOUT
the Author

Kandi Steiner is a bestselling author and whiskey connoisseur living in Tampa, FL. Best known for writing "emotional rollercoaster" stories, she loves bringing flawed characters to life and writing about real, raw romance — in all its forms. No two Kandi Steiner books are the same, and if you're a lover of angsty, emotional, and inspirational reads, she's your gal.

An alumna of the University of Central Florida, Kandi graduated with a double major in Creative Writing and Advertising/PR with a minor in Women's Studies. She started writing back in the 4th grade after reading the first Harry Potter installment. In 6th grade, she wrote and edited her own newspaper and distributed to her classmates. Eventually, the principal caught on and the newspaper was quickly halted, though Kandi tried fighting for her "freedom of press." She took particular interest in writing romance after college, as she has always been a die hard hopeless romantic, and likes to highlight all the challenges of love as well as the triumphs.

When Kandi isn't writing, you can find her reading books of all kinds, talking with her extremely vocal cat, and spending time with her friends and family. She enjoys live music, traveling, hiking, anything heavy in carbs, beach days, movie marathons, craft beer and sweet wine — not necessarily in that order.

CONNECT WITH KANDI:

NEWSLETTER
(http://www.kandisteiner.com/newsletter)
INSTAGRAM (http://nstagram.com/kandisteiner)
FACEBOOK (http://facebook.com/kandisteiner)
FACEBOOK READER GROUP
(http://www.facebook.com/groups/kandilandks)
(Kandiland)
TIKTOK
(https://www.tiktok.com/@authorkandisteiner?lang=en)
GOODREADS
(http://www.bit.ly/GoodreadsKS)
BOOKBUB
(http://bookbub.com/authors/kandi-steiner)
TWITTER
(http://twitter.com/kandisteiner)
PINTEREST
(https://www.pinterest.com/authorkandisteiner/)
WEBSITE (http://www.kandisteiner.com/)

Kandi Steiner may be coming to a city near you! Check out her "events" tab to see all the signings she's attending in the near future.

SEE UPCOMING EVENTS
(http://www.kandisteiner.com/events)

Printed at Repro India Ltd.